We'll Meet Again

Books by Bartle Bull

THE ANTON RIDER SERIES
The White Rhino Hotel
A Café on the Nile
The Devil's Oasis
We'll Meet Again

THE CHINA SET
Shanghai Station
China Star

HISTORY
Bull's Way
Safari- A Chronicle of Adventure

**For more information
visit:** www.SpeakingVolumes.us

We'll Meet Again

Bartle Bull

SPEAKING VOLUMES, LLC
NAPLES, FLORIDA
2022

The lyrics to the song We'll Meet Again by Vera Lynn are under license from and courtesy of Blue Pie Productions USA LLC.

ISBN 978-1-64540-785-0

For Kathleen

Kathleen Augustine and Bartle Bull on the Nile, 2019

The Characters

Olivio Fonseca Alavedo - A dwarf, the Goan proprietor of the Cataract Café in Cairo.

Saffron Alavedo - Daughter of Olivio. The fiancee of Wellington Rider, the late son of Anton Rider.

Algernon Blunt - An intelligence officer with Britain's Special Operations Executive.

Dr. August Hanger - Swiss physician in Cairo. Olivio's doctor.

Jamila - Cairo's most celebrated belly dancer.

Nada - A Jugoslav partisan. Daughter of Yanko.

Anton Rider - A professional safari hunter from Kenya, originally raised by gypsies in England.

Denby Rider - Anton and Gwenn's surviving son. In the 7th Hussars in the North African campaign.

Gwenn Rider - A Welsh surgeon, the separated wife of Anton Rider. Denby's mother.

Lester Simon - A U.S. Air Force officer assigned to Anton's mission to Jugoslavia.

Alistair Treitel - An intelligence officer with Britain's Special Operations Executive. An archeologist.

Ernst von Decken - A German soldier and old friend of Anton Rider.

Yanko - A Partisan commander in Jugoslavia. The father of Nada.

Prologue

The scout lay on his hard belly and watched the short-haired mongrel dart from side to side. Agitated, its head low to the ground, the dog whined and scratched at the stones and dirt. Pungent wild sage grew from cracks in the rock close to Anton Rider's face, covering the smells of the Mediterranean, the animal and the greasy goat bones in the cooking coals. The crisp dusty dry scent of the sage reminded him of acacia in East Africa. Behind Anton, the shepherd finished his morning prayers. Bowing to the east, still stiff and chilled by the night, the old man folded his rug and peered into the thick dawn mist that covered the north side of the mountain.

Captain Rider knew that the Tunisian's right eye was still sharp, not yet clouded, but that his ears were not what they had been. For an Italian bayonet, a few coins, a tin of cigarettes and some loose tobacco, the shepherd had accepted the three British soldiers of the Long Range Desert Group into his camp. The other two men of Rider's patrol were now a mile further on, to the west, also monitoring North Africa's only coastal road. Their Chevrolet lorry, overloaded with petrol and water, a tall radio mast and perforated metal sand channels, was screened by canvas and brush, hidden in a long meandering wadi. The bottom of the dry river bed was thick with silver-leaved bushes.

So far, all that had passed along the dusty road were five side-car motorcycles and a pair of Kübelwagens, light German reconnaissance cars, something like the new American Jeeps, perhaps scouting ahead for the mass of General Rommel's retreating army. For two years the

Germans had been on the edge of victory in North Africa, advancing East from Libya into Egypt, bombing Alexandria, mining the Suez Canal, threatening Cairo, as Rommel sought to turn the war with a triumph in the Middle East. But now, short of petrol and re-supply, Germany's desert general had been defeated by the British at El Alamein. His army, still dangerous, was fleeing West along the coast of the Mediterranean.

With his bad leg hobbling him, Anton hoped the other two men would be able to collect him on the way out. But after twenty-five years in the bush, the old safari hunter felt most comfortable on his own. His hands and face were tanned nearly as dark as the old shepherd's. Today his job was to observe and report, not fight.

Bundled in his shaggy sheepskin coat, the long cold night had given Anton Rider too long to think about his own problems back in Cairo. Particularly his wife, Gwenn, and the complications of her medical work and her new lover, this time an Englishman with a poncy school accent. Despite all that, and his own foolishness with other women, he loved her still, perhaps more than ever. And he prayed that, at bottom, Gwennie still loved him, too. Or was that just a wishful attachment, a last pining for a romantic ideal that he might have lost forever? They had shared and endured too much. Struggling to build a farm in East Africa, long absences, misunderstandings, cruel loss.

The war seemed to defer some problems, like work and money. But others, such as uncertain love, it aggravated and intensified. He thought of the son he had already lost in the war, and the pregnant fiancée the boy had left behind.

Of course the dog, barking now, would sense sounds and movement even before Rider, and well before his master. The mongrel had been a useful sentry, and the camp and goats a perfect cover for Anton's forward position as he stalked the German retreat.

The old Tunisian hissed sharply to calm the animal, not knowing what had disturbed it. The dog moved closer to his master's side, twitching and pressing against his frayed *gallabiyah*. Suddenly its legs grew rigid. The grey hairs on its neck stiffened against his touch. What danger could this be? Thieves? A wild boar? Not a giant cat. The last black-maned lion in these mountains had been hunted and killed by the French soldiers when the shepherd was a boy.

Then all three heard it.

A grinding clanking sound rose through the morning mist, as if great chains were being dragged across the crags and boulders of the massif. The old man crouched near Rider beside the fluted fragment of an ancient column. The dog trembled between his hands. Gusts of warm salty air blew up from the Gulf of Gabes, clearing the mist from the road and the sea below them. The captain smelled the remains of the cook fire when the wind stirred the ashes. The shepherd glanced around and watched his goats nibbling and scrabbling among the scattered stones of a fallen empire. Perhaps once a villa, Carthaginian or Roman, Anton Rider guessed, or a watchtower, where one ancient invader had waited for the next. He knew what must be coming now.

Anton used both arms to scrape out a deeper position between the rocks. His heavy shoulders and long body nestled into the depression. He pinched a bit of sand from between his teeth. His thick dark hair, even his pockets, always seemed full of the stuff. His desert boots, torn khaki trousers and faded tunic were covered in grit and dust. Only his bolt-action rifle was clean, with one round already up the spout and the ten-shot magazine loaded with regular .303 rounds. One of his canvas belt pouches held several tracers.

As the air cleared, the din grew louder and they discerned the monster that was approaching. Anton drew his field glasses from a canvas pack. He wiped the lenses with his *diklo*, his red gypsy kerchief, before raising the binoculars to his light blue eyes.

A sand-yellow steel machine, long as a bus, massive as a village house, was advancing along the coast road close below them. A thick black cross was painted on its side. A man's head protruded from the top of the vehicle, another from a low opening near the front. Both wore dark leather helmets and heavy round glasses. Their faces were tanned and dusty as the desert. The long barrel of a heavy gun extended before them, its muzzle wrapped in canvas against the blowing sand. Ten wheels drove the track on the left side of the machine. A Mark IV, Rider recognized, General Rommel's desert work horse, this one up-gunned with the lengthened 75mm barrel, one of the finest weapons of the war.

A dense plume of dust rose behind the vehicle. Cannon and armored cars, lorries and motorcycles, radio trucks and ambulances and half-tracks, captured Russian anti-tank guns, all followed the lead tank. Risking reflection from the rising sun against the lenses, Rider studied the column through his binoculars before taking out a small notebook and beginning to log the numbers and types of heavy armor.

Now the lead tank was directly below them. The shepherd shielded his good eye and squinted into the rising light that reflected off the choppy sea, bright and sparkling like the silver scales of a fish. Behind the tank, as far as Rider could see while the mist dispersed along the winding coast of the Mediterranean, a solid column of moving vehicles, over twenty miles long, was sliding forward like a great serpent from Libya into Tunisia.

Erwin Rommel and the Afrika Korps were racing west.

Two machines fanned out as the head of the column passed. An open eight-wheeled armored car and a large half-track with three sets of seats. Rows of jerry cans were strapped to the sides of both vehicles. The cans near the drivers were painted with white crosses. Rider knew these contained water. The others were the solid sand yellow of the Afrika Korps and held precious petrol.

An officer in the half-track removed his sand goggles and took a pair of field glasses from a case that hung from his neck. He focused the lenses and scanned the coast to his right and the hillsides on the left. As the officer stared up, Anton caught the reflection from the man's binoculars. He had the sense that the German officer must have done the same with Rider's glasses.

A squad leaped down from the big half-track. The men stared up the hillside as the officer pointed. Luftwaffe paratroopers, Anton reckoned by their rounded helmets. Rommel's best. Hardened veterans of the long retreat from Egypt. Most wore britches and tall canvas lace-up boots because leather dried out and shriveled in the desert. By now, the third year of the war in North Africa, both Germans and British, and even some Italians, had learned how to fight and survive in this special landscape.

The troopers began climbing towards Anton's position as a heavy machine gun mounted on the vehicle swivelled to provide covering fire. Still prone, Rider shouldered his Enfield. The round bolt felt smooth and comfortable before he flipped off the safety.

The shepherd stood and began collecting his goats just as the MG 42 opened up. His white robe billowed around him like a sail snapping in the wind. The mongrel dashed about barking, its head low, gathering the goats. Suddenly bullets cracked off the rocks. Stone splinters flew. The dog collapsed, dragging both hind legs, whining as it struggled to reach its master. Its guts trailed to one side. Its open belly scraped along the rock. The shepherd cried out. He bent to lift the dog as two bullets stitched across his body. Their blood joined when he fell across the animal.

Anton fired once, hitting a German in the chest. The other paratroopers slowed and crouched before advancing from rock to rock. Leading his men forward, their officer ran from cover to cover at the base of the slope. The men in the armored car behind them scrambled down to join the other soldiers. Rider waited until the officer rose again, then shot him in the throat. He fired two quick shots into a petrol can strapped on the side of the armored car. Gasoline flooded down over the second row of jerry cans. Satisfied all was ready, Anton chambered a tracer round and fired into one of the lower cans. Oily flames flashed amidst the moving paratroopers.

Rider instantly gathered his pack and rifle and began stumbling down the back of the hill, trying to slide on the loose rock and keep his weight on his good leg, hoping he could reach the protection of the wadi. He and his patrol were probably the first to spot the German army retreating from Libya into Tunisia. They must radio in the report. Out of breath, his leg heavy and aching as he scrambled towards the camouflaged lorry, Anton wondered how many more such missions he was good for.

Chapter One

Cairo. April, 1943

"You're done, Captain, all clapped out. Your war's over." The colonel shook his head and tapped the fitness report twice with his pipe. "Too old to start with, and after that Teller mine and your last patrol, too many broken bits." He paused and squinted across his desk at Rider, aware of the old hunter's stubborn temperament, perhaps considering how much he should say. "I hate to see a chap trying not to limp. Wrong edge of forty, are you not?"

"I can still manage what the rest of the men can, sir." Annoyed, Anton Rider pinched the bump on the bridge of his prominent nose, broken in a brawl many years before. Though he was a bit heavier than when he had first come out to East Africa at eighteen, he reckoned he could still shoot and fight with the best. More important, he knew how to do it.

"Medical officer tells me you're the only case he's ever seen where they were pinching out the shrapnel and found an old slug from some other campaign they had to cut out along the way." The colonel gave him a curious admiring look. "Said your body is like some field in Flanders after the Great War. More like archeology than surgery. Don't want to dig about too much. Never know what bits of metal you'll find next."

When Captain Rider did not respond, the senior officer continued. "Hate to think what you were up to before this punch-up came along. Abyssinia, was it? Culling Eyeties in thirty-six?"

"Something like that, sir." Anton Rider shrugged. Seven years before, he had been on safari with clients in Ethiopia when Benito Mussolini sent half a million Italians to invade the old African kingdom. The safari had been obliged to fight its way out and escape to Kenya. "There must be something useful I could do, sir . . ."

The colonel considered the possibilities. "Perhaps you could manage some training lectures, help get the new chaps sorted out before they trot off into the desert, that sort of thing, but I doubt you'd have patience for all the sitting about and talk-talk." He could see from Anton's face that the old hunter would hate that sort of duty.

"For the moment we've assigned you to GHQ, Press Relations, just to keep you out of further mischief. I believe they've already fixed your first appointment with one of those correspondent types. American or some such. By the name of Bouvet." The officer frowned at the French name. "They all like to tell their readers they're writing from a Bren gun carrier somewhere in the Western Desert. 'Course, they're really hanging about in Shepheard's, swilling gin and over-tipping the staff."

The mere idea of press relations made Anton wish he were back in the bush, tracking and stalking, even putting up with spoiled clients. "Not really my sort of game, sir."

"You'd be surprised, Rider. Some of these wretched scribes, especially the picture weeklies and the Yanks, will be charmed by all that Great White Hunter business of yours. 'From the bush to Benghazi,' 'Nairobi to the Nile,' that sort of thing."

Apparently well pleased with his turns of phrase, the colonel paused again. As he waited for Anton's reply, the colonel scraped out his pipe with the small blade of a pocket knife.

"They say some of these scribblers are proper lookers, girls out here for a little wartime entertainment," he observed without looking up from his pipe. "Where else can they dance with a new hero every evening and drink champagne one day's drive from the front, like Brussels before Waterloo?"

Anton leaned forward and prepared to rise. The entire notion disgusted him. He must find some way to hook up with the next patrol of the Long Range Desert Group. He wanted to wake up again to the exhilarating crisp morning air of the desert, before sharing the day's hazards with his men.

The colonel wiped the bowl of his pipe along both sides of his nose until the dark wood shined. "Frankly, packing it in might not be all that bad." His tone softened. "Your family's done its bit, Rider. I believe your wife's just back here from that field hospital. You've lost one brave boy already, God bless him. And I understand your other lad's on some special mission with the Rats in the race for Tunis. No doubt they're hoping to get there before the Yanks join in and spoil the natives with their nylons and chewing gum."

Anton Rider stood up. He appreciated the colonel's concern for his family, and it reminded him of the imminent arrival of an illegitimate grandchild. But the muscles tightened in his jaw at the thought of a desk junket. So far, despite a couple of wounds, he had felt fortunate to be out in the desert with small informal patrols assigned to reporting on Axis movements and behind-the-lines raids on German air bases.

"Meantime, everyone's waiting to see where the first Allied landing's going to be. Big question is whether the French army and navy will fight our boys on the beaches if it's Morocco or Algeria. So far most of the Frenchies seem to be siding with Corporal Hitler, both at home and out here."

The colonel sucked on his pipe. "But as for you, Captain, I must say you're looking surprisingly fit, or at least hard, on the outside anyway. Perhaps you could find something else to do on your own till this show sorts itself out. Maybe something in your old line. They tell us you used to be the finest rifle shot in East Africa."

"Not many safari clients about in wartime, Colonel." Rider saluted him crisply. Even in peacetime it was difficult to make a decent living as a professional hunter. "But please let me know, sir, if any active assignment turns up."

"We'll see, Captain." The colonel turned his attention to a stack of cablegrams.

Careful not to favor his right leg, Anton turned on his heel and strode to the door. It was time for a drink.

The hall porter bowed as Captain Rider entered the Moorish lobby of Shepheard's, the grand hotel on the Shari Kamil. Anton's mood was foul. The last thing he wanted was to spin war stories to some pansy correspondent posing in desert khaki with a dangling cigarette and a schoolboy notebook. But at least most of them knew how to drink and, unlike him, had the cash to pay for the cocktails.

"Madame Bouvet has been waiting, effendi," said the boy. Surprised by the gender, Anton squinted about in the dim rosy light that filtered through the colored glass dome high above his head.

"*Capitaine Rider*?" said a woman as he paused beside a tall potted palm.

"Yes, ma'am." Anton looked down, then smiled at the prospect before him.

"Cerisse Bouvet. *Enchantée!*" Seated at an inlaid octagonal table between two officers in French naval uniform, the woman in a skirted herringbone suit looked up at him and indicated an empty chair.

"You're just like they told me at the Press Office," she said, evidently pleased. "Impossibly tall and handsome, Captain. But I almost gave up on you. I thought you English were *toujours à l'heure*."

The two men rose only slightly from their seats when Anton saluted.

"I'm with *L'Exprès de Montréal.*" The lady put down a small lined pad beside a flat gold cigarette case and gestured towards her companions. "Admiral Auphan, Captain Berval. Their ships have been interned by the English in Alexandria, to make sure they don't join the German and Italian fleets." She turned to Anton, flashing lively brown eyes. "Captain Rider is with the famous Long Range Desert Group, gentlemen. Always dashing about behind the German lines. Something of a hero, are you not, Captain?"

"Wouldn't have thought so," Rider said, annoyed by such talk. He called to the barman. "Double gin, Abdu."

"These sailors were just explaining to me why the French ships and shore batteries might not welcome an Allied landing in Morocco and Algeria."

For a moment no one spoke. All were aware that French Africa was garrisoned by troops loyal to Vichy, not to de Gaulle. Cooperating with their country's Nazi occupiers, France's Vichy government had spared Germany the need to occupy French Africa and nearly half of France itself. All believed that in exchange, old Marshall Petain had promised to keep the Führer's enemies out of French North Africa. Now the world was waiting to see on whose side the French army in Africa would fight. Vichy and Germany, or America and England? Were their radios tuned to Hitler and Mussolini, or to Roosevelt and Churchill?

"The talk is that your chaps will be throwing in with the Huns and Eyeties," said Anton, not reluctant to provoke the French officers. "Shouldn't make too much difference either way, but it'll be a shock to the Yanks. They'll be coming over to fight the Krauts again and the Eyeties, not the French."

He paused to sip from his drink, noticing the lady's reasonable legs when she crossed her ankles. Not young, but young enough. She had thick dark hair and the sort of high lavish figure that no doubt made other women say she would not look so good as life went on.

"The Anglo-Saxons have no business invading French Africa," said the admiral, stiffening. "Tunisia and Morocco and Algeria belong to France. *Il faut défendre l'Afrique contre quiconque.* Would not the Americans fight if we landed in Hawaii?"

"Or the British if we invaded Gibraltar?" added the captain, leaning forward.

"We'll never know," said Rider, "will we?" He felt himself growing hot. His wife's last lover had been a Frog, and he'd seen enough of them. They always wanted someone else to fight their wars: colonial troops, Foreign Legionnaires, Brits or Poles or Yanks.

"Gentlemen," said Bouvet, touching Anton's arm firmly, "please. Here at Shepheard's there is no war."

"Madame Bouvet," said Captain Berval, "I thought you were French. *On ne parle pas comme ça.*"

"I am," she said. "*Plus ou moin.* French Canadian. But perhaps Frenchmen should be killing the *Boches*, the Germans, instead of our friends." She laughed lightly, without humor. "No? *N'est ce pas?*"

"Madame!"

"You must forgive a foolish woman, Admiral, for not understanding why we might soon have more Frenchmen fighting the Americans in Africa than are fighting the Germans in France."

"Perhaps we have fought the Germans too often." Captain Berval sat forward. "Let the Americans try it."

"I believe they already have," said Cerisse Bouvet.

Enjoying the exchange, Anton lifted the gold case from the table, hoping it contained proper Virginia tobacco, rather than army-issue "V" cigarettes, said to be made in Calcutta from street droppings. "May I?" he said, catching the lady's eye as she nodded to him and spoke again.

"Who was that deputy from Paris who said it was dangerous to be a friend of France?"

"That was years ago," said the admiral rising huffily from his seat. "When Hitler invaded Czechoslovakia and France was not able to help." He shrugged and pinched his cigarette butt from its holder.

"In any event," said Anton, relishing the fine tobacco, "I hear some of your Foreign Legion battalions are fighting each other near Damascus or Beirut. Who is your fleet for this afternoon, Admiral?"

"For France, Monsieur," said Berval in a deep tight voice. "*Toujours pour la France.*"

The admiral began to rise. "Good afternoon." He kissed the air above Madame Bouvet's hand, and the two Frenchmen left the table.

"For a press officer, you have little talent for diplomacy," said Cerisse. Then in a softer voice, looking in his eyes, "Have you time to buy me a glass of champagne, Captain? Or have you more battles to fight this afternoon?"

"My time is your time," Anton said, relaxing, grinning at last. "After all, you are part of my new job." He turned to call for the barman. Even with Gwenn back in Cairo, he and his wife were not together and had not been for a very long time. Though presently in uniform, and English for a change, her new caller was the sort she now preferred, intellectual and said to be rich. Of course, Anton himself was neither. "*Abdu!*" he said. "*Shampanya!*"

The two flirted, and for an hour it seemed that there was no war. Finally Anton emptied the bottle into the glass of the Canadian correspondent, then tipped it upside down into the bucket.

"You English soldiers always look like schoolboys." Cerisse leaned back with her shoulders squared, regarding him with large open eyes. She had removed her jacket. Her creamy silk shirt was tight against her chest. He wanted to open the buttons. In her tent, a client had once advised him that you could discern a woman's intentions by how she dressed and presented her body in her clothes.

"In your khaki shorts and long socks and all those little decorations, like Boy Scouts. *Adorable!* Who else would wear a scorpion on his shoulder patch? *Quelle bêtise!*"

"All men are boys." Anton smiled. The deadly desert scorpion was the symbol of his regiment. "All we want is flattery and ice cream."

"Ice cream?"

Rider frowned at the question. "Why are intelligent women so literal?" he said wearily. "There are many kinds of ice cream, miss. Mind if I scribble something in your notebook?" Without waiting for a reply he picked up her pad and flipped to a new page.

Cerisse passed him a pencil, then tapped a cigarette on the case while she watched him write something brief. She noticed his powerful tanned hands and long fingers. His ring finger betrayed a pale line but nothing more.

"May I ask if you are married, Captain?"

She leaned forward and touched his hand as Anton lit her Lucky Strike. He looked at her through the smoke, admiring her heavy shapely lips, almost those of an Ethiopian or Somali. Cerissee seemed to have unbuttoned the second button of her shirt. He had the sense that she had already made her decision. He had learned that it was always the woman who decided.

"I believe I am separated," Anton said.

"By what?"

"The war. Age. Choices. Sometimes the desert." He paused, not explaining that though his wife was ten years older, she still excited him more than any other woman. "And perhaps by too much of my own foolishness." Not to mention temperament, tastes and interests. With their son Wellington gone, young Denby was now all that Gwenn and he truly shared. That and a tempestuous past in East Africa. Anton shrugged, feeling suddenly awkward. "I'm really not quite sure where things are now."

He recalled what his little friend Olivio Alavedo did whenever someone pressed him with a personal question.

"How did you get assigned to Cairo?" Anton asked. "Something of a plum these days, is it not?"

"My father owns the newspaper."

Just then Abdu appeared at Rider's elbow. "Excuse, please," he said urgently. "Telephone, effendi. Cabinet number one, please."

Relieved by the interruption, Anton walked to the telephone kiosk, his leg stiff. Behind him, he heard the hotel band tuning up for the afternoon's tea dance, beginning with *Down Mexico Way*, probably to be followed by *Donkey Serenade*. One of the advantages of wartime Cairo was that the city provided unceasing entertainment for every taste, from Tea Island in the Zoological Gardens at Gezira to the Melody Club, where boisterous squaddies were separated from the band and the belly dancers by a barbed wire fence.

Rider closed the door of the kiosk so he could hear the thin voice on the telephone.

"Captain Rider? Is that you, sir? Anglo-American hospital here. Miss Alavedo asked us to ring to say she's about to have the baby. Her father has been here all day."

At last the baby! The child of the son he had lost. Anton cradled the phone and hurried back down the hall. Wellington had been killed in the desert shortly before his wedding day, he thought sadly. Now Wellie would be absent at the birth of his own baby.

"Sorry," he said to the startled Canadian reporter, tossing two banknotes on the table. "I'm off to the Anglo-American. Someone's having a baby." No need to mention it would make him a grandfather.

"Mind if I come with you? I have one or two friends at the hospital myself." Cerisse rose abruptly from her seat. "These days the hospitals are the best spots for interviews. No one's in a hurry, and they can't get away."

"Of course," Anton said. All the while he was thinking that forty-two seemed a fine age to become a grandfather. He had been raised by gypsies in England and had spent most of his life under canvas on safaris, and recently on missions in the desert. The thought of a grandchild, illegitimate or not, cheered his heart. Now he would have something to come home to, an anchor in his life, even if it was not the woman he still loved. Maybe he could become a fat old desk jockey after all.

Chapter Two

Not waiting for the lift, Rider left Cerisse in the lobby of the Anglo-American Hospital and dashed up two flights to the maternity ward, now compressed into a small suite to free space for the flood of wartime casualties.

At first he thought the long dim corridor was empty. Dark wooden blinds were drawn across the tall windows to keep out the heat of the afternoon, lining the floor with thin stripes of light. As Anton's eyes adjusted, he saw the small familiar figure that waited at the end of the hall, unmoving as a stout stone Buddha. Olivio Fonseca Alavedo.

The little man reminded Rider of one of the squat statues of Bes, the ancient Egyptian deity of dwarfism. Olivio collected these images in his gallery on the lower deck of the Cataract Café. How suitable, thought Anton, for he knew that Bes, despite his deformities, was also the protective household god of families, and of women during childbirth.

Seated on a brocade cushion on a child's high chair, clothed in a dark three-piece pinstripe suit, Olivio raised one small hand in greeting. A green tarbush with a silk tassel rested on the bald globe of the dwarf's head. The Goan's round face, strained tight by age and pain and the proud flesh of burn tissue, seemed glazed, almost amber in the shadowy light. His ears hung in empty loops like the open handles of a vase. His nose was button-flat and smooth as a baby's.

Tariq, Alavedo's personal servant, stood directly behind the dwarf. The arms of the massive Nubian were crossed over his grey gallabiyya as he nodded respectfully at his master's closest friend.

Though now he could barely walk, Olivio despised the confirming helplessness and the diminished stature that a small wheelchair would provide. He preferred the ambulatory convenience, the formidable presence and the sense of menace that he gained when the mighty black man carried him in his heavy arms. Instead of pathetic, the dwarf felt enhanced, like a cavalry officer well mounted.

"Greetings to you, Mr. Anton!" called Alavedo. He knew better than to comment that Rider seemed to be favoring one leg. "Ha! Ha! Soon we will be grandfathers, you and I. Grandfathers!"

"Hullo, Olivio, Tariq," said Anton in his easy way. "Is everything all right?"

"It has been made clear to the doctors that everything must be all right," Olivio said severely. "And I have directed my personal physician, Doktor August Hänger of Zürich, to watch over this procedure as closely as he attends his own reflection."

The wealthy dwarf would be generous if the doctors did well, but vicious if things went badly for Saffron Alavedo or the baby. For once Anton detected anxiety in the dwarf's demeanor, and nervousness in his voice, qualities unthinkable in the little man even in times of brutal stress. Both in Kenya and in Egypt he had seen Alavedo threatened and in pain, impatient and enraged, but never fearful.

"I have sent word to Miss Gwenn," added Olivio to Anton, warning Rider of his wife's imminent arrival. The dwarf never changed his form of address even with his closest friends. "I understand that today she is operating at a military clinic in town."

A surgery door opened at the far end of the corridor and an Egyptian nurse appeared. A Kopt, Anton judged. A Christian Egyptian. Her quick steps echoed as she approached them.

"It is taking longer than we thought, *Senhor Alavedo*," she said, her voice crisp as her white cap. "There are complications. Would you prefer to wait in the doctor's office? Perhaps a cup of tea, coffee?"

"No, thank you." The dwarf shook his head as best he could on his short stiff neck. "You may advise Dr. Robinson that I will wait here where you see me. What are these complications?"

"Oh, nothing too serious, but we are not certain how long it will be."

"My dear," said the dwarf, his tone hardening. Alavedo was not amused by the need for repetition. He wriggled forward in the high chair with quick jerky movements until the pointed toes of his velvet slippers touched the foot rail. "I asked you: what are these complications?"

Tariq raised a hand so that his master would not slip from the seat.

Anton marveled at the little man's gift for authority. In an instant Olivio transformed the nurse's impression of him from one of misery to one of command. Rider had seen brigadiers in the field, enhanced with all the luster of uniform and staff and discipline and crisis, yet not able to convey such confidence of leadership.

"There are two problems, sir," said the nurse, abashed. "Miss Alavedo, though in perfect health and normal in every way, is narrow in the hip, and the baby has a large head that has not descended and approached delivery as we would wish."

"Thank you, nurse," said Olivio in a quiet firm voice. A large head? "You will please advise Dr. Robinson that I await his next report."

The dwarf's single grey eye met Anton's. Though never having spoken of it, both men feared that this infant might enter the world with the burdens of a lifetime of deformity.

Anton knew that an outsize head was a forewarning of dwarfism. But to Olivio, with his small only son already sharing his life of freakish isolation, it signaled yet another generation of haunted peculiarity. Though Saffron herself had escaped his curse, he knew it was still buried within all his daughters like an evil dormant egg. Olivio had learned to master, even to exploit his diminutive condition, but it was not a test he wished for his grandchildren.

Rider wondered if their grandchild was to begin life with such an inheritance, and with no father and an unmarried mother? He also dreaded that his small friend might blame himself for the first of those hardships. Anton's own wife already blamed her husband for the others.

He paced the hall for the next hour while Olivio sat silent and still in the tall chair. Rider knew that Alavedo's demeanor might appear passive, but his senses were as alert as those of a leopard crouching flat on a branch. His mind was more active than Napoleon's before a battle. Tariq knew better than to speak until addressed. From time to time the dwarf tapped together the sides of his Ottoman slippers with sharp slapping movements. His expression, always inscrutable, was flat and clear as glass.

The surgery door opened. A short lean man emerged in a starched white surgical coat and heavy black wing-tipped shoes. He wore rectangular gold spectacles on his high beak-like nose. At least seventy, with knobby cheekbones and furry white sideburns, he bore three deep parallel lines across his forehead. A ruff of white hair circled around the back of his otherwise bare head from ear to ear.

"*Herr Alavedo*," began Dr. Hänger with a tight tone and an accent that could be either Swiss or Austrian, perhaps even German. "I must speak vith you."

"Do." The dwarf was disturbed to see August Hänger reveal anxiety as he curled and uncurled the fingers of his hands. Hänger's surgical rubber gloves made a slick slipping sound as he squeezed his hands together. His long white coat seemed stiff enough to stand on its own.

"Ve have known one another for many years, *Mein Herr*," said the doctor.

"Seven and a half."

"I have always done my best to honor our understanding. To attend first to the unusual needs of you and your family, living and dead."

"Of course."

All three men understood that the Swiss physician was referring to the cruel infirmities that attended aging in a dwarf. Each year increased the progressive imbalance of every organ, the constriction of each muscle and nerve. Few dwarfs survived to the age of fifty, let alone to the age of Olivio Alavedo.

"But today you must understand that there is not much that I can do." Dr. Hänger paused nervously. "Dr. Robinson is the finest birthing specialist in Cairo. He delivered the sisters of King Faruq. The princesses Fawzia, Faiza, Faika and Fathia. Now he tells me that in a few moments he may have to decide whether to save the child or the mother. What would you have me instruct him, sir?"

"You ask me to choose, Doctor, between my daughter and my grandchild?" Alavedo glanced sidelong at Anton. "Our grandchild."

The dwarf stroked both his lips from corner to corner with his thick pointed tongue. First the upper lip, then the lower. It was a movement that Anton had observed only in lizards and certain snakes. Olivio employed it at moments when he sought to contain and direct his mounting fury.

"For this, Dr. Hänger, I brought you from Switzerland to Egypt?" Alavedo exclaimed. "For this I brought you from the Alps to the pyramids?" He did not mention the more intimate arrangements he had provided to enhance the physician's personal life on the Nile. In Zürich would this thin-lipped surgeon have been fulfilled on his seventy-first birthday by a dancing girl whose enticing embrace had restored him to life itself?

The dwarf turned his eye to Anton Rider.

"My daughter or our grandchild?"

Slowly the small man raised both hands, then his shoulders to the extent the contractions of his muscles permitted. He blinked. His good eye glistened with the same hard moistness as his false eye of hippopotamus ivory.

Rider took his friend's tiny left hand in his own hard fingers. Rarely had they ever touched. He found the appendage as smooth and cold as that of a porcelain doll.

"Whatever you decide, Olivio," said Anton, "that will be our decision. Yours and mine."

Olivio Alavedo turned his attention back to Dr. Hänger.

"You will save both, or neither," said Alavedo sternly, aware that neither Rider nor Hänger would understand the difference between what he said and what he intended. He was certain the doctors would still save one, but he feared that his own choosing might incline them to avoid the more arduous hazards of compromise. He was determined to compel them to take the difficult risk of attempting to save both.

"Both or neither."

Dr. Hänger gave no response. He turned stiffly and walked back to the delivery room. In the silence, his hard heels were sharp and measured like the clicks of a metronome against the wooden floor of the corridor.

As the doctor opened the door, a shrill scream sounded from the delivery room, then another as the door closed after him. They were the cries not of a baby newly born, but of a woman at the peak of pain.

In the corridor the three men froze as if dead themselves. For a moment none breathed. Inside the cold stiffness that gripped him, Anton felt all the pain of his old wounds: the thick burn scars from the fight on the rusting *Garth Castle*, the bumpy broken ribs from his buffalo thumping in the Aberdares, the bullet wound from Ethiopia, and the shrapnel in his legs and the broken collarbone from the mine in Libya not long ago. But no wound would be like this.

Minutes later they heard a muted cry. The door opened. The wailing cries of a baby carried down the hall with the clarity of a church bell, followed by the swift steps of the nurse.

The Kopt approached the dwarf. The face of the nurse shone with perspiration.

"You have a grandson, sir. A lovely baby boy. Nearly seven pounds." She hesitated. "He is perfect," the nurse said to Olivio and, smiling, to Anton, "and you, Captain Rider, have the son of your son."

"And Miss Alavedo?" said Anton, his eyes wet, feeling that his own son, and he himself, had been reborn. He thought how happy Gwenn would be. Nothing could replace Wellington, but this child would give her one more cause for which to live, in case, God spare us, Denby was one day lost as well. "How is she, how is Mrs. Rider?"

Astonished to hear the surname, the dwarf stared at his friend, welcoming the consideration, knowing they would never speak of it. Now the boy would not be a bastard.

"Well enough," said the nurse. "She should be fine, I think, but it was not easy." She bit her lower lip and spoke directly to Alavedo. "Though it is too soon to be certain, Dr. Robinson doubts if your daughter can have more children."

As she spoke, Anton recognized the hurried steps of a woman's heels behind him at the end of the corridor. His stomach tightened. He brushed his eyes with the back of his hand, certain who it must be.

"Miss Gwenn! Good afternoon to you," said Olivio Alavedo with affection, buying his friend a moment to collect himself.

"What's happened?" said Gwenn Rider urgently, out of breath. A military surgeon's field cloak hung unevenly from her slender shoulders. Her short tawny hair was in disarray, her face tired, but the green eyes Anton had first loved flashed with animation. "How is Saffron? Has she had the baby?"

Chapter Three

Too much learning can get you into trouble, his father used to say, and now that seemed too true.

Seconded from his regiment due to his fluent Arabic and passable French, Lieutenant Denby Rider had been sent ahead on the submarine *Seraph* to link up with the first shore parties from the imminent Torch landings near Algiers Bay. Three Free French officers accompanied him. While the *Seraph* surfaced and recharged her diesels on a dark night, the four-man team had transferred to a North African fishing boat. With a net draped over their shoulders, they had then climbed the beach unnoticed under a thin new moon. After breathing the thin foul air of the submarine and repeatedly knocking his head against the ship's low pipes and valves, Denby was relieved to be breathing the fresh salty air of the coast.

For two days the men lay under dusty scraps of camouflage canvas near the ruins of an abandoned lighthouse high on a *djebel*, a rocky hill above Cap Matifou. Gnarly grape vines grew in tight rows all around them. They had been unable to repair their old Marconi wireless. But they knew that if the weather was tolerable for a landing, the Allied fleet, hundreds of ships altogether, should appear off the coast at first light. Staring through binoculars in shifts, they counted the military traffic on the coast road and scanned the shimmering sea that sparkled in the gusting *khamsin*. Except for the shoreline breakers, the waters were calm. The defending French fleet and the *Armée de l'Air* were busier than expected, patrolling actively, though never venturing far out over the Med.

Ever since the Americans had joined the war in forty-one, everyone knew it was a matter of time until they landed in Europe or North Africa.

Denby's mother, a Volunteer Ambulance Driver in the last war, had told him what a difference the Yanks had made then. As a young but exhausted V.A.D. in Flanders, she had watched the Americans marching to the front in endless brown lines, big and fresh and young, with inexhaustible supplies, food and cigarettes. After a few cruel lessons, the Yanks had fought well. Would it be that way again?

The last time, in 1917, the French had cheered the Americans as they crowded down the gangplanks in Cherbourg and Le Havre to fight the Huns. But this time no one knew how the French army, 130,000 strong in North Africa, would receive the Americans and the British. Like unoccupied Vichy France itself, Tunisia and Morocco and Algeria were defended only by French troops, sparing the Nazi army for other battle fronts.

Denby Rider realized that the Gaullist Frenchman on the dog watch had fallen asleep with his shoulder against a rock. Denby sat up and rubbed his face. He scratched his fingers through his hair, dark and thick like his father's. He was tired of the sand that penetrated everything, even each tin of bully beef as soon as a ration was opened. One of his mates in the Hussars used to show off several grains of sand that had penetrated under the glass of his wrist watch.

Denby raised the collar of his heavy rough jacket and leaned forward with his arms around his knees, wishing he could light a smoke. Six empty bottles of Algerian red lay nearby.

Then he thought of his older brother, Wellington, killed in the breakout from Bir Hakeim. His lorry had been blown apart, probably by one of Rommel's eighty-eights. Denby hoped he himself would fight well enough to have made his brother proud. He thought of the lovely pregnant fiancée Wellie had left behind and wondered how his parents and the dwarf would look after Saffron and the child. Perhaps being grandparents would bring his parents together again. He had wished that for so long. He knew they had shared hardships and adventures but never inclinations.

A truck or bus rattled by on the coast road below, its headlamps hooded into narrow slits like snake's eyes, guarding against Allied air raids. He thought of the Roman legions that had tramped the same dusty coast road, following the same *fasces* emblems that Mussolini had now brought back to Africa, the bound reeds and axe that represented the power of ancient Rome.

To the east the sky softened over the Mediterranean. Soon the sky was lighter than the sea as the low band of light grew broader and taller. This morning the world would change. The war should start to turn. El Alamein and Stalingrad had been the beginning. Denby lifted his binoculars and scanned slowly westward. Seeing nothing, he stood and relieved himself behind the shelf of rock that sheltered them.

He wondered if his Free French companions would actually fight their own countrymen if the Vichy defenders of French Africa resisted the landing by what they called "*les Anglo-Saxons.*" He knew the three were not certain how well he understood their language, underestimating his fluency because of his schoolboy English accent, not aware that thanks to his mother's old French suitor, his comprehension was near-perfect though his grammar was garbled. He had heard them repeating the bitter French complaint about Churchill's decision two years before to sink French warships in their ports rather than let them join the Axis fleet.

Denby raised the glasses again and felt his stomach tighten at the sight. His breathing caught in his throat. At first he was not certain, then he whistled and kicked two of his sleeping companions.

The tall slanted grey funnel of a heavy cruiser rose on the horizon like a gibbet, black smoke trailing aft. Then another, followed by a fence of funnels as warships large and small seemed to climb over the horizon as they sailed south towards the coast.

"*Mon dieu!*" exclaimed the French major. "Give me the glasses!"

"Thirty-one," said Denby, passing them over as the three men stood beside him.

"*Bravo!*" one said, clapping the young Englishman on both shoulders. "*Enfin ils arrivent.*"

"*Americain,*" said another. "*Et les Anglais aussi.*"

Further to the west, they suddenly heard the heavy distant echo of the 15-inch guns of the French battleship *Jean Bart* duelling with the Allied fleet. Closer along the coast, the French 75mm coastal guns were firing at the Allied vessels.

Now Denby and his companions could discern a swarm of smaller vessels, low in the water, first gathering in circular groups, then steaming for the fortified harbor to their left. Six destroyers escorted the landing craft in close formation with the bigger ships following. One had the low powerful profile of an old British dreadnaught from the last war. With all three heavy turrets mounted forward, he knew she could only be the aging battleship *Rodney*, or perhaps her sister ship *Nelson*.

Denby clenched his fists and pounded them together as the Allied ships drew near. He looked at the *Tananarive*, the French light cruiser moored in the harbor, and at the fortress above her. He prayed that her guns would stay silent. He knew the pro-Vichy *Richelieu* had fought off British and Free French vessels in Dakar earlier in the war. Wounded by a Swordfish torpedo bomber, the French battleship had settled on the harbor bottom of the Senegalese port. But the flagship's fifteen-inch guns, still sticking above the water, supporting the German cause, had continued firing at her own countrymen and her former allies.

The fleet's crowded square-bowed landing craft seemed incredibly slow as they churned through the water in clusters. Denby wondered how fit the men could be after nearly three thousand miles at sea.

He saw two puffs of smoke from the fort, then heard the crack-crack of artillery as the French shore batteries opened up on the Allied landing. Two waterspouts rose in front of the landing craft. At the same instant the triple turret of the French cruiser turned to face the invaders. Three more waterspouts blossomed in the midst of the little boats after the cruiser's six-inch guns lowered and began to fire.

At least now we know what side the bloody Frenchies are on, thought Denby.

"Damned French bastards!" he exclaimed, forgetting himself as a shell burst directly inside a landing craft. He saw a man hurled in the air as the boat broke open and disappeared. The craft following ran straight over a knot of struggling men, each heavy in the water with boots and sixty pounds of equipment, including weapons, gas masks and wire cutters, ration packs and magazines of ammunition. An American flag floated in the oily water beside them. The French major lowered his glasses and stared at Denby without speaking.

Denby and the Frenchmen fell to their knees as a flight of twin-engined fighters flew low towards the sea from their French base in the desert. Denby recalled his weapons-recognition training. The three Potez 631's, normally flown as night fighters, had the red-white-and-blue rondels of the Armée de l'Air. They were followed by an *escadrille* of the *Aéronavale*, three naval torpedo planes. The Latécoères were twin-float seaplanes designed for marine support and torpedo bombing. Each plane carried one large torpedo suspended like a silver shark beneath her fuselage. He saw the orange licks of flame through the white puffs as the big guns of the heavy Allied warships fired back at the French defenses.

A British destroyer took a torpedo hit at the waterline and listed heavily to port as she swerved across the line of attacking landing craft. Several of the little vessels were snared in the chain and nets that crossed the mouth of the harbor. Soon an American destroyer smashed through the cable. The small craft followed her through. French machine guns began firing down into the crowded open boats as they approached the shore. From the quay at the other side of the harbor, the deck gun of a moored French submarine fired directly into a knot of advancing landing craft as the brightening light illuminated the targets.

Sickened and angry, Denby tightened his boots, checked his Webley revolver and prepared to run down to meet the first men ashore. He wished his squadron of Hussars was with him. He missed the most exhilarating part of soldiering: sharing hazard with one's mates. This lonely adventure was more his father's line. His own squadron of armored cars could be attacking the French from the rear, drawing fire away from the defenseless boys in the open boats. He thought again of Wellington and what his brother's last moment must have been like as his column of thin-skinned lorries raced for the open desert to escape Rommel's encircling panzers.

The French fighters dove in tight turns with one wing low, trying to avoid the anti-aircraft fire of the destroyers as they strafed the landing craft. One Latécoère plunged into the sea close to a British destroyer. The others, climbing swiftly without their torpedoes, banked and turned back for the desert as formations of Allied aircraft, Spitfires and War-hawks and Hawker Typhoons, flew in from their base at Gibraltar. Submariners on the *Seraph* had told Denby that the Allied planes had been waiting, crowded together on Gibralter's cemetery and racetrack, some with the wings removed, while the airstrip of the fortress was extended into the sea. In the evening the young pilots drank navy rum in crowded smoky subterranean bars with coal miners brought out from the pits of Lancashire and Wales to excavate new tunnels under the island fortress.

During a brief less noisy moment, Denby heard loudspeakers blaring from the lead American destroyer: "*Ne tirez pas! Nous sommes vos amis. Nous sommes Américains. Ne tirez pas!*"

The first landing craft crashed through the breakers onto the rocky beach. Some washed sideways in the surf before the bow ramps were lowered and the men could disembark. French machine guns began to chatter from the breakwater, sweeping the edge of the craft as the heavily encumbered men jumped down from the tilted sides. Bodies and tangles of equipment washed along the beach as the surf threw them up and sucked them back down like sodden rag dolls. French bullets stitched through the water in neat lines, occasionally punching into a soldier's pack or coloring the water with his blood.

Denby flung off his jacket, revealing his regulation khaki trousers and tunic, required even on this mission due to Hitler's orders to shoot all non-uniformed combatant prisoners. And why not? thought Denby Rider. Fair enough. The Americans, after all, had been executing non-uniformed German saboteurs who had landed in the States from U-boats.

"Come on!" he hollered to his three companions.

The Frenchmen hung back and disputed among themselves as Denby grabbed a sack of grenades and set off running for the unpaved road that led to the breakwater. He guessed they were waiting to see which way the battle would go.

With rocks and pebbles shifting and sliding beneath his boots, Denby scrambled down the hillside and ran through an old olive grove towards the harbor.

Two four-wheeled armored cars were stationed at the end of the rough road. Denby recognized them as Panhard et Levassors. The forward one was equipped with a 25mm turret cannon, the nearer one with twin 7.5mm machine guns, probably the *Mitrailleuse modèle 1931*. "Quick firing but prone to overheating," the training sergeant had said. "Typically French."

The crews of the empty cars had joined the French forces firing from the breakwater down into the Allied landing craft. But the driver of the first four-wheeled vehicle sat smoking on the side of his car away from the harbor, his leather helmet resting on one knee. A large orange cat lay licking itself on the seat beside him.

Denby recalled a lesson of his youth. When stalking, approach the game obliquely, at an angle, tacking towards them like a sailboat, left and right, so they do not think you are coming directly for them. Get close, hunt like a Gypsy, his father had urged him that morning near Mt. Kenya, always at his best in the bush. Though his heart was pounding like a kettle drum, Denby felt confident, excited in his belly as the moment approached. He knew he was more suited for this sort of thing than his brother had been.

He paused as he came close to the armored car. He lit a cigarette before walking towards the driver in the dim early light. He waved once as he approached. The French soldier looked up without concern as Denby came towards him with no weapon in his hands. The cat rose and arched its back. The driver cupped his hands as he sought to light another cigarette against the coastal wind. Without warning Denby drew his Webley and fired the heavy pistol twice. The Frenchman slumped back against the vehicle, his head flopping at an angle inside the open door.

Denby Rider pulled the body free and climbed into the car. He hissed at the cat as the animal crouched on the floor against the far door. The hinged steel window shield was fully raised. He heard the chatter of machine gun fire, the pop of light artillery and the whistle of heavier incoming shells. The car seemed rather like the Humbers used by the Hussars in the Western Desert. He set the sack of grenades on the seat beside him, pumped the gas pedal and pressed the starter button. The engine coughed three times and turned, almost soundless in the rising din of battle. Denby untied the sack and placed a grenade on the seat, folding the top of the rough cloth across it so it would not roll onto the floor.

The Panhard lurched forward in low gear, bouncing hard over the broken ground on the rough top of the breakwater. Ahead of him two machine guns were firing from their protected positions into the advancing boats. Other French soldiers, some black, probably Senegalese, were firing bolt-action rifles from behind the concrete parapet on the inshore side of the embankment. On the mole that jutted into the harbor, a party of French marines was picking off swimming Americans with steady rifle fire. Two Renault light tanks were shooting over the men's heads with cannon and machine guns as the landing craft grounded on the steep beach and their bow ramps lowered.

Twice Denby's car almost stopped. Once it became lodged when the forward wheels caught between the jagged rocks that decked the top of the breakwater. He backed up a few feet, then forced the car forward until it jammed fast.

Denby moved into the gunner's seat as several soldiers from the line of Frenchmen on the breakwater glanced back at him, their guns trained on the harbor. Behind them, more Americans and British were storming ashore as their boats crashed onto the beach. He checked the side-mounted drum magazines of the twin machine guns, praying he would have a chance to use all 150 rounds that each one should carry. He took hold and aimed at his targets.

Denby's guns began to fire, sweeping steadily back and forth across the line of exposed Frenchmen before him. He felt lost in the crackling roar of the gunfire, entirely absorbed in his own concentration. Frenchmen's bodies twitched and crumpled as the bullets struck them. One soldier turned in time to release a line of shots through the open window of the armored car before Denby could cut him down. The Englishman flinched as a bullet punched into the back of the driver's seat. Denby swung his machine guns back, shooting steadily into the line of firing men. Then one gun jammed and the other began to smoke and overheat before he was able to turn his fire onto the first machine gun nest. He struggled with both weapons without success. Bloody French incompetence.

He saw two men in the first nest scrambling to shift their gun from its embrasure onto their new enemy.

Denby opened the door and jumped down with a hand grenade in one hand and the open sack in the other. The cat sprang out and dashed under the vehicle. Just like cricket, he thought as he pitched the first grenade towards the French. It landed beside the first machine gun. Crouching low, he waited for the explosion as he pulled the pin from the second grenade. There was no explosion. The Frenchmen adjusted their gun on its heavy tripod and turned it towards him. Denby threw another. The second grenade fell in the midst of the gun crew and exploded as it touched the ground.

Denby ran to the first machine gun as the crew of the next one screamed and struggled to re-aim their weapon. He glanced up as a Warhawk dove towards the breakwater. He saw for the first time the white star of the United States Army Air Force. The plane's piston engine screamed as its six machine guns strafed the French defenders. Stone splinters whistled and rose in a line as the American gunfire stitched along the rocks of the embankment.

Denby Rider felt a cut to his face and a blow in his shoulder as he threw himself down beside the gun that had been set free of its harbor embrasure. At least he had played a hand to help the attack. Then he saw nothing as the world went black.

Chapter Four

Anton Rider stepped out onto the sidewalk of the Shari el-Gezira, squinting in the bright sunlight of the late Cairo afternoon. He leaned against the front wall of the Anglo-American Hospital and closed his eyes. Stamping out his cigarette, he wiped his face with his red kerchief. The difficult delivery, the glory of Wellie's leaving a boy in the world, and the confusion he felt on seeing his wife, all left him feeling as if he had gone ten rounds in the ring with a younger and stronger man.

Soon his wife and Olivio would be down. He knew Gwenn would insist on talking to the doctors on her own. Wellington's baby boy was her grandchild, too, and as a surgeon herself, she would want to understand everything.

The dwarf's maroon Mercedes Benz waited nearby, parked directly across the road. A barefoot street boy, no doubt retained as a guardian, stood proudly beside it. Discouraging the approach of other youths, he wiped a rearview mirror with the long cuff of his outsize gallabiyah. Formerly black, now painted in the dwarf's livery, the motorcar had been the personal vehicle of the ambassador of the Third Reich. Olivio would have preferred green, but in the land of the pharaohs no one other than King Faruq was permitted to possess a green motorcar. A spare white-walled tire was mounted in the back of each front fender. The auto was a gift to Alavedo from Nahas Pasha, the Prime Minister, in appreciation of the little Goan's contributions to flood relief in the Delta. As a general rule, Olivio favored Daimlers, but Anton suspected that his small friend enjoyed the powerful provenance of this gift.

A column of khaki Morris ambulances drew up in front of Anton and lined the curb. The large red crosses on their sides were brown with the gritty dust of the Western Desert. Most had battered fenders and arcs of clear glass where their windscreen wipers had cleaned away not rain but the desert itself.

Egyptian medical orderlies and Indian Army stretcher bearers, many in turbans, began busily unloading the worst cases. The latest casualties, Anton reckoned, from the pursuit of Rommel and the Afrika Korps across Libya and into Tunisia. Reminded of his friends, always more at ease in the field than the city, Rider sometimes missed the fraternity of warfare.

"Can I help?" asked Anton, holding open a rear door of one ambulance. Sand was scattered on the floor of the vehicle. Two orderlies reached inside and lifted the handles of a stretcher. "Thank you, effendi, but we can manage," said one of the Indians as they started across the sidewalk towards the hospital with their burden.

Rider looked down at another stretcher, certain the man must be already dead. The broad bandages that bound the soldier's head were glazed dark with dried blood and set thick with sand like an emery board. Anton looked into the open double door of another ambulance. Two figures lay side-by-side on stretchers. He saw one reach across the narrow space and rest his hand on the other man's arm. As he passed, Rider set his precious pack of Senior Service on the edge of the first man's stretcher. In wartime there was never enough tobacco.

The rear door of the next ambulance opened. A glance at the high canvas lace-up boots and lime-green breeches of one casualty and at the gaiters and ankle-length desert shoes of the other, told Anton these were Germans, most likely a Panzergrenadier and a tanker. He was not surprised. Rommel had started this generous practice when the Afrika Korps captured a British forward aid station in Libya over a year before. German and British medical teams had worked side-by-side for weeks, treating casualties from both sides as if they were their own. On no other war front, he had heard, was this true.

Then Anton saw Gwenn Rider appear at the door of the hospital and wait on the step as Tariq emerged holding his small master in his arms. Gwenn seemed more collected now, slightly flushed, and smiling like a schoolgirl. He was certain she had cried. He wished he could hold her.

"Mr. Anton," said the dwarf in a voice that did not invite rejection, "I am inviting Miss Gwenn and you for a cocktail at the Cataract Café to celebrate the birth of our grandson."

Anton held up a hand and led the three across the busy street, swarming with horse-drawn gharries, a small herd of fat-tailed sheep and old bicycles laden with panniers of figs and charcoal. The usual chaos of Cairo mixed feverishly with staff cars and lorries and armored vehicles, all the varied transport of warfare. They avoided a motorcycle dispatch rider as the man swerved around a broken-down donkey cart loaded with vivid green *birsiim*.

Tariq settled the dwarf high on a throne of beaded cushions in the back seat as Anton held open the rear door of the magnificent machine. Then Gwenn joined the little man. Rider sat in the front as Tariq drew on his driving gloves.

Anton looked out the window, startled to see Cerisse Bouvet step out the door of the hospital and gaze up and down the street. He hardly noticed her legs and figure. Was she looking for him? When the Mercedes pulled away, he had a flash of interest and wondered if the Canadian girl had seen him.

As they joined the traffic, Anton was just as pleased that the heavy glass partition was raised, making it impossible for him to hear Gwenn and Olivio conversing behind him. The events of the day and now motoring along the Nile with his wife and the dwarf, made him think how quickly the time between the two wars had passed.

At eighteen, just after the Great War in 1919, Anton Rider had crewed out alone from Portsmouth and jumped ship at Dar-es-Salaam, making his way across Tanganyika and Kenya to the White Rhino Hotel in Nanyuki. There he had met the two men who were still his true friends: Adam Penfold, a lonely impractical English gentleman from a bygone time, and Olivio Fonseca Alavedo, then the Goanese dwarf bartender of the up-country hotel owned by Lord Penfold and favored by farmers and big game hunters. And on the way out from England, on board the rusty steamer *Garth Castle*, he had met Gwenn, now again the lost love of his life.

Back then, with Africa before him, Anton had been young and sound, entering a land and a life that suited him and his training. It had been a youth of stalking and poaching, gambling and fair-ground boxing, wandering England in a wagon with his mother and her gypsy lover, Linares, the man who had given him his first diklo and the slim Romany knife he still carried.

He glanced at the overhead mirror and saw Gwenn's profile as she talked with Olivio. Although appearing tired, she was still lovely, and more than that, courageous. Had their marriage always been hopeless, or should he have done better? She was ten years older, better educated and decently ambitious, and he had been young, craving adventure and all the foolishness that came with being a professional hunter with spoiled clients in the bush. Somehow in Kenya the two of them had seemed to manage to survive it all. But their move to Cairo in the thirties, with Gwenn at medical school and him on long distant safaris in Ethiopia and the Sudan, had tested both of them too thoroughly, especially when war had come to Abyssinia while he was there on safari.

For years she had tolerated his brief flings as inevitable mischief in a younger wild husband. But when Gwenn took on more serious romantic relationships in her own life, neither he nor she could reconcile that with any sense of marriage, despite their children. Now she was living with

Major Alistair Treitel, a poncy scholar attached to the intelligence service, reportedly with the education and money to satisfy her needs.

Alavedo tapped on the glass and the Nubian lowered the window between the seats. No longer spared by the ambassador's old diplomatic amenity, Anton could not avoid the conversation.

"It seems the war is taking a better turn," said the dwarf brightly, no doubt thinking to avoid awkward personal matters. "At least in Africa. And who thought Cairo could be so busy? We have never seen so many uniforms at the Cafe."

"A few of the smoothest ones never make it out of Cairo," said Anton over his shoulder, wondering if Gwenn understood this reference to her new gentleman caller.

"There are many ways to help win the war," said Gwenn, understanding very well. "Some men contribute their intelligence. You just act like it's one more jolly safari, although everyone is getting killed."

"They say the very smartest ones are campaigning at the Gezira Club rather than in the desert," continued Anton, trying to keep his voice easy. "Seems that sort prefer to spend their evenings at the Long Bar rather than under canvas."

"Not everyone is best at killing people," said Gwenn, knowing how to gall him.

Before he replied, becoming angry, Anton thought of brave friends both he and his sons had lost. He stared at the Roman numerals of the clock on the dash of the Benz, counting as the long second hand turned. Perhaps he should teach Gwenn the true meaning of her words.

"Thank heavens Wellie killed a few before they got him." Anton knew he should not be saying this. Now Gwenn would not let go, torn between cold anger and emotional pain.

"God bless the boy," the dwarf interjected with a distant voice.

"And I... ...nby's potted a few more . . ." Anton managed before Gwenn's cut in.

"Wellington might still be with us, Anton Rider, if he had not signed on so early, in that first frenzy of patriotic madness. I told you not to encourage him." She leaned forward. "I told you. You know I told you." She paused. "Then Saffron would have a husband and their baby would have a father."

"The whole world is at war, Gwenn. You know all his friends joined up." Anton turned in his seat and faced his wife before continuing. "What would you expect a good proud boy to do? Hide in Cairo like that rich professor of yours?"

"Ah, here we are," interjected the dwarf as if he had heard nothing, though for some time he had been interested in this new suitor of Miss Gwenn's. "Here we are. The perfect time for a cocktail." He clapped his tiny hands joyfully as the car drew up alongside the embankment. "The day is cooling. The sun is low on the Nile, my dear friends, and the Café is not yet crowded."

They crossed the embankment and approached the sloping gangway that led to the dwarf's floating Café. Gwenn Rider followed behind Olivio, her lips closed tight like the lid on a jar. With his master in his arms, Tariq, normally silent, called out to the waiting barman on the deck below.

"Allah is great!"

The man on board beamed and raised both hands. The good news was understood. The uncertain celebration could go forward. The barman clapped twice. Servants in white gallabiyahs and maroon sashes swarmed onto the deck with trays and ice buckets. Two girls, six and twelve, ran forward to greet their father. A small boy in a white tunic followed more slowly. Strangely dignified, he carried an adult fencing mask in one hand and a short épée in the other.

"Papa! Papa!" the girls cried, kissing the dwarf gently as Tariq held his master lower, turning him left and right for each embrace. "It's a boy! It's a boy! We knew it!"

"We must behave," said Gwenn quietly to Anton, without looking directly at her husband.

"Of course," he said, resenting the instruction.

"Olivio is always so charming," said Gwenn, as if gracefully changing the conversation.

"One might think so," said Anton, smiling to himself. Yet that was only one side of the little man. Anton recalled how back in '21 Alavedo had slowly drowned Vasco Fonseca, a Portuguese planter from Mozambique, in a tank of molten creosote. For Anton Rider, then a young man without education, the dwarf had served as an example of how to serve both one's enemies and one's friends. Gwenn understood only one part of that lesson.

"I was told there was no more Heidseick in Egypt," said Gwenn, accepting a glass of that champagne.

"So they say," said Anton, bending to kiss Olivio's daughters. "Hullo, Ginger. Cinnamon, dear. And this squire with the sword looks like my young friend and god-son, Tiago himself."

The two girls curtsied. A short heavy boy with an outsize round head, Tiago Fonseca Alavedo shifted his mask and slipped his épée under his left arm, hilt forward. It was difficult to guess his age. His face was not that of a child. The little boy bowed stiffly as he shook Gwenn's hand. This lad, thought Anton, is truly his father's son.

They all climbed to the poop deck to join the dwarf at his table.

"There is a God!" announced the little man. Welcoming them, he raised his glass in celebration and gazed down at his three children on the deck below. His body was painful and weary, but his mind was singing.

"To our grandson." And if there truly is a God, thought the dwarf, then one day this infant will have the strength and stature of Anton Rider and the brains and cunning of the Alavedos.

They drank and a steward appeared and held out a salver with an unstamped tan envelope addressed to Captain A. Rider, Long Range Desert Group.

"A dispatch rider brought this for you, effendi." The words "On His Majesty's Service" were printed across the top of the envelope above a single black line.

"Excuse me," said Anton, tearing the envelope open and quickly reading his new orders.

He had not escaped the war for long.

***

Nothing like a nap enhanced by the gentle rocking of his houseboat on the river Nile. A brief repose for the pure of heart, thought Olivio Fonseca Alavedo. He reached for the pigskin handle suspended above his bed and slowly pulled himself up with a long groan. There were so many ways to celebrate important personal events, the dwarf reflected. He wondered if there were any with which he was not familiar, in some cases, too familiar.

He sat up and tried to arch his uneven rounded shoulders one by one, back and forth, while his mind began to work and his schemes flowered again. He was concerned about his friend, Anton Rider, setting off on another campaign for which he was not fit, in a hard land where he knew neither friends nor language. And leaving behind his wife, once again encumbered with an unsuitable romantic partner. Perhaps this was where the dwarf might be of help.

Already Olivio had begun to make a study of this academic Englishman of hers, the professor's habits, his attitudes, his associations. Alistair Treitel, a major in intelligence, known as "the Don," seemed to have a relationship with a coterie of expatriate English self-considered intellectuals, some who had paraded in that civil war in Spain, on the losing side, and others who admired what Alavedo's physician called "those decadent Marxist philosophers." There were whispers that an associate of Treitel's, an officer called Blunt, might have a hand in military contraband, a massive market in Cairo and Alexandria.

The dwarf's informant at the Department of Antiquities had advised him that both these Englishmen were interested in a dig on the Upper Nile that, due to the limitations of wartime, was not being properly monitored by the authorities. Any one of these concerns might give Olivio himself an opportunity to assist Mr. Anton by complicating the affairs of his wife's suitor, Major Treitel.

Alavedo grunted as he slowly swung his legs to the edge of the low bed and tried to wiggle his baby-like toes. His favorite green brocade slippers waited, their pointed toes curling up in the old Turkish style.

Jamila would be arriving shortly, with the lofty expectations he had earned. He must be prepared, both for their private recreation and for the more varied entertainments that sometimes followed. As the *doyenne* of Cairo's most celebrated belly dancers, Jamila was renowned in the Nile valley for her ability to bend a thin gold coin in her navel. But she was no longer the inspired young woman she had been when Olivio had first arrived in Egypt twenty years earlier. Now she was a woman jaded with knowledge and experience, though never in her enthusiasms when she was with him. For the dwarf was more than a client, more even than a lover.

He alone gave Jamila what other men did not: her own pleasure. Long ago the dwarf had learned that to be desired, he must give women what other men, preoccupied with their own brief pleasure, did not. The less appealing one was physically, the more one was obliged to perform the sexual toil. Accordingly, Olivio sought to share fully the purpose and dream of a woman's most intimate satisfactions. Other men, diplomats and bankers, generals and archeologists, saw Jamila for their own delight and excitement. They desired the dancer for her movement, her breasts, her skin, her scent and her patient provocations. None of them possessed the inclination, skill or imagination to transport the woman, Jamila herself.

Her favorite treat, one she and Olivio limited to her private birthday celebrations and to his own saint's day, arose when the dwarf insinuated a small but ripe Delta fig near her intimate center and then drew back its petals with his lips. He worried the moist seeds about her until at last he pursued them one by one with his peculiar long pointed tongue, finally devouring Jamila and the fig as if they were a single fruit.

At such merry times, his own little body, normally stiff and painful with the hideous premature aging so common to dwarfs, came alive again and he became limber as a boy, or so it seemed. These privileged figs, of course, were no ordinary syconia, but were a little mutation cultivated on his own farms. Easily planted, they yielded three crops a year, their ovaries contained in succulent receptacles. Alavedo was not surprised that figs were domesticated thousands of years before dates, grapes or olives.

This evening Jamila would oil and massage him, then dance on her knees above him, occasionally sweeping his yellow dome-like belly with her heavy breasts and with the curtain of her long thick hair. Today they would have to finish early, before the new dancers arrived, her training class of the young women who would be the divine belly dancers of tomorrow. The hold of the Cataract Café was the perfect studio for this university of the senses, where the pupils learned an ancient trade that combined discipline and abandon.

Some new dancers, of course, were still confused by their own personal combination of youthful lust and innocence. As the young women passed along the gallery of the lower deck for the first time, a few were alarmed by the precious images assembled there. Middle Kingdom statues in clay and stone, later fragments of papyrus and murals, all depicting the dwarf god Bes, sometimes magnificently rampant or precocious, in other depictions innocent or aged. Later, relaxed, most would stop to giggle behind their hands as they studied these artifacts more closely.

Occasionally, aroused by her own dancing, a young woman became too excited to contain herself. In time they would learn to direct that sexual energy into the dance itself. When their studies were finished, and their arts complete, his Café would be the setting to which each one aspired, and its owner would be her patron in the fullest sense.

As the vessel rocked gently and the musicians played on deck with their instruments echoing below, as if contained inside a drum, incense would cloud the hold as the dancers practiced under Jamila's eye, singly and finally together, joining in each other's intoxication as the little man passed among them, sharing favors, distributing his own. What more could a gentleman ask? What more could each young flower ask of him?

Even before he heard her gentle double knock at his cabin door, Olivio's fine nose detected the scent of her perfumes. A blend of sandalwood and something French, the finest intoxicants of Europe and the East.

With a rustle of silk, Jamila entered. A short dark figure in cape and hood waited between two tall candle holders. He shuffled two small steps towards her. A faint snuffle of excitement escaped him as he loosed the golden cord at her waist. Her robe spread open. She reached down and lifted the cape from the shoulders of the dwarf. His hard yellow belly protruded forward shamelessly as he stepped to her and buried his face between her legs.

Chapter Five

Waiting for the senior officer to speak, Rider touched his pocket to be certain that the small leather box was still safely there. As soon as he was finished with this Major Treitel, he would take it to the hospital. But first he must tolerate this meeting with the lover of his wife.

"Ever made your way to Jugoslavia, Captain?" said the Don. The major glanced through a folder of papers as he spoke, carefully allowing their meeting no more importance than it deserved.

Dignified and at ease, with tight sharp features and wavy grey hair, the older officer seemed at home with his position, if not his uniform. Clearly from one of the better Cairo tailors, probably Collacott or Phillips, the sort of luxury Anton could not afford, the well-cut cotton khaki drill of his shorts and tunic fitted him too well, failing to enhance his thin wiry arms and angular shoulders.

A long blackboard was mounted behind the major's table. The other three walls were covered in maps of southern Europe and North Africa. Certain that this pedantic officer enjoyed his classroom tools and authority in Cairo as he had at Cambridge, Anton turned his attention to the battle map of North Africa. He wondered how Denby was faring in Tunisia.

Rommel's German and Italian army, identified by tiny black swastikas and green fasces, was in flight to the west along the Mediterranean coast. Squeezed from the east by Montgomery's pursuing Eighth Army, and from the west by the recently-landed forces of Alexander, Eisenhower and Patton, the wily German field marshal seemed caught between the small Union Jacks of the British forces and the Stars and Stripes of the Americans.

"I say, Captain Rider, have you been to Jugoslavia, or is that beyond your range?" said Major Treitel sardonically. "Not enough elephants, perhaps?"

"Jugoslavia?" retorted Anton with a touch of cheek, not willing to be lectured by the one officer he was keen to avoid. "Jugoslavia? No, no, can't say I have, sir."

"Well, now's the time for you to catch up. Jugoslavia's becoming more important to us every day. We've been sending in teams for some time now, mostly SOE, Special Operations Executive, occasionally with a few Yanks added on."

Alistair Treitel was one of the instant majors assigned to intelligence and special operations. Before the war he had been a tutor at King's College and a professor of classical history, more at home bickering about the Caesars than directing men under fire. Some whispered that he had been part of an intellectual Cambridge coterie that for a time celebrated Karl Marx and Leon Trotsky. Worse, the professor's friendship with Anton's wife had become more than that. Treitel had just the sort of cultural patina and independent means that Gwenn now seemed to favor. If the old girl wanted stark contrast with her husband, she had found it.

The last thing Anton expected was to find himself taking orders from this skinny sherry-sipping pansy. He looked to one side, noticing the books on the crowded shelf behind the Don's desk: Polybius, Webb, Shaw, Bukharin, whoever they were. In front of the books was a picture frame laying on its face. Gwenn? His wife?

"The job of these missions and the makeup of the team depends on where they're going."

Major Treitel spoke slowly, as if to a dull student, all the while scratching his ankle with a blackboard pointer jammed down inside his long khaki sock. He continued in a distant drawling voice, perhaps aware that even his accent and tone annoyed Anton Rider.

"If it's Jugoslavia or Albania, the idea is to help the locals fight the Jerries. We fly them out of Egypt or Libya straight across the Med. Shorter and safer than flying across Nazi-occupied Europe from home." He tapped a map twice with his pointer as if Anton could not otherwise identify the sea.

"Basic theory, Rider, is to tie up as many Heinies as possible in those ghastly Jugoslav mountains, the Jura Alps, so they can't go and play about on the French coast or the Russian front, where the real fighting is going on. Uncle Joe's doing most of the dirty work for us, of course."

Real fighting, thought Anton bitterly. What did the Don think Tobruk and Alamein were about? Not to mention Bir Hakeim, where his son Wellington had perished in June.

"If they're dropped into France," continued Treitel, "the grub's a bit better, and the teams are meant to be setting things up for the channel invasion, whenever that is, but they end up spending most of their time dodging about, trying not to let the Frogies sell 'em to the Gestapo."

"Of course." At least they could agree about the French, thought Anton. Their army had just changed sides again, after first sinking a British destroyer and killing over a thousand Americans and Englishmen as they struggled ashore in Algeria. Once the landings had succeeded, the French commander, Admiral Darlan, had changed sides, abandoning Petain and Vichy, and declaring for Free France and de Gaulle. The next day Darlan himself was murdered by another French officer.

Irritated by the lecture, Rider stepped behind the professor to study the arrows and lines on the blackboard.

"I say, Rider, are you with me?"

"Right you are, sir. Just having a glance at your map of the Torch landings in Algeria and Morocco."

"Quite. First time anyone's seen an American in uniform in Africa. We've been fighting out here for three hundred years. Against the Dutch, the Sudanese, Ethiopians, Zulus and what not. Now the Germans for the second time. No telling how the Yanks will take to it."

"Perhaps they'll be our Italians."

Treitel did not smile. "Well, you'll find out about that firsthand, on your own mission. You'll be meeting up here first thing tomorrow for a little education, Rider. Learn something about what the real Nazis are up to. They're not all gents like the Desert Fox."

"My mission?" Anton reacted sharply. "I'll be going back to the desert soon, out in the blue, rejoining my squadron for the push to Tunis. We're just refitting all the jeeps with Brownings, and the Bedfords with new tires and radiators." Anton shifted his stiff leg.

Major Treitel shook his head slowly from side to side, enjoying his authority. "For the moment, Captain, you're assigned to us. To the SOE. Intelligence in the field, if you like." He paused, obliging Anton to wait for him to go on. "That's why they sent you down here to see me. Even said you wanted a spot of action."

Anton wished he could give the Don a challenging assignment in the field, perhaps something involving thirst and hunger and German steel. When Rider did not respond, Treitel continued.

"If it's the Balkans you're after, this will be your go. Straight on in to Jugoslavia, Bosnia to be exact. Maybe with a sideshow in Croatia on your way home. And you won't be lolling about in jeeps and lorries."

"Sir . . ."

"I'd wager, Rider, that you're a bit light on Bosnia-Herzegovina, so I'll just give you a short course."

Anton did not reply. No doubt Gwennie had told this smooth scholar of hers that Rider had been spared what most people considered an education.

"Trouble all began about 1400 when the Pope declared the Bosnian Catholics heretics and urged Hungary to destroy them. So the Bosnians

49

sought protection from the Ottomans, who were already just across the way in Serbia." The Don identified Jugoslavia with sharp taps of his pointer. "That invitation brought the Turks right into the center of Europe, finally to the gates of Vienna, and in time made most Bosnians into Muslims, blue-eyed ones at that. All the fault of the Holy Father in Rome, of course. Typical Italian intrigue, not to mention messy church-craft."

Despite himself, Anton found that he was growing interested as he studied the map. Except for Dickens, he was not much of a reader, but after Ethiopia and the Western Desert, he was an old hand with maps.

"Four hundred years later, the Austrians invaded Bosnia and op-pressed all of them, Muslims and Christians alike. Then, in 1914, a young Serbian Bosnian murdered the Austrian Archduke in Sarajevo. So Austria invaded Serbia and began the Great War. After that Bosnia became part of Jugoslavia until Hitler moved in to sort them all out again. Now we're trying to mess up the Jerries by stirring up the Jugo-slavs, mostly Tito's red Partisans."

Major Treitel stood in one spot, his thin legs spread apart, rocking backward and forward like a metronome as he lectured. Anton could tolerate him now that he was being useful.

"Mihalovic and his royalist Chetniks are on our side as well, but they are not good for much, so we're better off helping the Reds. On the opposite side, the Croatian Ustashi are supporting the Germans and the Eyeties. They're running death camps where they're killing off their Serbian enemies and Jews and Gypsies and what not. Worst camp seems to be at Jasenovac, on the Sava River, right on the border of Bosnia and Croatia. Reportedly the Ustashi hang bodies from trees along the riverbank, even the children."

"Very interesting, sir," Anton said as his stomach tightened. He wondered if Gwenn had told this man that he had been raised by Gypsies in England, and whether Treitel was trying to stir him up. He decided not to rise to it. He tried not to think of gypsy girls and boys hanging from trees. He remembered playing with the Romany children in England under the narrow wagons in the gypsy camps and learning their tricks of sleight-of-hand and card play. "But what about this mission?"

"There will be only three of you on this one, Rider. Major Sparrow from SOE will be in charge. Bit mad, they tell us, but speaks all those beastly languages and knows the Jura mountains from his days hiking about and drawing before the war. Seems he'd rather sketch or watercolor than eat or fornicate." Treitel stroked his hair back with both hands as he glanced at some notes and yawned. "The other fellow's an American Air Force officer from ACRU, their Air Crew Rescue Unit. Captain Simon, he's called." Treitel eyed Anton shrewdly. "You'll enjoy that one. They say he's a bit prickly. Chap's meant to set up escape routes across Jugoslavia for downed American fliers. Don't know how much use that might be," he scoffed.

Though irritated, Anton reminded himself to think like a hunter, not like a soldier. Instead of being annoyed, he should study this man as he would an animal on a stalk. There was something in the way the officer spoke that caught Anton's ear. Not in his words but in his tone, a note of detachment, almost disinterest, as if none of it really mattered, as if the war was for other men.

"Just now we're a bit short-handed. That's why you're on loan to us." Treitel frowned at the acknowledgment. "Luftwaffe out of Crete caught two plane loads of our chaps over the water. Our old Halifaxes are no match at night for Goering's one-tens, you know. Damned twin-engine Messerschmitts come at you in the dark like a bat after a mosquito. Best night fighters in the sky."

Rider could imagine how many nighttime missions Professor Treitel had flown over the Med. Before Anton could ask, the major continued.

"Still, we have to keep trying. Meant to 'set Europe ablaze,' says the P.M. And he wants us to work like twins with the Yanks even if they're rather awkward. So we're having to fill up the next flight or two with men from out here who haven't had our usual Highland schooling, Rider. Probably skip parachute class altogether. Better to risk losing men on the jump that counts rather than losing them in training, eh?" He nearly chuckled at Anton's look of discomfort. "Jump masters tell us you're less likely to have an accident in one real jump going in than if you do five or six practicing."

Rider tried to put the thought aside. He had always hated extreme heights, especially the jagged cliffs and escarpments of Ethiopia. When he had been fleeing the Italian army fifteen years before, the land had often been harder than the enemy. Even the mules and camels had sometimes perished when they lost their footing.

"Any event, we've no time for beginners," continued Treitel. "We need men with special skills, who already know what they're about. Explosives, languages, radio, long-range sniping, whatever. That's where you might help."

"How's that, Major?" Anton asked skeptically. He was no religious scholar, but he knew enough of his Bible to be familiar with the tale of the king who sent his lover's husband into battle in order to free her bed for himself.

"They say everyone's good at something, and you're meant to be rather handy with a rifle, are you not?" For the first time the Don betrayed a twinge of envy. "Probably all that fooling about in the bush in BEA, the great white hunter saving infatuated clients from tigers and pythons and what not."

"We have no tigers in Africa, Professor," Anton commented quietly.

Major Treitel ignored the correction, and the inappropriate honorific. He bent down and pulled one sock up his leg before he spoke again.

"There are two things Tito's Partisans seem to care about: killing their enemies and protecting their wounded. Seems it's bad for morale when the Nazis overrun a field hospital and kill all the wounded. But that's not your worry," he said with a tight smile. "We know you'd be better at the killing end of it."

"Thank you, sir."

"There are one or two men in Jugoslavia we need to kill," he went on. "A German general and a Ustashi colonel, the founder of the Black Legion, the Croatian fascists who run the death camps. It's time we gave Tito's Partisans a bit of a hand. There's no favor like a good assassination, and if we do the job for them, the other side is less likely to take reprisals against the locals."

***

"May I?" said Anton Rider later, standing beside Saffron's hospital bed in the best corner room at the Anglo-American. The antiseptic smell of the institution was overwhelmed by the lavish scent of the jasmine and fresh roses that crowded against the radio on the bureau. He heard the BBC broadcast "Sincerely Yours" playing quietly in the background, the gentle bittersweet voice of Vera Lynn, the 'Armed Forces Sweetheart,' singing one of the songs that were breaking the heart of every lonely soldier.

> *We'll meet again,*
> *Don't know where,*
> *Don't know when,*
> *But I know*
> *We'll meet again*
> *Some sunny day.*

Anton had been waiting impatiently at the door of Lattès on the Shari el-Manakh for Cairo's finest goldsmith to open early that morning. Now he watched as Saffron stared at the wedding ring in its red leather box. She looked up at Anton with trembling lips and shining eyes as he gave the girl what his dead son could not.

"May I?" he repeated softly, trying to smile, conscious of Olivio Alavedo standing behind him. The dwarf's face appeared just over the foot of the bed, his smooth round head framed against a wall of flowers.

The girl nodded and held out her left hand, the palm down. Anton lifted the gold band from the box and slipped it onto her wedding finger. She smiled at her father, then bit her lip. Now the child would be a Rider, and his mother would be an honorable woman, widowed by the war.

For a moment no one spoke. Olivio raised one hand to his shiny eye. The only voice came from the radio.

> *We'll meet again . . .*
> *Keep smiling through*
> *Just like you*
> *Always do*
> *Till the blue skies*
> *Drive the dark clouds*
> *Far away.*

After a loud knock the door opened. Anton turned, noticing that his little friend was blinking furiously. A nurse entered carrying a pink-faced baby boy that she set in Saffron's arms. The child squealed and began to grapple with his mother's tan swollen breast.

"Excuse me, please," said Anton, gently cupping the baby's forehead with the fingers of one hand. Then he kissed Saffron on the cheek before stepping to the door. "I'm due at HQ."

Chapter Six

"We're the lucky ones," said the young Irish staff officer to Denby Rider as the two emerged blinking into the sunlight outside the Hôpital de Dey in Algiers. "Live to fight another day and all that." Ten days had passed since Denby had been wounded during the Allied landing.

Behind them, Arab sweepers were mopping the wide portico of the old French military hospital. Originally built for the *Armée d'Afrique* in 1833, it was now occupied by Allied medical teams and served both the French themselves and the Yanks and Britishers the French had shot up as they came ashore.

"I'll stand drinks at the café tonight if you can find out where I can meet up with my regiment." Denby set his new cap above the dressing that covered one side of his head just above his ear. "The Eleventh Hussars." Under his tunic another bandage covered his left shoulder where they had taken out three small bits of shrapnel. He knew he had been lucky. "They should be pushing west somewhere, scouting for Monty's link-up with your lot." The Hussars, as usual, would be in the van of the Eighth Army, most likely well south of the main coast road, the Via Balbia. They would be searching for a soft spot to get around Rommel's Afrika Korps and his dwindling Eyeties.

Denby took a pedicab to the bottom of the Casbah. Three small boys, skinny and nimble and barefoot, followed him like a pack of hounds. They begged and whistled as he climbed the steep winding alleys and hundreds of narrow stone steps that rose between the old crowded buildings. Finally he found a small open restaurant at one end of a courtyard. The proprietor promptly drove off the youths.

Denby settled in to eat and drink, relishing the contrast with the privations of the desert. He drank red wine from the hills near Casablanca while an old Arab with a copper-trimmed box filled with a wonder of rags and polishes knelt and shined his new boots. The bootblack finished by treating the edges of each sole with a dark liquid stain. Then he bowed and gestured at his work with pride.

Feeling spoiled, Denby gorged on pigeon and couscous. He still had a fistful of French-Algerian francs from his mission, and he suspected they would not be good much longer. As he ate, images of his parents came to mind. The war had not been kind to them. His mother should be safe enough with her medical duties, but Denby worried that his father was getting old for the sort of hard service he seemed to favor.

His thoughts then turned, as they often did, to the older brother he had lost. He thought of Wellington's sunny confidence and courage. He wished he could be more like Wellie, both with the girls and with his mates. He recalled the boys he had seen killed by the Frenchies on the beaches and in the boats, all the cruel waste of it. The killing he himself had done did not disturb him greatly. There had been too much war, too much loss for that, not to mention the Gallic perfidy.

After a time Denby leaned back against the wall and covered his eyes with one hand. He had drunk too much, and he wanted more.

He ordered coffee and another bottle. He drank and nibbled dates dipped in honey.

Wellie would have been twenty-two next week. By now he would have been married and had his first child. Denby did not know whether it was a boy or a girl.

He thought of Saffron and how enticing she had been. Younger than Wellington, she was almost exactly Denby's age. But until he went to war, she had always seemed far more grown up. The two families used to share holidays. Saffron and Denby had always gone to each other's birthday parties. Hers were the most desired in Cairo, by the children at least. Saffron's mysterious little father would turn his vessel on the Nile into a magic party boat. Lanterns hanging from the masts, costumed pirates swinging from the rigging, brandishing cutlasses. Music, tumblers, clowns and acrobats, games of hide and seek on three decks and in the hold. More than any young person might imagine. And the child-sized host himself, each year in a different costume: Buonaparte, a Prince of the East, a one-eyed gladiator with net and trident. Always funny, dramatic and formidable.

Once Denby and Saffron, perhaps thirteen, had hidden in the same closet in the hold of the Cataract Café. She had pressed close to him in the mysterious exciting darkness. He could still remember her sweet perfume and the effect of her touch. It was the first time he had ever been kissed or had felt a girl's breasts. "Do you like them, Den?" she had asked after she unbuttoned the top of her pinafore and encouraged him. It was a secret experience he had never revealed to his brother. He wondered if Saffron ever thought of it.

Denby rested his bandaged head on the table and closed his eyes.

"Effendi," said the Arab proprietor after a time with gentle respect. "Effendi, please, it is time to place candles on the tables. We have dinner guests arriving for a party. An important American general. Please. "

Lieutenant Rider rose and made his way down the worn winding steps to the appointed café at the edge of the Casbah. There he found the Irish staff officer and two others well ahead of him, surrounded by overloaded ashtrays and empty bottles. He recalled his promise to pay for drinks. Seeing several dark cigars on the table, Denby took one and cut off the tip with the small blade of his pocket knife.

"Wine or gin, Lieutenant?" asked his friend from the hospital, holding a bottle high in each hand. Denby chose wine and the Irishman continued. "I have a secret for you. Since it concerns your own regiment, I may tell you. The Eleventh Hussars are on their way, with one squadron cutting far south through the Tunisian desert, bound first for the old French fort at El Adiyah, or thereabouts."

"Thank . . ."

The Irishman was not finished. "And here is a blank requisition slip for the motor pool with our HQ stamp on the bottom. What you do with it is your show, Lieutenant," he said. "But they have impounded a mass of French transport." He handed Denby the paper. "I'll count on you to use this for something French. They've got hundreds of Peugeots and Citröens, Simca motorbikes, Renault lorries. None yet repainted."

"And French camels, donkeys, street girls," added another drinker with a grin. "The girls get repainted twice a day."

Denby rose and left the others. Feeling dizzy, he washed his face in the loo from a bucket of cold water, then walked down the steps of the Casbah with the excessive slow care of the partially inebriated. Near the bottom of the ancient quarter he stopped in a café for two cups of coffee before finding a pedicab and making his way to the motor pool.

"Voilà, monsieur," said the slender Senegalese mechanic, smiling brightly beneath his red fez, his shiny face black as death. The man slapped his hand down on the broad high fender of a Citröen staff car. He pointed to the two spare wheels. He opened the boot and gestured towards a wicker picnic hamper. *"Convenable pour un colonel."* He pulled a long rag from his belt and wiped the windscreen. "Only the driver's door does not open as it should, monsieur."

The two climbed into the automobile. Denby pressed the starter button twice. The engine turned over. His mother's old suitor, Giscard de Neufville, had driven a motorcar very much like it and had taught Denby how to drive it. Denby had never been certain what had happened to Monsieur de Neufville, who had suddenly gone missing after his exposure as a Vichy-Axis informer.

From a friend in the Cairo Special Police, Denby had heard a rumor that Mr. Alavedo might have been involved in the Frenchman's disappearance, even that the dwarf may have had the brilliant Frog scholar prepared for the after-life by having him eviscerated and mummified in the ancient Egyptian manner. Any other man, killer or not, would seek to suppress such scandal. But Olivio Alavedo was known to foster and embellish such rumors to enhance his fearsome reputation and to confuse and discourage his adversaries.

"Voulez-vous un chauffeur superbe, mon lieutenant?" said the Senegalese, still in his French army shorts and long socks. *"Pour moi, pour Raoul, la guerre est terminée.* My battle is finished."

Why not? thought Denby Rider. It would be a long hot drive southeast across the Mzab to Ghardaia and Ghadames, and there might be scatterings of French garrisons along the route, not to mention mechanical problems with the Citröen.

"Let's have a look at the engine," he said after struggling to open the balky door and get out. The Senegalese unclipped the clasps that held down the long hinged bonnet and folded it back. Despite his training with armored cars, the sight was not much help to Denby.

"Clean it up, Raoul." He handed the man more francs. "Check everything. Air filter, tires, radiator, the lot. Fill the back seat with petrol tins and water. *Tout ce qu'il faut.* I will be back at noon." With food and wine, he thought. When he met his mates in the desert, the first thing they would ask was what had he brought to drink.

***

As the Morris ambulance slowed in the thickening traffic of central Cairo, Gwenn Rider untied the scarf she had wrapped around her nose and mouth for the long drive back from the military hospital north of town. She had taken a lift in the ambulance to help the two men who were being transferred to one of Cairo's better surgeries.

The mixed chaos of the city's traffic replaced the opposing columns of military transport and ambulances that had passed each other on the road since early morning. The Sikh driver and Gwenn had kept the windows lowered, agreeing that the confined heat and the smell from the back of the ambulance would be worse than any sand and dust. Perhaps she should have brought her gas mask, used by many old hands as protection against dust and sand storms. Gwenn reached down and unstrapped her medical pack, folding back the cover flap with its large faded red cross. She searched under her emergency surgical kit and pulled out the amenity she wanted, an army-issue metal shaving mirror. She removed her sun goggles.

Her lower face was relatively clean once she brushed away the gritty dust. But her green eyes, centered in pale circles like an owl, were red and tired. Her forehead and hair were filthy, dark beneath the edge of her service cap. Gwenn shook her head and pressed apart the tightening wrinkle lines between her eyebrows. She was still slim enough, she thought, but she was beginning to show her age. She was tired, tired all the way through. She knew her face showed it. No woman's looks lasted forever, though good legs and bones were said to last the best. She had been blessed with both. Gwenn closed her eyes and pressed one hand against her short tawny hair. In wartime Cairo, of course, European girls were as scarce as orchids in Wales. Any woman could have her pick of men. But all the same, as one got older, one had fewer romantic choices and opportunities, though right now all she wanted was to be alone.

She prayed that Alistair would not be home when she arrived back at the flat in Gezira. He would be after her at once with questions and some awkward demand for the confirmation of intimacy, or at least affection.

Most troubling were his recent outbursts of anger, after he had too much to drink, of course.

This damned war was changing everyone, including how men drank and smoked, and Alistair was no exception. His wartime job seemed to be affecting his temperament, and his behavior towards her. In the past, she had always enjoyed discussing his archeological interests, but now that he was in military intelligence, they no longer discussed his work.

A week ago, after Gwenn had poured out his drink before he finished it, he had taken her face in one hand and held it hard, pinching in her cheeks between his fingers. For an instant she had feared he was going to strike her. But finally he had controlled himself and let her go. Clearly upset with himself, he had apologized the next evening, but it disturbed her that she had, as never previously in her life, tolerated rough behavior.

Gwenn's mother had warned her that less imposing men, unable to fight or bully other men, sometimes used their frustrated violent impulses against their women. But Alistair had never been this way before. Always he had been gentle, even graciously affectionate. And now something else seemed to be bothering him as well. For the first time, she felt he was concerned about money.

Occasionally Gwenn wished she were on her own again, but Cairo was crowded and she could not afford a decent flat. Sometimes a girl had to be practical, as long as it did not compromise her too much. There was never a perfect choice. Gwenn knew she still loved Anton. She had always been enamored of his qualities, but his shortcomings had hurt her too many times. Alistair was brilliant, and was still said to be rich enough. He seemed devoted to her, and was extremely handsome, in a different way than Anton. Of course, she could always stay at Olivio's and be pampered like a princess, but generous as the little man was, that option, too, would have its complications.

The one person she was desperate to see every day was her new grandchild. The boy was a gift, from Wellie, and for him.

Right now, she thought, leaning back in her seat, all she really wanted was a bath, long and hot, then a nap, and later a glass of wine and a fine dinner in Cairo. That was one advantage of this desert war that her relationship provided, the luxury of being spoiled once home, only hours from the front.

For years, Anton had been absent on safari. Now he was absent on long-range missions.

The only news she craved was about Denby and that was probably impossible to obtain, though sometimes Alistair was able to learn about the larger campaign involving whatever unit Denby was with at the time. At least most of Morocco and Algeria was now in friendly hands. She just hoped her handsome boy was all right, perhaps carrying on with his mates in some unspeakable haunt in the casbah in Algiers. His father's son. She shook her head and smiled tightly.

Gwenn turned in her seat to examine the two figures strapped to the narrow stretchers on the floor of the ambulance behind her. One poor lad had been groaning continuously, the morphine inadequate to protect the young lieutenant from the perpetual painful bounces in the road. They had stopped once to change the dressings on his upper legs, but now the bandages were red and wet again.

"Allah save us!" shouted Mansur as he suddenly slammed the breaks.

Gwenn's left arm struck the windshield as she clung to the back of her seat with the other hand. She stared out as the ambulance skidded and her door crashed against the high wooden side of a donkey cart loaded with sugar cane. The other wounded man started cursing and moaning. The driver of the donkey cart screamed at Mansur and waved his stick, pointing at the left foreleg of his donkey. The animal turned its head and nibbled a sweet stalk of cane.

Dazed, Gwenn finally reached through the window and handed the carter a crumpled Egyptian banknote. The man spread the bill flat on one palm, squinting at the portrait of King Fuad before he nodded. Gwenn smelled the sweet cane as she turned around to speak to the wounded men while Mansur spat out through his window and drove on to the hospital.

Chapter Seven

"You are late, Captain," said Major Treitel without turning away from the wall map. Two other men assessed the new arrival. Three envelopes rested side by side on the table. "Major Sparrow, Captain Simon, this is your third man, Captain Rider, Long Range Desert Group. He'll be doing the shooting."

"Welcome on board, Captain," smiled Major Sparrow, a wiry man with a smallish head, lined face and a trim speckled mustache. The slight officer reminded Anton of a small bird he could not identify, a sand bird of some sort, perhaps a tern. "We've heard a certain amount about you, Rider. Old Africa hand, they tell us."

"Very old, sir." Anton gave a relaxed salute, palm forward in the British way. The American looked him over carefully before acknowledging him. Rider shrugged curtly in reply. The Americans had not proved much yet.

"Tomorrow morning we'll be kitting you all out," said Major Treitel to the three men. "Then you'll be off for Derna, just across the way in Libya, the closest aerodrome to Jugoslavia. Most likely they'll run you up there by Dingo. The army is ferrying up some new Mark II's. This afternoon you'll each be getting a little topping up with some specialized instruction. Major Sparrow already knows all about the old zoo we call the Balkans, but there's always something new." The Don paused and looked at Sparrow, as if inviting a comment from a pupil before he continued.

"In Jugoslavia the old men say, 'War in Croatia means blood to your ankles. War in Bosnia means blood to your knees. War in Serbia means blood to your neck.' You lads are off to Bosnia, so you should be able to wade nicely through it." For the first time the Don smiled. "In peacetime

Balkan politics are a jungle. All savages really. Wartime's even better, gives 'em a chance to refresh the vendettas, open the old wine, so to speak, educate the next generation about whom to hate. Our job is to make them all think they hate the Jerries more than they despise each other, for now, anyway."

Major Treitel pulled down a sheet of tracing paper over the wall map that featured Jugoslavia. "Bosnia is divided into ninety-five regions, each centered around an important town or city. Vitez and Travnik, Mostar and Tuzla." He tapped each with his pointer, identifying drop zones and escape routes, Partisan strongholds and railway bridges, and troop concentrations of Italians, Germans and Bulgarians. "Just remember, we've got two lots of good chaps who hate each other other as only brothers can: General Mihalovic's royalist Chetniks, who're mostly Serbs, and Tito's communist Partisans, who're a bit of everything. Chetniks wear beards. Partisans wear mustaches, like Stalin. You'll be dropping in Friday night if the weather holds over there."

The Don turned to the Yank before continuing. Anton noticed the Army Air Force wings on the jacket of the man's uniform. "Captain Simon here will have a cup of tea with the wallahs from what passes for RAF intelligence. Maps, German dispositions, target assessment, air crew escape routes, all of that."

The American nodded without expression. A heavy-shouldered man with a broad face, thick joining eyebrows and large spreading pores on his nose, Lester Simon had the solid hard bulk of a Graeco-Turkish wrestler. "As you say, sir," he said, pulling at the hair that curled from his ears, "but I already have my orders from the Air Force."

Treitel ignored the response. All were aware that the British regarded the American participation in such missions, perhaps even their late entry in the war itself, as essential but amateurish and cumbersome.

"As for you, Rider, your job is to do a mighty favor or two for Tito's Partisans, to encourage them to work harder on our side. Some of them are holding back from taking on the Germans, saving their strength to fight their brothers later, especially the Royalists, the Chetniks, after we and the Russians have finished off the Huns for them."

"Hope I can be useful, sir," said Anton, growing bored with political theory.

"The Germans have a commander who's been doing his job too well. He's trying to pacify Bosnia by killing villagers instead of by hunting Partisans in the mountains. That way he doesn't need so many men, and the Huns can keep their best troops on the eastern front or the Atlantic wall. Whenever a German soldier gets killed, this chap gathers a village together in the town square, strips the men and boys naked, and shoots ten or twenty against the wall of the local church or mosque. *Pour encourager les autres.* Usually comes himself to watch. If he's in a foul temper, he has the bodies pitched down the village well." Treitel looked up to gauge the men's reactions. "Müeller, he's called. General Manfred Müeller. Commands an SS mountain division. He's a proper Nazi, old chum of Heydrich from the early days in Munich, and he's after Tito's boys, not the Royalists, because they're supported by the Soviets. If we can kill this Müeller, the Partisans around there say they will do whatever we want."

Anton nodded. "And if I get him, sir, or if I can't get him?"

"The second chap we're after is that Ustashi colonel, Francetec of the Black Legion. His specialty is hunting down Partisan hospitals in the mountains, keeping them on the jump and killing them off while they're on the mend." He dragged his pointer along the Jugoslav coast. "You might even want to try a recce on that Jasenovac death camp before you pack up, then make your way to the coast somewhere near Dubrovnik, or else slip out by one of the escape routes Captain Simon will be setting up for the flyboys."

He set the pointer down, done with that task. "There's a car outside waiting to take you to the range, Rider. The armorer, 'the Bowman,' they call him, will fit you up with one of the new Number 4 T's, the finest sniper rifle in the world." Treitel turned to the other two officers and explained, "The T is for telescope."

Anton nodded again, beginning to understand why Gwenn liked this bookish major. Like a good hunter, the professor seemed to approach each part of an exercise in the most suitable way.

Sensing that at last he had attracted Rider's interest, Treitel continued. "Basically it's one of the new Enfield .303 service rifles converted by Holland & Holland. Sergeant Drummond, the 'Bowman,' used to run the sniping school. Won all the long-range medals at Bisley. He believes in three things: range, concentration, trigger control. He's hunted all over the Empire, though probably different sorts of game than you've been after, Rider."

The Don stood without saluting, and turned to face a different map. The meeting seemed to be concluded.

"By the way, gentlemen," said Treitel as his visitors approached the door, "each of you must take one of these envelopes. Your allowance is inside. A few Maria Theresa silver dollars and some gold coins for emergencies." He paused and added as if performing a generosity. "Plus an American Zippo cigarette lighter. Each lighter has two L-pills hidden at the bottom, something to put you to sleep forever if the Nazis catch you and might torture something useful out of you. Cyanide, of course. Never takes more than four minutes."

The three men gathered outside in the hall. Messengers, girls from the typing pool and young officers clutching papers passed one another busily. Rider heard the clack of typewriters and teletypes from a nearby room. All the encumbrances of running a war from the rear, he thought. How fortunate Rommel was always to be travelling light, without war correspondents or visitors from Whitehall or Horse Guards Parade. He led from the front, either in his mobile map van or scouting ahead, piloting himself in his light Fieseler Storch.

"Seems we have only two more evenings left in Cairo," said Major Sparrow to his new companions as an attractive WREN hurried along the corridor. She had a pencil over one ear just below her cap and smiled at Anton as she passed.

Rider dreaded that the superior officer was about to announce the requisite departure drink for his new band of men. This Captain Simon seemed a dour lot.

"Shall we meet up for a glass or two at Shepheard's or Groppi's?" said Sparrow with crisp cheerfulness. Neither man rushed to reply. "Which would you rather," continued Sparrow, "this evening? Or perhaps in Derna?"

Simon announced gruffly, "I'll be having a drink both nights."

"Actually, sir," said Anton, "I became a grandfather yesterday, and I've one or two things I should sort out myself before I leave . . ." Including completing his obligations with a certain foreign correspondent, he thought.

"Of course," said Sparrow, as if just as pleased himself. "Perhaps we'll catch that drink in Derna, shall we?"

***

Out at the range on the edge of the Western Desert, the Bowman seemed relieved to be outfitting a man who knew how to shoot. A bobby's silver police whistle hung around the old Scot's neck from a braided red lanyard. Anton noticed a captured "German camel," a small open motorcar with the doors missing, sheltered under a nearby shed. The tropical military version of the Volkswagen *Kübel*, or Bucket, the sand-colored vehicle looked as if it had seen hard service. A dark Indian Army soldier in a striped turban was wiping down the car.

"Most of these young subalterns are at home with a shotgun," said Sergeant Drummond in a clear powerful voice. His Scots accent with its rolling r's was thick as a Perthshire fog. "But rarely with a rifle, unless they've been on the hill, out stalking red deer up my way in the Highlands."

Although protected by the long canvas roof of the firing shelter, the sergeant's ruddy face and thick forearms were inflamed with sunburn. A long wooden chest painted desert khaki rested behind him. "Once you get the hang of it, shooting Eyeties is a deal easier than bringing down high-driven pheasant in the wind and rain," he observed. "No need to swing through the target, sir, just stay right on it as it runs away."

"I doubt your Scottish pheasants shoot back, Sergeant," said Rider. In East Africa, the old hunters had taught him always to respect the animals, and the same was true with an enemy, even Italians. In the bush, of course, the thrill was that while you were stalking one animal, another could be hunting you. Sometimes the same was true in war.

"Range," said the sergeant. "We'll start with that, sir. Range. I like two methods: either estimate distance in hundred-yard increments, or by calculating from the appearance of a single specific object that you have memorized at various ranges. If in doubt, average the two. But the first way is difficult in different lights and different terrain. See that third petrol drum out there, the red one? How many yards would you call him?"

Anton Rider squinted across the hard rocky sand into the heat shimmer. He tried to relate the barrel to the height of a man, and the distance from that.

"One hundred eighty, eighty-five yards."

"Two hundred, sir," the sergeant said flatly. "No good. You wouldn't get the drop right." He gestured towards the distant target. "Easiest way to measure distance in this work is by figuring from the size of the human head. Everyone has one, and it's what you'll be looking for anyway. Say every petrol drum is as wide as three or four heads. But from here it looks about like one. That makes it two hundred yards. Get used to figuring what a head looks like at every distance." He gestured towards the waiting soldier, who nodded stiffly. "Here now, sir, we'll use Singh. As he walks off and comes back to us, I want you to call out his distance every ten paces. Just watch his head. Ignore the turban."

"As you say, Sergeant."

"Singh!" bawled Drummond. "Singh! Quick march out to six hundred yards and back again. Hop to it."

The Sikh soldier set off at a trot into the firing range.

"Range?" asked the sergeant.

"Ninety yards. One hundred twenty. One hundred fifty. One hundred eighty," said Anton steadily, attempting to freeze the images in his memory. "Two hundred ten. Two hundred forty."

The sergeant shook his head. "Let's try again, sir. How far is that blue drum?"

"Three hundred yards."

"Right you are, sir," he said cheerfully. "Might have sighted down a barrel once or twice, eh?"

Drummond opened the wooden chest until the lid hung back on a short metal chain. "Here's the way the Royal Small Arms Factory ships these out to us, with the full Equipment Schedule. There's more in here than you'll be jumping with," he said, waving at several pieces. "You'll already have your own compass and glasses. Best part's the new Number 32 telescope sight. On a clear morning you could see Goebbels clipping hair from his moles."

The sergeant lifted the rifle from the chest, drew the bolt and stared at the sky through the long barrel before passing it to Anton.

"What did Holland do to it?" asked Anton, referring to his favorite rifle maker. In the old days he had taken heavy game with his double .375, usually when he was backing up an unsteady client or dropping a wounded animal.

"Mostly, sir, they stripped it, machined the body and drilled the rear pad," he said. "The telescope can be fitted on with thumbscrews and removed when you don't want it. So let's give her a try, shall we?"

Anton settled himself and calmed his breathing. He squinted through the telescopic sight. When Drummond blew the whistle, Anton fired five shots each at one hundred, three hundred and five hundred yards. His purpose was to learn his weapon and adjust it, not to impress the sergeant with his shooting. The Enfield was well-balanced, smooth in the hands and delivered only a modest punch in the shoulder if held in tight. That would be easier to control, he noted, if they extended the stock. A comfortable wooden cheek rest was already screwed to the butt. As Anton adjusted the scope, he noticed the Holland wartime code mark, "S51," stamped on the underside of the butt near the knuckle.

"Tight groups, Captain," said the Bowman, nodding, staring through a heavy pair of field glasses. "But all about eight o'clock. Some of them damned near punched the same hole." His tone was matter-of-fact. "We'll adjust the sights, then try some real shooting, sir."

Rider understood. At a stationary unsuspecting target, the first shot was the easy one. But to confirm the kill or if the target moved or was only wounded, an instant second shot on a moving target was essential. That was one reason why double-barrelled rifles with two triggers were used for heavy game in the bush. An immediate dependable second shot might save your life.

With the kick from the first shot, the target moving, one's brace now an impediment and the inevitable distractions that followed, the second bullet was always far harder to place. The trick was, as Anton had instructed clients many times, to keep your cheek on the rifle and your eye on the target, seeing nothing else as you combined accuracy with speed of fire.

Drummond leaned down and held the Enfield into Anton's shoulder. "We'll add an inch and one quarter to the stock," he said. "You've got arms like an ape, if you'll pardon the expression, sir." He glanced at Anton's large hands. Recognition bloomed on his face. "Captain, weren't you the chap who hammered Sergeant-Major Stoner in the ring about six months back? Broke the old pug's nose." Drummond smiled at the memory. "Turned his face into a proper pudding after he kidney-punched you in the clinch, if I recall, sir?"

"Luckily, my own nose was broken many years ago, Sergeant, while boxing for the Gypsies at a village fair," Anton replied. "But Stoner cracked two more ribs for me."

"You cost me a guinea, sir, you did," grumbled the Scotsman, shaking his head. "Never thought you'd get him down."

He called to one of the Sikh range boys. "Three hundred yards, Singh," he ordered in his drill-sergeant bark. "When I whistle, start running the stick to your left. Left!" Then, quietly to Anton, "Just call 'em all 'Singh.' Seems to work."

The Indian Army private ran to the three-hundred-yard target trench and dropped down. A six-inch black circle attached to a stick rose above the trench near the larger fixed target.

"When I whistle, Captain," said Drummond, "shoot the first target, then see what you can do with the second, moving target. We'll see how far it gets before you fire again. The idea is to finish your man with the second shot before he can take a full step. After that, you've lost him."

For a time the sergeant idled about, fiddling with his lanyard, turning his back. All the while Rider kept his cheek on the rifle, his elbows steady on the brace of the firing parapet. Without warning the whistle shrilled. Anton fired into the bull's-eye of the big target as the small target darted to the right. He raised the Enfield from the brace and fired again.

"Three yards. You nicked it, sir," said Drummond with scant satisfaction. "Unless your first shot killed him, the bugger survived." Their eyes met, and Anton nodded in agreement. "Let's try again. Prone this time. No brace."

Anton stepped in front of the parapet and groaned as he lowered himself onto his belly on the hot desert, outside the shade of the firing shelter. He spread his feet and braced his elbows on the grit. He was reminded of the clean smell of the dust and the acacia when he knelt or stretched down for a shot at home in Kenya.

The whistle blew at once. The small target leaped sideways as Anton fired. The two shots echoed together. The small target splintered into fragments. Several of its flying bits struck the larger target, perhaps a yard or less away.

"That's got him, sir," cried the armorer. "Chappie barely had time to wiggle his toes." Regarding Rider differently, the Bowman took the rifle from him and rested it on the wooden chest. "We'll just try one more. Something different," he added, climbing into the driver's seat of the German camel.

Anton joined him in the battered Kübel as the sergeant punched the starter and the vehicle shook to life. They drove down-range until Drummond stopped near a wooden stake set in a small cairn. The top of the stake was split into a tight fork. Anton squinted through the shimmering light of the desert at the firing shelter. Perhaps seven, eight hundred yards, he reckoned, maybe even a bit more.

The Bowman reached into a pocket of his tunic and drew out a clam-shell.

"That's come a long way," said Anton as the sergeant blew sand from it. The shell of the molusc was lined and rough on the outside, pale pink and smooth as a pearl on the inside, almost round.

"I always carry one for special occasions. It's usually safe enough over seven hundred yards," said Drummond. "Had this old shell for quite a time." He wiped the shell against his shorts. "In the old days, thirteen something or thereabouts, when the Black Prince sent his captains out into the counties to pick his longbowmen to fight in France, they had two tests. First, each archer had to hold up the first two fingers of his draw hand, in a V, to show he still could pull a bow, because the French-ies often chopped off those two fingers of a captured bowman so he couldn't come back and bother them again." He wagged his own two digits. "That's why Winnie holds up two fingers. It doesn't mean V-for-victory. It means ready to fight."

Anton nodded, understanding at last why they called him "the Bow-man." He shielded his eyes with one hand against the sand that suddenly gusted past in the rising wind.

"The archer's second test, sir, was to hit a clamshell. One hundred yards with a single three-foot arrow. Usually set the shell in the fork of a tree." The sergeant wedged the thin edge of the clamshell into the cleft at the top of the stake. "We don't have any trees out here, but it's your turn to hit the shell, Captain."

On the way back to the firing shelter, the sergeant stopped to pick up the Sikh. "Don't want to pop young Singh before his appointed time," said Drummond as the man squeezed into the tight back seat. "We'll let the Jerries do that."

Anton lay on his belly with the Enfield, squinting at the clamshell through the rising heat shimmer and the blowing sand. He considered the wind and the distance before adjusting the range screw of the telescope.

"Don't mind the sand, sir," called the sergeant from the shelter, a pair of field glasses in his hands. "There's always something special to every shot. Where I'd guess you're going, it'll be snow, and the glare will come from the ice, not the desert."

Concentrating, blanking out everything else, Rider fired. Before the fragments of the shell touched the ground, he fired again, splitting the post from its fork to the cairn.

Sergeant Drummond strolled over. "No need to waste any more bullets, Captain," he said as Anton rose, groaning, and handed him the rifle. "Looks like it won't be your first time. Let me work on the stock and clean her up for you." He smiled briefly. "And by the way, sir, if it ever troubles you shooting at an unsuspecting target, just think of the chap's head as a clamshell."

Chapter Eight

"Coffee, excellency?" said the cotton trader, lounging in his office near the entrance to the warehouse. He set aside the stem of his hookah and rose from the low copper table with a cheery smile but wary eyes. He laced his fingers over his stomach and bowed as he insinuated both feet into his slippers. The merchant's flesh shook inside his gallabiyah. A broad brown sash bound his belly like the center hoop of a barrel. "A sweet coffee?"

Olivio Alavedo stared down at the man from his seat on the heavy crossed arms of his Sudanese retainer. Three large young men, with shoulders like charcoal bullocks, crowded the doorway behind him. He would need them.

The dwarf did not extend his hand. Ever since the fire in Nanyuki twenty years before, he had an aversion to being touched. Occasionally he was reminded of the morning after the fire. With the ruins of the White Rhino Hotel still smoldering nearby, Miss Gwenn had pasted him with tannic acid jelly and swaddled him in bandages like an infant mummy. Only his eye and mouth showed life, his hidden body skinless and raw.

"I come, Hassan, for my cotton, not your coffee," snapped the little man. Restrained anger ground in his voice like gravel under the wheels of a cart. "My drivers are outside, waiting in my lorries. Tariq's nephews are here to assist with the loading."

"Cotton? Cotton? I have no cotton for you, effendi . . ."

"You promised me thirty thousand yards of the finest khaki drill. The price was fixed." The voice of the dwarf lowered. "Yesterday, I have learned, you sold my cotton to another buyer at a higher price. You will not see his money, or mine." Alavedo's speech slowed as his words took command of the office. If he tolerated one such abuse, his fortune would vanish with his reputation. Fear and integrity were brothers. Both required nourishment.

"I guaranteed your loan," Olivio almost whispered. "I procured you credit with the Zilkha bank. And I pledged the cotton to the suppliers of every officers' tailor in Alexandria, Cairo and Faiyûm. My word is on it. Are these brave gentlemen to have no shorts and tunics when they go to war?" Alavedo stiffened in his servant's grasp. "I will have that cotton if I must flay it inch by inch from the bleeding bodies of your idle sons."

"But excellency, there is no cotton!" the trader protested. "The crops were spoiled. Floods and weevils, bolls and Jew worms. Blights and weeds." Hassan raised trembling hands above his head and rolled his eyes to the ceiling. "All the fellahin are busy with the rice and with the road repairs demanded by the British for the army. The cotton is rotting in the fields. And the war has stolen all the transport . . ."

"Are you yourself not wearing cotton when you owe it all to me?" cried Olivio, further incensed by the defiance of argument. Unable to sweat through the poreless glazed skin of his old burns, Alavedo endured the heat of aggravation that blazed inside him like an over-used furnace deep in the bowels of an old tramp steamer. "I will have every stitch and bale. Tariq, open that door behind this dog, the door to his warehouse."

Hassan backed against the door. His hands gripped the edges of the walls on either side.

"The goods in there are not mine. I beg you, effendi! They are being stored for others."

"Open the door, Ali," Tariq ordered. One of his burly nephews strode up to Hassan. With stout arms he lifted the trader by his sash and flung him backward onto the glowing brazier of the water pipe. Hassan screamed and rolled wildly against the wall, swatting the charred hem of his robe. Another sturdy lad opened the door and bowed as Alavedo passed through it in the arms of Tariq.

The nephews shoved aside several workmen who were laboring in the warehouse, shifting stacks of folded army tents and khaki blankets, camp cots and cases of tinned bully beef. One man was busy repainting a row of captured German gasoline tins. Half of the four-and-a-half gallon Jerrycans were still in Rommel's desert yellow. A few were marked with large white crosses. The other cans, drying in a shiny line against one wall, were already British khaki.

"Aha!" exclaimed the dwarf as two nephews strode ahead of Tariq, holding lanterns aloft before them. He pointed at several crates marked with large red crosses.

"Aha! So it is! This evil rogue steals not just from me. He steals also from the soldiers, even from the valiant wounded." The little man flushed with agitation. His voice rose. "Here I find all the contraband of Cairo, the black market of the black market!"

The workmen cowered in a corner. Hassan stood at the entrance wailing and wringing his hands. "These things are not mine, excellency! I only store them."

"Aha! Whose are they?" snapped the dwarf, twisting around in Tariq's arms to face the trader. "Who owns these things? Give me a name."

"I do not know. How can I say?" the man blustered. "They are only stored here. The lorries come and go at night."

Alavedo did not believe the dog. "Then I will return with Omar and his skinning knife. He will flay you until you recall the names. Sometimes his blade is a trifle dull. But if he can peel the hide from a camel, I wager he can do as well with you."

The dwarf turned back to his waiting helpers.

"Load the lorries! Leave only the tents and medical supplies. Seize all those cans, wet or dry. Now this dog Hassan will pay with interest the interest that he owes me." Not to mention, thought Alavedo, that the Special Police and the British will be in my debt when I report this.

"Set me down, Tariq, on those medical chests. Then you will strip the cotton robe from the back of this hyena. Let his men see their master as he is, without his cotton."

"I beg you, effendi!" cried Hassan as Tariq tore away his sash and robe and undergarment. A leather money belt was wrapped around the trader's naked waist, nearly covered in the drape of his hanging flesh.

"Empty that thief's belt and throw whatever it hides to these men he cheats each day."

Tarik ripped open the four pouches of the leather belt and flung folded currencies and a few bright coins at the feet of the workers. The men stared down at the money as if at manna.

"Take it," ordered the dwarf with lordly impatience. "It is yours. Take it and leave us."

The warehouse workers gazed at the ground, then at their naked weeping master. At last one man, the oldest, bent and picked up two small gold coins. He held them against the light of a torch before hurrying past his master and out the door. After a few frantic moments, all the money and the men were gone.

Now there would be no witnesses, thought Alavedo as he stepped to his automobile. Only one more rumor of his fearsome generosity.

Olivio rested on a cushion in the Daimler while Tariq supervised the loading. He felt an alarming tightness in his chest. These moments of crisis and heroic enterprise made him feel young once more, but they were not what his physician recommended. In one act, he had combined profit and justice, largesse and reputation. He should have brought his son, Tiago, to learn the lesson of generosity without cost.

"Now we will call at Saint Francis Xavier's Home," said the dwarf as Tariq approached the car and requested instructions. As a young boy in Goa, Olivio had been raised in an orphanage. There a matronly nun, astonished by his juvenile manliness, had eagerly given him his first arousal while she bathed him and tickled his tummy with her mustache. Here in Cairo he had become a patron of the most wretched of all the orphanages.

In the courtyard of St. Francis', the dwarf rolled down the window. He sniffed, always proud of his exceptionally acute sense of smell. The orphanage was close enough to the camel market for him to smell the mounds of precious dung being raked together and turned to dry in the sun. His spirit brightened.

Two boys were busy in the corner of the yard pummeling a smaller schoolmate. The younger lad clenched his teeth but did not cry out. Olivio was reminded of the cathedral school in Goa, where he had learned to turn the larger boys from brutal bullying masters into willing pawns.

He watched the younger lads, jolly hopeful creatures of his own size, wrestle and play while the older boys helped to empty the trucks of everything except the corded bolts of khaki cloth. Those would be assigned to fulfill the pledge he had made to the tailors and to the quartermaster of the British army.

He knew that here every cot and blanket, each tin of old beef would find a grateful needy youth. Tonight, thanks to Olivio Fonseca Alavedo, the children would eat and sleep as they should.

**

"May I have this dance?" said Anton that evening, pleased that Cerisse was enjoying the champagne. He was keeping up with gin.

81

"My card is empty," replied the correspondent, taking his hand as they rose. The small dance floor of the roof garden was crowded, as it had been every evening since Mussolini invaded Egypt in September, 1940.

Without the money for many such evenings and unknown to the over-tipped maître d'hotel, Anton had been obliged to call on Senhor Alavedo to secure a favored table. One side of the dining terrace was set against the windowed wall of the top floor of the hotel. Another was the roof bar with its eight tall cushioned stools, always taken by a few drinkers out scouting on their own. Ladies, of course, never sat at the bar. The other sides of the terrace were open to a view over the rooftops and swarming streets of Cairo, normally illuminated by a thousand lights glowing on both sides of the Nile. But with the blackout, only tiny dots of light were visible in the streets as every vehicle drove with masked headlights, part of ARP, the air raid precautions that controlled much of life in Cairo and along the Suez Canal. The glitter of the stars and moon had replaced the sparkling ancient city.

"In the mountain greenery, where God paints the scenery," crooned the singer in his white shawl-collared dinner jacket. "Just two crazy people in love." This was the sort of dance, a subdued fox trot, that Anton Rider could manage. He had always been lighter on his feet in the boxing ring. He knew he would never master the dances of today, the jitterbug or the crab walk.

Anton's shoulder brushed against another couple. He glanced at the pair turning close beside them. The woman's slender arms were reaching up, her hands clasped around the young soldier's neck. Her eyes were closed and her cheeks were wet.

"Glad the Yanks are on our side at last," said Anton quietly. "They always give us the best dance music."

"The Jerries are rather good at that as well," said Cerisse, drawing back a bit and smiling into his eyes.

"The Huns? Dancing?"

"Waltzes," said Cerisse, her soft cheek and full breasts touching him again. "Liszt and Mozart, to name two. Don't you waltz, Captain Rider?"

"I've never tried," said Anton, somewhat irritated. He had spotted Captain Simon pressing his way through the bar crowd. The boor took one of the high seats recently abandoned by a dancer, but still reserved by an unfinished drink. Be friendly, he reminded himself. Gwenn had often scolded him for making his dislikes too hastily, and too obviously. Worse, she deplored his propensity to confront other men, too often leading to violence.

"When are you leaving?" Cerisse asked softly as he guided her to the far side of the dance floor. Her lips and breath were on his ear.

Distracted by a thought of Gwenn, Anton replied, "I'm not at liberty to say, but I doubt we can dine tomorrow."

Both knew what was expected of each other before a man returned to war. Far from home, and sometimes less than a hundred miles from the front, it was understood in Cairo that the moral restraints of peacetime were designed for a different time and a different place. Here and now, one should take advantage of what might be life's last moments.

When Anton was younger, he thought that this was the eager objective only of the man, but he had learned that experienced women also appreciated such moments of romantic intensity, even of erotic desperation.

He had the sense that Madame Bouvet already assumed how this evening would conclude, that there need be no negotiation of seduction. She had removed her wedding ring.

The band stopped playing. The dancers returned to their tables as the live music of Jimmy Dorsey and Harry James was replaced by broadcast tunes coming from two scratchy speakers.

Finally a woman's clear warm English voice came over the crackling military wavelength of the BBC as Vera Lynn sang, *There'll Be Blue Birds Over The White Cliffs Of Dover.* The terrace grew silent as the nostalgic words drifted into the Egyptian night, accompanied by the high-pitched breathy background of the clarinet. Then there was a pause as diners whispered and lit cigarettes and waited for one other song.

We'll meet again.
Don't know where,
Don't know when,
But I know
We'll meet again
Some sunny day.

Anton gazed out over the subdued lights of Cairo to the Nile. Aware of Cerisse regarding him with softer eyes, he tried to smile as he filled her glass, but he was thinking of another woman. He turned the bottle upside down in the bucket before raising his hand for a gin.

Vera Lynn sang as Cerisse rested one hand on his. Anton was enjoying her, and he would, but he wished the warm hand was Gwenn's.

Chapter Nine

No way to spend the morning, thought Anton Rider, red-eyed as the Dingo banged along the Desert Road that led north to the Med and west to the big RAF base at Derna. Yet in a way, these impulsive evenings and urgent departures suited him, perhaps too well.

By mid-morning the light armored car was hot as a saucepan. "Toasters," the old Tommies called the Dingos. With the hinged steel roof folded back and the window plates battened open, dust and sand covered the interior like fresh earth in a grave. The exhaust of the endless column of motorcycles, staff cars, lorries and light armor poisoned every breath. The driver's red beret was pulled down to the rim of his sun goggles. An unlit cigarette was tight between his lips. Snug in the Bren gunner's seat, Rider made no effort to scream conversation over the racket of the rear-mounted six-cylinder engine. He raised the knotted diklo from his neck until the red gypsy kerchief covered his nose and mouth. Directly before them, a six-wheeled Saracen churned up the rough road with giant tires.

At least, thought Anton glancing down, the .303 should arrive clean and intact. Properly oiled, wrapped in a camouflage mantel, the N.4(T) sniper rifle was tight inside the parachute cannister that rested between his feet and extended back towards the sloping metal plate at the rear of the Daimler scout car.

The Dingo passed orderly cities of khaki bell tents, graveyards of damaged vehicles and artillery, Italian and German and British, and petrol dumps where fifty-gallon drums were stacked between sand berms that disappeared into the distance like the smooth low dunes of the Sahara. With one such dump, thought Rider, Erwin Rommel's panzers would have taken the Suez Canal in 1941.

To confuse the enemy and make the Tommies feel at home, at every crossing London street names were mounted on wooden stakes set in petrol drums filled with sand and rock. Today "Chelsea" indicated the right turn for Alexandria. But their own route lay ahead, with all the trouble that brought. The column had stopped twice when some tie-up blocked the road. Each time Gypies appeared like eager phantoms at the windows of the vehicles, hawking dates and oranges to the soldiers. During the delays, Rider could feel the hot breath of the Sahara in the *khamsin* as the wind swept across from the south on its way to the Mediterranean, tumbling clumps of camel thorn across the road.

All along the route a hedge of destroyed or damaged machines was pushed to one side of the track. Some were painted in the perfectly chosen sandy yellow shade of Rommel's Afrika Korps, others in British desert khaki or the uneven yellow-green of the Italians. Many vehicles bearing German markings were actually British under the paint, captured in the early days when it was all going Rommel's way.

Anton saw a high-turreted armored car lying on its side, two massive torsion bars exposed where a mine or shell had blasted away the protective armor. He knew what it had been like for the brewed-up crew inside. Not just "creased," as Tommies put it when a man was wounded, but finished, done, "toppled off one's perch."

Every few miles transport recovery teams were repairing and cannibalizing vehicles and painting over the swastikas and fasces of captured trucks and armor. At one stop the long barrel of a captured German .88 was being used as a crane to lower a new engine into a Scorpion minesweeping tank.

Anton knew his side were amateurs at this salvaging compared to the Panzer Korps. By now over half of Rommel's transport was captured or repaired British vehicles.

Starved for fuel, supplies and reinforcements, Rommel's tank-recovery squads accompanied his sand-colored Mark III's and IV's directly into battle. Young German mechanics in high-laced cut-down desert boots, sun goggles and worn olive-green shorts, tanned dark and blond like boys at the beach, levered damaged treads from tank sprockets as they made heavy repairs in the desert. All the while, the .88's whistled over their heads and battle raged around them.

Anton's squadron, firing machine guns mounted on their jeeps, not proud of the work, had shot up one such unit themselves. The enemy mechanics had been armed with nothing more than giant spanners and heavy crowbars. Afterwards, when they picked up two of the German walking wounded, they found that both men, like English tars of the eighteenth century, had the loose teeth and patchy skin sores that come with bad diet and no water for bathing. The standard ration of the Deutsches Afrika Korps was greasy tinned Italian sausage meat, the captives explained after sharing the squadron's bully beef and some treats from Cairo, including Springbok cigarettes, a spoonful of marmalade and one gulp of whisky.

Thirsty, his temples throbbing, Anton peeled a blood orange and recalled sitting around the cookfire in the evening with the young German mechanics, one with both arms in slings, the other with his chest wrapped like a mummy. The fire was like one of theirs, the captives said, with sand filling most of a cut-off German gasoline tin, a "Jerry can," and a splash of petrol burning at the top. The German fuel tins were superior, sturdy and well sealed, practical for repeated use, unlike the fragile British "flimsies" that had to be boxed in wooden cases.

One mechanic explained that each Italian sausage tin was stamped with the grim letters "AM," *Administrazione Militare*. Rommel himself, who ate what his men ate, said the letters stood for *Alte Mann*, Old Man, but most Jerries favored the earlier title *Alte Maulesel*, Old Mule, or

Asinus Mussolini. Their Italian allies, said the other German prisoner, still called the sausage meat *Arabo Morte*, Dead Arab.

Today only ambulances seemed to be driving the other way, east and south towards the big civilian hospitals of Alexandria and Cairo, carrying men too badly injured for the dusty field hospitals where surgeons like Gwenn Rider were doing their best.

He carried one thing of Gwennie's in his kit. A sleeveless khaki sweater she had knitted for him, useful in the desert cold at night. "Happy Christmas, Anton," the note said, though that was still some time away. "Forgive the wrapping paper." Two recent pages of the *Cairo Daily Mail* had wrapped the sweater, one with the headline, "French Prepared to Fight Yanks and Tommies in Algeria." She had left the parcel for him at the Press Office. Gwennie was not much of a knitter, but it reminded him of what their love once had been.

Anton thought of his last drive with his wife less than a year ago. After his final surgery, Gwenn had collected him at the hospital in Alex and driven him to Ramleh for more personal recuperation. For a time, she had made him feel himself and loved again. It was the last time they had made love. And the last time that their love for one another, and even their affections, had been in reasonable harmony, as if briefly blessed by both opportunity and mutual inclination. He bit his dry lip and cursed himself for all his destructive wasteful foolishness, and hers.

Now he was doing it again, and so was she. His wife's relationships were more selective, longer lasting, deeper for her, and therefore, he thought, worse for him. His were lighter, foolish flings that for him were transient adventures. But to Gwenn, he now knew, his shallow preferences suggested how unimportant their own relationship might sometimes be to him. At first she had tried to understand this in a husband ten years younger, but by now his boyhood was too long past.

This new mission, she had warned him, was a further extension of his boyish hunger for the next excitement, whether in adventure or romance. She had reminded him that he was now too old, and too often wounded, to serve on active duty.

Even he was worried about his latest deception, pretending he was fit. The Gypsies had taught him gambling, cunning and dissemblance, and other useful skills with his fists and his wits. Sometimes he used these skills too readily.

In order to rejoin his squadron, he had lied about the condition of his leg. But instead of long-range jeep patrols, where his leg might have been a modest hindrance and his experience a substantial advantage, they would be dropping him into the freezing mountains of Jugoslavia, a young man's two-legged adventure if ever there was such a thing.

Anton Rider cared about it all, but somehow he did not. He had lost one son, and the other was far off on his own, doing what a young man must. His wife was doing the same, in Gwenn's own way. The world itself was injured and at risk. Why should he not be? Anton thought as his eyes closed and his aching head collapsed on his chest.

As the Dingo banged along, his dreams were dizzy with confused details about Turks and Christians, Serbs and Bosnians and Croats, and who was Orthodox or Holy Roman, communist or Muslim. There was one shadow of nightmare: two barefoot gypsy children swinging by their necks from a tree on a riverbank.

***

By the time Derna rose modestly before them, a low Arab town of broken white walls and slender minarets with tiny platforms like demitasse saucers, Rider resolved never to drink again. Grey sand stuck to his throat like a coat of plaster. He was too dry to speak. He was almost looking forward to the cold mountains of Jugoslavia.

Anton drained his canteen and studied the aircraft scattered about the edge of the desert. Hurricanes, Halifaxes, Liberators were all widely dispersed to reduce damage in an attack. Lying about in the sand among the limestone outcroppings past the end of the runways were the ruins of old Axis aircraft. Fiats and Bredas, Dorniers and Messerschmitts, burned out, engines removed, wings broken, propellers missing, yesterday's scarecrows rusting into the Sahara like the armor of long-dead crusaders.

Cairo belonged to the army, thought Anton, all of it. County regiments, Canadians, Rhodies, Indian Army, South Africans, Anzacs, the Guards. Together they overflowed the barracks, the tent cities, the hospitals, the restaurants and clubs, the bars and brothels.

Alexandria, Port Saïd and Suez belonged to the Royal Navy. In Alex the Senior Service kept the French fleet imprisoned and the Eyeties and Jerries at bay.

Now Derna belonged again to the Royal Air Force, ever since the Eighth Army had captured it for the second time in the seesaw campaign along the coast of North Africa. For the Luftwaffe, the RAF and the Regia Aeronautica, the fighter bases, with their short flat strips, easily graded and repaired, were low maintenance and quick to establish.

As the airstrip closest to the Balkans, Derna also supported the bombers, the long-range Mediterranean patrols and the special missions over Nazi Europe.

They were quartered in a single-story Italian farmer's villa at the edge of Derna, with a walled garden, a few date palms and touches of Rome in the columns, arches and tiles. A profile in mosaic of the block-like head of Benito Mussolini was set into the thick garden wall. His robust visage, with its Fascist cap and black tassel, stared out towards the desert that he had attempted to make part of the new Roman Empire. A small flower bed, now dried out, was dying beneath the Duce. Vines of Italian tomatoes struggled to climb the wall to reach him. Mussolini's face, however, was now smeared and extravagantly touched up with camouflage paint and less tasteful materials, apparently the work of wags from the RAF fighter base nearby.

The house came with an elderly native cook trained to serve one dish: sandy linguini with tomato sauce. Anton preferred to take his meals on his own in town. Once the mission was under way, the three men of the team would be seeing enough of each other.

Major Sparrow seemed to understand. He liked to wander on his own with a sketch pad and his swagger stick, drawing faces and landscapes and buildings. Insulated by his English sense of privacy, he appeared relaxed, confident, as if off for a day's sport with companions who were not quite his style. Captain Simon, however, although no more sociable than Rider, appeared to resent these separations. Anton imagined that this American resented most things. In the mornings Simon rose late, his lips sometimes black with wine. Last night he had not returned at all.

For five days they waited for the flying weather to improve over the Balkans. Each morning Anton would check his rifle again and set out his ten shoulder bandoliers, each one holding fifty rounds of .303 ball, five rounds of tracers and five rounds of armor-piercing ammunition. Then he would stroll into town, looking forward to an expresso and several square pieces of breakfast pizza. He also hoped to strengthen his leg with the exercise. His favorite café, the Borgia, was on the waterfront, run by a cheerful mixed-blood Italian woman who knew enough English to make ordering easy but not enough to pester one with conversation. Anton could smell the coffee and the sea as he turned the corner of the short dusty street.

This morning, as he admired the orange-brown froth on his first expresso, he considered what lay ahead. Jugoslavia would be a different world. He had never been to the Continent. The undefined adventure before him, no matter how foolish and hazardous, made him feel young again, at risk.

As he sipped, Anton twisted his gypsy diklo, the red scarf knotted at his neck, and thought about the drop. Twenty-four long years before, he had voyaged to Africa. But this time, instead of sailing down the Red Sea on a rusty passenger-freighter, he would be flying across the Med in a four-engine bomber. Instead of plunging ashore in a surf boat in the African sunlight, he would be floating down under a parachute at night. Bosnians and Croats would be waiting, instead of Waliangulu and Masai. But in Jugoslavia, as in Tanganyika, there would be Germans waiting as well.

His thoughts turned to the Gypsies in the death camp at Jasenovac. He wondered what sort they were. There were many tribes of Romanies, from Spain and Roumania and a dozen other countries, but all with their ancient roots in India and a belief in isolating their children within their own traditions and dialects. The term 'Gypsy,' Anton recalled, had its misplaced origin in nearby Egypt, where the Romanies were once thought, mistakenly, to have originated.

Rider nodded as the maternal hostess, known as "the Duchess of Tripoli" to the young pilots and bombardiers, set down a generous glass of grappa beside his coffee. Her dress and coloring suggested a relaxed mixture of southern Europe and North Africa, the sort of blend that seemed more comfortable and natural in the Italian colonies than in the British.

His mind returned to the jump. Having taken off twice across the Med, only to be turned back by weather, the three members of his mission had become more friendly with their Australian flight crew than they were with each other. None of the airmen was over twenty-one years old, and they all took war for granted, like school. Two had fathers who had fought in the last war. "Now it's our turn," shrugged the tail gunner, offering a handful of barley sugars, "the pilot's candy," better than caffeine to keep a man alert but continent on long flights.

The two aborted runs had turned into training simulations for the final flight, but they did nothing to lighten Anton's concern about the jump itself. Rider had fought Italians in Ethiopia and Germans in Libya. He had been hammered by a buffalo and mauled by a leopard in the Din Din forest, but the notion of falling from an airplane made him want another stronger drink. He knew this was not his game.

"It's a lot worse falling out of the hole in the bomb bay than it is jumping out a door in a real drop, especially at night," Sparrow warned him, pointing at a ring secured to the fuselage. "But when the moment comes, you won't have any choice. Your chute will be hooked to that ring, and it will open automatically after you fall out."

"In American operations we always have a reserve chute," Simon put in. "But the Brits are too flint cheap to pay for the extra silk." The two Englishmen exchanged a weary glance, and Simon bristled. "Who's dropping first, anyway?"

"On British jumps," replied Major Sparrow quietly, pinching his thin nose, "the senior officer always jumps first."

Before boarding the Handley Page Halifax, Major Sparrow and the captain of the air crew had checked the binds that secured large containers under each wing of the long-range bomber. These contained weapons, explosives, medical supplies and radios being parachuted to the same band of Partisans that would be their reception party. The containers would be dropped first to lighten the aircraft. Once the navigator identified the ground signals, the plane would slow, circle and descend to three or four thousand feet to improve the chance for the containers to fall into the drop zone. Then the Halifax would be obliged to climb steeply to avoid the mountains before coming around again and descending as low as possible to drop the three men with minimal drift.

The spirited lads of the air crew made Rider think of Denby as he sipped his grappa. He gazed idly at the grey gulls wheeling above the oily lapping water only a few yards away and wondered if there was any use in trying to send a last letter to Gwenn or his son. Anton wasn't much at writing, but during the war even a short letter was always intensely welcome.

As he asked the Duchess for a bit of paper, three women approached and sat at a nearby table. It was early for working girls, he thought. All were dark-haired, honey-skinned and relaxed in caftans, sandals and European silk scarves. They giggled and whispered in Italian at the table beside him. The loose robes made it hard to guess their bodies. They sipped coffee from small cups and nibbled dates from a copper bowl.

"En-glish sol-dier?" said one.

Anton turned towards the prettiest one, a little heavy, but with dark oval eyes, full lips and a merry smile. Arab and Italian, he guessed as the Duchess handed him a small sheet of paper. He was about to reply when he caught himself. No information. He was wearing desert boots and military shorts and shirt, but with no indication of rank or regiment. They had been told not to wear their jump boots when they went to town.

"You write to lover girl? *Amore?*" Her pink tongue licked the side of a date. "*Amore?*" As she held Anton's gaze, she nipped off one shiny end.

"No." I wish I were, he thought.

"You like to buy Gina drink?" She sucked her sticky thumb.

"Delighted." Rider held up his hand, and Gina drew her chair up to Anton's table.

The Dutchess set down a bottle of Bardolino and two short glasses and wiped them with a soiled towel, holding each one up against the sky. The girl rested her hand on Anton's leg while he poured the wine. They drank and laughed as they struggled to understand each other. This was just what Gwenn would resent, he thought, as he resolved to restrict the flirtation.

A battered Fiat rattled up to the café while they chatted. All the side windows were broken. Both running boards were gone. A spare tire was lashed to the roof. The word "TAXI" showed underneath the dirt on one door. The driver jumped down and opened the back door, leaning in and disputing in a high voice with the passenger inside.

Suddenly the driver screamed and stumbled backward, his mouth bleeding. A man burst out with a rush and slammed the door behind him. Captain Simon. Anton thought he saw a second person pressed into one corner of the passenger seat, a slender dark figure.

"You cheating bastard!" The American, his face red and sweating, swung with his entire broad body and punched the driver in the stomach. Lifted off his feet, the Libyan collapsed in front of the café, gasping on his side with his knees drawn up and vomit spread on the dust around his head. Simon pulled one leg back and kicked the man in the belly. The girls screamed. Anton stood up.

Gina stepped in front of the fallen man as Simon reared to kick him again. His boot caught her in the leg instead, and Gina fell crying on top of the driver.

"That's enough." Rider grabbed Simon's right arm. He felt the thick hard muscle that filled the man's sleeve. Behind them, another vehicle pulled up beside the taxi.

Simon turned on Anton, unable to shake his grip. Twisting his arm, he finally succeeded with a third violent effort. "You're too late with your whore, Rider. I had her last night."

The American clenched both fists. Anton saw the swollen neck and the small raging eyes under the thick black eyebrow. He reached back and lifted the bottle from the table, never taking his eyes from Simon. "You first."

"Gentlemen!" Major Sparrow banged his swagger stick on the table like a gunshot. "You forget yourselves!"

Two British officers stepped out of the Dingo behind the major, though they seemed less concerned about the brawling. "Gentlemen," Sparrow said sternly, "you will both get your kit and report to the aerodrome. You can settle this another day in Bosnia."

Trembling, Captain Simon pushed his flushed face close to Rider's. Anton smelled the sour odor and the hot alcoholic breath as the man spoke.

"Touch me again and I'll kill you."

Chapter Ten

After they descended from the coastal massif south of Algiers, the paved French road with its Napoleonic shade trees and kilometer markings became a *piste* in the desert, a packed track of gritty sand and rocky outcroppings set amidst a level gravel plain. At first they passed clumps of low scrub bushes and occasional herds of brown hairy sheep or small lonely goats. Then the desert grew hard and dry.

Lieutenant Denby Rider drove eagerly, his sleeves rolled up, a pair of Zeiss sun goggles pinching his nose. Tight against his cheekbones, their broad rubber rims kept the sharp flying sand from his eyes. The lucky red bandana his father had given him was knotted at his throat. He had found the glasses several months ago on the charred black-lipped face of the turret gunner of a brewed-up Panzer Mark III.

Hot dry wind blew in through the open windows. A hundred and fifteen in the shade, Denby reckoned, munching a fresh brioche. Sand scratched his teeth, and he frowned. He should have known better, he thought, and driven either at sunrise or late in the afternoon. But he was eager to rejoin his mates and get back in the game. As he drove, he picked idly at the edge of the bandage on his scalp. The cut on his cheek had healed to a thin scar. At least, he thought, he had brought an old sheepskin coat for the nights. If things went bad in the desert, one never had enough supplies. As one of Rommel's generals famously said, "North Africa is a tactician's paradise and a quartermaster's hell."

Raoul sat forward on the seat beside him, concerned with the Englishman's driving. He squinted at their old French map, fluttering in the wind, and shook his head.

Three hours later they came to a fork in the piste. One track led south, the other deeper track roughly to the east. A cairn had been knocked over where the paths joined. A wooden road marker had been broken off near the top of its post, standard practice in wartime to complicate the travels of the enemy. Denby needed his black military compass, now in its oval leather case in his knapsack on the back seat. The Citröen had no sun compass. That horizontal metal circle, divided into 360 degrees set around a central needle, was mounted on the dash of most British scout cars. Magnetic compasses were little use inside a vehicle. But as the circle of a sun compass was rotated to follow the movement of the sun, this simple instrument, invented by the Light Car Patrols during the Great War, always found a true bearing. Denby braked and switched off the engine before reaching back for his pack.

He saw a thin line of steam rising from the edges of the bonnet. He recalled his father saying after one long patrol that moisture evaporated so rapidly in the desert, you never knew how the radiator was doing until it was too late. The same was true of men, an old desert hand had told the Cherry Pickers, his regiment of Hussars. "Losing moisture can kill you. The more you sodden chaps sweat, the more you must drink to stay alive." The covering layered garments of the Tuaregs and Chaambas and other desert tribes, and the graceful arrogant stride of their patient gait, conserved both moisture and energy.

Denby had a sudden image of his father lying on his belly in the Samburu country. He picked out the slender figure of a tiny antelope amidst the acacia. "Gerunuks never have to drink," the old hunter had whispered to his son. "They collect their moisture from the wait-a-bit thorn bushes when they browse." But a European soldier needed at least one gallon a day.

In Libya some Bersaglieri prisoners had told how, during more carefree days, they had hunted a herd of fifteen addax in the Sahara on their Lancia motorbikes.

"After a long dusty hunt and an accident with a broken leg, we finally ran the antelope down and shot two handsome males from our sidecars, each one a good two hundred pounds," a young Italian lieutenant had recounted. "We skinned and cleaned the big white buck in the desert, and rode back with their spiraling horns, two feet long, lashed to the front of our bikes like chariots. A feast for the whole squadron." Trying to be sporting, the Italian soldiers had spared the females and the younger males, but later the Bersaglieri found the entire herd had perished in the desert, hopelessly dehydrated, unable to replace the moisture they had lost during the chase. It might be a lesson to remember.

"You better take a look under the bonnet," said Denby before strolling into the blue with his canteen and the map. It was like walking through a wall of heat. He relieved himself as Raoul opened the hood and leaned over the engine with a rag in one hand. Denby sat on the edge of a jagged shelf of dappled rock that thrust through the crust of the desert. He drank and wiped his face with the diklo before spreading the wrinkled map across his knees.

Averting his eyes from the sun, glancing down, he discerned a small strange bump on the narrow rock shelf that lay beneath the upper edge of the outcropping. He scraped along the rock with the edge of one boot. The bump opened and blossomed into a sand scorpion. It extended its eight legs and two claw arms and raised its curved tail as if to strike. Denby instantly drew back his foot. The poisonous creature scuttled off.

The map showed not only the national borders and the transportation routes but also the traditional names of the underlying regions of the Maghreb: the Barbary Coast, the Mzab, the Erg and all the other exotic names that had captivated Denby as a boy studying geography in Cairo. After a lifetime in Egypt and two years with the Hussars in the Western

Desert, Denby was a student of the desert tribes and clans, both nomads and villagers.

Occasionally, eccentric British travelling scholars would give the Hussar officers a talk, explaining how the nomadic tribes could not survive without the sedentary oasis communities that provided them with vegetables and dates, salt and cotton. Occasionally a lecturer would speak of what the French called "*caffard*," a sort of desert madness that sometimes afflicted thirsty and lonely travellers. Most of the young lieutenants would doze in the back row, more interested in the polo and dances that Cairo provided. Their interest would sharpen, however, when the speaker spoke of certain tribal customs: how wealthy Mzabite families provided Negro concubines as trainers for their sons, how widows married again into the families of their late husbands, and of "children of the trousers," as they called infants born to women whose husbands had been away more than nine months.

To rendezvous with the southern scouting parties of the Hussars or the Long Range Desert Group, they would probably have to drive southeast through the Mzab and the Eastern Erg into Tunisia. "Might catch your Cherry Pickers at one of the oasis towns," his Irish friend had said in Algiers. "Perhaps Ouargla, Ghadames, or a bit farther east." Denby wasn't sure if the car would make it. The rule was never to travel in the desert with fewer than two vehicles.

He went over to examine the motorcar more closely. The Citröen had already acquired the dusty colors of the Sahara, a pale yellow-grey in this full bright light. He thought he saw a dark shiny patch in the shadow under the car.

"*Mon lieutenant!*" called the driver. Denby walked over to him, offering the canteen to the Senegalese with its cap hanging by a tiny chain.

"*Trop chaud,*" said Raoul, after drinking slowly and wiping his mouth. "She is running too hot. Boiling."

"Drive her forward a bit, and I'll see." Denby knelt beside the vehicle. His squadron had learned to care for their armored cars the way generations of Hussars had looked after their horses, as if they were their children, always watering and feeding them and brushing them down before they drank or ate themselves. He stared at the ground as the car rolled forward. Then he dipped two fingers in the small slick pool and smelled them.

"An oil leak." He wondered if they should turn back or carry on.

Raoul groaned when he saw the shiny oil. Both men dropped onto their backs and edged forward under the Citröen until their two heads nearly touched. They stared up at the engine block and suspension. Thick black drops were collecting slowly on the bottom of the engine block and falling one by one into the dust. Both understood the incendiary danger of an overheated engine and leaking oil.

"How far can we go with this, Raoul?" asked the Englishman after they emerged. "And how bad is the radiator?"

The Senegalese pulled up one long sock and shifted from side to side, shrugging like a Parisian. "We have one liter of spare oil, and this leak is not yet so very bad, Lieutenant," he said. "But the radiator is too hot to open. I brought all that water in the back seat. We must drink less. The car will drink more."

Denby knelt at the fork of the two trails and traced the depressions of each with his fingers, as his father might do with an animal track. The southern piste was packed lower and far harder in the center, suggesting a track pounded down by caravans of baggage camels, whereas the eastern route was more defined by the parallel depressions of wheeled vehicles. He recalled tales of Arab caravans bringing gold dust, salt and very young Negro slave girls, north from Timbuctoo and Tamanrasset.

"*À gauche*," said Denby, wiping his face as he climbed in the back and pointed to the left fork, hoping he was correct. He decided not to scold his companion for the condition of the vehicle. "You carry on, Raoul," he said, removing his boots and stretching out on the broad seat. "I'm going to catch a bit of kip."

The Senegalese smiled weakly as he took the wheel, glancing at the other track.

"How was I to know about the motor car, Monsieur?" Raoul hunched his shoulders in resignation. "This was the colonel's personal machine, sir. And the French took down the road signs, in case you British came."

Asleep in the back seat on his sheepskin coat with containers of water piled on the rear window shelf and his boots and the petrol tins crowded into the footwell, Denby Rider dreamed of an evening picnic at one of the luxurious party tents near the pyramids. He felt the heat of the cook fire as the lamb roasted, and smelled the scent of the smoky herbs and meat. Then the smell changed and he coughed.

"Lieutenant!" screamed Raoul, reaching behind the driver's seat and striking Denby with his arm. "*Du feu!* Lieutenant!"

Denby awoke as thick oily smoke filled the automobile and obscured the windscreen. He looked out a side window into the night. Only a bit of moonglow brightened the desert.

"Stop the car!" yelled Denby, but the machine continued to roll forward, bouncing and jarring as it left the piste. A water bottle fell onto him from the rear window shelf. "Stop the car, Raoul! Out!"

Denby opened a side door, grabbed the water bottle and flung himself from the vehicle, tangled in his sheepskin coat. He rolled free onto the crusty surface of the desert. He sat up, stunned, then crouched on his knees and watched the car bump away in an uncontrolled curvy line.

Suddenly a streak of light flashed from the Citröen. The automobile turned in profile two or three hundred yards away. Denby stood and began to run after it in his stocking feet. He saw a dark figure struggling to clamber out through the driver's window.

Now the vehicle was in flames, moving more and more slowly as Denby hurried after it. He smelled the fire as he ran. Orange and red flames flared at the center of the dense cloud of dark oily smoke.

The car stopped as Raoul fell from the window, his hair and clothes on fire. The Citröen exploded. A wave of heat gusted over Denby as the burning vehicle rose on two wheels before bouncing and finally coming to rest on the passenger side. He inhaled the bitter stink of burning oil, rubber and petrol. Flung from a fender, a spare tire rolled flaming into the rocky desert before settling and burning steadily like an abandoned camp fire.

Denby saw Raoul rise on his knees, a human torch shaking and waving his arms. He heard one long shrill scream through the crackling of the fire. A second, then a third explosion followed as the gasoline cans inside the car exploded like fire bombs.

When he reached Raoul, the man's body was still, but his clothing continued to sizzle and flicker with flame. Denby flung himself on top of the Senegalese, crushing out the final flames. He stood and turned Raoul onto his back. He stared down, then knelt beside the dead body in the light of the burning car. He closed his eyes to the ghastly sight. Was it his fault?

After a time Denby stood unsteadily and went back to find the water bottle and his coat. He collected them and then looked at Raoul's singed boots. They were hopelessly too small. He could not do anything more here. He started walking and continued on in the moonlight until he found what he believed must be the piste. Glad to have his coat in the cold of the desert night, he followed the track as the sky slowly brightened. He scratched above his ear, where the dressing from his wound seemed to have fallen away during the accident.

Raoul and he had already driven for ten or twelve hours, he reckoned, perhaps three hundred or more miles. If he was on the right track, it should only be another forty or so to the ancient oasis town of Ghadames. There was no way he could avoid the scorching heat of the oncoming day. At first he tried to force himself to hurry. Then he recalled the lesson of the antelope hunters. Accelerated dehydration could kill him.

When the sun appeared, blazing like a fire rising on the rim of the desert, he sat and took several sips of water. His socks were already in rags, his feet cut and blistered. With every step the desert seemed more hot and sharp. He opened the large blade of his pocket knife. He stood on the bulky coat and cut around the outline of his right foot, careful to include one of the heavy bone buttons at the top of the scrap of wool-lined leather. He bent the leather up around his foot and cut a hole to secure the button across the front of his ankle. It was a messy job. So loose he knew it could not hold together if he walked. He started over and did the same thing twice more, getting better at it as he worked. Then he cut a few thongs to lash the leather across his feet. At least it should help for a few miles. His blisters had become open bloody sores.

He rose and continued on. Soon it grew infernally hot and he draped the remains of the coat over his head and shoulders. After a few more miles he stopped, conserving himself as he had been taught, sipping water and sheltering until the day cooled. Before sleeping briefly, he cut more leather strips from the coat. Then he walked all through the night, sometimes shuffling slowly on bleeding feet, certain he would never leave this desert alive.

As the following morning brightened, he stopped and drank almost all of his remaining water. It could not be too far. Dizzy, Denby staggered forward.

He was not certain what he was seeing, but he blinked and saw again the illusion of a slender tower rising from the sand.

He hurried forward, his feet bare again. He fell on his knees and finished the water. In the depression in the desert in front of him was a walled town, a *ksar* or old fortified village of flat-topped houses and one minaret. Palm trees and irrigated gardens spread beyond the walls. The oasis lay before him like an island in the ocean.

Chapter Eleven

A narrow crescent moon rose sharply behind the Halifax as the bomber crossed the Med and flew up the Adriatic towards Dalmatia. This time they could leave on their winter kit. It was cold enough in the big trembling belly of the bomber, and four more hours remained until their scheduled TOT, time over target, of 02:30.

Anton felt his stomach tighten as they left the coastal mountains behind and dropped swiftly to five thousand feet. He thought of what might happen if their landings went wrong in Bosnia. Germans instead of Partisans. Torture instead of friends. Perhaps even Ustashi, Croatian Fascists, often reproached by the German troops for excessive cruelty. These were men who knew their fate if their side lost. As the last briefing officer put it, "If you've a choice, lads, let the Jerries grab you. They'll shoot you if you're not in uniform, but they probably won't pull your teeth out first."

As the time drew near, the bombardier removed a wooden hatch cover from a hole set in the metal floor of the bomb bay. A shock of winter blasted apart the air of the desert. The three fastened their chin straps. The American had a first-aid kit attached to the front of his helmet, above his forehead. Sparrow's and Rider's, in the British way, were secured at the back.

Anton touched the modified F-S British commando knife strapped to his right calf. It had a skull-crusher knob at the top of the hilt and a "fingerprint" on the ricasso at the top of the blade to remind a man where to place his thumb when delivering a thrust to the carotid. Captain Simon carried a different knife strapped on his leg, an Everitt Knuckle Knife with four brass knuckles along the hilt. Rider groaned as he noticed the swagger stick jammed into one of Sparrow's boots. Would they have to put up with that in Bosnia?

The three men checked each other's harness. Rider felt Simon pull his shoulder straps with hard quick movements, grunting as he forced his hands between the canvas straps and Anton's shoulders. Sensing the man's hostility, Rider wondered how far the American could be trusted. He was relieved when Sparrow checked both his and Simon's jump gear.

All three knew that the navigator and the pilot were searching for the plateau where the Partisans should be waiting with a beacon fire, this one in the shape of a cross of Saint Andrew.

"The Jerries have learned to set false beacons to mislead our drops," the Australian pilot had warned them. " 'Night fishing,' the Krauts call it. So the Jugos have to keep changing the patterns of the fires. It's become a game, and the SS mountain troops know how to play it."

A red light came on over the bomb bay. Anton heard the engines throttle back. He felt the aircraft slow as the flaps were lowered and the plane lost altitude. After the wing containers dropped away, it gained speed and climbed once again.

Now it was their turn. The left wing fell. The big aircraft banked, throttled back and came back around for the drop. A small bulb blinked green in its wire mesh cage overhead. The bombardier raised his right hand above his fleece-lined leather collar. Thumbs-up.

The three secured their static lines to the jump hooks as the Halifax circled. Anton knew this was a dangerous trade-off: doing it in two passes made for a tighter drop zone, but it gave the Germans a better chance to spot them. They would have to scramble once they hit the ground.

The three men sat facing each other around the rim of the open hole. Simon, perhaps more experienced, had taken the position with his back to the engines. He would not be facing into the wind when he jumped.

Their legs dangled just above the slipstream. Sparrow shouted through tight lips, but Rider could not understand his words over the roar of the engines. He seemed to be hollering something about the wind.

Anton looked down through the bottomless blackness, trying not to feel sick as his stomach twisted in a hard knot. Suddenly a cluster of fires sparkled past below them. Could that be it? He checked again that the static line was hooked to his parachute. He forced himself to recall the instructions: do not try to anticipate the instant of impact by tensing your legs. Keep them together, bend your knees and roll. Protect your head by raising your arms to grip the shrouds of the chute.

Anton clenched the cold edge of the metal opening with both hands. He felt the tension in his palms and fingers. His rifle cannister was beside him, tethered to his belt by a coiled twenty-foot cord. He checked again to make certain it was attached. He saw the signal fires come into view. Dear God. The green light flashed.

"Tally-ho!" yelled the bombardier through a mouthful of crunched barley sugar. Sparrow was gone. Rider felt Simon punch his shoulder. Resisting the urge to punch back, Anton pushed off over the hole and fell into the night.

After an exhilarating instant of free fall in the darkness, Rider felt his canopy snap open. He found himself carried diagonally in a strong wind, facing back towards the four dwindling sparks that were the Rolls Royce engines of the Halifax.

Bosnia rushed up at him like a monumental black slab. Anton hit hard, taking too much in his legs instead of rolling. The parachute dragged him across the rocky ground like a small boat with too much sail in a storm. At last he pulled on the cords and collapsed the canopy. He lay still for a moment as it settled over him like a shroud. He felt pain in his right knee and hip. He gulped in the cold air to steady himself.

Anton rose slowly and unclipped his harness before gathering in the chute. A dusting of light snow or frost covered the ground. Given the barren solitude, he reckoned he had been blown outside the waiting circle of Jugoslav Partisans. Rider heard the bomber's engines soften into the southern sky.

If the Partisans found him immediately, he knew they would cut up the precious parachute to use the silk for bandages and clothing. If not, he was instructed to bury it in twenty minutes.

Anton freed his rifle cannister from the tethering rope. Opening the clamps of the container, he removed the bandoliers and the rifle case. He sat on a rock to wait and stretched out his legs. A few minutes later he rose and took the folding shovel from his pack and tried to dig a grave for the chute. The point of the spade found nothing but impenetrable rocky ground. Welcome to Bosnia, he thought. Instead, he stuffed the parachute into the cannister and covered the long container in brush and rocks.

Rider climbed onto a stony hillock and squinted about in the pale moonlight. He seemed to be near the edge of the plateau, a valley falling off to the east and a ridge of mountains rising on the other side. A cold wind gusted down sharply from the north, a harsh breath of winter that slipped inside his collar. He saw no sign of a fire. He heard no faraway voices. His two commands conflicted: link up with your mates, and flee the drop zone at once. Staying in place was too dangerous if the Ustashi or the Germans had spotted the flight, but he decided to wait the rest of the required time.

Finally Anton settled the pack on his back and slung the heavy canvas bandoliers and the metal telescope case over one shoulder and the Enfield over the other. Unable to read his compass clearly, he took a bearing on the north star and set off at an angle of twenty degrees. He felt comfortable again. At heart he was a hunter, not a soldier. This should be more his kind of drill. He hoped his leg would loosen as he walked. Back on the ground, and in hard country, he might still be a match for any man.

Rider paused every few minutes and listened for any sound of his companions. Each time he stared into the night in all directions. He'd been told to identify a small double-crested mountain that was the team's second rendezvous if they lost touch after the drop. "Cotswold" they'd called it in Cairo.

After half an hour Anton found himself climbing steadily. His knee and hip were hurting with the exertion. Entering a small cleft in the hillside, he found a softer patch of ground. There he buried five ammo belts and chipped a mark into a nearby rock. He sat and rubbed his swollen knee with both hands. He ate a Cadbury chocolate bar, one square at a time.

It was only October, but he was not used to the cold that reached into him as he continued sitting. This was no good. All around him, farther than he could ever proceed in any direction, thousands of square miles of German-controlled territory extended across Europe. He shook off that thought. He should focus only on what he must do. He was carrying enough food for two days. By then he must link up, if not with his team, at least with the Partisans.

Anton climbed for another hour. His limp was slowing his progress. Sometimes he had to grope forward hand by hand to advance up a steep slope. At length he settled under a pine tree and loosened his boots. He opened the rifle case and removed the oily Enfield. He lifted the twenty-nine-inch barrel to his right eye and stared through the sleek spiralled tube at the moon. He checked each part with his hands and assembled and loaded the weapon. The familiar drill made him comfortable and confident.

Just then a sound startled Rider from the trees behind him. A low wailing echo. Anton stiffened as another low call answered, the ghost-like hoot of an owl. He remembered camping in the woods as a boy in Lincolnshire, exchanging just such signals with his Gypsy friends.

Putting aside the distraction, Anton wiped the eyepiece of the sniper scope. He studied the broken surface of the moon through the slender three-power telescope before mounting it on the rifle. He leaned against the rough trunk and closed his eyes. He should rest for a couple of hours, then search for his companions. The rifle lay across his legs. He heard the owl hoot, now a friendly call. The fresh pungent smell of the fir tree provided another memory, of Christmas in the north of England, with the vardos circled around a large fire and children playing under the narrow high-arching gypsy wagons, practicing old tricks of dice and cards. Soon he felt himself drifting into sleep.

"*Ustani!*" a voice said through his dreams. "Stand up! Who are you?"

Anton felt the barrel of a shotgun punch into his chest. He blinked and instinctively tried to roll to his left. A hard kick in the ribs stopped him. Rider grunted and looked up.

Four men and a young woman stared down at him in the early light. All five were armed and clad in rough winter clothing. Tall worn boots and thick grey wool trousers. Short ragged black coats and cloth caps. Grenades, holsters and bayonets hung from heavy leather belts and shoulder straps secured outside their coats. The men wore mustaches and several days of dark beard. One carried the five ammo belts that Anton had buried. The girl supported her left arm in a dirty sheepskin sling. He tried to suppress any reaction when he saw that her hand was missing. A short single-barrelled shotgun was slung over her shoulder. In her right hand she carried Anton's Enfield.

"Who are you?" the girl said in slow English. The four men spoke to each other in what Anton took to be Serbo-Croat. He had always been a quick learner with languages in Africa, and several long sessions in Cairo had taught him a few words of this one.

"A friend," Anton said. He stood, trying to conceal that his bad leg felt rigid as a board. "From England. Egypt, really." The girl looked at Anton carefully with eyes more blue than his own.

"From Churchill?" said the oldest man. He had eyes like the girl's, a thick white mustache, yellow teeth and a broad hard face cut with deep wide lines like bark on a cork tree. It reminded Rider of photographs they had shown him in Cairo. "The face of Bosnia," Major Treitel had said.

"*Da*, from Churchill," Anton said. "By way of Cairo. I am Captain Anton Rider, British Army."

The girl spoke to her companions. They studied Anton and passed around the Enfield before nodding and consulting with each other. The man with the white mustache held up a hand to silence the others.

"Have you a message for us?" the girl asked.

"Yes," Rider said, using the special words he had learned in Egypt. 'You do not fight alone.'"

"Those are the words," she acknowledged, "and when we see you kill a German, we will know they are true. We are Partisans. With Tito."

The older man seized Anton's hand in a huge rough fist. Anton met his grip as the girl continued to translate for the big man. "My name is Yanko. I am commander."

"And he is my father," she added.

The leader took the rifle from the girl. Another man opened a leather pack and quickly built a low fire.

"What is this rifle?" Yanko shouldered the weapon and closed one eye. "With this I could see Hitler's belly button." He sat down laughing loudly. "Ha! Ha! Ha!"

The girl smiled and took a bottle and a dark loaf from the pack. She pulled a knife from her boot and cut thick slices of bread, pinning down the loaf with her left forearm. She passed a slice to Anton on the tip of the knife. "I am Nada. Are you hungry?"

"I am Anton. Yes, I am hungry."

"Sit. We will drink." Yanko drew Anton down by his arm. He pulled the cork from a long oval bottle of pale yellow liquid. A man beside him forced a handful of coffee beans into an engraved copper cylinder. The man fitted a lid on top of the cylinder and turned a handle at its center. Anton smelled the fresh-ground coffee. An old custom from Bosnia's Ottoman days, he reckoned. Three tin cups of water soon simmered at the edge of the fire.

"Ah!" Anton gulped a mouthful of the oily liquor and passed the bottle to Yanko. "Plum brandy."

"*Da. Rakija.* Now you are in Bosnia. For each drink you owe me one dead Fascisti. If it is Italian, he counts for half. Ha! Ha!"

Anton nodded, his expression confirming that he would not hesitate to shoot two Italians. He had already killed his share of Eyeties in Abyssinia in '36, he reflected.

Yanko abruptly stopped smiling and looked Anton hard in the eye. He directed Nada to translate for him as he spoke:

"In Travnik, to avenge one German officer, they shot forty-five Bosnians. There were not enough men left to shoot, so they took fourteen boys from the school. First they made them all, boys and men, undress before the women and the other children, under the lime trees by the old Turkish tombs. For two hours they stood naked, shivering and urinating from fear. Finally the Nazis had the Ustashi do the shooting to remind everyone which side they were on. These killers wore black. Colonel Francetec's men, the Black Legion, the Nazis of Croatia." Yanko scowled. "For that devil, I will give you a bottle of brandy, and all the colonel's medals."

"Bosnians never forget," Major Treitel had said.

The group drank noisily and ate the bread while the water boiled. When it was ready, Nada removed the copper top from the coffee grinder and emptied the bottom into the cups. The scent rose sweet and strong in the sharp air.

"We are on our way to help one of our field hospitals move deeper into the mountains. The Germans are trying to encircle us before the winter comes, so we must move now," Nada said. Warmed by the blaze, she took off her jacket and looked into the fire. "We cannot leave any wounded, or the Germans and Ustashi will kill them," she explained. "Near Vitez they put our wounded in a field and drove over them with tanks."

As Anton absorbed this, she paused and picked lice from the seams of her coat, cracking them one by one against the heel of her boot with short chipped fingernails. He had seen baboons do something similar.

Rider passed around a packet of Senior Service. The Partisans smiled and each took a cigarette with restrained eagerness. Anton noticed the men's hands, grey, the skin indented rather than lined, rougher than old boards. Even Nada's was no longer youthful.

They all smoked and drank the thick coffee to the grounds. As he smoked, Anton dropped his ashes into the cigarette box.

The respite was over soon. "Now we walk." Yanko stood and pointed through the pines and birches up the rocky ridge to the first mountain. He handed the Enfield to Anton.

"I must find two other men," said Rider. "An American and an Englishman. They jumped with me last night."

Yanko spoke to Nada and she said, "Other Partisans look for them. Perhaps we meet them at the hospital in the mountains. But now we must move. The Germans and Ustashi, and their jackal Italians and Bulgarians, are closing the ring to clean central Bosnia of Partisans."

They began the slow arduous climb with Anton and Nada placed in the middle. Swollen and stiff, Anton's right knee was soon throbbing. A deeper duller pain cried from his hip. He tried to ignore the leg, and for a time it seemed to loosen as they hiked uphill.

"Can you walk long?" said Nada, concerned.

"Of course."

At the top they passed furtively over the crest of the ridge and descended to a stand of pines. Yanko took the Enfield, wanting to use the scope. For ten minutes he scanned the valley below them. Then he put down the rifle and held up a fist.

"From how far can you shoot my hand?"

So the old man did know some English.

"Six hundred yards. A bit less in meters."

"Six hundred? Impossible."

"If there is no wind, and you keep your hand still, six-fifty." Anton sensed that Yanko had a specific reason for asking. "Shall we try it?" he offered.

"Follow this path with the glass down to that road in the valley." Yanko handed Anton the Enfield. "Then right along the road. There is a stone bridge. At this end you see a guard post. Sandbags. A wireless mast, one motorbicycle. Two German soldiers."

Anton was already sighting through the telescopic sight. "I see them."

"How far are they?"

Anton tried to measure off the distance in hundred-yard increments, but the slope and the changing rough ground made it difficult. Then he concentrated on the heads of the two soldiers.

"Five hundred yards," he said to Yanko. "Five-twenty at the most."

"At the end of the day, just before darkness, I want you to kill those Fascisti before they have the chance to use the radio. If so, we can cross this bridge and escape to Mount Vlashitch above Travnik. Others will bring your friends there."

"Perhaps I should shoot the radio first?" Anton suggested.

Yanko waved that idea away. "The radio is valuable. And so is the *Schutzmantel*, that rubberized motorcycle coat the big German is wearing. Perfect in the snow and wind," he added with a note of longing.

During the afternoon, the six took turns sleeping and watching. Once when Anton woke, his knee throbbing, he opened his eyes to see Nada studying him intently, like an object in a museum. Caught, she turned away. She made a show of removing her cap and shaking her head. Long filthy hair fell loose about her face, thick dark brown curls with highlights of red. Her face was strong more than pretty, with a prominent nose and bold cheekbones and a high clear forehead.

They regarded each other steadily, almost as if they were touching. With the attention, Nada smiled. Her eyes became the color of the sky. Anton grinned as well. She rose and came over to him.

"Let me see your leg."

"It's all right."

"No, it is not. With the Partisans I am a nurse. I was training to be a doctor." Like Gwenn, he thought. The best way for a woman to make a difference, his wife had told him once.

Nada looked down at her sling. "But perhaps now I must become a teacher. Pull down your trousers to your ankles."

116

Uncomfortable, Anton did as she told him. With the other men near-by, he tried to appear indifferent to her examination.

Nada gripped him firmly above the right calf. With a deliberate touch she moved her hand along his limb. Then she felt the inflamed area around his knee and the muscles above it. Her hand was cold and strong. Like a boy at the dentist, Anton hoped she would not discover the place that pained him most. She flexed the leg, first bending it like a double hinge, then sideways, rotating the joint in the hip socket. He made no sound but knew she sensed the shrieking pain.

"The knee is a bad sprain. I think no fracture," she offered. "And there is something wrong in the hip. You should not be walking."

Anton shrugged. "There should not be a war." Hastily he pulled up his khaki trousers. As he turned, he realized Yanko had been watching.

***

"The post, master." Tariq centered the salver on the folding map table set each morning near the helm of the Cataract Café. The brass-hinged table was rumored to be that used by Nelson on the deck of the *Vanguard* before the battle of the Nile. When Napoleon's flagship, *L'Orient*, had exploded during the great sea battle at Aboukir Bay, the table silver that the Corsican had stolen from the Knights of Malta had showered down like spring rain on the decks of the surrounding British warships. Olivio Fonseca Alavedo liked to think that a fork or two had landed on the very table on which his small hands now rested.

This morning the dwarf wore a green brocade vest against the dawn chill. He enjoyed these early morning ceremonies after his mighty Nubian carried him on deck. The balance of light and temperature before the sun rose and steamed away the coolness of the river. The downward stroke of daylight as it first illuminated the balconied tips of the minarets and then their lean supporting stalks. The first feluccas gliding down-stream, light as water bugs. The slowly rising distant din as the great town on the river Nile came alive. At first light, like Admiral Nelson in his salty domain, the city and the river were still his.

Today his mail was weighty with the estate manager's report from Oporto. The season in Portugal had been bone dry. The deep-rooted vines had sucked up what moisture they could from the fissures in the rock, veritably squeezing blood from stone. The wine would be low in volume but intense in color and flavor. The immense storage barrels, each one an oaken castle, two of them filling a vaulted stone barn centuries old, were nearly topped up with the port of previous harvests. For a moment Olivio imagined himself on the broad verandah of his *quinta* in Portugal, nibbling toasted almonds as small glasses were presented for his judgement and he employed the discerning weapon of his extraordinary nose.

Olivio set aside the dreary unopened envelopes of lawyers, account-ants and fournisseurs. He turned to what always carried more interest for him, correspondence belonging to others. In this case, he was attending to it by invitation.

His friend, Mr. Anton, had no home. So the dwarf stored his few be-longings like baggage in the hold and collected Rider's correspondence here at sea, responding to whatever required attention. The dwarf had as many friends as thumbs, and he knew well who they were.

Of the two envelopes for Captain A. Rider, one contained a bill from Groppi's restaurant, a minor matter he himself would settle and would never mention. The other was of deeper interest. This second envelope was from the Anglo-Swiss Hospital on the rue Sign el-Hadra in Alexan-dria. It was formerly the German Deaconesses' Hospital, a title no longer fashionable after the Luftwaffe bombed that city. Above the name of the institution, penned in black gothic writing, were the words: Kapitan Ernst von Decken.

Von Decken! Could that brutal rogue still be alive? Of course, smiled the dwarf. This German was the sort you could never kill.

He knew von Decken was Anton Rider's oldest friend in Africa. Rider had told Olivio he had met Ernst as a boy, on the dusty road north from Dar es Salaam in German East Africa in 1919. They had shared mischief and troubles in Tanganyika and Egypt, Libya and Ethiopia, where the German had lost a leg after the Italians shot down his Potez in 1936. The light aircraft had been loaded with stolen Italian coins, crates of the Maria Theresa silver dollars Mussolini had sent to bribe the Abyssinian priests and princes.

A year ago, Captain von Decken, now attached to the Afrika Korps, had helped Rider to escape from one of Rommel's desert prison camps. So Anton Rider was in the debt of this German, which put Olivio in the same dangerous position as Mr. Anton himself, he thought as he slit open the square brown envelope with his dagger and read the contents.

Mein Engländer-

I am with five other wounded German officers by the British to this hospital sent. I used to complain that it was a waste for General Rommel, himself exhausted and over-burdened, to spend his time seeing that our English prisoners proper medical care received. But they say that is why we are now it receiving.

There are even a few old nurses here trained in Heidelberg and Dresden, but the naughty one who likes me most has only ancient charms, and a grey mustache.

So Engländer, soon, when I am better, I trust you to do for me what last year for you I did. Help me find my way. My escape.

Perhaps you also remember my dear Father, who after you
looked when young we were.

Your only true friend-

Ernst

Only true friend? The little man grew hot. What did this savage Hun
know of friendship? What did he think Señhor Alavedo himself was to
Anton Rider? What was it this brute demanded now? Of course: to be
rescued and released, and no doubt much money and the risk of others to
assist him.

Olivio tapped the dagger on the letter and stared out across the river,
his eye lead-grey. "Coffee!" he called. "*Qahwa!* For two."

The dwarf read the letter once more, wary of the burden of friendship, but appreciating the cleverness of this German. Anton Rider had
spoken with affectionate memory of his first host in Africa, old man von
Decken, the father of this savage.

If that friendship required a service of Mr. Anton, it required it of
Olivio Alavedo.

The little man grumbled to himself. He was also going to assist Anton in another matter. His mind turned for a moment to a scheme which
would develop in two evenings in the high-stakes card room at the Royal
Automobile Club of Egypt: a game that would not be a game.

Just then Tiago climbed the steps to the poop deck with his schoolbooks hanging over his hunched shoulder in a belt. Alavedo would spare
a few minutes for his son before the child left for the Lycée. It was the
dwarf's practice to impart each day one lesson from his own life.

"*Bom dia*, Tiago," said Olivio as they kissed, trying to keep his son
familiar with Portuguese.

"*Bom dia*, Papa."

"Why are there so many water craft on the Nile, Tiago? Why are there so many carts and lorries on the roads?"

"For business, Papa," said the small boy, eager to demonstrate his filiation. "For commerce."

"Correct. Cairo supports many economies. Native and imperial. Agricultural and military." The dwarf spread his hands and stared into his son's eyes, communicating the energy of his teaching. "Some as ancient as the sandy camel tracks of the Sahara. Others as modern as the steel warships passing through the great Canal. But they all require one thing to make them work together. And what is that, my boy?"

"Money, Papa! Money!"

"True," the dwarf nodded. "But something else: lubricants. Like oil in a cooking pan, or grease on the axle of an automobile. Lest things stick or grind together. And in commerce the greatest lubricants are human. Sometimes they are men who have no business, my child, except for the business of others. The traders, the brokers, the agents, the fixers . . . Ah, here comes one now, that scoundrel Demetreos. Off you go, my lad. *Bonne journée*."

The boy left for the waiting Daimler, passing a slope-shouldered figure in a wrinkled linen suit hurrying up the gangway from the embankment. Tariq waited by the motorcar, his demeanor friendly to the child, stone-like to the visitor. The man had a short dark mustache and slick black hair cut long and parted in the center like a villain from the films. Tiago ducked to prevent the man from patting his head as the two passed.

"Sit," said the dwarf as his guest bowed. "Serve yourself some coffee, Demetreos."

"Thank you, excellency," said the Greek, squinting into the rising sun and removing his thick spectacles. "How may I be of service?"

"Only a little business information. To do with Cairo's latest industry, what some call profiteering, or military contraband. For every ship that unloads at Suez or Port Saïd, for every convoy to the front, each truckload or freight car that passes from Cairo to Alexandria, there is a sort of tax, Demetreos. Here a crate of boots, there a thousand blankets. Tents, bolts of khaki cotton, even medical supplies. No doubt you know how these things are managed."

"Me? I know nothing of such things, excellency." The Levantine looked down and picked at one of his long finger nails. "How would I . . ."

"Careful, Demetreos." The dwarf raised a small hand. "You are speaking to Olivio Alavedo. Have you forgotten? Would you like Tariq to take you for another drive into the open desert?"

The Greek shook his head. He had once tried to mislead the little man in a shipping transaction. He did not require a second lesson.

"We are discussing a request, not an accusation, Demetreos. I need to learn who is providing and controlling the military supplies that enter a certain warehouse and who is benefitting from their sale. Who is the bridge between the British and the thieves?" Alavedo pushed a folded piece of paper under the edge of the Greek's saucer. "There is the address of the warehouse and the name of the wretch who manages it from day to day. Please join me again for coffee tomorrow morning at this hour."

Chapter Twelve

"It is time, Englishman, to see you shoot your first German," said Yanko roughly as he came over and stepped between his daughter and Anton Rider. "You and I will go closer to the bridge. Leave your pack and things for the others. The rest of you," he ordered, "run for the bridge as soon as he fires the first shot."

Anton checked the rifle and reloaded. He slipped the leather lens cap from the scope and cleaned the sight. He grunted to show he was ready.

By now the sun was setting behind them. He and Yanko eased down the slope until they reached a cluster of grey birch trees three hundred and fifty yards from the German guard post. Anton studied his targets. Like rhino, he thought. Seemingly harmless at a distance, but dangerous if provoked.

One soldier, slender and young, perhaps Denby's age, was leaning against a sandbag, smoking and gazing downstream along the sparkling river. In one hand he held a crumpled letter without reading it. On his grey field cap he wore the emblem of an edelweiss, the spring mountain flower that was the symbol of the *Gebirgsjaeger*, the soldiers of the crack German mountain divisions. His lean shoulders were hunched. The collar of his field-grey greatcoat was raised around his neck. Thinking of home, Anton guessed, perhaps missing his girl or mother.

The other soldier, a big man tightly packed into his rubberized coat, was cleaning a machine gun with a dark rag. On his collar Anton recognized the double lightning bolts of the SS. Probably a Jaeger of the Prinz Eugen Division.

Below the two Germans, the water flowed fast and emerald green. Anton recalled the map, guessing this river must be the Lasva on its way to Travnik and Vitez.

Yanko tapped Anton's shoulder and pointed at the dying sun. Nodding, Rider stood behind a tree and faced to the right of the target. The crotch of the tree would provide a stable platform but would make it harder to swing cleanly for the second shot. Better to sit.

First, he opened his packet of cigarettes, tapped it sharply and watched the ashes fall out. Almost no wind. He wet three fingertips and tested it again.

Moving slowly, Anton crossed his left foot over his right foot and sat down. Methodically, he assumed the position he wanted. He braced his elbows on his thighs and settled the rifle like a child in his arms. Extending his legs, he spread the heels of his boots three feet apart. He bent forward at the waist and aligned his left upper arm against the inside of his left shin. With his right hand on the butt, Anton pushed the Enfield forward before settling the rifle into his right shoulder. He advanced his right hand until it grasped the small of the stock. He lowered his upper right arm against the inside of his right knee. To prevent his knees from spreading, he pointed his toes inward. That would also maintain steady pressure on his upper arms.

Balance and tension, Anton reminded himself. He relaxed his weight forward and took a long slow breath. He thought of the Bowman and his three fundamentals: range estimation, concentration, trigger control.

Rider studied the big German, the barrel of his machine gun, his head. Three hundred and twenty-five yards. Anton allowed for the drop and adjusted the elevation of the telescopic sight. He selected a dark stain two-thirds up the man's back, a bit to the left of the spine. Just at the moment of firing he noticed the younger soldier starting to reach for the radio. Anton ignored the movement and squeezed the trigger.

The big German slumped over the gun. In the same instant Anton swung to the second, now moving target. He heard the Partisans rushing forward through the brush behind him. The young German was turning the crank handle on the radio as Anton fired. The soldier fell back against the sandbags, pulling the radio down with him, his hand still moving. For a second Anton saw the boy's face through the scope, his eyes open, as if amazed. Blood ran from one corner of his mouth. Rider fired again and hit the clamshell between the eyes.

Anton rose to join the running Partisans. His leg gave way and he stumbled forward. Yanko jerked him to his feet and helped him swiftly to the bridge.

One Partisan was already making off with the radio. Two others were lifting the machine gun and a metal case of ammunition. Anton removed the round edelweiss badge that was pinned to a pocket of the young German's tunic. Yanko took the big German's coat and washed the blood from it at the edge of the stream. Nada set her foot in the crotch of each dead German and pulled off their boots.

"You ruined my *Schutzmantel*, Englishman," said Yanko. "You should have shot him in the head." Rider shrugged and the older man grinned. He directed Anton's attention to the vehicle parked nearby. "Can you drive a motorbicycle?"

"I believe so."

Anton slung the Enfield across his back and swung his good leg over the bike. For a moment he thought of an afternoon over twenty years ago in East Africa, fleeing on his motorbike as a pack of wild dogs tore after him through the bush. He supposed this situation was not much different.

He kick-jumped the starter pedal. The engine sputtered then caught as Anton turned the handle throttle and fed it petrol. Yanko placed the machine gun and ammunition in the sidecar. Nada tossed in the boots. As her father watched sternly, she mounted behind Anton and grabbed the raised metal ring at the back of the driver's saddle. Anton put the bike in gear and they followed the others across the humped stone bridge.

Yanko led the group off the dirt road onto a trail that cut up towards the mountains. The motorbike ran out of petrol just as the path became too steep and rough and narrow to accommodate it. Two men wheeled the machine to the edge of a precipice and pitched it over the side.

Their uphill flight continued until they reached the bank of a fast cold stream. They paused to rest and exchange their burdens. Flat high rocks, covered in thick moss, indicated the natural crossing.

Habituated to doing more than his share, Rider was ashamed that he was slowing the pace and not carrying as much as he should.

"Soon we will come to the secret hospital," Nada said, sitting on a rock beside him.

They watched Yanko advance to the stream. He carefully bent and turned each mossy rock upside down. Then he led the way across the stones. The last man turned each stone back to mossy side up after he stepped from it.

"If the moss is worn, the Germans will know many men have come this way," Nada explained, not knowing what Anton's life had been. He smiled to himself, recalling how some Africans taught their children to track small turtles by the tiny scratches their claws left on the rocks. He doubted that any Kraut could hunt and track like a Bushman.

"Usually, only our medical people know exactly where the hospital is," Nada continued. "Our stretcher bearers set down the wounded in certain places in the forest. Then hospital workers collect them."

They continued onward and at length a picket whistled from behind a tree. Yanko went ahead and conversed with the man, then led the party forward.

Anton rose and followed, feeling stiff but pleased that these Partisans had a style of warfare that suited him better than discipline and tank battles. He should have known that a hunter would make a fine guerrilla.

***

"My trick," said Major Treitel quietly, exposing his last club and gathering together the final four cards. "And my over trick."

His bridge partner, Algernon Blunt, a fellow scholar in uniform, tallied their modest winnings in the quadrants of the narrow score pad. The patches of raised veins on his neck were not inflamed, indicating relative sobriety and evenness of temper. Seated between them, Olivio Alavedo's elderly physician was reviewing the calculation with the precision and spirit of a *chef de caisse* in a Zurich bank. The old Hun, or Swiss or whatever he was, was dressed like one as well. A black suit with a boxy unfashionably-short jacket, typical of dressy Europeans. And a bright white shirt with an overly high starched collar. Did this surgeon costume himself like that when he was carving or suturing?

But even Dr. Hanger's few guineas would be useful, thought Alistair Treitel. Wartime inflation was making Cairo less inexpensive, and maintaining the appearance of solvent ease was becoming more costly every day. He knew Gwenn Rider appreciated his generosity, in contrast to her husband's near penury, but he himself was not as rich as he let her think, and tonight would not be much help. But every guinea, every farthing, always counted.

Algie Blunt and Treitel had learned two things when they were up at Cambridge: the philosophy of Marxist social justice, and how to cheat at cards. The two were not unrelated. The young bloods in the set to which they aspired took Edwardian privileges for granted, while townspeople and less advantaged undergraduates struggled in the capitalist Depression. Where was the shame or injustice in stealing back some of the wretched lucre?

Due to their early academic aptitudes, Blunt and Treitel had met as Scholars at Rugby and there had acquired the accent and manners to play in the world of young toffs. Returning from dreary holidays at home in Reading and Nottingham, the two had found their schoolmates tan and worldly after Biarritz and Deauville. Occasionally Blunt's resentment would flare in anger. Solidly built and far better at games than Treitel, Algernon sometimes punished another, smaller boy on the football pitch. In their final year, he had broken a classmate's knee with a side tackle, sending him to St. Moritz to celebrate Christmas on crutches instead of skis.

The injured lad had jested once about Algie's smell, a notoriety even among his schoolmates not used to bathing after sports. "Like a bucket of old fish heads!" the boy had declared with a hee-haw laugh. "Fish-head" had been Blunt's name thereafter, usually whispered behind his back, depicted in chalk on a blackboard, or written by another in Algernon's schoolbooks. With its prominent nose, sloping forehead and receding chin, Blunt's big head earned the title, especially in profile. But the word was never used by Treitel, not even in jest or anger, though often he thought of his friend by that name.

On school weekends, at first their pockets had been empty. The two had watched with envy as their classmates bought pork pies and sweet rolls and tea and treats in the village. Then one market day Treitel bought a slender volume for ninepence from the cart of a used-book dealer. Quentin Trill's classic, *Cards in the Back Room- Or, How to Get Away With It,* was the beginning of a long study.

Cards soon gave them the money to buy the tweeds and waistcoats of a better world. At university Blunt went on to read Greats, while Treitel studied Hume and Hegel, Rousseau and Engels. One morning they attended a lecture on Heinrich Schliemann's discovery of Troy. From that they developed a shared interest in archeology.

During weekday evenings they practiced card tricks and read *The Social Contract* out loud. "Man is born free," they would say to each other instead of good night, "and everywhere he is in chains." Each Friday and Saturday they played cards at Trinity or Magdalene. Drink was their best friend, sometimes too good a friend.

Knowledge was the key. As it was in their studies and during this war. If you knew where the enemy had positioned his heavy armor, or which card was a king before you turned it over, the game was yours.

Only once had they been caught. At a house party at an old pile near Huntingdon, the father of their host joined the younger set for a few hands. The old soldier had wheeled his chair tight against the card table and adjusted the blanket across his legs before calling for more brandy. No doubt hardened to drink and gambling at Buck's or Blades', he was never as inebriated as he seemed. On one occasion he had taken Treitel by the wrist the way a farmer seizes a chicken by the neck before the strangling. His other hand spun one wheel of his chair, forcing Treitel to rise as the wheelchair turned from the table. Astonished by his grip, Treitel could still remember the old man's pinched lips, his face gone white except for the cherry of his nose.

"Go to your room," their host commanded quietly. "We do not shelter cheats." A chambermaid was already packing their bags when they arrived upstairs. At six the next morning there were two sharp raps on their door. A servant entered and carried their cases to a waiting car. The house was still asleep. Blunt and Treitel did not speak as the chauffeur drove them back to Cambridge in the rain. Staring out the window, Treitel had reflected that the old gent's grip came not just from outrage, but from years of driving his body with his hands.

"My fault, Treitel. We underestimated the old boy," Algie had said as they set down their bags inside the college gate. "If we are going to do this, we must learn to do it better." Part of that, they learned, was studying their opponents, not just the cards.

Like so many details of school life, Blunt's nickname had survived his youth, mysteriously following him wherever he went, first to London, now to Cairo. Even when he entered the Turf Club or the Long Bar at Shepheard's, someone would say, "Ah, there's old Fishhead."

Alistair Treitel rubbed his wrist and put the recollections aside. He looked around the card room as the losers confirmed the score and settled the account. It was remarkable what one could win at cards, one way or another. Last month they had been paid with land, nearly three fedan of date palms and rice fields near the great oasis of Faiyūm. "Fine shooting, too," said the bleary loser, settling the debt. "Mostly dove, you'll find."

From their portraits across the table, Ismael Pasha and King Fuad gazed down at the players through the thick smoke with dark eyes and manly Ottoman dignity. Both rulers wore the fez of Egypt, the decorations of Turkey and a uniform jacket with gold braid akin to the European military. Around them in the card room, French and Arabic, English and Greek blended together in the low rumble of voices. The green felt tables, newly covered every year, already bore the stains of thick coffee and the ring marks of port and brandy. War and its commerce might be flourishing from Cairo to Casablanca, but on the Shari el-Madabigh the Royal Automobile Club remained true to itself. Only at the Muhammed Ali Club did men play for higher stakes.

Obliged to honor the etiquettes of a club of which they were not members, Treitel and Blunt joined the losers for drinks in the Guest Bar.

"The war seems to be going rather better," said Dr. Hänger's partner, a grand Kopt unconcerned by losses, as he pumped soda from a silver siphon into his long brandy. How many fellahin had starved and labored like serfs and for how long to pay for this man's foolishness? wondered Treitel as the Kopt continued. Of course now Blunt and he possessed a few barefoot fellahin themselves, laboring for them near Faiyūm. And why not? Fabian ideals aside, these Egyptian peasants had to work for somebody.

"Stalingrad and Alamein are heavy blows, even for Berlin," the Kopt observed. Like Blunt, he had been drinking like a dromedary at the last oasis. Sometimes, when not playing against the very best, Algie's thirst could be useful, encouraging other players to do the same. "And now the Americans will be turning out tanks and planes the way we produce camels and dates."

Algernon Blunt puffed out his red cheeks like a blowfish and shook his head twice. "It's Stalin and the Soviets who will win this war for us, not capitalism or the Yanks." He had spent nearly two years fighting in the war in Spain, or at least living in Barcelona, working in a hospital kitchen and reading Marx to the wounded Republicans. "Thousands of Russians are dying for us every day," Algernon added, outrage bitter in his voice. "Even the women are fighting."

"And when it's done," said Treitel more calmly, having had enough to drink himself, "the Americans will go home again, and at last we will have socialism from Edinburgh to Vladivostok."

By the time Alistair Treitel parked in the courtyard behind the apartment building, even the streets of Cairo were quiet.

"Good evening, effendi," saluted the old guardian as he staggered up from his tall stool near the entrance and rubbed his eyes. "Madame is at home."

Upstairs, Treitel had difficulty in finding his key. Once he slipped inside at last, he closed the door too loudly. Now he would have to deal with Gwenn. She liked to be well rested when she reported to a surgery early each morning. Tonight he was in no state to discuss her anxiety about where they were going to live if they lost the flat. But he was angry with himself. He knew he had promised Gwenn too much, trying to distinguish himself from her husband's penury, leading her to believe that he was better off than he was.

In Cairo, rents had tripled during the war. The damned Americans were making it worse. Even their ranks were inflated. He leaned against the wall by the door, balancing carefully as he took off his shoes before walking down the hall. He opened the bedroom door with his shoes in one hand.

"Alistair," Gwenn's voice called, sleep heavy, at first not unfriendly. "What time is it? Oh, God. Why are you always so late?"

"I was at the Royal Automobile Club, as you know. How could I leave before the game was done?" He sat on a corner of the bed and undid his tie. His head hurt. "Won a few quid. Not enough to pay the rent, of course."

"Rent?' she said, stirring to wakefulness. "You told me money would never be a worry."

"Money is always a problem." He tossed one shoe into a corner of the wooden floor. He was in no mood for this. All my life, he thought, even at school money was the problem. He threw the other shoe.

"Alistair! Please. I'm trying to sleep. You know I have to operate in the morning." She sat up with a pillow held across her chest. "What do you mean, there are money problems?"

"Go back to sleep," he said, unbuttoning his shirt.

"After you've woken me up like this? It's two thirty." Gwenn rubbed her face. "Tell me what you meant about money problems. I've been through enough of those."

"If you're going to talk, I need a nightcap." Treitel draped his dinner jacket on a chair and walked down the hall. Back with a cigarette and a dark brandy and soda, he sat on the corner of the bed with his back to her.

"Alistair, if we have problems, I want to know about them," Gwenn said in a tight tired voice, "Please be honest with me. What did you mean? I moved here because you asked me to."

"If money is so important to you, Mrs. Rider, how could you marry someone who never paid for anything in his life? Not even his own sons' school fees."

Her tone became rigid. Anton was out of bounds.

"This is not about him, Alistair. It's about us. You are meant to be a distinguished professor, a collector of antiquities, an officer. How can money be a problem? Why do you play cards if you can't afford the rent?" Even more of an edge entered her voice. "If you are not honest with me, I can't live with you."

"You mean 'live off me,' not 'with me,' don't you, Gwenn, dear?" He sat closer to Gwenn, with his drink and cigarette in one hand. "Half the time you avoid me now."

"I've had enough money problems."

"Of course you have." Treitel turned towards her and rested one hand on the covers over her leg. "With that poor cadging idiot you married." He gripped her leg hard through the thin bed clothes.

Gwenn struggled to free her leg from his hand, outraged by his man-handling her. "In every other way, Anton Rider is twice the man you are."

Treitel's face reddened. He reached for her clumsily.

"Leave me alone," she said, shifting to the far edge of the bed, uncertain whether he wished to strike her or seduce her, though he had probably had too much to drink for the latter.

133

"I'll leave you alone," Treitel announced as he dropped his cigarette butt into the remains of his drink. "You deserve to be alone."

He stood and threw the drink over the bedcovers.

Chapter Thirteen

The stench greeted them before they reached the mouth of the surgery cave. As they approached along the trail, they passed fewer guards and more wounded. Some were awaiting treatment. Most huddled silently on rocks among the dark pines and oaks. Other men trimmed poles for stretchers or scraped earth and stones into burial pits.

Three women in black shawls bent over the body of a mule, edging their knives under the hard dark skin as they pulled back the animal's coat. Untouched, the head and neck still appeared as they had in life. Beyond the cut, one shoulder was a clean filmy white where the women had already flayed it. A large iron pot boiled nearby awaiting the meat. Here and there men clustered around small fires, cleaning bolt-action rifles, carving canes and fabricating crutches. Bony-hipped horses and mules were tied to trees, rubbing their pack sores against the bark.

A murmur of groans rose from the stretchers clustered outside the entrance to the cave. Some men lay silently in bloody ragged clothing. Two torn canvas sheets covered the opening of the cave. One bore a five-pointed star with a red hammer and sickle at the center. At the far edge of the camp, Anton saw men seated on the ground listening to a commissar who stood on a tree stump with his back to the cave, gesturing with his fists whenever his voice rose.

Yanko and Nada bent down to attend to an elderly man who lifted himself on his elbows as they passed. Anton caught up with them and sat down against an oak. Slowly he straightened his leg before him. A long scream came from the cave. Setting down her pack and gun, Nada pulled back the coat that covered the old man's lower body. Yanko held the man's shoulders while she examined the soiled dressings that wrapped the stumps that were his ankles. A mine, Anton reckoned. He removed the first-aid pack from his belt and tossed it to Nada. He prayed he would not need it himself.

"I say, Captain Rider!" called an English voice behind him. Major Sparrow.

Anton stood and turned around.

"Sir!"

Sparrow lay on a makeshift stretcher with a pack under his head. He was shaving himself with a straight razor. He looked ten years older, gaunt as an old bird, though only four days had passed.

Anton knelt beside the Englishman and touched his arm. "How are you, sir?" Sparrow's swagger stick lay between his legs. "What happened?"

"Rather a messy drop. My chute tangled and I made a rocky landing on my backside," he said, matter-of-fact as always. "Worse than the Wall Game. Seems I messed up my spine. Can't feel much below the waist. These Red bandits have been dragging me about for days. Now they're threatening to open up my back." The major dipped his razor in a tin cup full of soapy water. "Glad you've come to join the party. Simon's hanging about here somewhere. 'Fraid he's making a little mischief."

"How can I help, sir?"

Sparrow wiped his razor on some leaves and leaned forward to lift his head from the pack. "Take a handful of tea from my kit here and fix us a cup, won't you, Captain?" He emptied his tin cup before scouring it with a handful of dirt and passing it to Anton.

"Right you are, sir." Rider withdrew the packet of tea and handed the major his sketching kit.

"Oh, and Rider, do make certain the water is really boiling."

Anton found another cup and threw in some tea leaves. To get water he had to pass the mule skinners. Now only the head and legs were black, he noticed. Two women struggled to turn the animal over to get at the other side. The third was cutting the raw hide into strips to make lashings for the stretchers. Anton stopped to help lift two legs and flip the mule. He filled the cups from a large black kettle nearby and returned to the major's side.

"I gather we haven't popped in at quite the best time." Sparrow closed the razor and took his cup in both hands. "But what can you expect from that lot of intelligence wallahs in Cairo?" he said, shrugging. "They tell me the Jerries've got five divisions trying to trap the Partisans, even held back two from the Eastern Front to have a better crack at it. This lot's racing to break out before the noose tightens. Tito's told 'em they can't leave the wounded. They'd all get shot." The major blew across the cup and sipped his tea. "Suits me, I must say, now that I'm wounded myself." He raised his eyebrows at Anton and said quietly, "Nobody takes prisoners out here. Not like our desert war. Even the Eyeties don't like surrendering anymore, though a mob of 'em are serving here as porters."

Anton had never heard the major talk so much. Before he could reply, Sparrow continued.

"So in the morning we'll be off. Amputees, limpers, the whole wretched lot. We're to meet up with two other hospitals and make it out to the north, crossing the Bosna River and back up into the mountains scampering on to the west. Should be quite a parade. Sporty, too, evading Ustashi hunting parties. The Huns use 'em as beagles to run down and pin the fox till they catch up and finish us off." The major handed back his cup. "Not bad on the tea, Rider. And what've you been up to? Had any good shooting?"

"A bit, sir. That group over there found me and led me here."

Major Sparrow gave them an appraising glance. "Who's your fair dolly? She'd do at a garden party."

"Nada is a nurse," Anton said. "Should I have her look at you, sir?"

"Can't do much good, but why not? Oh, I think she just slipped into the butcher shop."

Anton finished his tea and walked to the cave. Trying to ignore the smell, he raised the edge of a canvas sheet and stepped inside. Four smoky paraffin lamps hung from bolts driven into cracks in the top of the cave. A camp dog whined in the shadows. Wounded men lay in the darkness at the back of the long rock shelter. Women knelt among them. Several discarded limbs lay against the wall. The dog slunk towards them. Anton tried not to breathe.

Two half-naked patients lay on makeshift tables, one apparently dead, one still under the knife. The wounded Partisan was strapped to his table. Three men tried to hold his twitching body still. A leather bit was wedged between the man's teeth. His face glistened with sweat and tears. Empty brandy bottles lay under the table. Holding a short saw, Nada stood behind the surgeon, a tall hollow-eyed woman with rubber gloves and a bloody smock. Sickened, Anton went outside and walked off among the elders. He seized an overhead branch with both hands to steady himself. Then he closed his eyes and vomited.

"What's the matter with you, Rider? Need a drink?" The speaker belched. "Schnapps?"

Captain Lester Simon drank from the cup of a German canteen. "Where the hell were you at the meeting point, Rider?" He watched Anton spit and wipe his mouth on his sleeve. "Sparrow made us wait for you. You could have got us all killed."

Rider remembered one of the lessons the dwarf had repeated to him: only say what you yourself wish to say, not what someone else wants you to say. No need to explain yourself.

"We're all here, Captain." There was no apology in Anton's voice. "How bad is Major Sparrow?"

"He's had it." The American rubbed his eyebrow and shrugged. "Useless, but he still thinks he's in charge."

"He is."

Anton woke before dawn when he heard wolves howling in the distance. At home it would have been hyena. His face was wet. He touched his cheek and licked the snow from his fingers. Was it not too early for winter? He sat up and looked about him. Large snowflakes fell slowly through the trees. He remembered one winter when he was young, at some gypsy camp near the New Forest, lying on his back in the snow with his arms behind his head until he was completely covered, hoping no one would ever find him, blinking and trying to catch the snowflakes on the tip of his tongue while he imagined poaching deer with Robin Hood and Little John.

As the sky greyed, Anton watched the white forms take perfect clean shape around him. Trees, each rock on the hillside, the outlines of sleeping men, the motionless horses bunched shoulder to shoulder in a single pale sculpture. Sparrow lay beside him, still and silent as the white marble carving of a dead knight atop a catafalque.

Like a great wounded animal the camp awoke and stirred, rising and shaking itself, coughing. Dark shapes and colors broke through the light snow. Yanko and the other leaders moved among the men, kicking some awake, helping others. The scouts and advance parties were dispatched.

The hospital was broken into groups of fifty or sixty, sorted by degrees of immobility. Each was escorted by a political commissar and a unit of armed Partisans. The seriously wounded and slowest left first, a few mounted on mules or horseback. Most were borne on stretchers carried on the shoulders of four men or women. Long files of walking wounded arose and followed with their sticks and crutches, many helping each other and carrying weapons over one shoulder. Ninety typhus cases, Anton was told, were isolated in their own camp on the next hillside and would set off in a separate column.

The mule train followed. Seventy or eighty lean animals carried medical and military supplies packed on wooden frames and lashed with ropes of cord and leather and parachute harness. Following a dispute between an officer and two party commissars, the strongest animals were loaded with wooden chests of silver coins, typewriters and a small printing press and reams of paper.

"*Agitprop*," whispered Nada to Anton. "All the materials for propaganda and political education. That man with the star on his cap and the ear flaps was trained in Moscow by the Comintern."

The senior Partisan commander came over with a commissar and gave Major Sparrow the Red clenched-fist salute. Four Italian prisoners stood shivering behind him. Anton noticed Nada watching from a distance. She nodded at him, smiled and blew on her hand. He saw Simon staring at her.

"Introduce yourself, Captain Rider," said Sparrow. "Hop to it. Don't be modest. Tell these Bolshies you're with my mission and a specialist in long-range murder. Then they'll see you get fed." In a quieter voice he added, "Please don't let them think I'm going under."

Anton complied and accepted a flask of cold coffee and brandy from the commissar, a stocky woman in a fur cap with a felt hammer and sickle stitched across the red star on its front.

The Partisan commander examined Rider's rifle. "They tell me you already have killed two Germans with three bullets," he said, stroking his long dark mustache with thick filthy fingers. "How many bullets have you left?"

"Two hundred and ninety-seven," replied Anton crisply. "Please look after Major Sparrow. He is an important English officer with messages from London for your commander. He will be ordering parachute drops of weapons and medical supplies."

The commissar turned to the lightly clad Italians and pointed down at Major Sparrow. She spoke to one prisoner in rough German. "You will carry this Englishman to the next camp. If he does not arrive there safely, you will end up like that." She pointed at two boys who had emerged from the cave carrying between them an oval basket filled with severed arms and legs.

One Italian translated for the others. They nodded and stepped hastily to the stretcher.

Anton saw Simon hurrying towards them through the trees with a map in one hand. He already looked like a Partisan. Rugged, hard-faced, unshaven.

"Major Sp . . ." Rider began.

"Tell these people I want to know where we are going," Simon said to Sparrow, interrupting. Looking down, he assessed the Englishman's condition. "I have a job to do, and I must speak to someone close to Tito."

The two boys, perhaps fourteen or fifteen, dropped the basket under a pine tree and sat down beside it. No one else seemed to notice them.

"We should get ready, sir. Probably strap you into your stretcher, if you don't mind," Anton said to Sparrow. He tried not to watch as the boys began to tie the limbs in bunches of three or four with what appeared to be lengths of cord cut from parachute risers. They secured each bunch with tight knots around the wrists and ankles, chatting and working easily together. A new level of savagery, he thought, perhaps worse than he had seen in any campaign in Africa, even in Ethiopia.

Nada appeared beside Rider and commented, "Sometimes the Germans use dogs, big hungry shepherds and Doberman pinschers, to try and find the hospitals. We drag severed arms and legs through the forest to mislead the dogs."

Anton nodded at the thought.

"Carry on, old boy," Sparrow said to Anton from the ground. "What's the show?"

"The whole camp is moving deeper into the mountains, sir." Anton knelt and slipped a belt under the officer's stretcher. "Consolidating with two other hospitals in a safer place, what the Communists consider a 'Free Territory' under their control. The men call it 'Titoland.' Probably near Bihac. Marshall Tito's command should be nearby."

"Better be," Simon snapped, "or we should be making our own plans. We didn't come to Bosnia to play nurse."

"You could always stay here, Captain Simon," Sparrow said, tapping his swagger stick sharply against one boot, "and wait for the Jerries on your own." Smiling, Anton gently secured the buckle across Sparrow's chest. "They will not be long."

The first day the hospital made progress, crawling along the trails, keeping below the ridge lines as the light snow blew off, weaving through thin birch forests on the rocky plateaus, losing only a few men while they descended towards the Sava River.

Habituated to leading a safari or a squadron of the Long Range Desert Group, Anton Rider soon found himself at the head of one column. His injury was modest compared to those of the men around him. Cutting and stripping a stout staff, he ignored his leg and took naturally to the work. An Italian prisoner struggled to keep up with him, encumbered by Anton's pack and bandoliers.

The march was brutally flogged onward by small parties of Ustashi. The black-uniformed Croatian fascists harassed the retreat, stalking stragglers and shooting any wounded abandoned on the trails. The wounded understood their future, asking to be left behind with a rifle or a few grenades. They were determined to lighten the column and take at least one enemy soul with them. A screen of Partisan escort teams tried to protect the hospital column. They had ambushed one Ustashi hunting party, which fought with the desperate ferocity of men who knew surrender was unthinkable.

In early afternoon an unarmed German light reconnaissance aircraft, a Fieseler Storch, hummed towards the sprawling columns, hovering on their flanks, then floating into the distance, slender and harmless as a dragonfly. Anton was familiar with the graceful aircraft from their use by the Afrika Korps. General Rommel, always leading from the front, flew a Storch himself, preferring to make his own battlefield observations.

Rider knew what would follow this reconnaissance.

The Stukas were on them within half an hour. Anton recognized the stubby angled wings and tail swastikas as the flight of Junker dive bombers arced down like a deadly grey and black rainbow.

Jumo engines shrieked and howled like demons as the Stukas dove and their dive sirens screamed. Terrified, three Italian bearers dropped Sparrow's stretcher and flung themselves into the forest. Cursing them, Anton and the fourth Italian hurriedly dragged the stretcher off the path. All around them men and animals scattered and fell as machine gun and cannon fire swept the trails and hunted groups of fleeing figures into the mountainsides.

A mule, shot in the back, one leg dragging, bolted close past Anton with a wounded man lashed to its back. Rider grabbed at the rope halter but missed the plunging animal. The mule kicked and screamed before falling and crashing down the rocky slope. Anton heard a line of bullets cut through the trees, biting into the ground like a row of perfectly driven nails. Tat. Tat. Tat. Beside him the fourth Italian cried out when two bullets caught him. Anton held the man's shoulder as he died. His own porter seemed to have vanished.

The Stukas ended their runs and turned back to the south in tight formation with empty guns. As the hospital survivors got to their feet and searched for their comrades, a heavier drone filled the sky. Once again, as if identifying a bottle of wine or an old friend, Anton recognized the sound. A flight of Dorniers. One of his squadron's missions behind the Axis lines had been to destroy these bombers on the ground before they could raid Alexandria and the British bases.

Anton dragged Sparrow under a ledge and stared up through the branches. He heard the singing whistle of falling bombs before a stick of explosives tore the trail above. Fragments of stone and earth fell on the two men. "Good thing I can't feel anything," muttered the English major. The twin-engine bombers continued to the north. Only five or ten minutes had elapsed since the first Stuka attacked.

The remains of the hospital columns regathered slowly. Grouping themselves according to the line of march, they settled in camps under the trees. Fresh casualties had replaced the wounded that had fallen back along the way. Many animals and at least three nurses were dead. Anton walked back along the trail under the trees with his rifle, searching for Nada, Simon and the Partisan commander. He saw dead horses already being butchered and drawn to the fires in pieces. One large cook pot was filled with snow and old bandages taken from the dead. As the snow melted, the water bubbled pink. Two women wrung out the bandages and draped them over branches to dry near the flames. Nearby other women were making bread with straw and boiling birch bark and wild roots.

Anton arrived at the last encampment near the end of the forest and walked out onto the open mountainside. He gazed down across the rugged profile of gorges and narrow steep valleys leading to the next, lower line of mountains.

From the still bright sky to the southwest Anton heard the fluttering sound of a light engine. He stood motionless and listened. The Storch was returning to survey its work.

Rider quickly tore a branch from a birch and lay down beneath it with his Enfield. His teeth ground together in determination. It was his turn to join the game, to hunt the hunter. It reminded Anton of Africa, where the sport would change as an unexpected animal hunted the hunter.

He heard the busy pitch of the single engine change as the Storch moved up the line of valleys. Echoing at first from each rock wall, then growing stronger as it flew over the next ridge. Anton removed the scope from his rifle and checked the barrel. He loaded the weapon with two tracers and five regular .303's.

Hours seemed to pass as he waited on his back, the cold settling into him. When it finally came, the plane missed him, climbing, flying on a higher line along the top of the ridge to his left. It continued past him. Anton heard small arms fire as the Partisans tried for a lucky shot. The firing stopped when the observation plane flew on to the north.

Then he heard the engine again. More shrill as it dove. Gaining speed for a second, faster fly-over as it passed along the line of march. A few weapons fired.

Suddenly Anton saw the Storch directly above him. The right wing was tilted down to permit the aviator to study the ground beneath him. The side window was open. Anton saw the pilot's face. The man's chin strap was unbuckled, his mouth open, goggles high on his forehead.

Anton swung his rifle through the line of flight and fired the first tracer. At that instant he was certain the pilot saw him. Anton fired again. A hit, just behind the cockpit. The plane continued, then turned and climbed in a tight circle, passing in the distance over the ridge behind Rider.

In a moment the aircraft was back, swooping down behind him, perhaps three hundred feet above the slope. Anton heard a movement in the forest nearby but held his concentration. He raised the rifle and looked up along the barrel. He saw the airman drop a stick grenade out the window. Rider ignored it and focused on the diving Storch. He squeezed the trigger. The canopy shattered before the pilot's face. At the same time the grenade exploded. Splinters of rock cut into Anton's face, blinding him with a sheet of blood from his forehead.

As the small plane continued on, Anton freed himself and stood, wiping the blood from his eyes with one sleeve. He found Yanko kneeling behind him, staring at the sky as if his life were suspended there.

The Storch abruptly changed direction and veered west into the setting sun. Anton followed the aircraft through his scope. Slowly, almost casually, the plane's nose fell. It dove steeply over the last ridge and out of sight. A moment later a thin column of black smoke spiralled up in the distance.

"I think you got him, Englishman," a female voice said. Anton turned to see Nada standing behind him, fresh blood on her sling. She raised her hand and touched his face. "Why don't you come with me? You need a few stitches."

Chapter Fourteen

Denby Rider rose and shuffled towards the village on bleeding feet. The desert grew softer as the hard crust became more like a dune. The surface sand was light and loose enough to be swept and sculpted by the wind. It slipped under his feet as he stumbled and slid, descending into the depression that held the walled town before him. One of the four Mzabite villages, he guessed, perhaps Guadames.

He paused at the bottom, then walked towards a cluster of date palms, arriving first at a rock shelter perhaps five feet high where a thin bearded man with wrinkled brown skin sat cross-legged on a mat. His eyes were closed, his arms folded across his chest. A large wooden cross hung from his neck on a thick leather cord.

Denby stopped in front of the man and tried to speak. His throat was parched. The man opened his rheumy eyes. As if sun-blinded, he stared at Denby, then reached behind him for a jug. He passed it to Denby, who sat down with his legs extended and drank, thinking it was water. But it was milk. Heavy, sweet and slightly warm. Denby gagged. Camel or goat's milk, he was not certain. He drank a bit more.

"Thank you," said Denby. Patches of sand were stuck to the open wounds of his feet as if they were part of him. "Can you tell . . ."

The angular ascetic shook his head and closed his eyes. One of the Christian desert hermits, Denby realized at last. Even the smallest Muslim towns held scatterings of distant cultures. Tribal blacks, for instance, the Haratin, had first come as slaves. Travelling Jews were known for digging the 80-foot wells that kept these towns alive.

Denby staggered on towards the walled village. He admired the small perfect irrigation channels that watered the apricot and orange trees planted between the palms. For the last two days he had valued water like a Bedouin. Low ridges of earth separated small plots of onions, tomatoes and red peppers, orderly as diamonds and rubies set in a bracelet.

Soon Denby found himself chewing tobacco and sipping small cups of mint tea with three elders of the town. They were seated in the court-yard of a two-story dwelling that was entered by a tunnel and had no outside windows. The thick adobe brick walls were mostly covered in a coat of clay. Children played with a young goat on the rooftop terrace amidst fluttering laundry. One woman, veiled in a shawl and a *haik*, worked on a loom in a corner of the yard. Another roasted a hedgehog and several lizards in the opposite corner. Both women wore baggy belted robes of printed cotton cloth. He smelled smoky herbs and spices over the fresh scent of the mint tea. A dead spotted dog hung from a hook by its hind feet, waiting to be skinned and cooked.

All three Mzabite men were short, with long arms and broad hips, and flat oval faces with narrow noses and dense beards under tightly wound white turbans. They wore striped cotton shirts and baggy indigo blue trousers under their voluminous white *gandoura* robes. Denby was surprised by the whiteness of their skin when the men pushed back their sleeves and reached their fingers into a bowl of steaming couscous that the cook set before them.

The village barber and physician, a short professorial figure with a neat white beard and lined face, had first bathed and cleaned Denby's feet. Then he had treated them with a soothing paste of palm oil and several minerals he ground in a pestle in one corner of his stall under the arcade that surrounded two sides of the dusty central square. An aged camel paced patiently back and forth on a narrow ramp in the middle of the square, drawing water from a deep pulley well. While the barber attended him, a mangy yellow cat appeared and dropped a small dead snake at his feet. Then the barber washed the Englishman's face with a warm wet oily rag and sharpened a straight razor on a belt before giving Lieutenant Rider the finest shave he had ever enjoyed. Denby had closed his eyes and listened to the comforting scratching of the blade before luxuriating in the hot towel the man had pressed against his eyes.

Two of the elders understood French. The son of one had served as a sergeant in the French Camel Corps. When Denby asked to meet him, the elder clapped his hands. A young boy appeared and was sent running to fetch the veteran.

Rashid, the sergeant, soon stood at his father's side. For the last of Denby's French currency, he agreed to provide camels and to ride with the English soldier to the coast road. But first, pointing at the sky, Rashid and the old men discussed in Berber the only thing they feared: wind, the chance of a desert storm. Denby had once seen a lorry that had survived a sand storm. The Fiat had been entirely stripped of paint, every touch and trace, as if burnished by giant steel brushes. The Libyan driver had told him a yellow wall of sand sixty feet high had closed the sky and raged across the desert on the wind.

In the morning a baggage camel and two riding camels stood outside the headman's house while Denby took tea with his host and Rashid. The barber waited outside. There he again treated the Englishman's feet and wrapped them in cotton rags before Denby climbed awkwardly onto his kneeling camel. Two pairs of yellow goatskin slippers waited in one of the packs on the baggage camel, a shorter, darker and more thickly-furred animal than the finer-boned riding camels.

Occasionally Denby and his mates in the Hussars had messed about with camels, racing each other behind the pyramids until most lost their seats, their long falls softened by the desert and the drinks they had downed at Mena House.

Denby's camel rose with a quick jerky rocking motion when the sergeant hissed and threatened it with a fly switch. Rashid handed him the switch and mounted his own beast, leading the baggage animal by a leather cord. Denby had watched the women pack long salted strips of camel meat for the riders to eat as they journeyed north and east. A goatskin was tied to one side of the pack frame of the baggage camel. The skin was swollen, stuffed with a stiff gluey marmalade made from the dates of the village palm trees.

Denby wished to hurry, but Rashid ignored him and held the camels to a steady ambling pace. A rifle and cooking pan hung from his saddle. A leather bandolier crossed from one shoulder to his waist. The bottom of each leather pouch revealed the shiny tips of three bullets. The only sounds as they rode were the padding paces and the snuffling of the camels. Occasionally a low whistling wind blew the loose surface sand. Denby felt he was riding on the moon. For the first time, he understood why the old Sahara hands adored the silence and the crisp clarity of the desert. After a time, cradled by the gait, he dozed lightly in a mesmerized half-conscious state.

Twice they stopped and relieved themselves. They adjusted the saddles and packs before drinking water and eating handfuls of dates and dried apricots. In the early evening they camped in a small depression between two hard sand hills.

Rashid untied a bundle of old palm fronds and built a modest fire. Denby unwrapped his feet and was pleased by how they were healing. After eating, the two men chewed tobacco and conversed in French about the old desert campaigns. Yesterday's Arab slavers and *razzias*, bands of marauding Bedouin raiders. The Italian and French battles with the Senousi and the Tuaregs. All had been replaced by the Afrika Korps, by tanks, artillery and fighter planes. While they spoke, Rashid tightened the single string on his *imzad*.

"*Toujours la guerre*," said the Algerian with no regret. "Always, always we will have war. The desert welcomes young bones."

"How far can we ride tomorrow?"

"By midday, *mon Lieutenant*, we should be in the hills about fifty miles from the coast, close enough to your soldiers. It will be safer to go a bit to the east, then wait above the road until your English army finds us, monsieur. No need to go looking for the fighting." Rashid closed his eyes and cocked his head to one side against his instrument. "But first the desert may have a surprise for you."

As the night cooled, Denby treated his feet with more paste and smeared a bit above his ear. Then he lay on his back with his head on his camel saddle, listening to Rashid stroking his violin.

He gazed at the stars, seeing them as he never had before, wishing that, like his father, he knew each by name. He thought of his brother and the war. He worried about his mother's romance and his father's appetite for campaigning. Finally, with a shadow of guilt, he thought of Saffron Alavedo, her lips and breasts, and how she had always had her mother's high tight African derriere.

Was it possible? he asked himself the next day. A small pink lake hidden in the Sahara?

"*Voila!* Here is the surprise I promised you." Rashid stopped the camels on the slope of a long dune. "The lake of the *Dood*, the worm men, blacks who live by eating worms from three little lakes like this one."

Denby shifted uncomfortably in his saddle and gazed down at the sheet of salmon-colored water. It was not a mirage. He could see the reflections of the date palms at its far shore. Distracted, he failed to check the animal when the camel swung its head around and bit him savagely on the leg. He jerked back the braided reins and struck the animal's neck sharply with his switch.

"Every camel is like an old woman," said the Algerian, winking. "Always wishing to punish you and be the master."

Denby smelled the water as they descended. Salt water? He had the impression that his eyes and nose and ears had all become more sensitive and acute with his time in the desert.

Five women were wading knee-deep in the lake. They paused to close their veils as the two men descended towards them. Then they resumed their fishing, wading parallel to the shore, sweeping the water with long sleeve-shaped cloth nets.

The two riders dismounted near a cluster of *zeribas*. The round huts were built with palm fronds woven between sticks. Several children were playing with a donkey, tormenting the motionless animal with small cruel attentions. Rashid bargained with two black Africans for a basket of tiny pink shrimp-like creatures that the men were carrying from the lake.

Greeting them, Denby lifted out a handful of the shrimp and ate a few. They were salty from the lake water. Each one was smaller than his little fingernail. There must be masses of them to give the lake its color. Rashid hung the basket from his saddle and they rode on from the village.

In the evening they made a fire and cooked the shrimp in Rashid's pan, gorging themselves on the tiny creatures before lying down. A breeze rose from the north. Looking up at the stars, feeling slightly ill, Denby thought he could almost smell the sea, but he was not certain. Perhaps it was the salty shrimp. His feet were not as swollen, though one seemed to be infected.

They rose early and heated mint tea before mounting the camels, eating dried dates as they rode. The land changed, becoming harder, less and less sandy, with patches of low dry bushes and gravel-covered slopes. Finally they came to a line of hills with the first green vegetation. Rashid stopped the animals. He would go no further.

"Now you are there, Lieutenant. Close enough." The camels sat and the men stepped down. Rashid gave Denby a sack containing dried apricots, a skin of water and a strip of camel meat. Denby squeezed his feet into the larger pair of goatskin shoes. He shook hands before his companion could salute. He watched Rashid remount and ride back towards the open desert without looking back.

Denby looked to the north and climbed to the top of the hill facing him, wishing he had a pair of field glasses. The slope below was covered with the overgrown vines of an abandoned vineyard. Beneath it were patches of uncared for but cultivated land, with no people or habitation. In the far distance he saw what must be the Tunisian extension of Libya's Via Balbia, the Roman coast road that ran from Alexandria to Algiers.

Small as ants, silent in the distance, a double line of vehicles was advancing slowly from east to west. He was too far away to discern their types or markings, but their direction identified them as British, on their way into Tunisia to hook up with the Allied armies that had landed in Algeria and Morocco.

Denby paused and looked back. Now a distant still figure, Rashid seemed to have turned and waited. He rose in the saddle and waved his rifle twice. Denby returned the wave. Then he slung the sack over his shoulder and started down towards the coast road.

Chapter Fifteen

"I don't want to slow you down, Captain," said Sparrow to Anton the next day amid the chaos of the fleeing field hospital. Another hospital had joined them on the trail. The route was harder, and there were fewer animals for food and transport. The Ustashi hunting parties seemed more numerous and active. "Tell these Jugos to leave me with the rest of this hopeless lot," said the major.

Anton leaned on his staff and shook his head. "I cannot do that, sir."

"Just help me change out of this British kit first," added Sparrow. Four Italian bearers, two of them near collapse themselves, were hunched on nearby rocks. "If they leave us some weapons and a little lead, we'll take a few Blackies with us and slow down the chase."

Behind Sparrow a team of Partisans and a female commissar were passing among the severely wounded, seizing weapons from the protesting men as the sky darkened. Henceforth the columns would travel by night to avoid the German aircraft.

"What are you doing?" said Yanko to the commissar with anger in his voice. "If they have guns, they can kill a few Germans and slow down the enemy."

"Do not dispute with me," the woman said, moving on briskly. "If we leave guns with the wounded, many will shoot themselves before the Ustashi find them. This way a few may survive, and the Black Legion will not get our weapons."

The hospital began moving again. Ignoring Sparrow's instructions to abandon him, Anton gave nettle broth and scraps of goat cheese to the Italian bearers. Then he followed the Englishman's stretcher, occasionally pausing to lean on his staff or walking beside the litter when the trail was wider.

As they marched through the darkened forest, they passed groups of the abandoned wounded. A few cried out, cursing, demanding to be carried along or to be given weapons. "*Sreca!*" others called to their departing comrades. "Good luck!" Most watched without speaking, knowing they were already dead, lying among the stones and trees or leaning against boulders with blankets pulled over their heads and shoulders, their gaunt faces shrouded and invisible.

Three times during the night the column stopped, each time discarding a few more wounded. At the final stop, in a patch of forest high on a steep ridge, Yanko and Nada came back and found Anton Rider.

"The colonel asks me to reconnoiter the next march. We are going where Nada and I lived before." Yanko passed Anton a bottle of plum brandy while Nada translated. "We are almost at the Sava. A few of us must cross the river before it is light and find where it is safe for the others to come. The ones who can will follow late tomorrow." Yanko eyed Rider's staff, then his bad leg. "If you can, I want you and your rifle with me. We may need you."

"Of course," Anton responded, "if you make certain they will bring Major Sparrow."

"Nada will stay with him," Yanko assured Rider.

As the two men walked through the settling camp, Yanko pointed out, "We are the lucky ones. We will be crossing the gorge over the old footbridge. Most of the others will get wet tomorrow down below."

When they arrived at the edge of the ridge, Rider looked down in the dim light and saw they were on the rim of a deep chasm. Perhaps two hundred feet below them a river roared fast and black. Here and there scouts were descending the face of the rock, searching for the best routes down to the riverbank.

Walking along the ridge towards a narrow suspension bridge, Anton saw swarms of dark shadows moving through the forest towards the camp. In the half light before morning, hundreds of men on stretchers and horseback drifted in and settled under the trees. A third Partisan hospital had arrived to join the break-out across the river.

He surveyed the uneven wooden planks of the slender bridge. One side was suspended a bit higher than the other. Deep in the gorge below he saw two scouts wading into the rushing river with rifles held over their heads, searching for fords.

"How many are down there?" Anton asked uneasily.

"They say three thousand wounded, plus escorts, medical and political staff, stretcher bearers, followers, maybe five thousand altogether."

Yanko tested one of the bridge stanchions with his powerful hands. The tall metal post was driven into a cleft in the rock and supported by two cables of twisted wire attached to spikes in the ground. Yanko jerked back on the stanchion. A ripple of movement danced along the two sloping rust-colored cables that suspended that side of the bridge. One cable supported one edge of the line of planks. The other, drooping severely, served as a low handrail. "But they won't all be coming with us."

"What do you mean?" asked Anton.

"Most of the bad cases will never make it across. And the commissars plan to kill the Italian prisoners, the bearers. That's why they haven't been feeding them."

"Kill them? Why?"

Yanko's voice turned stony. "The Ustashi and the Germans have been shooting Bosnian prisoners. We must remind them who we are. In Travnik they buried the prisoners in pits with the remains of pigs. In the night our people came to bury them again. They found dogs eating the arms and legs that were sticking up through the earth. We are not savages like them, but these outrages must be answered."

Yanko set off across the bridge. When he reached the center, it sagged like a rope hammock, swaying out from side to side. The big Partisan hesitated, crouching on the rocking narrow planks to keep his grip on the low hand cables. Yanko advanced slowly upward. Near the end he allowed himself a short rush of hurried steps as he dropped the cables and lunged for the metal stanchions. Anton recalled staring up at a beautiful trapeze artist under the tent of a travelling gypsy circus somewhere in Derbyshire. Even the practiced aerialist had quickened her pace as she approached the tiny platform with small urgent steps.

Rider peered across the Sava into the early morning gloom. He made out Yanko gesturing at him impatiently from the opposing cliff. The Partisan's last words had been a warning: never place all your weight on one plank. It might be rotten.

Anton adjusted the straps of his pack and tightened the leather sling of the Enfield to secure it behind his shoulder. Hurling his staff into the gorge, he gripped the twisted wire cables and stepped onto the gently swinging planks. His footing felt precarious. After a few steps, he was alarmed by the slippery frost and the steepness of the decline.

As he pressed on, he felt one board bend dangerously in the center under his right foot. The planks would be stronger at the edges, but if he stepped on the sides, the bridge would tilt. Anton took two more steps, then paused as the rocking worsened. He tightened his grip on the cables until the frayed ends of rusty broken strands cut into his palms.

He looked down, trying to concentrate on his boots and the planks, instead of the plunging gorge and the foaming river two hundred feet below. But the planks were set two or three inches apart, probably to give the bridge flexibility and inhibit the accumulation of snow and ice. Far below he heard a jarring crack. He peered down between two planks. In a patch of river directly below him a long tree trunk dashed and tumbled against the rocks. It leapt high, like a matchstick in the spray, and rushed out of view. At the sight of the river's force, Anton felt his stomach clench. He closed his eyes.

For an instant he was back in Cumberland fishing with Linares. He was ten years old, bursting with excitement, thrilled to be adventuring on his own with the Romany companion of his mother. He carried his short fishing line coiled around the handle of his slingshot. They came to a branch of the Caldew. It seemed a mighty raging river. "There's two ways to cross a stream, boy," the Gypsy said, kneeling to tighten Anton's boot laces. "Wet or dry." Then Linares stepped onto the rough bark of the narrow sloping wet log that crossed the creek. He walked steadily across, erect, never looking back or down as he continued on into the trees. Anton had watched, biting his lip until it bled. At last he followed, stretching to place his feet exactly where Linares had. He was almost across when he looked down and slipped, plunging sideways into the stream, losing his slingshot and line. Soaking, ashamed, he found the Gypsy waiting for him, squatting on his heels and smoking his short clay pipe while he built a small almost-smokeless fire, a specialty of poachers. Linares grinned when he saw the dripping boy.

A rifle fired downstream followed by the brief stutters of an automatic weapon. Drawn from his reverie, Rider opened his eyes and cautiously advanced to the dip at the bottom of the bridge. A plank cracked under his foot. He slipped, then scrambled forward, pulling himself upward with his hands. Yanko waited at the top, one hand gripping a stanchion, the other extended. Anton moved towards him, deliberately unhurried as he stepped off at the top before taking Yanko's hand. The Partisan slapped Rider on the back and offered him the flask of plum brandy.

"We must go down to the river and help protect the crossing," Yanko said, pointing. Anton was beginning to understand his language, and the Bosnian was learning to clarify his words with gestures. "Already the Ustashi are coming to cut us off."

By mid-morning, they were two miles downstream. Many Partisans had arrived before them at an old cattle crossing. They had already secured a heavy guide rope across the river. Even at the ford the water was high and fast, alive with spray, violent and bumpy where rocks forced the water to rise. Men were busy establishing defensive positions in an arc beyond the bank. Others fanned out into the woods to meet and delay the enemy while the hospitals crossed the ford.

"You have walked enough," Yanko said to Anton. "You're limping like an old woman. We'll find you a comfortable place to sit and rest. You will do some killing," he added, his finger pointing, "while our friends come from one side and our enemies from the other."

Yanko headed on to the riverside and spoke to two Partisan commanders. Soon he returned to Rider and led him to a rocky eminence overlooking the crossing. Anton took a position where he could sweep the country in all directions through the scope. On the far side of the hill, running west, he found a long trail winding towards the river. That was probably the way the enemy would come. Beyond the track, perhaps six hundred yards distant, was another, slightly higher rise. West of both hills, the forest resumed, denser at this lower altitude, extending into the hard grey-green landscape of central Bosnia. If the hospital columns could reach that forest, they might survive.

"We might do better from the next hill," Anton said, gesturing towards it.

"Too exposed." Yanko shook his head. "We'd never make it from there into the forest."

Rider nodded. He sat down and stripped his rifle, cleaning each part with an oily rag. He took twenty cartridges from a bandolier and polished each one, searching for imperfections. While he worked, groups of men were digging rifle pits on the hillside below him. Others set up light mortars on the edge of the forest. Yanko cut thick branches and arranged them around Rider's position. When the rifle was ready, Anton studied the trail to the west, calculating the range at each bend. When he was satisfied that he was prepared, he stretched his leg and turned to watch the river, hoping to see Nada and Major Sparrow.

The mule train came first. The animals bunched together at the water's edge while Partisans tightened their packs and others joined them from the hillside paths. Men led and flogged the mules and horses into the icy river. Some animals missed the uneven rocky ford and lost their footing in the deeper water. Panicked, weighted by their packs, a few swam desperately, only their noses pointing above the surface. Burdened by the printing press, one mule went under, rolling over as the weight of the machine forced the animal upside down. A man was capsized nearby, still holding its lead rope. The man's head disappeared, then rose again in the faster current. Anton saw the legs of the mule thrashing and spinning above the water as beast and man vanished around a bend. In the distance Rider heard the thud of a heavy mortar.

Within an hour the steep slope opposite the ford was swarming with Partisan soldiers and stretcher bearers. Hundreds of dark figures emerged from the clusters of thin pines, sliding and scrambling down ledges, limping along the narrow tracks, passing heavy packs from man to man. Unseen on the mountainside behind them, Anton realized, thousands more were descending along the trails as best they could. Anton saw two bearers stumble, dropping their burden clumsily. A blanket-wrapped figure was pitched from the litter and came to rest twitching against a rock twenty yards below. Scattered farther back, discarded on the way like the flaking skin of a snake, would be the newly dead and dying, waiting for the wolves and the Ustashi hunting parties to find them.

At the sandy riverbank three crude rafts were being assembled from logs cut by an advance party. Nurses with dark scarves tied about their heads bent like pecking crows among the scores of stretchers that waited by the rafts. Medical stores and ammunition were stacked among the rocks nearby.

One unit emerged on the hillside and dressed in tight order at the riverbank. An *odred,* a trained formation of the Partisan army, two hundred strong, stood in four rows in a gravelly clearing. Men checked their rifles and tightened the leather belts and shoulder straps they wore outside their varied coats and heavy jackets. At one end of the front rank a tall Partisan unfurled a flag and rested the pole across his shoulder. The Communist red star was centered on three horizontal stripes. A commissar strode up and down the ranks addressing the men. After a few moments they laid down their weapons and stripped off their clothes, knotting them into bundles.

"The Ustashi will come soon." Yanko pinched his nose, sniffing. "I smell them." He sharpened his knife on his belt and cut a slab of dark smoked meat into two pieces. He passed one bit to Rider on the tip of the knife. Mule, Anton reckoned.

"You must not be greedy with your rifle," Yanko counseled. "Do not shoot too soon. Our men will fight them as they come along the trail to the river. You must wait. If you shoot the easy ones, the others will not expose themselves and they will attack this hill."

Anton Rider listened patiently though he did not require the instruction. He had ambushed Bersaglieri in Ethiopia and Afrika Korps columns in Libya. Yanko tapped the butt of Anton's rifle before gesturing with his trigger finger. "We want them to come to us. Then you shoot the *satniks,* the captains."

By now all three rafts were in midstream, two of them packed with litters. Several dogs sat upright like guardians among the prone figures. Small waves washed over the wounded men. The third raft floated even lower in the rough green water, weighed down by the money chests. A

Partisan sat on a chest in the center of the raft, a machine gun across his legs.

Waist deep, escorted by Partisans holding rifles high over their heads, Italian prisoners surrounded the rafts, pushing and hauling them across the ford. Around them others, weakened by hunger, jostled and struggled to keep their feet as they forced their way through the cold water. The odred and a few others, men and women, walked naked into the river carrying their clothes and weapons above the stream. Hundreds of walking wounded were clustered at the end of the guide rope on the far side, waiting their turn to cross. Far behind him, Anton heard occasional gunfire and the explosions of mortar shells.

As he picked up his scope, he noticed another stretcher nearing the river. Its bearers, three men and a woman, lowered their burden to the ground. Anton raised his telescope to his eye: Nada and Sparrow. He saw Nada bend over the major, then search for a clear path into the water. Four horses passed in front of her, prancing and splashing, nervous and resisting as the mounted officers forced them forward. He watched Captain Simon enter the river farther upstream.

Suddenly a mortar shell whistled and exploded close downstream. Knowing their time was limited, the figures on the hillside descended more swiftly, rushing and stumbling downhill. Men shouted and pressed forward through the water. Two prisoners abandoned their positions at the edge of a raft and began to swim. In response, a commissar lowered his machine gun. A line of bullets dimpled the water before finding the shoulders of the swimmers and traversing them one by one. Their coats spread around the two men like skirts as they floated downstream on their faces.

Simon and most of the odred were now across. Some, still naked, dropped their equipment on the near bank and turned back to help their comrades. Others drew on their dry clothes. In the meantime, shells continued to explode in the river. Columns of water shot into the air.

Below them a raft crashed into the rocks, pitching up with one edge over the boulders and spilling the wounded into the stream like coal from a dump truck. The raft with the money chests careened beside it, the Partisan on his knees as he clung to two chests of silver. "If he lives," said Yanko without humor, "that one will be the richest man in Bosnia."

***

It was the hour for lunch with August Hänger at Celestino's on the Shari Alfi Bey. Standing on his own, the dwarf removed his fez as he entered the fashionable restaurant, advancing slowly under his own sail.

"Excellency," bowed the head waiter, leading the way to a corner table. Alavedo moved carefully between the tables with a steady rocking motion, shifting forward first the left side of his body, then the right. The smooth dome of his head appeared just above the tabletops. Several guests nodded in respect. Others whispered discreetly. A low stool waited at the foot of his chair, with a cushion on the seat. The physician rose from his chair but knew to offer no assistance as Olivio clambered up.

"Tell me, *Doktor*," said Alavedo, pausing to watch his guest stir his cup of warm pink vinegar water. The sour acetic fluid was essential to the man's regime for staving off arthritis, the greatest threat to Hänger's skills as a surgeon. "You are acquainted with this intelligence major, this Alistair Treitel, the suitor of my dear friend, Madame Rider?"

"Too well, sir," said the doctor. "He plays cards for money. Yesterday he beat me again at bridge. Sometimes I think he knows the cards too well, especially in the final hands."

"Who makes the cards?" asked the little man.

"B. P. Grimaud, of course. They are French."

Olivio nodded his round head with a bobbing motion. His expression did not change, but his old physician guessed his intention before he spoke. "Could you beat this Englishman at bridge, and play for higher stakes?"

"If I had the money to play with, and a better partner."

"You will have both." The dwarf's mind turned to James Kotsilibis, once a youthful sufferer of smallpox, now a Greek professor of logic in Alexandria. A master of memory, a collector of statistical trifles, the professor could recall exactly how many steps he had taken to any destination. The man ran sums in his head like a usurer on an abacus. He had grown into a type Alavedo understood: a man with a soft body but a hard mind. Years ago, as a teaching fellow, already married, the Greek had made pregnant a plain but lusty Alexandrine girl *de bonne famille*. Olivio had compelled a son of his cotton trader to marry the suicidal girl and had himself provided her dowry. Like a number of other debts, the dwarf had not yet called in this obligation. These were not favors, but investments. That principle, too, he must teach his son, Tiago.

"What else do you know about Major Treitel?" asked Alavedo, comfortable that the brilliant Greek professor would be the doctor's partner at cards.

"I am told that he and his bridge partner, Mr. Blunt, fancied themselves fashionable Marxist intellectuals when at university in England. This Blunt has patches of tight prominent veins on his neck. Some evenings the two join a circle of such thinkers here at the American University. Now the two seem dedicated to helping Russia even more than England. It may be that they are not always doing His Majesty's work."

Already Olivio disliked the two Englishmen. "You must learn more about this, as well as how their politics affect their duty." He scratched the scaly lid above his dry ivory eye. "Arrange for another evening of cards. I will see that you have what you require. Take them to dinner first and give them the best of everything the two care to drink. Englishmen always enjoy their drink, especially if someone else is paying for it."

"There may be an additional approach, sir," said the physician. To Olivio's annoyance, before continuing, Hanger twisted and pulled the swollen knuckles of his thumbs until they cracked like snapping sticks.

"Treitel's bridge partner, Major Blunt, also favors a different sort of entertainment. Long evenings with a pipe and a dancer, a woman known to your admirer, Jamila. On occasion I have used this woman myself," he added, pursing his lips. "Suda has told me how Blunt, loosened by gin and his pipe, bores her as he unburdens himself of all the wartime secrets he spends his days protecting. He thinks her English is not good enough for her to understand what he relates, but Suda's comprehension is far better than he suspects. To get him to desist, to keep still, she distracts Blunt with attentions that otherwise she would prefer to avoid. The man carries a peculiar odor, and among some Britishers is known as 'Fishhead.' "

How strange it was, thought the dwarf, that some men reveal secrets to an indiscreet woman that otherwise even torture might not elicit from them. Was it that they trusted the women, or that they had so little respect for them that they were not concerned what they disclosed?

"Next time, Doktor, you will have Suda ask him more about his work, and tell you all."

Chapter Sixteen

Nearby, Anton saw Nada lead the way to the river. Closer now, two shells whistled overhead, hesitating at their peak, then screaming as they began their descent straight to the ford. A spotter must be sighting for the mortar crews, Rider thought.

Anton jumped to his feet, intent on dashing to the river. But Yanko held his belt from behind. He could not move without straining against his leg.

"We have work here," said the Bosnian harshly. "You can do nothing in the river." His hands gripped Anton's shoulders. "Do what you are in our country to do. Kill our enemies."

Rider understood. He wiped his telescope and scanned the distant hills and rocks. Finally a brief sparkling reflection caught his eye. Light was glancing off metal or glass high in the rocks downstream, among a cluster of poplars on a crag across the river. The Ustashi spotter was perhaps seven or eight hundred yards away. Anton braced his elbows on his knees and focused the scope. He watched the wind riffle the silvery leaves of the poplars. Behind the fluttering leaves a single shape did not move. A dark uniform among the trees, black as a sable antelope. Anton fitted the scope to the Enfield. He put a bullet in the chamber and settled himself, slowly scanning the trees with the cross hairs.

As he focused, he heard shells explode among the rocks across the river. Shrapnel scythed along the bank. Splinters of rock and metal ricocheted and whistled. Screams filled the air as Anton kept his right eye fixed to the glass.

The river became a chaos of struggling men and women. Fresh arrivals plunged into the water, as if replacing the bodies that floated past. Horses and mules bolted and swam on their own. The prisoners abandoned the rafts they were escorting. Laden with the wounded, the crude wooden craft gathered way and rushed downstream. They spun like toys in the current, sweeping over waders and swimmers.

Anton spotted twin sparkles glinting among the poplars. Field glasses. He made a final consideration of the wind, raised the elevation and fired, instantly reloading. Yanko knelt beside him with his binoculars trained on the poplars. A violent disturbance shook several trees. Rider fired twice more and the movement died.

Yanko clapped him on both shoulders. "You can shoot, Englishman."

Anton looked back to the river, searching for Nada. He spotted her in midstream, up to her waist, struggling to raise her corner of Major Sparrow's stretcher with one hand. The current swirled against Major Sparrow and washed over him.

A wounded mule dashed against the upstream side of the litter, knocking one bearer from his position. Anton saw the other three struggle to keep Sparrow's stretcher above water. A few yards away wounded men clung to the severed guide rope as it swung in a loose arc like a giant fishing line drifting on the current.

Anton hurried to the river to help Nada and Sparrow. As he approached, he saw Simon disappear into the alders with a group of Partisans. At the forest's edge others returned fire with light mortars. The riverbank was lined with crawling figures dragging themselves from the water. Half-dressed men of the odred were hauling the wounded to shelter. A scrawny horse, bleeding from the shoulder, screamed and kicked and bucked at the water's edge, trying to free itself of the pack that hung below its belly.

Yanko appeared beside him in the river as Anton reached Sparrow's stretcher. Seizing one shaft, Rider tried to steady himself in the icy rushing water. Sparrow's eyes were closed. He was still lashed to the carrier. Yanko pushed two Italians aside and grabbed the rear handles.

They transported their burden ashore among the willows. The shelling had stopped. Occasional rifle and automatic weapons fire sounded in the distance. A group of Partisans gathered the Italian prisoners as they emerged onshore.

Yanko seized Rider's arm. "We must get back to the hill. The others will move on to a safe camp. We will find them tonight." He turned and hurried towards a group of porters.

Anton put his hand on Nada's shoulder to comfort her. Her body shivered violently under his touch. Terrified, she stared up at him without speaking. Her upraised face was wet and drawn, her eyes wide and shining. Anton wiped Nada's cold smooth face with his open hands to comfort her. His thumbs touched her closed eyes. His palms swept her cheeks.

He glanced down at Sparrow. The stretcher seemed to float among the slender pointed yellow leaves that covered the ground around him. Still tied into his soaking blanket, the English officer shivered and opened his eyes. "Step to it, will you, Rider?" he sighed in an impatient voice. "Do as you're told. Off with you, Captain. I'd rather be with the girl, if you please."

Anton smiled at the unexpected humor, and Nada joined him.

Yanko assigned four men to the major's stretcher, then led Anton back to their hide. Rider had no sooner assumed his former position than he heard machine gun fire and screams rising from the riverbank. He turned to see the remaining Italian prisoners, sixty or seventy men, being knocked back into the water by the bullets of the Partisans. Anton recognized one of Sparrow's stretcher bearers. The man was on his knees, his feet submerged in the lapping water behind him. His hands were raised in supplication to the armed Partisan before him.

As the Red turned his weapon towards the kneeling figure, a mortar round exploded beside them. The Italian was decapitated. The Partisan's body rose in the air. A wave of shells burst along the bank.

"They are coming." Yanko gripped Anton's shoulder and turned him towards the trail above.

Three crouching black figures dashed around a distant bend. They dropped by the side of the path and began to set up a heavy machine gun. Anton studied them through his telescope. Grey shirts, black tunics, with the red and black checkerboard insignia of the Ustashi's elite Black Legion. A few of these Croatians, Yanko had said, were hardened survivors of the Russian Front, sent back by the Germans to fight on their home ground. Now they were in Bosnia settling old scores. As Anton watched, the machine gun crew was joined by a small man wearing a black side cap, the *bustina* favored by Italy's fascist militia and adopted by the Ustashi. The front of the man's cap bore the U and the grenade flash of the Ustashi. An officer, a satnik.

Staring through his field glasses, Yanko placed a restraining hand on Rider's shoulder. "Wait," he said quietly. "There will be more targets."

A squad of uniformed men rushed up the trail passing the machine gun crew and the officer as they advanced towards the river. One fell as rifle fire greeted the Ustashi from the woods. The rest of the squad retreated into the forest.

Anton focused again on the distant bend in the path. He saw the satnik stand and salute. Beside the officer in the shelter of an oak on the far side of the trail, stood a tall figure in a black helmet, wearing a mustache and an eyepatch. The tall soldier turned his head. Anton made out three braided circles and a braided bar painted in blood red on his helmet.

"Pukovnik!" whispered Yanko with excitement. "A colonel." Gunfire intensified on the hillside below the hide. "It must be that animal Francetic himself, the founder of the Legion!"

The Ustashi colonel turned his back to the trail and spread a map against the trunk of the oak. Anton could just see his helmet through the branches. It was the man he had come to kill.

With an old hunter's instinct, even more critical than his skills, Anton Rider could almost feel the man thinking as he studied the map. The other officer joined the colonel and raised one hand to the map. The leaves of the oak shadowed the two men.

Anton felt Yanko's mustache as the Bosnian put his mouth to Rider's ear. "One eye. It is Francetic! This one is worth dying for! You must take him. Forget the other man."

The wind rose. Branches brushed the shoulders of the two Ustashi officers. Anton calculated the range by the size of the helmet. Six hundred and fifty yards. But his estimate for the bend in the trail was five hundred, perhaps five-fifty. He calculated again. He would shoot for six hundred and aim two inches low. He braced his knees and studied the movement of the leaves. Directly below Rider, near the rifle pits at the bottom of the slope, a mortar round exploded. Wounded men screamed.

Oblivious to everything else, Anton set the cross hairs on the left side of the colonel's back. A bit to the center to be certain.

He steadied his breathing, then fired a shade too late. He hit the colonel in the side as the officer turned and lowered the map. The man fell forward on his knees. His face struck the oak. Cursing, Rider fired again. The hurried shot took the colonel in the right arm. The nearby Ustashi machine gun opened up as Anton fired a third time.

"We cannot stay." Yanko pulled Rider to his feet. Bullets whistled all around them. Together, the two men broke for the forest. Anton wished he had done better.

***

"I am looking for a prisoner, a German officer," said Dr. Rider to the medical orderly as she entered the door of the crowded ward. The shades were drawn against the heat of mid-day Cairo. And the better to conceal the bruise on her cheek, Gwenn thought. "Captain von Decken. He is missing one leg."

"Yes, ma'am, I mean yes, Doctor. I know the fellow." The orderly lifted a clipboard from a table by the entrance. "Big noisy chap. Always fussing and asking for extra rations and what not." He squinted at the roster in the dim light and handed it to the physician. "Bothers the nurses a bit."

"That sounds like von Decken." Gwenn smiled and tucked her short hair over one ear as she glanced down the list.

"Last bed on the left, Doctor. He's probably asleep. Seems to keep his own hours. You'll know it's him by the snorin'. Sounds like an old sow drowning in a swamp."

Gwenn walked down the hall with her stethoscope coiled in one hand. Several patients whispered in Italian as she passed. A young handsome one winked. Harsh grunts arose from the far corner, the sounds of a heavy man lying on his back and gasping for air.

"Captain von Decken," she said, tapping the edge of the clipboard against the metal foot rail of the bed. "Captain von Decken!"

"Ah! Ach!" The big man rubbed his face with both hands and sat up, making no effort to cover his broad hairy belly. *"Mein Gött!"* He scratched the grey bristle of his scalp. "Can that be you, Gwenn Rider? The only woman who would marry my only friend?"

"Yes, Ernst, it is I." She could not help smiling at the old memories of East Africa. "First I want to thank you for helping Anton to escape last year."

"Yes, I was foolish. I risked my life for him," laughed the German. "*Mein Engländer* belongs in prison. Is he off somewhere now, killing more of my countrymen?"

"Something like that, but I really can't be certain."

Von Decken lowered his powerful voice. "Now it is I who need help to get away. How did you find me? They are always shuttling us about from hospital to hospital."

"Olivio set me on the trail. I believe you wrote him from the old Deaconess Hospital in Alex."

"Yes," van Decken nodded. "I had been expecting that wicked little man, not you. And you are still so beautiful, Gwenn Rider. Always too good for my friend," Ernst added, looking at her closely, squinting in the dim light. "Is that a bruise on your face? Were you in a fight?"

Gwenn blushed. "Not exactly, I . . ."

His voice softened. "And those four bruises on your arm. As if someone had squeezed you with a death grip."

Without replying, she sat on the foot of the bed and felt about to cry. Gwenn had never mentioned Alistair's behavior to anyone. She was ashamed that she had put up with it even for a short time. Never in her life had she tolerated such treatment. She would not do so again.

"If you out of here take me, I will punish the man who did this," said von Decken. He added in an undertone, "If Anton Rider knew, he would kill him."

Chapter Seventeen

"Another march like that and there will be nothing left but one mule and the surgical needles." Yanko shook his head as he watched his daughter examine Rider's leg.

The knee, dark and swollen, filled his trouser. His hip was stiff in the socket. He tried not to holler when she tested it. Nada removed the leather lace from Anton's right boot and pulled his trousers down to his ankles. She measured around the two calves with the bootlace, then did the same around his thighs.

"Your hip is worse than I thought," she announced gravely. "The knee is swollen, but the calf and thigh are already smaller than the other leg. Your right leg is atrophying. It is dying," she clarified. As Nada gazed up at Anton, the circles around her eyes were like two holes burned in a blanket. "Your leg needs two things it cannot have with us. Rest and proper surgery."

Anton smiled forlornly. "No one is getting what he needs."

"I think there's damage in the socket, where your hip bone meets the pelvis," she said. "If we do nothing, you could lose the leg."

"Do you really think so?" Unsettled by the news, Anton pulled out his Zippo and the last cigarette. He thought of the poison capsules hidden in the bottom of the lighter. The three sat silently and shared the tobacco and blew smoke into the frosty air. Around them, men and women of the march were making camp. Yanko cut pieces of bread from a small hard loaf, then passed Rider the plum brandy.

"What should be done?" Anton said to Nada as he replaced the boot-lace.

"Put you to sleep and open up the hip."

"Sounds like fine sport for our camp butchers," Yanko said sourly. He flipped the tiny butt into the fire. "There's only one proper place to do it. Travnik, the big hospital."

Anton pulled back slightly. "Isn't Travnik full of Ustashi and Germans?"

"Plenty of Ustashi, and plenty of our people, too. But the Germans have handed over garrison duty to the Italians. It's all they're good for, and it frees up the Krauts to hunt us in the mountains." Yanko jammed the cork back into the bottle. "We could dress you up in a Ustashi uniform and slip you into the hospital. With a bandage around your neck, they won't expect you to speak. It's chaos in there anyway and the staff never ask questions. They know the war will be over one day, and they know Bosnians will never forget. We've already tried it once. One of the commissars, lung shot."

"What happened to him?" Anton said.

"Don't know. We never saw him again." Yanko shrugged. "Someone probably recognized him. Even the Reds hate the commissars."

Anton wasn't eager to be recognized himself. "I have a job to do with you."

"Perhaps you can do it in there. Kill someone important." Yanko sat back thinking, warming to the notion. "No telling who comes to the hospital. Always a few Italian generals working on their syphilis, trying to share it with the nurses." He smiled. "They're hardly worth killing though. And you couldn't use the rifle. Have to strangle them while they're masturbating. Ha! Ha!"

"If we're going to try it," said Nada, scowling at her father, "we must do it tonight. Tomorrow the column is heading west for Titoland, back into the mountains."

***

The bearers, three women, left Anton Rider in a torn grey blanket on the floor of the entrance hall of the Travnik hospital. He appeared to be one more still figure in a long line of new Jugoslav patients. He wore the motley Croatian uniform of the Ustashi auxiliary. Some men sat against the cold chipped plaster walls, their eyes closed in the near darkness. A few hung on crutches. Others lay silently like Anton. Nada sat behind him waiting to have her arm examined and to offer to assist at the hospital. Everyone looked up without speaking whenever senior military patients, Ustashi or German or Italian, were led past to the front of the line. For a few hours most of the patients slept slumped over where they were.

Anton woke in the night to find Nada holding his hand. He was not certain how it had happened or who had reached out. From time to time he felt her hand twitch and clench. Her skin was rough as a farmer's. Nada had warned him that she would say they were engaged to be married, to make it natural when she sought to look after him in the hospital. Anton moved his fingers gently, feeling no response, but stroking her thin wrist where the skin was smooth before falling back asleep, her hand comfortable in his.

Early in the morning a group of women, Muslim and Christian, un-trained volunteers from the town, passed through the chilly corridor waking each patient and ladling out wooden bowls of thin lukewarm broth. Slowly the patients advanced towards the examining room. While they waited, the morning light streamed down the hall from the convalescent sun room at the end of the corridor. A small generator, powered by precious fuel, was used only to light the lamps in the surgery.

A commotion stirred the hall as both entrance doors opened and cold air swirled inside. Four neatly uniformed Ustashi in black tunics and field caps carried in a stretcher. Two others, machine pistols slung at their waists, held open the doors. Anton saw a Black Legion sergeant push ahead of them along the crowded corridor, hollering for a surgeon. Anton looked up as the stretcher passed but was unable to see the wounded figure. With both hands the sergeant grabbed a passing physician by the collar of the doctor's white gown. A stethoscope struck the floor as he demanded, "Hurry, clear the surgery. Now! The colonel needs immediate attention. Lead us to an operating room!"

The sergeant pushed the doctor forward with jabs to his back. The two men hurried down the hall and turned the corner out of sight, with the stretcher following.

Nada bent over Anton pretending to adjust his blanket. She moved her lips almost silently. "I think it's Colonel Francetic. They must have tried to look after him in the field first."

Anton cursed himself. Time to finish that bungled hunt, he thought. Never leave a wounded animal.

Doors banged and protesting voices echoed down the hall followed by the sounds of a struggle and hard blows. Anton heard metal wheels scrape the floor. "She will die!" a woman's voice cried. "Finish the stitches!" In the corridor no one spoke, and the hospital's routine quickly resumed.

Three hours later, it was Rider's turn. The line divided inside the examining room. At one end two young doctors with tired eyes diagnosed the new patients. Four orderlies in soiled pale green smocks lifted Anton by the edges of his blanket and set him on a wheeled enamel table before rolling him into one line. Anton noticed several patients jockeying to get into the other line.

An orderly questioned Anton, who pointed to his knee and hip. The man helped him remove his boots and trousers. Rider was embarrassed by the smell of his own body. Watching anxiously, Nada stood silently in the second line. Stacks of reused bandages, some reduced to shreds, lay on the long metal table between them.

The doctor tested his leg, causing Anton to groan in pain. "We must operate. Bit tricky," he announced, rubbing his eyes. Anton was aware of Nada trying to listen. "We'll go in from the back of the pelvis." The physician spoke as if he were talking in his sleep, as if Rider had already rolled on. The surgeon glanced at the next patient and continued. "I'll do it now. There's more fighting in the mountains, and tomorrow they're sending most of us out to help the army. Wouldn't be surprised if we never come back ourselves."

Anton soon lay in the operating room face-down on a dirty sheet. Leather straps secured his body to the table. He recognized the smell that had permeated the surgery cave. Dead flesh. He closed his eyes and prayed as a nurse raised his head and held a gauze pad to his mouth and nose.

"Quickly!" the nurse warned him. "Breathe deeply. We don't have any anesthetic to waste." He gasped in the sharp odor of the ether and lost himself as he floated.

During the next hour, distant voices reached him. Anton dreamt he was impaled on a giant pitchfork. He struggled to free himself. The long tines stabbed deeper, working themselves into his flesh. Anton heard his own voice howl, coming closer and closer. Pain cut through him like a bolt of slow lightning burning open his body. Something struck his face.

"Hurry, doctor," the nurse said. "He is waking up." They were speaking about him, Rider realized. Under his face the table was slick with blood where he had smashed his nose in the struggle. Pain tore him as he came awake.

"More ether!" The surgeon rubbed his forehead, upset. "I cannot finish while he is moving."

"There isn't any. We only have enough for one more operation," said a nurse. "The girl on the table outside. An amputation."

"I'll do my best," the doctor said, sighing. "Help hold him steady while I stitch him up."

Anton had never known such pain. He screamed and pressed against the straps that bound him as the stitching needle pierced along the wound of his hip. He was aware of two men helping to hold him down. The nurse slipped a leather pad between his teeth before the doctor continued stitching, closing the long wound.

***

"For a price," said the dwarf, lying on his aching rounded back as the physician examined his organs with evil probing fingers, "anything can be made in Cairo. Anything, whether it be false eyes or Third Kingdom antiquities." Alavedo tapped his own eyeball, carved from the hard off-white ivory of a hippopotamus tooth, slightly more porous and easier to lubricate than elephant ivory.

"Please roll over, *Mein Herr*," said Dr. Hänger respectfully as Olivio Alavedo continued.

"In the back alleys of Khan el-Khalili, the market of markets, behind the shops of the jewellers and the spice merchants, the knife grinders and the sandal makers, you will find the vendors of stolen goods, and behind them the stalls of the forgers and the counterfeiters. Ach! Ach! Curse you, Hänger!" Before continuing, Olivio Alavedo groaned and wriggled as the Swiss physician explored his yellow flesh with merciless finger-tips.

"Among those artists are one or two who specialize in marked playing cards. The best of these experts, originally trained by a Corsican master in Monaco, works alone in a shop no larger than a broom closet. He fled here to avoid the finger-breaking vengeance of the chief dealer at the Casino de Monte Carlo. He is a Rembrandt, though he fancies himself a follower of some old German engraver, called Dürer, I believe. His work is so fine that the cheat who buys his cards must himself study them for days so as to recognize their details when they are swiftly dealt and handled."

The dwarf moaned as Dr. Hanger kneaded two knobby vertebra at the back of his short neck. Both bones protruded as if eager to burst free from the little man's body.

"It seems that Alistair Treitel is a client of this artist, who in the market is known as Albrecht," continued the dwarf. "He is one of the finest forgers on the Nile. Albrecht prepares passports, letters of transit and other government documents, usually working from original stolen papers. At times like these, he is very popular."

The session was soon over and the dwarf and his physician reconvened under an umbrella on the poop deck of his cafe on the Nile. The table was prepared for three.

A gentleman arrived on time at the canopied ramp that led down from the limestone embankment to the main deck of the Cataract Café. Tariq stood behind his master's chair as the dwarf waved at his ascending guest.

"Professor Kotsilibis holds the chair of logic at the university in Alexandria. When he can spare the time, he occasionally plays a hand of cards in Alex at the Sultan Hussein Club or the Royal Yacht Club," said the little man in introduction. The heavy-set Greek bowed and raised thick speckled eyebrows until they creased his pitted forehead. "And Dr. Hänger has brought the medical science of Zürich to our betterment here on the river Nile. He has extended my own life longer than nature would otherwise permit."

Olivio clasped his hands over his hard belly, neatly contained inside the waistcoat of his tan linen suit. Both men, he knew, were aware of the importance of their assignment: to create an obligation for the losers.

"You will make a splendid pair at bridge, gentlemen. I will finance your bets, and the winnings will be yours."

After the Nile perch was consumed and the custards and sherbets had been taken away, a green felt cloth was spread on the table and secured at the corners. A young Sudanese boy, black as an ace of spades, served coffee in a white robe and turban, an elegance of presentation that the little man had first observed in Lisbon at his favorite grand hotel, the Aviz. "I trust the beans are to your taste?" he said. "They come to us each year from my family's *fazenda* in the hills north of Rio."

"Hot lemon water and red vinegar, *bitte*," said Dr. Hänger. The tall white collar of his shirt was stiff as porcelain.

Suddenly the whistle and scrape of steel on steel rose from the deck below.

"*En garde!*" cried a fierce young voice.

The three men looked over the railing and saw a short child with a mask and a white fencer's jacket. The boy saluted his opponent, extended his épée and stepped forward with the mannered concentration of a bullfighter, intensely self-absorbed but aware of his audience.

The small barrel-chested youth slapped his right foot forward and straightened both short arms in a lunge. His tall opponent parried and retreated. Despite the advantage of his reach and height, the fencer gave the sense of a swordsman defending himself against mortal attack as he retreated from the narrow fencing carpet to the steps of the companionway. Only their weapons were the same length. The child pursued him like a young ferret in a mole tunnel, pressing relentlessly, blade to blade, as if determined to exterminate his adversary.

"Signore Rossini is the finest swordsman on the Nile," observed the dwarf. "I have instructed him to teach Tiago to fight as if each joust is real, and not just on the fencing *piste*, but throughout my vessel, as if they are two men fighting for their lives. One never knows. Tomorrow, as a special treat, Tiago will begin practicing the traditional Royal Navy cutlass drill, using a sabre, of course."

Alavedo did not add that other parents had complained to the fencing master about his son's terrifying ferocity during lessons and junior matches at the Gezira Club. Such complaints were better than awards, of course, promising harbingers of a life-enhancing aptitude.

He himself had not so long to live, if Dr. Hänger was to be credited. Who knew when Tiago Alavedo would be obliged to fight with no button on his sword tip?

As the men sipped their *digestifs*, an Egyptian servant appeared on deck bearing a silver tray with two decks of cards, sharpened pencils and a narrow rectangular pad quartered by vertical and horizontal lines. Olivio nodded in his direction.

"On Friday and Saturday evenings, Akbar here is the senior steward of the card rooms at the Muhammed Ali Club on the Shari Suliman Pasha. On other occasions he is employed by me. His father manages my principal estate in the Delta, though rarely as well as I might wish." The dwarf sighed before continuing.

"Akbar will reserve for you one of the two tables in the high-stakes room at the Club. He has advised me that occasionally, when much money is at play, your two Englishmen, Blunt and Treitel, first provide him with their own cards, though each box bears the name B.P. Grimaud and each card is correctly printed with the emblem of the club. After the first hand or rubber, one of the two Englishmen asks for fresh decks, and Akbar, well paid, provides those that they themselves have furnished. Now, gentlemen, we will replace their cards with our own, identically marked, save for certain details." The grey eye of the dwarf brightened. "The markings of the kings and knaves will be reversed, as if by accident."

"Sir," bowed Akbar as he offered the cards to Alavedo's guests. Each man opened a box and removed one deck, tightly sealed in its transparent cellophane wrapper.

Dr. Hänger removed his gold-rimmed spectacles and wiped them on a fresh napkin. He tapped one deck sharply on the table and studied it before tearing open the wrapper. In the bright light of the Cairo afternoon, the white ruff of hair low on the physician's scalp framed his head like an Elizabethan collar.

Professor Kotsilibis turned his deck over on the lunch table. He set a monocle in his left eye. Twice he brushed his fingers across the seal of the cellophane. "Perfect." He twitched one eyebrow. "Perfect."

"I have arranged for six such identical decks," said their host. "Two here, to help you learn the markings. And four at the Club to be presented by Akbar as required when you play Major Treitel and his partner, Blunt." Olivio's eye twinkled in delight. "You will cheat the cheats."

Each man opened his pack and studied the backs of the cards one by one. The initials MAC were centered on the back of each card in overlapping script surrounded by a complex pattern of fine blue and grey lines. Neither man spoke. The Greek professor laid down his cards according to suit in four neat rows, first face up, then face down from ace to king. He rested both elbows on the table. His long fingernails picked at the pits in his temples.

"In addition to the cards, Doctor, our guest from Alexandria will advise you of a facial code he may employ to assist your partnership." The professor cocked one eyebrow, then the other, before scratching at a smallpox sore and removing his monocle.

"Now you will excuse me, gentlemen, while you rehearse." The dwarf nodded and Tariq lifted his master in his arms. Olivio knew his guests would memorize the markings and would drill against each other like British regiments before an Aldershot tattoo.

Refreshed by the beginning of a fresh scheme, the little man clapped the insides of his feet together in anticipation.

Chapter Eighteen

Nearly three weeks had passed. Anton was thinner than he had ever been. Each day, he thought, his wound was healing, or at least closing, but he was getting weaker. Convalescence did not suit him.

Only the ward for the Axis soldiers and Ustashi received real meals. The senior officers sat in tall wooden wheelchairs in the bright conservatory. Warmed by large lumps of coal glowing in an open grate, they ate from trays, their legs draped in blankets, convalescing as they cracked walnuts and talked about women and the war. For the others, such as Rider, it was bread and tea or thin coffee in the morning, and, in the afternoon, soup thickened with potatoes or turnips or old crusts.

Anton had learned to live with the throbbing pain. Nada told him the young doctor had done what he could, cleaning out bone chips from the end of the hip, trimming off the edge of the damaged pelvis, and finally stitching together the muscles severed during the surgery. The operation had not been perfect, but he should be able to walk. It could have been worse, Anton thought, eyeing the invalids around him. One of the reassuring benefits of a hospital was that there was always someone in more serious condition to make one feel better.

Occasionally, when he felt the newly re-broken bump on the bridge of his nose, he smiled to himself and thought of Nada's words: "The doctor says you are the first man to break his own nose during surgery."

Nada had joined the half-trained nurses working in the civilian wards and halls, only assisting with the soldiers when military casualties flooded in. She had washed her hair and asked Anton to cut it. At last her own arm was healing cleanly. She finally explained that a fragment of shrapnel, deep in her wrist, had progressed to infection, gangrene and amputation.

Each day her cheeks were brighter. Lying on a low cot at the end of the main hall, near the conservatory, Anton stared up at her whenever she passed. In ways she reminded him of Gwenn. Nada was younger, of course, her figure fuller, her hair darker, but she also had a perfect oval face, high rounded cheekbones and eyes that drew him in. Both women had found medicine as the way to make something of their lives. Both had learned to suffer. With both, some hardening had come with the wisdom.

Hearing the enemy wounded recounting their battle stories, Anton was sometimes reminded of a training lecture he had received in Cairo. "Forget the dispatch cases, forget code breaking," the instructor said. "If it's intelligence you are after, you will learn more in any bar, and if you wish to know how a war is truly going, try a hospital."

He was learning to understand the hostility between the Italians and the Germans, the Ustashi and the foreign soldiers. In addition to the occasional wounded Bulgarian or Hungarian, Rider was surprised one day when two injured Spanish soldiers were admitted. Men from a battalion of Franco's Blue Division, veterans of Stalingrad, diverted now to this less brutal duty, reported the hospital chatter.

"Perhaps our Japanese partners are coming next," said one exhausted orderly.

Each evening Nada found the opportunity to sit by Anton, sharing a scrap of sausage or smoked goat cheese stolen from the officers' kitchen. She would change the dressing on his wound and they would talk. She would ask him about Egypt and Ethiopia and whisper about Bosnia before the war. Some nights, exhausted, she sat beside him without speaking, her eyes closed and her back to the wall. When it grew dark, she took his hand. But usually she wished to talk, to speak of other times and places, to learn about his life and a world far different from her own.

"This evening, after the kitchen closes," she whispered late one afternoon as the hall darkened, her lips close to his ear, "I am going to give you what you need most."

He felt himself grow warm. "Do you mean it? What would your father say?"

"No." She slapped his cheek. "For that he would kill you." She held something scented under his nose. "A hot bath in the doctors' washroom." Anton knew that access and opportunity were her rewards for these weeks of helping at the hospital. Two years of medical studies in Zagreb had made her less than a doctor but more than a nurse. "This soap came from the Danube, the finest hotel in Sarajevo," she whispered.

Later that night steam rose as Nada lifted three big pots of kitchen water from a service trolley and poured them into a chipped enamel tub, filling it about halfway up. Anton, feeling strangely shy, undressed in the candlelight. "Stop being foolish," she said, examining his surgery scars and dropping his clothes into one of the pots that still held some water. "I am your physician and your nurse." Ignoring his protests, she helped him as he lowered himself in, keeping his right leg just above the water.

Anton leaned back and closed his eyes and sighed. Then he felt her hands on him, wet and slick with soap, wiping the grime from his body, massaging his chest and good leg with a warm wet towel, exciting him. He could not help himself. She began to pay attention.

"Do the European ladies in Cairo wear makeup every day?" Nada whispered a bit later as he moaned, slightly embarrassed by his reaction to her touch, all tension lost, his eyes still shut.

"Whenever they leave home."

"I could be more pretty if I had rouge and lipstick."

"I do not think so," he said honestly.

She squeezed his hand. "Would they like me in Cairo, or in London?"

"I would." He put one wet hand behind her head. For the first time, he drew her face and lips to his.

The next day she sat on the floor beside him in the early afternoon, her shoulder almost touching his cot, her quiet voice lost in the din of the crowded hall. "Here's some medicine for you." She slipped him the stub of a thick brown sausage. "And, I have news." Alerted by her tone, Anton was careful not to turn his head towards her.

"That was Francetic, all right, the one who had the boys murdered at the Turkish tombs. You hit him twice, once through the upper right arm, shattering the bone, and a shot across his chest. Just missed the heart and lungs. The bullet lodged between two ribs above his heart. The German military surgeon finally came and removed it, said he'd never seen a bullet quite like it. They want to know where it came from."

"Wouldn't hurt to help them lose it," Anton said, slowly chewing the greasy sausage. "If you can."

"I will try," Nada said. "And I have received a message from our friends. They say that we must kill Francetic. The order came from Tito himself. The marshall wants to set an example of the most vicious collaborator. Tito said he will drink plum brandy with the man who kills him."

"Won't the other side execute more villagers in reprisal?"

"Of course, but the commissars don't care about that. It just gains us more support."

Rider shook his head. This was a different sort of war, with all this civilian bloodletting, but that wasn't his affair. His job was to carry out the assassination.

A suitable idea came to him immediately. "Who prepares Francetic's food?"

"The officers' cook. An Italian from Trieste. Rosario, working in the doctors' kitchen."

"Does he like you?"

Her lips smiled. "How do you think Nada got your sausage?"

Anton was not surprised. "Take the cigarette lighter from my jacket pocket. I have something the Colonel might enjoy with his dinner. What is he having tonight?"

"Probably nothing solid." Nada ferreted about in his jacket and handed Anton the Zippo. "But Francetic is getting stronger. Tomorrow they're moving his bed to the sun room, and he will want what he orders every day, boiled potatoes with two eggs mashed into them. Typical Croat peasant."

"Perfect." Anton opened the Zippo beneath his blanket and removed one of the two cyanide tablets hidden beneath its mechanism. "Mash this in as well. He'll be the first man killed by a potato. But do it soon, so they will think it was caused by his wounds." He placed a restraining hand on her arm and added, "Don't let that Rosario see you near Francetic's food."

Anton Rider lay on a cot near the end of the corridor, his head raised on a folded blanket and his doubled jacket. He ignored the smells and the sounds, the familiar frenzy of the hospital, increasingly overburdened as the war in the mountains became more cruel.

Before him the scene was very different: orderly, clean, warm in the sunshine that entered the floor-to-ceiling windows of the officers' conservatory. The large panes were frosted at the corners. Thin pine needles, blown from the tall evergreens at the back of the hospital, stuck to the outside of the glass, reminding Anton of long-ago winters in the north of England. The wheelchairs of the convalescing officers were arranged in two rows with their backs to him. Four had been removed to make place for Colonel Francetic's bed near the coal fire.

Anton could see the top of the colonel's head between the bars of the officer's bed frame. The black band of the eyepatch pinched the thin brown hair at the back of his head. Francetic appeared to be getting better. A young nurse, round-faced but pretty enough in a voluptuous way, perched on the edge of a stool beside the bed, leaning forward and smiling at the colonel's conversation while she poured his tea and lit his cigarettes. Once she wagged her finger playfully and pursed her lips, chiding her patient for excessive flirtation, Rider guessed. Occasionally other officers would turn their chairs and speak with Francetic, listening and nodding attentively when he spoke. Even the German major to his right appeared to treat the Croat with caution.

A brown robe and a heavy braided cord swept along the side of Rider's cot. He was surprised to see a monk walk briskly by and enter the conservatory. The chubby cleric carried a wicker basket containing a small wheel of cheese set in a napkin. He approached Colonel Francetic and the German major and nodded his round tonsured head.

"A small gift, gentlemen, from our monastery near Karlovac. A delicacy of our order." He stroked the heavy cross that hung from his neck. Francetic crossed himself, and the German inclined his head. The three men conversed as the colonel cut slices of cheese with the military dagger he kept on his bedside table.

Anton recalled Yanko's contempt for Croatia's Fransiscans. Trained in Siena and in league with the Ustashi, the monks proselytized relentlessly among the Serbs at the death camp at Jasenovac, persecuting the Orthodox prisoners into forced conversions. Meanwhile, each day, the Gypsies and Jews and anti-fascist Croatians were exterminated, usually after digging mass graves for each other. Challenged, one monk had explained: "I shall burn in hell, but at least I will burn for Croatia."

The plump nurse returned to the sun room with a tray and a napkin over one arm. Anton saw three glasses of red wine, a bowl of yoghurt mixed with dark stewed fruit, probably plums, and, in the center, a plate of mashed potatoes and one thin slice of meat. Had Nada mixed in the poison?

The nurse set the tray on the bed beside the colonel and leaned across him as she cut his meat while he ate some cheese. Anton recalled with satisfaction that the man's right arm was useless. Francetic lowered his face to the woman's neck, forcing her breasts into his stomach. The nurse squealed and wiggled. Francetic and the major laughed. The priest stood at the foot of the bed and sipped his wine. The German raised his glass and offered a toast Rider could not hear.

Flushed and smiling, the nurse sat back on the stool and drew it closer to the bed. She wagged one scolding finger at her patient before spearing a piece of meat and feeding it to the Ustashi officer. Francetic snapped the meat from the fork like a hungry terrier jumping for a treat. He spoke to her and she loaded the fork with mashed potatoes. As Francetic ate, the nurse paused to wipe his mouth. She fed him four more helpings of the white puree before she offered him a second bite of meat. That should be enough, Anton judged. He looked at his watch and began to count.

Colonel Francetic drank, then took his food more slowly. The priest refilled the glasses. The potatoes were almost finished. One more bite of meat, then two forks of mashed potatoes and the plate would be clean.

Rider checked his watch with concern: four and a half minutes. That was already a bit too long. The delay must be caused by the absorbent qualities of the potatoes and cheese. Or had Nada not been able to crush the cyanide tablet into his food? The nurse lifted the glass to the colonel's lips. He raised his left arm and took the glass.

Nada appeared behind Anton's cot and leaned against the wall without speaking. Anton glanced up at her, his eyebrows raised in question. She nodded.

Suddenly Nada gripped Anton's shoulder. He saw her eyes narrow, oval and bright like a lioness on the chase. Her hand tightened. Rider looked towards the conservatory.

Francetic appeared to rise entirely from the bed, like a man shot from beneath. Red wine and bits of meat and potatoes sprayed from his mouth and struck the monk and the nurse. Francetic's body convulsed forward. The covers fell back. He leaned on his knees, crying out and spitting. He bent sideways, rocking and twisting in the bed. His eyepatch drooped around his neck. For an instant his spine arched and his head bent back, revealing the dead naked socket as Anton gazed into his single transfixing staring eye. Francetic convulsed forward again. His hand clawed his stomach and he screamed three words:

"You poisoned me!"

As Francetic fell from the bed, he seized the throat of the nurse with his left hand. Locked together as if embracing, his right arm large and stiff in its cast, the two collapsed across the German major, knocking his wheelchair on its side against the fire. One wheel spun madly in the air. The major struggled at the foot of the bed amidst a scrambling mass of patients and moving chairs. The nurse fought in vain to free herself from the colonel's grip. Her face grew red. The last Anton saw was blood leaching through the bandages that bound the Croat's chest and shoulder. Then Francetic pitched backward, his body rigid. His face dripped with chunky vomit as he stared upward with his head and neck resting in a halo of hot bright coals.

Rider felt a charge of excitement rush through his body, but he controlled himself and covered his mouth with his fist. Nada joined the nurses and doctors who dashed to the sun room. The priest stood behind them, a stained dark figure against the wall of glass, repeatedly crossing himself.

Anton closed his eyes as Francetic's body was carried past him down the hall. He smelled the colonel's burned hair and tightened his lips.

Restored to his chair, wiping his face and trembling with rage, the German major rolled to the end of the hall. He positioned himself a few feet from Anton's cot with his back to the conservatory. Rider kept his eyes almost closed, his face turned to the wall.

"Secure the doors!" the major screamed down the long corridor. Black-uniformed Ustashi bustled in compliance.

"Bring me the cook and that nurse." The major seized a black Luger from the holster of a guard and racked the slide.

The young nurse stood before the German, one arm twisted high behind her back by a Ustashi. Her neck bore the red marks of Francetic's grip. The top of her uniform was ripped open to her waist. Her white breasts swelled and heaved. One seemed larger than the other.

The major raised the Luger.

"No!" screamed the nurse. "It was the cheese!" She pointed at the priest. "Of course, the cheese! He did it, the Fransiscan! That devil, the priest!"

The holy father clasped his hands and opened his mouth as two Ustashi emerged from the door to the kitchen. A sobbing figure in a filthy apron hung between them, knees trailing on the ground, feet dragging.

"Rosario, the cook," said one Ustashi as they flung the man down at the major's feet. The Italian chef stared up with huge brown eyes, his jaw twitching, his fingers laced together. The priest knelt nearby, his cross raised in both hands.

"Excellency!" Rosario cried as the major fired into his forehead. Bits of bone and soft tissue sprayed the two Ustashi. The nurse shrieked.

The German fired twice more, this time into the chest of the nurse. She collapsed across Rosario's body. The major slowly spun one wheel of his chair, then both, until he faced the Fransiscan, now prostrate in supplication. He fired two more times. The priest fell at his feet.

The major rested the Luger in his lap and wheeled himself back to the center of the sun room.

Nada turned and in the slightest of whispers said to Anton: "One less butcher."

Chapter Nineteen

"Sorry, sir," said the duty sergeant with a bit of Scots in his voice. "Thought you wuz a Wog, sir."

"I have been for a bit, Sergeant," smiled Denby Rider in his white robe, removing his head cloth. His face was dark and gritty from days of sun and sand and desert dust. His goatskin slippers, almost worn through, seemed part of his still-swollen feet. After leaving Rashid and the camels, he had walked down from the hills to the coast road, limping the last two miles, surprised it was so much further than it had appeared. His left foot seemed badly infected.

The sergeant stepped aside and permitted Lieutenant Rider to approach the open entrance to the large khaki tent. The flag of the 7th Armored Division flew from a tent pole. Beneath it was a triangular pennant featuring the division's mascot, a jerboa. Built like a tiny kangaroo, the long-tailed "desert rat" was able to jump six feet in one bound. The men of the 7th Armored had been contending with Rommel's Panzers for over two years of desert warfare back and forth across fifteen hundred miles of the North African coast. They were as familiar with the symbol of the Deutsches Afrika Korps, a palm tree atop a swastika, as they were with their own desert rat.

A Bren-gun carrier, a half-track and a Kübelwagen with large sand tires were parked near the tent beside a Dingo missing one front wheel. Two vehicles had mounted machine guns pointed at the sky. A hundred yards behind the tent, a dusty double column of military transport wound along the coast as far as one could see in both directions, almost all heading west for the Mareth Line and Tunis. For the most part, wheeled vehicles moved in one column and the slower tracked machines were in the other. Matildas, Grants and captured half-tracks ground up the old

Italian road. Only a few tanks, mostly those needing repair, moved on wheeled carriers. Some light vehicles drove east along the right edge of the road, generally ambulances and lorries under canvas.

Three officers in shorts and long khaki socks were bent over a map table in the center of the tent. "It's time we did a Rommel," said one colonel, tapping his swagger stick on the map before they all looked over at Denby Rider. "Swing south and attack with impetus and weight."

Glancing at Denby, dark tan in his robe and ragged slippers, the other colonel muttered, "Look at this, will you. Chap thinks he's Lawrence of Libya."

Relieved to be out of the sun, Denby slapped his heels together and saluted the senior officer. "Lieutenant Rider, General. Seventh Hussars."

"Good thing you're not a Cherry Picker, Lieutenant, I must say. Old Cardigan would have had your pips," said the general with amusement. All four understood the reference to the vain but courageous officer who had commanded the charge of the Light Brigade a century before. "Looks like you could use a wash and a drink and a long stop at the medical tent for those feet. Been out in the blue on your own, have you?"

"Yes, sir. It's a bit of a long story, sir."

"We've no time for it, Lieutenant."

"Yes, sir," said Denby, relieved. "I'm just hoping to catch up with my regiment, sir."

"You're a bit late for that. They're probably in Tunis or Rome by now. But the Eleventh will be coming up the road soon in their new armored cars. Don't know why the Hussars are always first to get the new transport." He glanced down at Denby's feet. "We'll see if you can shift along with them for a bit."

"Thank you, sir." Denby did not mention that his brother, Wellington, had served with the 11th Hussars. The general spoke again.

"Adolf promised Rommel some new weapons and they've arrived. Heavy tanks, Pak anti-tank guns and the Nebelwerfer, a mounted 150mm multiple rocket launcher with six tubes. The Americans call it the 'Screaming Meamie.' The Eleventh has a new assignment you might appreciate. Or possibly not. They're ordered to hook up with the Americans. Some sort of special Yank outfit, said to be their best, the Rangers. They're meant to link up together and go hunting the new German heavy tanks, the first Tigers sent out here."

"I look forward to it, sir," said Denby, excited at the prospect.

"Could be a bit tricky. First time the Eighth Army has had to work with these Americans," added the general. "Eisenhower and Alexander are keen to avoid command chaos at every level, but now that the French have switched to our side, at least in Africa, it's a sight harder. The Frenchies won't take orders from British commanders, and the French themselves are all mixed up with their own colonial troops. Foreign Legion, Senegalese, Zouaves and what not."

"'Course, Jerry has his own command chaos," said one of the colonels. "Rommel has to work with the Eyeties here and the Commando Supremo in Rome, and now he has to deal with General von Arnim at their Tunis bridgehead with a hundred thousand new men." The colonel looked at Denby more closely. "Where did you find those sporty slippers, Lieutenant?"

"Picked 'em up at an oasis sir, after my things got burned up."

"After you have those messy feet looked after, the quartermaster will fix you up with some new kit," said the general. "You are most welcome to join our open mess tonight. Roast goat and dago red. A sight better than what you'd find at the Savoy these days."

"Welcome, Lieutenant," said a cheerful major of the 11th Hussars a week later as he opened a khaki canvas map case. Denby glanced around the camp. One infection had proved a stubborn problem, but now his feet were nearly healed.

"We all miss your brother. Terrible loss, Wellington Rider. He was handy with everything. A spanner, polo mallet, a Vickers, whatever. Sometimes the best men seem to go first," he said wistfully. "Now half our lads are new, fresh out from England. But we've one old hand who shared a car with your brother, a hungry Scot, Graham Walker."

He continued before Denby could reply. "Anyway, you're just in the nick. We're short a couple of coves and we can use you in A Troop. Especially as I understand you can get about in Arabic and French."

"Thank you, sir," said Denby, uncomfortable in his stiff new boots and badly fitting tunic. "I'll do my best, sir, until we catch up with the Seventh."

"Wouldn't know about 'catching up,' Lieutenant. We're going on a recce with some Yanks." The major flattened a map on the bonnet of an armored car. "Looking for a way through the Dorsal mountains to the west. Somewhere near Sbeitla, or Kasserine, it looks like," he said, tracing the general route. "Hard dry ground, except when the winter rains flood the wadis. Fine tank country on the flats."

The major tapped the map with two yellow-stained fingers. "Our job is to spot Rommel's concentration of Panzers, call in the RAF and then let the Yanks sort them out with their new Shermans. Meantime, we have to meet up with their Rangers and hunt the Tigers with them." The officer folded the map. "You'll find your troop laagered just ahead along the wadi. The last camp. Happy hunting, lieutenant."

As Denby saluted and prepared to go, the major opened his map case. "Here's a spec sheet on the new German armor. Better have a peek. It might be Jack-and-the-Beanstalk time." He handed Denby the paper to show him why. "Don't know how we're going to stop their giants if they've made it across the Med to Africa." He offered Denby a Spring-bok and lit up as Denby started to read.

"Their new Tiger. Sixty ton. Twenty-five mph and an anti-aircraft eighty-eight in the turret. They say Mister Porsche was ordered to produce the first one in time for Hitler's birthday last year, and he did it, but no one's had to face one out here yet. Hope that little Nazi bugger doesn't have too many more birthdays," he growled. "If the old Desert Fox had Tigers six months ago, and some petrol, he would have taken Cairo. Your friends would be dining on wiener schnitzel and sipping schnapps by the Nile. But the Jerries have been reduced to bringing in petrol by glider and submarine."

Leaving the major behind, Denby slung his kit bag over his shoulder and strolled along the flat dry streambed until he found the three Humber armored cars and the single Daimler scout car of his new troop. A dozen Arabs and six donkeys were crowded around the soldiers. The lads were always keen for something other than bully beef and tinned pears.

"Welcome, Lieutenant," said the Cherry Picker captain, a trifle haughty, bending to scratch a desert sore just above his sock. "You'll be scouting in the Dingo with Walker." The officer pointed at the Daimler. "Reckon the rest of your lot are still lolling about, off playing a few chukkas at the Gezira Club."

"No doubt, sir," said Denby, declining the bait. Both men knew the 7th were always near the lead.

The captain looked at Denby more closely. "Ever done any killing, Lieutenant?"

"Yes, sir. 'bout my share."

"Huns? Eyeties?"

"No, sir. Frogs."

The captain's face lit with interest. "You don't say. Good on you. They give you that cut?"

"No, sir. That was the Yanks."

These Cherry Pickers were worse than the Guards, Denby thought, always certain they were the best. All started two hundred and forty years ago in a cherry orchard in Spain, where, grievously outnumbered, they cut up one of Napoleon's best regiments and earned the right to wear tight cherry-colored trousers. After that it was Waterloo and Balaclava. In the three-year war in North Africa, the 11th Hussars were the first to fight both Mussolini's Legions and Erwin Rommel's Afrika Korps. Now their ambition was to be the first regiment to enter Rome and Berlin. Just what his brother would have wanted, thought Denby sadly.

He was pleased to see that the Daimler's Bren gun had been replaced with an anti-aircraft mounting. One Humber carried a long-barrelled Boys anti-tank rifle, effective against armor at close range but disliked for their violent recoil. A grinning jerboa was painted on the gunner's door.

Denby chucked his knapsack into the Dingo. Then he joined the tanned young soldiers who were haggling with the Arabs without knowing the language. Panniers filled with oranges, eggs, peppers and onions and flat bread were balanced on the sides of the dozing donkeys, their eyes thick with flies. A short bald Hussar with bushy red eyebrows and a filthy tartan scarf around his neck was annoying the Bedouin by handling and pinching their produce before dropping it back into the baskets. "Walker," complained another Hussar, "leave off, mate. Stop fussing or they'll charge us double."

A black-robed Arab flung down a whimpering lamb with its feet tied together. The young animal bleated and flipped its head from side to side against the ground. The Bedouin knelt and slit its throat, wiping his knife on the lamb's coat. While the twitching animal bled out, the man settled on a price, then knelt and skinned the warm creature as part of the bargain.

Denby soon found himself in the thick of it, haggling in Arabic for every egg and onion. He went through each basket himself, finding six bottles of unlabelled red wine packed in straw under bunches of radishes at the bottom of one pannier. He bought the wine himself. Algerian, he reckoned. Soldiers whistled and clapped as he removed the bottles from the basket.

Every platoon or squadron seemed to have one man who took to cooking in the field. In A Troop it was Graham Walker. Denby had noticed him pinching the ribs of the lamb and insisting on a handful of herbs to go with it.

"Denby Rider," he said, introducing himself to Walker. "I believe you knew my brother."

The Scot ceased his haggling and gripped Denby hard by both arms. "Wellie was the best," said Walker. "The best of us. He used to talk about you, and that dad of yours. Sounds like he was once quite a chap himself."

"He still gets about," replied Denby Rider.

In the evening, the troop laagered about fifteen miles on, deeper inside Tunisia, some distance from the southern edge of the Mareth Line, said to be nothing but a series of crumbling French strong points left over from the Great War and now hurriedly re-fortified by the Germans. Like good cavalry, the men first checked their engines and oil and topped up their petrol tanks from the racks of jerry cans attached to each vehicle. The cold night settled swiftly. The soldiers buttoned their leather jerkins and raised the collars of sheepskin vests.

With better reception at night, a radio operator was stringing out a wire aerial, hoping to pull in Cairo's BBC radio service for some music and maybe even news from home.

Graham Walker quartered the lamb, ignoring the persistent but inconsistent advice of his hungry mates as he forced herbs into tiny slits cut into the meat. "What could a highland Scot know about food?" shrugged one. "They're still living in caves, barefoot for the most part."

The static lifted. Sentiment and nostalgia filled the cold desert night as Vera Lynn, the armed forces sweetheart, sang to each of them.

We'll meet again.
Don't know where,
Don't know when . . .
So will you please
Say hello
To the folks
That I know.
Tell them,
I won't be long.
They'll be happy to know
That as you saw me go
I was singing this song.

Some men gathered sweet-scented desert shrubs and brush and built a fire in the center of the ring of vehicles. Others cooked peppers and onions on sticks while they smoked and joked about the honey girls of Cairo and Benghazi. A few opened army-issue canvas khaki photo holders and studied or showed pictures of their families or girls. A bottle of precious whisky was quickly emptied. The camp grew loud and cheerful as the smells of cooking rose from the fire.

It was the sort of evening when a man might feel companionable and lonely at the same time.

When the lamb was nearly done, Denby Rider passed around the wine. A cold west wind rose. The sand began to blow, the curse of any desert meal. Denby heard it scratch his teeth as he ate. Clumps of camel thorn rolled and tumbled along the wadi.

By the time they posted sentries and curled up in blankets and under sheepskin greatcoats, the bottles were empty and the stars were desert-bright. Lieutenant Rider, content at last, made a pillow of his boots and turned his back to the wind and gusting sand. The khamseen howled like a lonely distant wolf as Denby fell asleep, his last thoughts of his family and Saffron Alavedo. We'll meet again, he dreamt.

"Rise and shine, fellas!"

It sounded like a foreign language, thought Denby at first. He sat up and rubbed his face in the early light. He watched a sentry hurry over and attempt to explain the sudden approach of the Yanks to the major as the British officer, surprised, rose with his Webley in hand.

"Sir . . ."

"Morning!" said the American, pleased to have slipped past the British sentries. "Excuse our arriving unannounced. Just practicing. But you must be expecting us, Major? First Rangers. I'm Captain Corrigan. Jack Corrigan." Three jeeps pulled up behind him. A dozen young Americans stepped down.

"We're here to blow up tanks," said a Yank. "Big ones."

Chapter Twenty

"We are almost there," said Nada over her shoulder. "Once we get to the stream, my satnik, you will be obliged to walk." Anton sat behind her in the wagon on a bed of stiff scratchy straw, facing back down the valley. In the fields the plowed furrows were already frozen hard. A fierce wind was gusting down from the Jura Alps in uneven wintry blasts.

The rattling iron-rimmed wheels of the wood-cutter's cart cut thin lines in the frost that covered the track into the mountains above Travnik and the village of Turbe. The neat rock-walled pastures and terraced cherry and plum orchards that girded Travnik had given way to patches of light forest and steep rocky fields as they climbed into the mountains to the west. Immense solitary pines were scattered on the grey slopes above, reminding Anton of the grave ink-black ravens they had seen in one low-lying meadow. The priest-like birds had stalked about with dignity, pausing and turning their shiny heads with sharp stiff movements, pecking at sheep droppings and searching for melon seeds at the edge of the field.

The lean-flanked mule, well fed for once, pulled willingly as Nada walked beside its head. She, too, walked with a light step, trying to avoid the deep ruts worn by farm wagons. Nada no longer wore a sling. Anton could see her red-brown curls at the edges of her flowered scarf. The rounded stump of her arm had healed smoothly just above the wrist. Now it was something that neither of them thought to notice. Anton was embarrassed that his own injury seemed more preoccupying.

Propped in the back and leaning on a sack of flour, he was exhilarated to be free of the congestion, suffering and rotten air of the hospital. Riding in the wagon reminded Anton of his young days travelling from village to village in the Gypsy vardos. Beside him now in the narrow cart were a well-used pair of Italian crutches and sacks of beans and potatoes, coffee and cheese, sausage and dried meat, some filched from the hospital kitchens, but most black market goods bought by Nada with Anton's Maria Theresa silver dollars. He missed his rifle and he worried about Major Sparrow. As soon as his leg was serviceable, he vowed to either make his way to Bihac and rejoin the fight or to find the death camp at Jasenovac and do whatever he could there. He could not suppress the image of Gypsy children hanging from trees.

Nada stopped the cart by the edge of a frothing mountain stream. She helped Anton down while the mule drank noisily. Rider hobbled about on one crutch, enjoying the movement of swinging his leg with less pain. Only the hip bothered him.

Together they unharnessed the mule and spread a blanket on the animal's back. Sensing mischief, the creature began to balk and shift from side to side. Anton stroked its hard shoulder then cut its harness into pack straps. They balanced the supplies on the restless mule as best they could.

When they were ready, Nada stepped between the traces and dragged the empty cart back down along the trail until she came to a steep rocky hillside. Straining, pushing with her shoulder, she shoved the cart over the edge. The wagon crashed down on its side, tumbling and splintering until it came to rest against a pear tree.

After Nada returned to Anton, they took off their boots and socks and hung them around their necks by the laces. Ignoring the cold, she followed him, leading the mule, but ready to help as he entered the shallow stream on both crutches, taking small steps with his good leg. Enjoying the sharp frosty sting of the rushing water, Anton turned in midstream, surprised to find Nada immediately behind him.

"Are there trout?" he asked with a grin, looking down, almost touching her. "Do you have a hook?"

"Of course," she smiled. "Do you have a line, Captain?" Her eyes were the grey-blue of the water.

Shaky on his crutches, unable to use his hands, Anton lowered his face towards hers. Nada dropped the lead rope and touched his cheek with her hand. She closed her eyes as they kissed.

When they separated, their feet were numb. Nada released him slowly and bit her lower lip. She went back for the mule while Anton climbed the far bank. He rested on a rock, embarrassed that he could not help. He watched her struggle towards him with the resisting animal. Anton looked past her to the distant valley floor and to the hard mountains beyond. He wondered what they would hold.

Once across the stream, they dried their feet on their coats and pulled on their socks and boots. She lifted her feet onto a rock and he tied her long laces with double knots.

They climbed slowly as the afternoon darkened and chilled. Low clouds scudded more and more swiftly against the mountainside. Nada paused once to button her collar. "In our mountains," she said, raising Anton's to cover his neck, "if you have no shelter, it is the wind that will kill you, not the snow or the cold. At night our wind will change a man to ice."

Occasionally Anton slipped on his crutches. Once he fell badly, striking his hip against the rocks as he came down, crying out despite himself. About a month had passed since the operation and he feared his leg would never be as it should. He missed feeling young and strong.

Higher up, they followed the shepherds' paths, pausing to rest in stands of pines or patches of flat grassland that were speckled with hard black sheep droppings. Near the top of one ridge, with the minaret, steeple and dark tiled roofs of Turbe barely in view far below, Nada pointed to the next crest. "Just past those rocks," she said, her face wet from the icy mist. "My uncle drives the sheep here every spring."

Two ridge lines met before them. Where the ridges joined was a small plateau. Pine trees were bunched at one edge. A low shepherd's hut was built into the opposing hillside.

They arrived an hour later. Built of logs caulked with dark earth, the cabin had a steep roof pitched directly into the edge of the mountain. Patches of moss and tufts of brown weeds grew between some logs. The long slender logs of the roof continued to one side past the stone chimney, providing a small open shelter for animals and firewood. A pair of short skis leaned against one corner of the shed. Anton picked up one. Hand-carved, Rider guessed, though he had never before seen skis.

Nada pushed at the narrow door without success. Anton forced it open and stepped into the darkness. Cold stale air greeted him, dank and piney-fresh at the same time. He squinted as his eyes adjusted. There was no window, save for a small hinged plank that could be held open. The floor was packed earth covered here and there with unfinished flat stones and plaited mats. Three log beams crossed the single room. Thick yellowed sheepskins, ropes of garlic and one large dark pelt hung from the beams. A rusty hatchet with a wide heavy blade hung from two nails behind the door. A wooden bed was built like a broad bench or shelf across one end of the cabin. A crude plank table and two short barrels were set between the bed and the rough stone fireplace. Two pipes lay on the jagged mantel formed by a flat stone set into the chimney just above the fireplace. Rider smelled one and wiped the rich burl against his trousers before oiling the pipe along the side of his nose.

Anton reached into the large dark jar that rested on the table. "How old are these?" he said, dropping a handful of dusty wizened prunes back into the jar.

"When you are hungry," she observed, "they are always fresh and delicious."

They unpacked the mule and fed it a few handfuls of grain before rubbing the animal down and tying it into the open shelter. Using pine cones for kindling, Anton built a fire from a small pile of cut logs. Tomorrow he would sharpen the hatchet and cut more logs. Nada lifted two wooden buckets from nails on the wall and walked to a small spring under the trees.

Anton felt her watching from the doorway behind him as he knelt and took out his Zippo. The dry pine cones caught and spat as the pitch flared. The branches lit. Flames filled the low fireplace. Smoke swirled into the cabin. Anton turned and sat on the floor against the edge of the chimney. He groaned as he stretched out his legs, pushing against one of the barrels as he did so. Surprised by its heaviness, Anton rolled on his side and heard liquid sloshing as he tipped the cask with his hands. He pried out the wooden stopper with the tip of his choori and put his nose to the bunghole. Plum brandy. A gift from the god of the shepherds.

Nada lifted down the sheepskins one by one, beating each of them clean against the outer edge of the doorframe. Then she spread them on the bed and set the bearskin on the floor before the fireplace.

The coarse dark pelt reminded Rider of a bear being trained to dance by the Gypsies in England when he was a boy. First they used a black-smith's tongs to wrench out the animal's front claws and lower teeth, leaving the more visible uppers to maintain its look of fearsome savagery. For the next three days the creature did not eat. The fourth evening the Gypsies dragged the weakened bear over a heated metal sheet while a boy beat time on a corner of the tin with a hammer. The center of the sheet glowed from the coals that smoldered beneath it. The animal's growls turned to whines and finally to childlike screams as the older boys hauled it back and forth across the glowing hot sheet by neck chains while the bear raised its paws and danced faster and faster as the beats of the hammer quickened. Emboldened camp dogs barked bravely from the edges of the coals. After five or six sessions, the bear would dance whenever someone repeated the sound with a hammer. After each dance, the bear was fed. When Anton had protested, Linares explained, "We Romanies do what we must in our own ways. We cannot live like other people and neither can our animals." Later, while local villagers laughed at the dancing bear, and the prettiest Gypsy passed among the farmers using her tambourine as a begging bowl, the Romany children picked their pockets and stole from their carts.

Anton watched Nada shut the door and lean against it and close her eyes. Neither of them spoke. At length she opened her eyes and put her fingers to her lips. Anton smiled up at her and listened to the fire strengthen. She set both buckets of water near the fire. The air cleared as the chimney heated and the smoke rose. The smell of the fire cleaned the room. In the morning he would cut some branches to scrape the flue.

Nada took one bucket to the other side of the fireplace. She turned her back and removed her jacket and boots, then all her clothes. Anton had never seen her naked. Nada dipped her shirt in a bucket, wrung it out and used it as a cloth to wash herself completely. He could not help staring at her breasts and her lean tight bottom in the firelight. She had the fit curvy body of a young woman ready to bear children. He was not certain whether the sight of her made him feel young or old.

When Nada was finished, she left her shirt and underclothes soaking in the other bucket with a handful of soda she had found in a wooden bowl. Then Nada bent over Anton and helped him remove his clothes.

"Tell me about your tattoo," she said, taking his wrist and turning it to study the dark short-winged bird in flight on his forearm.

"I had it done in Pompey, as the sailors call Portsmouth, when I was working as a docker." He did not know how much to tell her. "I was nineteen." He remembered the old docker he had saved during a loading accident saying to him, "Boy, you've got a grip like a freight-car hitch," then taking him to Zebraman for a tattoo. He thought of the bar girl who had sat very close behind him, teasing and distracting him during the tattooing as she touched him and filled his glass. He had never had a girl before.

"But why did you chose this beautiful hawk?" Nada brushed her fingers over the bird.

"The hawk was stencilled on chests of tea and cases of flax from Goshawk Plantation that we were unloading from Mombasa. The plantation was somewhere in the Kenya highlands. Nanyuki, BEA, it said. I traced the bird on a bit of light packing paper and gave it to the tattooist. I did it so as never to forget why I wanted to go to Africa."

"Why did you want to go to Africa?"

"I wanted to be free, in ways you never could be free in England, and to see the animals and make my fortune."

"Did you, my handsome satnik?"

"I saw many animals." Anton smiled at last. "And sometimes I was free."

No longer embarrassed, he let Nada wash him too. He watched her nipples stiffen as she touched him. As she bent over him, he held one breast between his hands and took it in his mouth. Her warmth and softness brought him to a different world. They sat on the bearskin by the fire until they were dry, touching, not speaking. When they were warm, Anton lay on his back and she settled slowly onto him. With her hand on his chest, Nada closed her eyes, arched her back and cast back her head. The urgent movements of her shadow danced on the wall behind her.

Chapter Twenty-One

"The Greek is here, master," said the voice of the Nubian in a deep whisper that penetrated the door to the captain's cabin of the Cataract Café.

What a choice, thought the dwarf. To pass time with that wart of Levantine corruption? Or to continue this session of intimate therapy, part of Dr. Hänger's rigorous schedule to help him gain a year or two of life, warding off the stiffening embrace of lordosis and arthritis by means of these nimble attentions from Jamila's young dancers in training?

Suspended upside down from the leather sandals of the harness, he swung gently like a fat yellow canary on its perch. His round bald head was red as a radish as the two women stroked and kneaded each limb and joint. There would be no sexual activity for them or him, but the stimulation of his sockets and circulation would give him life, and for them it provided an opportunity for the future. Not only would they be under the little man's protection, but they were learning early a fundamental lesson of their trade as dancers: cheerfully, without intimacy, to give pleasure no matter how unappealing the client. Already they knew better than to reveal the slightest indication of revulsion.

One dancer held him by the ankles, securing his slippery body, while the other loosened the leather straps that bound his little feet. The knobbed knuckles of each tiny toe were frozen cold and hard as marble. The dancers laid him on the divan and dried him front and back before easing him into his robe and slippers.

Demetreos bowed when Olivio Fonseca Alavedo, generally celebrated throughout Cairo for his hospitality, appeared on deck in his belted paisley gown. No stranger to indignity, the Greek was nonetheless annoyed at being kept waiting for an hour without the courtesy of either a seat or coffee.

"Ah, there you are, Demetreos," said Alavedo. "I trust you have made the enquiries I require and that you know where we must go to learn what is happening with all this military contraband."

"Indeed, sir," bowed the Greek, concealing his resentment. "I will direct your driver."

Demetreos sat in the front seat beside Tariq as they motored north from town, taking a turn east towards the Suez Canal at the village of El Abassa. After two further turns on the old cracked road, the dwarf anticipated their destination: Abu Sultan, one of several abandoned supply bases built eighty years before during the construction of the world's greatest maritime canal. Alavedo noticed the fresh tracks of many vehicles across the uneven patches of wind-blown sand that covered the way.

Two donkeys stood patiently by the side of the road just ahead. Wicker panniers were strapped to their sides. A boy squatted on his haunches between the animals. He waved a fly switch as the dusty Daimler passed. Olivio wiggled his fingers in reply.

Several men with rakes and shovels worked slowly on the sandy rocky slope behind the boy, turning the surface material.

"Scavengers, sir," advised the Greek. "Searching for anything of value from the old days of the Canal. Tools, scraps, buckets, whatever they can find. For twelve years this was an encampment of the fellahin. Thousands died as they worked like slaves toiling for the pharaohs. The French maintained the native clinic here, far from the Canal, lest the cries of the injured and the smell of the dying upset the workers or the visiting investors and dignitaries."

They approached the sand-covered wreckage of old structures. Fragments of cheap masonry, the rubble of workshops and shelters, bits of rusting iron framework were scattered on both sides of the road. Finally they came to a gradual depression that led down to the great Canal. Olivio saw the slanted funnel of a ship passing in the distance, though they were too far to see the water of the Canal itself. Two large structures loomed before them, tall unpainted masonry walls the color of the sand.

The Greek turned in the front seat and looked back at the dwarf through his dusty round spectacles. "In these buildings, Senhor Alavedo, were assembled and repaired the greatest machines then known to man. Giant dredgers, steam engines and conveyors, huge bucket chains that moved more material than had ever been done since the building of the pyramids themselves."

"Of course, Demetreos. What do you take me for? I am no new visitor to Egypt," snapped the dwarf. "I myself live and toil on the Nile. What have you to show me?"

Tariq slowed the car near a low wall that ran along the road. Behind the wall was a bedlam of transport. Old covered lorries, camels, donkey carts, heavy open-back trucks, all were busily loading and unloading.

"Here," said the Greek as if presenting a gift, "here is the market of the contraband."

"Stop the car," said Alavedo. He rolled down his window and crouched forward on the edge of his seat like a bird on a limb. He gripped the sill with both hands and squinted out at the scene. A cart labored past, close to his window. Hauled by four men pulling on the donkey traces, it was stacked high with rolls of heavy khaki canvas. Stolen tenting for the campaign in the Western Desert.

Alavedo felt like the last guest to be invited to a magic feast. Except for weapons, he was certain that everything required for the greatest war on earth was here at hand. Now he must find a way to combine honor and profit. To help the war his friend was fighting, while also turning it to coin.

He set a fine Panama on his head and tapped twice on the thick glass behind his driver. Tariq stepped down, opened the back door and lifted his master in his arms, raising him piggyback onto his shoulders and holding the dwarf gently by his right ankle. This gave Olivio the advantage of height and freed Tariq to use at least one hand if necessary.

"Stay in the car, Demetreos," said the dwarf. "See that no one disturbs it."

The buildings had no roofs, for there was never rain, but the high walls provided security then and now. Tariq and Olivio passed between passages lined with packing cases and rubber tires of every size, American and British, Alavedo noted, stacked higher than the Nubian's shoulders.

Olivio patted Tariq on the head, and they paused to watch an Arab pry open a large wooden crate, one of ten or twenty arranged in a single tight block and guarded by two other men. A board splintered and came free. The Arab struggled for a bit, then lifted out a round flat-sided canteen in a khaki canvas case. The standard British army canteen, used by every Tommy from Malaya to Libya. How many to a crate? wondered Olivio at once. Five hundred? A thousand? A clever theft, thought Alavedo, for in a country that was mostly desert, what could have more widespread utility than a canteen?

They passed on. Stacks of shorts and tunics. Boxes of belts and long khaki cotton socks. Heavy-duty zippers from Birmingham, to be combined with the tent canvas from Calcutta. Only the medical supplies turned Olivio's thoughts from greed to guilt. Every day of his own life depended on skillful medical care. And what of the wounded, like Mr. Anton and his boys? Here was a mountain of bandages and gauze. A flood of iodine and antiseptic. Finally, heavily guarded, small chests of surgical tools from Sheffield and Coventry, stacked in a far corner of the great enclosure.

"Back to the car," whispered the dwarf into the ear of his retainer.

Suddenly three men blocked their way, a tall Arab and two rough fellahin attendants. The Arab was trimly bearded, with fine riding boots beneath his costly cotton robe, a sign that he was not a man from Cairo, and so less likely to be familiar with Olivio Alavedo and his reputation.

"Move aside," ordered Tariq.

"Have you come to buy, little man?" asked the Arab, ignoring the Nubian.

"Are you for sale?" said the dwarf, seizing Tariq by the ears so that both his retainer's hands were free if need be. Both understood the signal. Olivio sensed a rush of excitement that made him feel young again.

The Arab cursed and spat near the sandals of the Nubian.

Instead of retreating, Tariq charged towards the Arab. The larger fellah stepped forward, one hand on the handle of a knife in the sash that belted his dirty robe.

Without releasing the dwarf's ankle, Tariq lifted his left arm across his body. He slapped the fellah open-handed across the face with a blow that knocked the man down and nearly broke his neck. The other fellah backed off as the Arab reached beneath his robe.

"I would not," said the dwarf, aiming a small double-barreled pistol at the Arab's face. Pearl-handled, it was the weapon of a lady or a gambler.

At that instant a fat trader in the striped robe and slippers of a successful Cairo merchant came to the Arab's side and whispered to him urgently.

No doubt, thought the little man, he is telling this rogue who I am.

"*Ahlan wa sahlan,* welcome effendi," said the Cairo merchant, rubbing his hands together, looking up at Alavedo before bowing. "My regrets for this foolish incident. I believe you have done business with my uncles, the Hameds, at their emporium on the Shari el-Maghrabi?"

"Follow me to my car, Hamed," said Alavedo, resting his pistol on Tariq's head. He had been preparing to cover Tariq's ear with the other hand had he been obliged to fire.

In the Daimler, Olivio asked Hamed to sit beside him while Demetreos and Tariq waited outside in the sun.

"Whatever comes of this," said the dwarf as he passed the thermos cup to his guest, "you will be protected. But one thing you must tell me. The name of the British officer who is most actively involved in this business."

Hamed sipped the cool tea.

"One name," said the little man.

"A captain of intelligence, who sells copies of the harbor manifests and schedules of all supplies. Other than weapons, of course."

"What is his name?"

"Captain Blunt, Algernon Blunt."

***

Time had passed quickly. Anton Rider did not consider himself naive or inexperienced, but this girl astonished him. He felt gentled, like a wild horse slowly broken. He had become expert at making love on his back.

"It is good for your hip, Captain," Nada assured him, and perhaps it was. Certainly there was no pain as there seemed to be in other postures. Best of all, there was no urgency. Never had he possessed the freedom of so much time to learn how to be with a woman, such time for dalliance, for the ease of pleasure.

Lying on a shaggy animal skin with the window panel latched open against the wall, Anton could see the snowy tips of the pines against the steep rise of the next ridge. Despite the changes of light and weather, the framed outdoor scene often seemed to be not a view but a painting hanging on the wall.

He watched the large slow flakes float and settle through the still crisp air. Today would be the fifth day of snow. The serenity of this life made him feel guilty. When the weather broke, he would have to work out how to get back to the war. This cabin, he realized, would be a perfect stop on the pilot escape routes that Captain Simon had come to arrange.

"Am I losing your attention, satnik?" Nada asked over her shoulder. She reached between her legs and stroked him with her short nails while she continued the supple rocking movements of her body. Her hand had become softer. She had been filing her nails against a stone of the fireplace, a practical surface for a person with one hand.

Each time Nada rose she arched her back and paused before descending. Anton noticed again the freckles on her shoulders and the smooth firm depression of her spine. He ran his fingers down her back. He felt her tighten, winding herself up. Then her slender muscled body rippled like a snake. She spoke over her shoulder with a soft casual voice. "Are you somewhere else?"

"No, nurse, I don't think so," he said, though his mind had turned to Cairo and a much older woman. How had Nada known?

"Tonight we are having a birthday party, Englishman. Perhaps I will teach you to dance the *kolo*."

"How many candles?"

"Sixty-four."

"You are sixty-four, sixty-three?"

"It is not my birthday we are celebrating, my dear satnik." She squeezed Anton with her fist. "It is Comrade Stalin's birthday. It is the duty of every Partisan, of every Communist, to celebrate. It is December twenty-first, the first day of winter."

"How appropriate," said Anton, not able to muster much enthusiasm.

"What is wrong with Uncle Joe? How could you not admire him?"

"Isn't Marshall Stalin rather rough, a bit brutal?"

"You Britishers are so soft. Josef Stalin is a man."

Later Anton made his way along the narrow packed track to the spring. He was still careful with his leg, but for the short walk he left behind the heavy cane he had made from a shepherd's staff found in the cabin. Thanks to the mountain air and a lean diet, chopping wood, hiking in the snow and learning to ski, he felt himself again. Bush-fit. Hard. Without his Cairo belly.

The snow rose higher than his knees. The thin spring still gushed modestly, then disappeared downhill under a crust of ice until Rider could no longer follow it beneath the snow. He studied the rounded tracks of a hare printed perfectly on the flat rock beside the spring. He heard the howls of wolves carrying from distant mountainsides on the bitter wind.

Rider offered a bucket to the mule. Leaning against the outside of the chimney, two blankets belted around it with leather straps, the mule drank eagerly, as if aware the water would soon freeze over. Anton scratched its forehead. The unfriendly animal shook its head irritably like a child not wishing to be kissed. Rider used his choori to cut a slender leather thong from the stiff remains of the harness that hung in the shed.

Anton went inside to prepare for the birthday party. It was his turn to clean the cabin. He held an empty pipe in his teeth as he worked, a new habit he found congenial, even though it was not his. First he took the

German edelweiss badge from his pack. For a moment he thought of the young German soldier he had killed. He polished the badge with sausage grease until the six brass stamens and each silvery petal gleamed. He hung the edelweiss on the leather cord and placed it neatly under Nada's plate.

After gathering firewood, Nada washed at the spring and ran back shivering to dry her hair. Pleased by the cabin's neatness, she prepared dinner. When everything was ready, they sat on the barrels eating the four final prunes, sipping hot plum brandy and talking about Anton's first voyage to Africa. He had the sense that there was something Nada wanted to tell him.

"Are all the European farmers rich in Africa?" she asked.

"It depends on the weather and the crops, but some are richer than others. For many it's always hard, and it takes money to start. Many never make it, no matter how long and hard they work." He shrugged. "About the same as England."

"Here in Bosnia, when this war is over, we will share everything and live together in great farms, like in Russia."

"That would not work everywhere." Anton chewed his last prune slowly before tossing the pit in the fire. He dropped an 1880 Maria Theresa silver dollar into the prune jar. Always leave something for the next person.

Nada filled their glasses and rose. "Comrade Stalin!" She lifted her glass. Her face was flushed. "And death to the *Fascisti*!"

Rider could drink to that. "Death to the Fascisti!" He looked up at Nada. He had never seen her so lovely. The strain had left her. The river was in her eyes. Her hair was longer, her face and figure seemed less lean. Tonight her frayed shirt, tucked neatly into thick grey wool trousers, was open one extra button. He felt young again, and hungry.

Anton turned his eyes down to the table. The last of their dried meat was cut in small chunks and arranged in the pan of red beans and garlic. He smelled the steamy sweet bread baking in the iron pot by the fireplace. Round like a cake, stuffed with scraps of potatoes. He raised his glass.

"Comrade Trotsky!" Anton drained his brandy and grinned.

"That is not funny. My people are dying for what we believe in."

"So did Stalin's old friend Trotsky, not long ago, with an axe in his head." Anton knew he should not have said it, but he was not feeling like a political lecture.

"Trotsky betrayed the revolution, and he ran away to Mexico."

Anton heard the mule bray and shuffle against the side of the cabin.

"Have you read Engels?" She looked down at him with hope.

"Who?" Anton tried not to smile. He took the two sides of her behind in his hands, squeezing and lifting her slightly as he kissed her between her legs, feeling her bone. He smelled her scent. She was so wet that he drank her when he sucked her into his mouth.

"Who?" He asked again when finally he raised his head.

Nada gasped and twisted away before she spoke. "The great philosopher, Friedrich Engels. You are so ignorant. Are there no schools in England?"

"Not for me. I was raised by the Gypsies. I just went fishing and poaching and played in the woods."

Nada put the steaming bread on the table and served the beans with the wooden spoon. As she moved her plate, she saw the necklace. "What is this?" Her plate rattled when she set it down unsteadily. She lifted the edelweiss and looked at Anton, her eyes shining. She formed a kiss with her lips.

"Happy Stalin's birthday!" Anton raised his glass.

Nada began to cry. She held the badge in one hand. After she recovered, she asked, "Do you know, Satnik, what a girl should do when a man gives her a necklace?"

Anton shook his head.

"Either she must give it back or she must do this." Nada took off her shirt and hung the cord around her neck.

Suddenly they heard the mule scream. Violent blows struck the cabin. They heard the shrill cries of an animal being torn apart.

Anton grabbed the hatchet and cane and flung open the door.

The mule struggled and kicked on its back under the shelter. Blood darkened the snow. A heavy shaggy figure was hunched over the mule with its face inside the mule's belly.

Rider plunged the hatchet to the handle into the bear's neck. The dark figure turned and rose raging in the snow with the weapon fixed in its flesh. Anton took a step back towards the door and clubbed the growling bear across the face with his cane. The animal slapped the cane from his hand and lunged forward.

Nada appeared and hurled the iron pot at the bear. Anton pushed her into the cabin and stepped inside. The animal hesitated in the dim light of the doorway, snarling and bobbing its head from side to side. Its snout shone with blood. Its black lips parted. Anton slammed the door. He shot the wooden bolt and braced himself against the door as the bear shook it with repeated blows.

In a few moments all was silent except for the groans of the expiring mule. Anton opened the window and peered out. The head of the mule twitched against the snow. A dark shadow fed at its stomach. The mule became still and they heard only the slobbering sounds of the feasting bear.

Nada and Anton lay awake through the night, feeding the fire and holding each other.

Anton thought of the small shining eyes of the bear, black with hate in the dark face, and remembered Captain Simon at the cafe in Derna. In the morning Rider looked out and saw the remains of the mule shrouded by a light dusting of fresh snow. The shoulders and head were intact. The guts and chest were a gory ravened mess. But Anton knew enough of animals and hunting to be certain that the bear could not survive the wound to the neck that he had given it.

Rider opened the door and stepped into the waist-high snow. With their meat finished, he was glad the bear had left what it had. He found the hatchet near the carcass of the mule and cleaned it in the snow. A red trail led towards the spring. He armed himself with his cane. Nada joined him with the kitchen knife. The blood grew heavier as they approached the spring.

They found the bear dead with its face in the frozen spring. Its paws were spread to either side like a man bathing his face. Smaller than it had seemed in the night, the dead beast was surrounded by a collar of pink frozen water.

"Fresh meat," said Nada. "Let's not leave it for the wolves."

They each took the bear by one hind leg and dragged the shaggy body to the cabin. Anton sharpened his knife and skinned the lean animal in the snow, using the edge of the blade to separate the hide from the pale membrane and flesh beneath. While he worked, Nada cut up what was left of the mule. Saving the tongue, she cast the head and the central mutilated section into the snow.

When he was finished, Rider hung the carcass of the bear and the remains of the mule from nails high in the open shelter. Scraps of mule and bear might not appeal to diners in Nairobi and Cairo, where eland and fowl and lamb were favored choices. But here in wintry Bosnia, they would be feasts.

Anton rubbed the bearskin clean with snow, wiped it dry against the door and draped it over a beam indoors. They did not have enough salt to waste on curing the skin. Nada and he washed their hands and arms in the snow and went inside to share bread and plum brandy by the fire.

Chapter Twenty-Two

"Not exactly Royal Navy style," said Graham Walker to Denby as they bounced to the bottom of the wadi in late afternoon. "These Yanks have pitched up like a bunch of Gypsies." They drew up thirty yards from the spread-out encampment of the American Rangers.

Four or five jeeps lay scattered in several directions. One half-track, a two-tonner, rested in the center with a stretch of canvas extending down one side. A bazooka was mounted on the back of a jeep, a fifty caliber machine gun on another. Open packs and grenade belts rested on the seats of the jeeps. A big black kettle sat steaming on some coals. The Stars and Stripes flew from an aerial mast. A pennant with a single blue star flew from another. Denby noticed two men leaning under the open hood of a jeep. A distributor cap, wrenches, some spark plugs and a bar of chocolate rested nearby on a scrap of canvas. The two Hussars motored over towards the Rangers.

"It's the sand, would be my guess," said Walker helpfully. "Not the starter."

"You don't say?" replied one Yank, raising his red face from under the bonnet. "We have sand where I come from, too."

"And where's that, laddie?" said Walker cheerfully.

"Arizona."

A heavily-muscled American in a sleeveless undershirt raised a hand and waved them into camp. Most of the Yanks were unshaven but not bearded. Several stood and wandered over as the Hussars climbed down from their vehicles.

One man, lathered with soap, stood at the far end of camp, shaving with a straight razor in the rearview mirror of a jeep. The stripes of a master sergeant were tattooed on his left arm.

"I'm Corrigan, First Rangers," said the American in an undershirt, saluting, then holding out his hand. "Captain Corrigan. Pleased to know you, Lieutenant."

"Denby Rider, sir, Seventh Hussars. These men are with the Eleventh." Denby had the sense that as the Rangers and Hussars mixed and chatted, they were assessing each other like teams before a rugby match.

Denby returned to Graham Walker. "Make camp here. But make it shipshape. Let's show these Yanks the difference. I want a perfect laager in thirty minutes."

Graham set the vehicles and gathered the men around him while Denby went back to confer with the American officer. He carried a bottle of whisky in one hand. Corrigan spoke first.

"If we're going to be hunting Tigers together, Lieutenant, I'd like to suggest a joint patrol, just to get the men working together."

"When?" asked Denby, concerned the waning light would not permit anything more than a quick recce in new country. "Night falls quickly out here. Might even be some rain."

"Right now," Corrigan said confidently. "Get started before it's dark. By the time they're back, the boys'll have chow ready and you and I can make plans for tomorrow."

Denby nodded in half-hearted agreement. Perhaps a short patrol was not a bad idea.

"Let's use two vehicles. We'll send out a jeep under Lieutenant Mendoza. He's a bit of a cowboy, but he'll do all right. Best eyes in the outfit. He can toss a coin with your man to see who's in command."

A few minutes later a jeep and an armored car set out on patrol driving northwest into the sunset along the next morning's line of search. Several Hussars examined the mounted 60mm bazooka, interested in any new weapon that might take out enemy armor.

Soon the evening was cold and starlit. Denby and Captain Corrigan sat smoking and sipping coffee from tin mugs on the rim of the wadi. A sentry was posted on the other edge of the dry riverbed. The men, a bit noisy for the desert, were gathered in camp below, where the low fire should not show. One could distinguish the Brits by their long sheepskin coats with the collars raised. The Americans seemed surprised by the cold. Fed up with their tins of bully beef and old mutton, the Hussars had eagerly swapped whisky for different rations and American tobacco.

"Where are you from?" asked Corrigan, offering Denby another cigarette.

"Nanyuki. And you?"

"Florida, Gainesville. Where's Nanooki?"

"East Africa. Up country from Nairobi. Coffee country and some tea and sisal. Plenty of game," replied Denby absent-mindedly, concerned that the patrol had not yet returned. The men camped below had already eaten, but the two officers were waiting to share dinner with the scouts when they came back.

"We've heard a lot about you guys. The Desert Rats, aren't you? That little jumping kangaroo on your pennant."

"That's us." Denby, restless, stood and stretched, stamping out his cigarette and staring west.

A flash of light flared in the distance, perhaps six or seven miles off in a line of hills, part of the Dorsal mountains that divided Tunisia from south to north. Immediately the boom of an explosion came from the same direction.

Captain Corrigan jumped up. The distant flash had become a fire like a candle flickering far off. "Could that be one of ours?"

"I'd say so," said Denby, stumbling down the side of the wadi. "They were headed on that line."

With Corrigan at the wheel, the jeep climbed nimbly up a slope and out of the wadi into the open moonlight. At least the Ranger could drive, Denby thought irritably. He should never have permitted the late recce. The fire glowed beneath the hills. The jeep crashed into a rock and the officer broke the rules of desert warfare by switching on the headlights. Denby searched anxiously as they drove towards the fire.

The American patrol jeep had been destroyed.

"A mine," yelled Graham Walker as Corrigan's jeep pulled up in the glare of the fire. "We lost two of them. Only the chap in the back was thrown free."

One man lay against the slope of the hill. A Hussar was kneeling beside him, bandaging the wounded American's head and shoulder.

"We must move, Captain," said Denby, knowing they were vivid targets against the oily blaze of the jeep.

He had learned the first lesson of joint operations. Never let the eager puppies lead the old hounds.

***

"I think I am pregnant," Nada said in a quiet neutral voice, looking up from the cook pot several weeks after Stalin's birthday.

Anton stiffened where he sat. He was already a grandfather. He felt his face grow red. He tried to think before he replied, careful not to be too self-concerned in his reaction. During the silence he heard the wind whistling and whipping against the walls of the cabin.

"Are you certain?" he said at last, aware that she, too, was seeking to control herself. "Isn't it a bit soon to know?"

"Yes, of course, but a woman can feel these things."

Anton rose and crouched behind her. He hugged her about the hips. She turned and pressed his head into her belly with her hand.

"Do you mind?" she said.

"I'm not sure. Do you?"

"No, but it's not an easy time for it."

"What should we do?" he said. "You know I am still married, and a father, and a grandfather."

"Nothing now, my satnik," she said, her eyes wet. She moved her fingers through his hair. "Do not worry. We are soldiers."

When they ate, Anton gave Nada most of the bread and all of their final plate of beans. Hanging in the shed, the tip of the mule tongue was dark and pitted and hard with cold. A strip of the tongue's curled rind rested on the edge of Anton's plate. Each evening the broth of the soup was thinner. Now it tasted only of garlic. The ribs of the bear rested clean and ungiving at the bottom of the simmering pot. If only he had his rifle, he could hunt. He knew the winter forest sheltered red deer, hare and birds. He had already built two traps some distance from the cabin. Tomorrow, like a Gypsy, he would build a poacher's snare and set it near the spring.

They lay together on the bed and listened to the wind gust against the roof. They had grown used to each other's smell and skin and taste. The touch of her bad arm seemed natural. He had never felt so physically close to a woman, even Gwenn. And more than that, comfortable and excited at the same time, effortless, beyond any need for athletic harmony.

All the next day it snowed. Nada had been teaching him to ski. The simple elements, she said: shifting his weight, control and balance, using his edges. In ways it reminded him of the bush, like tracking or learning how not to disturb the animals, finding a new way to be close to nature. He had learned to lash the short skis to his boots with thongs of hide and to use his cane as a pole before he made another one to match. Now he was comfortable on the skis. His hip hurt only when he had to climb.

In the late afternoon he braced the window open with a pipe. Banked snow lay like a grey blanket just below the level of the opening. Anton gazed across it as if he were lying on his stomach in the veldt.

The following morning Rider lay awake thinking what he must do. About the war, about Nada, another child, food and his leg. She slept beside him, tucked into his side like a puppy. How could he look after her and yet do his duty?

Loud knocks pounded on the upper boards of the cabin door. The bolt strained. Anton jumped to his feet. The blows grew stronger, violent. Save for a smoldering fire, the room was dark. He grabbed his knife as the bolt cracked. The door burst inward with a howling rush of snow and wind. A long heavy ski struck Anton in the side and slid past him into the cabin.

In the dawn gloom, three feet above the doorstep, Rider saw a pair of military boots standing like tree trunks on the packed snow.

With both feet free, the snow-covered man sank down like a hunkering animal and entered the cabin with one hand on his closed leather holster. Tied to the man's pack was what appeared to be a long rifle wrapped in a blanket. He slammed the door behind him as Nada covered herself and lit the oil lamp. The man lowered his stiff hood and pulled down his ice-crusted scarf.

"Rider!" said the bearded man. Frost hung from his nostrils and thick joined eyebrows. "I found you!"

"Welcome, Captain Simon," said Anton calmly, returning his Gypsy knife to its sheath. "How did you get here?"

"The Partisans gave me the Enfield and told me where you'd gone. One of them led me to the end of the valley." He pulled off his heavy wet coat and threw it in a corner. "As soon as the weather breaks, this'll be one of my escape shelters, a safe house for our pilots on the way west."

Simon wiped the snow from his face with the back of his hand. Water dripped onto the dark floor. The American squinted about the room. He stared at Nada standing by the fireplace. Her legs were bare beneath her shirt.

"There's a war on, Rider." Simon gestured at Nada with one thumb. "What've you been doing up here, hiding with this peasant girl?" He looked at Nada more closely. His eyes fixed on the stump of her arm. "Haven't I seen this one before, with her clothes on?"

"Mind your tongue, Captain. Don't talk like that." Anton felt the blood rush to his face. "The lady speaks English." He fought to control his temper. "Nada is with us. She's on our side, a Partisan. She's been fighting longer than any American."

"I don't care what she speaks," Simon sneered. "Two years ago the Commies were fighting on Hitler's side. Now they want us to save them."

Anton tried to defuse his anger by switching to another subject. "How is Major Sparrow?"

"I told you that Limey was finished. We had to leave him with the other hopeless wounded. I gave him an old revolver and two bullets. Maybe he knew what to do with it." Simon bent and tore loose the laces of his boots. He looked up and fixed Anton with small hard eyes. "You don't know what it's like out there, on the run, hiding in these mountains."

Despite himself, Anton felt his own guilt come alive with embarrassment as the American continued.

"SS Mountain Troops, the Prinz Eugen Division. Like mountain goats, even at night. The bastards have been training for this since they were schoolboys camping in the Black Forest. They had a picnic with these Reds." He kicked off his boots. "Give me something hot," Simon demanded. He lifted the scrap of rind from Anton's plate and put it in his mouth. "What's this?"

"Mule tongue," said Nada.

Simon spat the shreds into the coals. Then he lifted an empty mug from the table and smelled it. "And give me some of this. It's my turn. You've had your share of the booze and women, screwing this crippled Red bitch."

Swinging from the waist, his turning shoulder behind the blow, Rider belted Simon across the face with his open right hand. The slap sounded like a gunshot in the small cabin. More insulting than a punch, it was a blow that would have felled most men.

"*Svinga!*" screamed Nada at Simon as she lifted the kitchen knife from a barrel. "Pig!"

Simon staggered back against the door and reached a hand towards his holster. Rider struck him a similar slamming blow with his left hand and drew his knife with the other. Simon hunched down like a prize-fighter and shuffled towards him.

Anton held his choori to the American's belly. His other hand gripped the officer's wrist as Simon opened the holster. Rider smelled the man's stink and foul breath as he pressed close to him.

"Don't touch it, Simon, or you'll be holding in your stomach with both hands."

For a long moment the two men faced each other, panting, measuring each other's strength. Then Simon grew calm at last. Anton Rider released his grip.

Breaking away, the American officer rinsed his face in the bucket of drinking water. The soiled water fell back into the pail. Simon coughed and spat onto the hearth. His thick spittle sizzled on the hot stones. Then he poured a long drink into a mug and finished it quickly.

Anton and Nada watched him kick off his boots. Simon pulled off one sock and lay down on the bed with his Colt .45 beside him. Soon the American was asleep on his back, grunting with his mouth open. His sour odor filled the cabin and somehow made it his.

Rider was glad the American had passed out. He should be due for a long sleep. Knowing what must be inside, Anton unwrapped the damp blanket and found his Enfield and two bandoliers. He disassembled the weapon, annoyed but not surprised at its condition. He examined each part and cleaned them. He oiled the stock with a dab of bear grease.

Satisfied with his work, he slung on the rifle and one bandolier. At last he could hunt. A solid meal of fresh meat would help all of them, including Nada's baby. It might even improve Simon's humor.

Anton lifted Simon's pistol from the bed and handed it to Nada. "You're a soldier," he said quietly. "Keep your eyes on him while I'm gone. Use this if you have to."

Then he hugged her before stepping outside and taking the short skis from the shed. He lashed on the thongs. He knew Simon's long skis would be faster, but these were easy to use and fine for hunting. He took only his cane to act as a pole, leaving his other hand free for the rifle. He thought he knew where the red deer would be wintering, sheltered a bit lower in the next valley where bushes and young birch would yield shoots and tender branches under the snowfall.

Anton was right. Late in the afternoon, as the early shadows reached the cabin, he returned, satisfied with his hunt, feeling at home after a long day. A young red deer, already dressed, hung across his shoulders. He held two of its thin legs with one hand. He pinched the long hard tendons that ran like cables from hoof to hock. Nada would be pleased. If only they were alone.

As Rider approached, he did not see any smoke rising from the chimney. That was strange. He was also surprised to see the door of the cabin slightly ajar.

"Nada!" he called in a loud voice. "Nada!"

Anton dropped the deer and undid his thongs. He removed his skis and stepped into the dark room.

"Nada!"

Rider stumbled on the overturned brandy barrel and reached for the table with his hands to steady himself. He found it upside down. The fire had burned down to embers. He cut his right hand on the cracked glass of the lamp as he groped about in the darkness to right the table. Most of the oil had spilled out in a liquid trail on the floor. The wick cast only a low shadowy flame when Rider lit it. Without breathing he turned and looked about him with the lamp raised before his face.

Nada lay on the bed. Except for her socks, she was naked. Her shirt was gathered up around her neck. Her hand was clenched in a fist between her legs. The stump of her arm was ripped open where it had probably scraped the log wall. Her head was jammed against the rough wall next to the sharp corner of one log. Beneath her head the sheepskin was dark.

Anton's hand shook violently as he held the lamp over her. Dark shadows flitted about the room like bats. Blood dripped from his cut onto Nada's stomach. Anton collapsed to his knees with the lamp trembling in his hand. Her open eyes, dead black in the gloom, stared up at him. Shuddering, he dropped the lamp and closed her eyes. Gently he moved her head out from the wall. He felt her blood sticky on his hands as he found the dent of the wound at the back of her head. The bastard had killed her. Carefully he pulled down her shirt with slippery fingers.

Low flames from the spilled lamp spread across the packed dirt floor of the cabin as Rider hugged the cold body and pressed his face into her. Her blood smelled like old rust.

The cabin grew hot and smoky as Anton lay with her on the bed.

When he coughed and opened his eyes at last, the wall by the chimney was a shimmering sheet of flame. Numb to the danger, Anton kissed Nada's cheek, then her lips. He forced open her fingers and found the edelweiss badge on its leather cord. He hung the cord around his neck and carefully covered the body with a blanket.

Still dazed, Rider picked up his rifle, pack and bandoliers. He paused, returned to the bed and kissed Nada once more. Then, coughing, he staggered to the doorway and vomited. He wiped his face in the snow and stared about him. A thin moon hung over the pines. Simon could not have gone far.

Anton collected his skis and the carcass of the red deer. He walked back to the spring, gazing at the flaming cabin as he retreated. He dropped heavily onto the stone. A moan rose within him. He cried out with pain, howling without restraint like a wounded animal. All night he remained there, sobbing and rocking like a child. He should never have left her alone with that animal.

In the morning, half frozen, Rider warmed himself by the ashes of the cabin that had become a pyre for Nada and their child. Only the chimney, the iron pot and the hatchet survived. Around the black outline of the cabin, ice was forming from the melted snow.

Anton cut meat from the deer and packed the raw flesh in his knapsack. He was a hunter. He put a handful of .303's in one trouser pocket, where they would stay warm and dry. He scraped away the snowfall that had covered the short skies. With his belt fastened outside his coat, he lashed on the skis and set the hatchet in the back of his belt. Then he turned to search for the trail he must follow.

It was time to hunt.

Chapter Twenty-Three

"Another brandy and soda, Professor?" said Alistair Treitel as the four players settled at the card table in the Muhammed Ali Club. He was concerned that his own partner might already have had enough. Blunt believed that his own measureless brilliance would always prevail, no matter his level of impairment. Dr. Hänger had been unusually generous with the claret, ordering the third bottle from a different year, '37, saying he just wished to compare the vintage, though he himself only sipped it. Before and after the wine, the physician had offered champagne, too much champagne, Treitel thought. Now he had called for a hot *tilleul* with red vinegar for himself. What did this old Swiss witch doctor take for breakfast? he wondered. The blood of birds?

"By all means, sir," smiled Kotsilibis, nodding at Akbar, welcoming the brandy. "Shall we say a guinea a point, make a party of it? A bit rich for me, but today is my partner's birthday. Only happens once a year."

"As you like," said Blunt with a bland face. He cut the deck towards the Greek professor on his left while Treitel, excited by the possibilities of such a stake, shuffled the second pack. Kotsilibis dealt neatly and rapidly enough, thought the Don, and without the slick speed of too professional a player. That was what had worried him when the Greek first arrived with Dr. Hänger.

"Happy birthday to you, Doctor!" Alistair Treitel lifted his glass. With the right cards, or the wrong ones, a guinea a point could ruin any one of them but this fleshy Greek, he guessed. Having promised Gwenn a new flat on Gezira Island with her own room and a small terrace on the Nile, he had already lost the lease on his old apartment to a higher bidder.

In a moment each man was lifting and arranging his thirteen cards. The Greek picked at the unfortunate pock marks on his face. Occasionally one of his eyebrows twitched.

The hand passed easily, two no trump called and made by the Englishmen. Then another, two hearts for the same gentlemen. Game. Kotsilibis recorded the score while Treitel looked at his thumb, moist and red with a few drops of port. He gathered the tricks, soiling a card. With one game won, Treitel and Blunt were "vulnerable." A very profitable rubber was now possible, thought the Don.

"Boy!" he called to the steward. "Two fresh decks, if you please. I've made these a trifle sticky." Better to set it up now with a friendly deck, he judged. The new cards should make the difference. These two foreigners were not so slack. He could tell already that the twitchy Greek professor, although forever picking at those hideous pits on his temples, had a serious knowledge of the game. At over a pound a point, and with Fishhead not in top form, best to keep the game in control. This was one evening neither of them could afford to lose.

Akbar offered two decks on a salver and set down a box of the club's long cedar matches as everyone but Hänger prepared a cigar. Kotsilibis sliced open a cellophane wrapper with a fingernail. He freed the cards and passed them to Treitel. Smoke rose as the Englishman cut the fresh deck towards the doctor. Proud of his long elegant fingers, the physician dealt the third hand with care.

"One club," bid Blunt.

"One spade," said Kotsilibis between puffs, before resuming his ugly habit.

"I pass," said Treitel, studying the backs of Blunt's cards and holding his own well spaced so his partner could read the markings.

"Two hearts." The doctor coughed and waved the smoke from his face.

"Six clubs," said Blunt finally after another round of bidding. He's gone for a slam, thought Treitel, trusting Fishhead had it right. Since they were vulnerable, a slam would be a killing if they made it. He knew how much his extravagant partner also needed money, and his feral anger whenever anything went wrong.

"Double," said Dr. Hänger.

Algernon tapped his glass again and Akbar served him and Kotsilibis fresh brandy and sodas. We'll be either rich or poor, thought Treitel, alarmed, but still confident that his partner knew the markings. He had to suppress a sense of rising desperation, a fear of poverty returning that he had carried like an unhealing abscess since he was a boy at school.

"Re-double, gentlemen," said Blunt cheerfully.

Kotsilibis led a low heart. Now the dummy, Treitel set down his cards face up and held a fresh match to his cigar. He had a sick sense that something was wrong, that his partner was going to go down.

Treitel looked through the smoke at the cards as the hand played on-to the table. Suddenly he froze. He made an effort not to stare at a jack that should have been a king. He tried to confirm his recollection of the pattern of the marking on its back. Was he mistaken? Could the markings be wrong? Treitel tried to spot the marks on the card as Hänger collected the four played cards and put them into a neat trick that he placed in perfect line with the other two. But the back of the knave was covered too quickly, before Treitel could confirm its markings. Damn, he thought. Down two tricks already.

Before he finished his drink, the hand was over. Blunt and he were down five tricks. What the devil had happened? He felt he was back in school, his jacket cuffs lengthened but still too short, his only pair of grey flannel trousers shiny from overuse.

"Akbar," called Treitel, raising one hand, trying to keep his voice unconcerned. "Two decks of cards if you will." The steward presented new decks and refreshed the drinks.

The foreigners won the next two games as Treitel confirmed that the face cards were incorrectly marked. Vulnerable, with doubling and redoubling, they must be in for over a thousand guineas. Months of cunning cards and petty economies wasted in a night. Had that damned little Albrecht, working in that hideous dark alley behind the market, made some stupid mistake? They must call on the tricky bastard and learn the truth. Now the rubber was finished and the peculiar Swiss physician had his pencil poised over the score pad.

"Gentlemen," said Professor Kotsilibis as his partner tallied the score. "With respect, of course, but with the first rubber completed, and before we continue play, what assurance may we have that this evening's scoring will be honored?"

"We have always honored our debts, sir," said Blunt, his face flushing, his hands clenched on the table, the veins in his neck swollen and pulsing. "To whom do you think you are speaking?"

"I believe we understand to whom we are speaking," said August Hänger with measured gravity as Akbar stared down at the players. "Which is why one requires assurance, sir."

"Damned cheek," said Treitel, crushing out his cigar, surprised by the firm demeanor of their opponents.

"We will take your notes in hand, gentlemen," said the Greek with new authority, insisting on confirmation of the obligation. He nodded at the steward.

"Here you are, sir," said Akbar with a bow, handing one of the club's gaming record forms to Alistair Treitel. With one glance at his partner, the Englishman tore off a chit, wrote in the number from the score pad and signed his name with a bold stroke. He rose abruptly and slipped one face card into his pocket. He was going to examine this one at his leisure. Then he would correct this unspeakable injustice.

***

No new snow had fallen. The two packed tracks of the narrow downhill skis sparkled sharply with a thin glaze of night frost. At first, near the cabin, their pattern was set at uneven chaotic angles. Then the ruts became neat herringbones where the skier had pushed off from leg to leg. Finally it led downhill in tight parallel lines that merged as one in the white distance.

Anton Rider had been tracking since childhood, but never in the snow. He thought of the first time he had seen a mountain crowned with a startling whiteness. Waking in the bed of an abandoned lorry in Tanganyika, he'd been amazed to see the sunrise sparkling off the snowy shoulders of Kilimanjaro while the bush below was still dark. A glimpse of heaven, he had thought.

In Africa, every habitat was different: savannah and desert, tundra and rain forest, swamps and massifs. But everywhere, he had learned, hunting and tracking required respectful study of the detail of creature and landscape. As long as no new snow fell, he should be able to adapt to this new pursuit.

All day he followed the trail to the southwest, for Bihac, he guessed. Simon might not be aware that Anton had skis. On the downhill runs, or traversing, where Simon's long skis would be swifter, Anton placed most of his weight on his good leg and felt the alpine wind clean his face. But uphill or among trees, where his short light skis would have let him gain on Simon, his left leg defeated him. He cursed and felt the frustration of lost youth. Was that what Nada had lent him? He thought of her violated body lying on that bed in the cabin.

With the Enfield slung across his back and the skis in one hand, he dragged himself up through the snow until he could no longer feel his leg through the throbbing pain in his hip. Then he would collapse, sometimes almost weeping with agony and frustration, before rising again, his feet frozen, his hands numb. At one stop Anton cut a branch with the hatchet and trimmed it for use as a second ski pole. Revenge kept him on the trail. Thankfully, much of the route was now a gradual descent.

The track avoided villages and the valley floors, and Anton was glad for that. Simon had stopped frequently, three times removing his skis even on downhill passages. Rider did the same, resting his leg and searching for signs of the American's activity. Anton was determined to master the hardships of the mountains as he had learned to prevail over the challenges of the bush. That was who he was.

In late afternoon, Rider sheltered under a rocky overhang. A gibbous moon was rising like a distant ghostly observer. Only the brightest stars were clear. Pollux, Betelgeuse, perhaps Arcturus. His thoughts drifted back to rainy days in the wagon of a crippled gypsy astrologer, the *phuri dai*, the sage woman of the tribe. The low walls, ceiling and door of her vardo were pasted over with ancient star maps printed in Bucharest. Ropes of garlic, a chain of castanets and the skeleton of an immense bat dangled amongst the stars. "Never marry a girl who can't cook garlic," the phuri dai had told him. He had, of course. Then he thought of Nada, who used garlic with everything. Oppressed with guilt, his heart sickened at how it had turned out.

Anton gathered branches and built a lean-to as protection from the wind. He made a small fire shielded behind a ledge. He recalled the smokeless fires one could build with acacias at home, though he hardly thought Simon would spot him. Then he roasted the meat of the red deer and drank melted snow. He smoked the meat that was left and laid it in strips in the snow. He loosened his boots and wriggled his toes and stretched out with his head on his pack. At first the moon was encircled by a pale whitish haze. Unless it snowed again, he reckoned, the tracking should be easy.

Lying on his back, he stared up at the sky as the wind rose and the night clouded over. He was alone again, alone, and colder than he had ever been.

"A man always hunts and fishes best when he is by himself," Linares had told him when he was a boy. He thought of Simon out there hunkering bear-like in the darkness.

Bosnians never forget, Rider thought, and neither would he. He had some of the Gypsy in him, too.

From the mountainside above him, Anton heard a howling echo carrying on the wind. A wolf. Somehow a friendly sound. Other wolves, more distant, joined in. Perhaps some were young. Anton thought of Nada and their baby. A second child lost. He wept and listened through the night as the wolves roamed howling through the hills. His body trembled as the temperature dropped. The tears froze on his cheeks. Fearing the cold, he knelt and rebuilt the fire but fell into sleep despite himself.

When Rider awoke, his frozen fingers at first seemed useless. His feet, no longer part of him, were like two dead weights hanging from a distant scale. Peering between the branches in the early light, tired and stiff, his leg numb, he saw three or four inches had fallen. Enough snow to cover every track, he realized, cursing.

Anton sat up in the shelter. He knocked his feet together and rubbed his hands. Then he chewed a piece of frozen meat while he wiped the frost from his telescopic sight. He peeked between the snowy branches and scanned the long slope below him. Nothing. It was always movement that revealed the most elusive game, not color or configuration.

Patience, he told himself, the hunter's greatest weapon. He thought of Linares standing for hours in cold lonely rivers. Fishing with his hands, lest with a rod he be caught as a poacher. Waiting to tickle a trout and throw it up on the bank before falling on it.

Rider searched the smooth white bowl of the valley floor. Nothing. Across the valley the hills rose steeply, becoming a mountain above the tree line. Simon would not want to carry seven-foot skis that high. Instead Anton studied the elevated clusters of birch and pine.

Suddenly a block of snow moved between two trees. Rider adjusted the scope. He saw Captain Simon rise and shake the snow from his body. Anton stared at the American's head and estimated the range. Perhaps a thousand yards, eleven hundred. He considered the cold air and the strong cross wind. The distance was too far.

If Rider warned him with a bad shot, the pursuit would grow harder. Stalking patiently, he might have a chance to get Simon within range, six or seven or eight hundred yards for a fair shot. Calm now, Anton sat quietly, feeling his old powers return. He reminded himself that there were two things he knew how to do: hunt and shoot.

He watched Lester Simon stand and eat some snow from his cupped hands, spitting as he stretched and looked around before pulling off his hood. Simon wiped his skis clean, balanced them over one shoulder and moved off, making his way slowly uphill through the deep snow. After a time, Simon reached a crest line and paused to bind on the skis. Once the American was out of sight, Rider rose and set off himself.

In four hours he arrived at Simon's campsite, finding an empty biscuit tin and two cigarette butts. Anton was exhausted and he rested for an hour. He counted his advantages: a rifle over a .45, fresh meat and Simon's ignorance of Anton's pursuit. To get limber, Rider rose and swung his leg back and forth before lashing on his skis. He pushed forward, taking advantage of the path the American had cut through the snow.

A while later Anton found himself following the tracks on a gentle downhill slope through a thickening forest, ideal for his short skis. He jinxed from side to side between the birch, all his weight on his left ski. Once he saw where Simon had fallen, unable to make a tight turn between two trees. Several times Rider fell himself, and he took each opportunity to rest on his side.

Anton came to the end of the forest in the early afternoon. He sat with his back against a pine and studied the desolate valley below him. A grey figure moved on the far hillside. Anton pulled the telescope from the case on his belt.

He had closed on his quarry. Now he just had to get in range.

Chapter Twenty-Four

The labyrinth of Cairo's Khan el-Khalili market was a mad world of its own, like the inside of an ant hill or some distant planet. The frenzied hives and warrens of many varied creatures seemed scrambled together, yet each one was pursuing its own essential purpose. The twisting passages that wound between the stalls and shops and coffee houses of the largest market in Africa were narrowed by the congested press of traders and shoppers, beggars and thieves and travellers. Tobacco smoke and incense clouded above the denser odors of the leather shops and perfumeries. Open sacks and baskets held bundles of dried herbs and mounds of bright colored spices. Here and there shafts of late afternoon light glanced down through the narrow openings atop some lanes. The canvas and striped cotton awnings of the stalls filtered the light that touched the waiting wares.

Alastair Treitel and Algernon Blunt knew the way. Out of uniform, they cut through the crowd with easy imperial confidence, ignoring the grasping touches of mendicants and the welcoming entreaties of tur-baned purveyors and shopkeepers.

"Finest copper wares, excellencies!"

Treitel always let Blunt go first on this sort of journey. Fishhead had more of a taste for the physical side of pushing others from one's path. Tall, thick-shouldered, Algernon forged through without compromise, like an icebreaker or the nose in a rugby scrum. Occasionally his brutal streak came through a bit too harshly.

"Precious antiquities, oldest kingdoms, special prices for you sirs, effendis!"

It was always a bit theatrical, thought the Don with his usual de-tachment, these oriental solicitations. Each beggar or merchant attempted to play his part to complete a casbah scene in one of those American films from Hollywood. But now my own problems are real enough, thought Treitel.

A single game of cards had turned their financial affairs from awkward to desperate.

And today, for the first time, Blunt and he had crossed a line in their Balkan assignment. Instead of supporting Britain's Jugoslavian allies even-handedly to defeat the Nazis, the two were now assisting Stalin's plans for post-war Europe.

Until now they had merely tilted a bit in their allocations of parachuted supplies, favoring Tito's Communist Partisans over Mihajlovic and the Royalist Chetniks. As the link between the SOE and the RAF, that was easy enough, since the intelligence officers only gave the RAF physical target areas, not ground unit designations. More weapons, more medicine, more radios had gone to Stalin's Jugoslav allies.

But today the two officers had directed the RAF to drop even Mihajlovic's inadequate supplies into areas they knew were under Partisan control. The RAF, of course, would do its duty, as directed by the intelligence officers. The young pilots would be unaware of the hardship they were inflicting on the unsupplied Royalist fighters on the ground. This should help the Marxists not just during the war itself, but later when it really mattered: during the inevitable civil struggle that would follow it, the fight for the control and future of Jugoslavia and the Balkans.

Fortunately, so much was going on with the intelligence demands of the new battle front in Tunisia, and with the plans for Sicily and the rest of the Med, that their superiors had turned their own attention away from Jugoslavia.

The two Englishmen emerged into the quieter quarter of the specialists, the stalls of the men who served more particular, less popular interests. The sellers of orphans, the will forgers, the purveyors of stolen goods and war supplies, each had their place and discreet following in the back lanes of the Khan el-Khalili.

Albrecht's stall was at the very end of one such passage. They found the old forger as they always did, his long eyepiece fixed to the left frame of his spectacles and his head lowered over his workbench between the brightness of two lamps. A copper engraving plate was mounted in the steel clamp before him. The fingers of his left hand held a long fine-tipped engraving tool. "My fingers are my stock in trade," Albrecht had told them once. Now he set down the pick and lifted a thick badger-hair brush. On the wall behind his head was a framed engraving, the overlapping initials **A.D.**, the artistic symbol of Albrecht Dürer himself. Four playing cards were pinned to the wall beside it. Ace, king, queen and knave of hearts. "B.P. Grimaud" was printed on the side of an empty card box on the table beneath the cards.

"Gentlemen." the engraver said quietly, with no surprise in his voice. He leaned back on his tall three-legged stool. "Do you require some special new decks of cards?" Albrecht's long fine fingers reached under his workbench to a narrow shelf that ran beneath it. He drew out two new packs, each tightly wrapped in cellophane. He slipped them into Grimaud boxes and offered them to Treitel.

"What are these?" asked Treitel. Fishhead stepped behind Albrecht and rested a large hand on the old man's thin shoulder. "Are these the proper forgeries we pay you for? Or the frauds you created for our opponents at the Muhammed Ali Club, such as this king of diamonds?" Treitel threw down the single card he had collected at the Club. "Is this not one of yours?"

"I make only forgeries, sir," Albrecht said dismissively. He dusted the engraving plate with the badger brush as he spoke, then lifted the brush near his mouth and blew on the bristles to clean away the tiny metal filings they had collected. "Any fool can make a proper card."

"For whom did you make those cards, with the kings and jacks reversed?" said Treitel. At the same time Blunt turned the handle of the clamp. As its steel sides spread open, the copper engraving plate fell to the floor.

"You gentlemen know I never reveal my clients." The engraver looked up, his veined left eye huge and staring at Treitel through the eyepiece.

"Who were you working for?" repeated Treitel. With a jerk Blunt seized Albrecht's left wrist and forced his fingers between the jaws of the clamp. "For whom were you working? That Greek professor from Alexandria, or Doctor Hänger?"

"For neither, sir," said Albrecht, his voice rising, beginning to plead as Blunt tightened the vise on his fingers. "I do not know who you mean." He wiggled the smaller fingers of his left hand as the steel sides of the clamp were braced against the large knuckle of his middle finger. "I have never worked for either of them. Truly. Never."

"Who paid you for those cards?" said Blunt, tightening the vise as it compressed the joint. "Speak, or you will never work again."

Met with silence, Algernon turned the handle once more. The clamp tightened. Finally there was a sound like the cracking of a large walnut as the knuckle shattered. Albrecht's legs and arms thrashed like a mouse with one foot in a trap.

"Alavedo!" screamed the engraver as the clamp tightened against his smaller fingers. "That dwarf! Olivio Alavedo!" Blunt continued to wind the handle. "Ah! He made me do it! My grandson is sick in Trieste. I needed the money." By now blood was running down Albrecht's wrist. Fragments of bone were piercing through the torn skin of his fingers.

"Why?" asked Treitel with fierce curiosity. "Why did Alavedo want those men to cheat us? Why?"

"I do not know," screamed the engraver. Blunt ground the device until he could turn it no further. The two sides of the clamp nearly touched.

Concerned by Albrecht's cries, Treitel took the badger brush by its handle and stuffed it deep into the man's mouth. The engraver's face turned purple and he shook his head madly. Fishhead lifted the engraving pick.

Suddenly a burly Egyptian stepped into the shop with a tray and a small steaming cup of Turkish coffee. "Your coff . . ."

Seeing what was happening, the man dropped the tray and reached into his gallabiyah. With a grunt Algernon drove the pick into his heart. Coffee and blood splashed Treitel's linen jacket, making him wince in distaste. The big Egyptian collapsed with his head face-up in Albrecht's lap.

"And now for you."

Blunt withdrew the pick and with a savage grunt plunged it into the engraver's ear.

***

Anton closed his left eye and adjusted the scope. As he focused, his mind cleared. His senses brightened and he descended into concentration. Ignoring the cold and the glare of the snow crust, he followed the single figure below him as the man traversed the valley floor, striding flat on his long skis, his vision limited by the hood of his jacket.

Anton unwrapped the Enfield and loaded it with five warm dry bullets from his trouser pocket. He held up his fingers and tested the wind. He sprinkled a few flakes in the air. An uneven north-south wind from his right, less powerful than before. Anton mounted the scope, drew on his gloves and returned his right eye to the lens. He suppressed the pain that surged into his hip when he raised his knees and braced his elbows. His skis were still on, the left one flat to the ground, the right with the tip up and the heel set in the snow. Anton wiggled his trigger finger in his glove.

He watched Lester Simon arrive at a frozen river and test the edge of the ice with one pole. Apparently satisfied, the American turned parallel to the streambed. He lowered one ski onto the snow-covered ice. Slowly Simon dropped his weight onto the ski. He brought down his other foot to the ice, spreading the skis apart to distribute his weight. Anton noted the snow blowing along the surface of the ice where Simon disturbed it. A different wind, more northwest-southwest. This second wind would make a difference on a long shot, when the bullet would be travelling more slowly. He studied Simon's head, allowing for the hood. Seven hundred yards, maybe seven-twenty-five.

Captain Simon continued cautiously down the riverbank, evidently looking for a narrower stretch of streambed before he risked the crossing. His body was at right angles to Rider's position, presenting a narrower target. Anton surveyed the river himself, estimating where Simon might turn to his right to cross. He found a narrow section at a bend in the stream, perhaps another thirty yards distant.

Simon came to the bend. As Rider anticipated, he turned his skis to face the opposite bank. Anton pulled off his gloves and flexed his fingers before adjusting the range.

The American officer hesitated and tested the ice with his poles after freeing his hands from their straps. Anton understood what he was doing. If Simon fell through the ice with his skis on, he was finished. If he took them off to cross, his weight would be more concentrated and he would be more likely to break through the ice.

Simon spread his skis and slid slowly forward.

Anton breathed steadily and aimed the cross hairs at Simon's spine just below his neck, allowing for a drop of fifteen inches. Only the uneven crosswind worried him. He adjusted, aiming two inches to the right of the man's spine.

Stride by stride Simon approached the center of the river.

Anton squeezed the trigger. Instantly he drew the bolt and reloaded.

Simon crashed forward on his face. Jarred by the impact, his right ski broke through the ice. Rider fired again, striking him in the side just above his pistol belt. Simon's legs fell through the ice. He struggled with his arms, flailing for purchase.

Anton jumped up, jammed his gloves into a pocket, took the rifle in hand and pointed his skis towards the river. The surface of the crusty snow stayed hard as Rider tore downhill. He squinted into the freezing wind trying to keep sight of the struggling figure in the ice.

As he approached, Simon was now facing him. His left hand held a ski pole. The tip appeared to be planted firmly in the solid ice. With the other arm Simon sought to drag himself up onto the ice. The surface cracked and split at the edges as he thrashed. He seemed unable to move his lower body.

Anton stopped at the river's edge. Seeing him, Simon ceased his efforts. Gasping, he stared up at Rider with raving eyes. Anton raised the rifle and put a bullet in the chamber.

"Rider! I can't move my legs. Pull me out, you bastard!"

Anton hesitated. He could not murder a wounded man like this. He lowered the Enfield and removed his skis. He rested his rifle on one ski and stepped onto the ice with the other ski in his hands.

Simon stared up at him, screaming for help. His chin hung on the edge of the ice. His left hand gripped the pole. His right was underwater. Rider advanced cautiously towards him. When Anton was six feet away, he knelt down. He held the ski in both hands and extended it towards Simon.

"Grab the end of the ski with your free hand," said Rider. "I will try to pull you out."

Captain Simon struggled to approach a few inches closer along the edge of the ice. As his right arm came out of the water, he fired his .45.

Anton felt the heavy bullet burn his side. Immediately he drew the hatchet from his belt. All the conflicts of his life united in the instant that he raised it.

Rider slammed the hatchet down on the wrist of Simon's gun hand. He heard bones break. Simon screamed from the depths of his belly. The hand and the pistol dropped into the water.

Anton twisted back to his right and raised the ski in both hands. Like a wood cutter aiming at a notch in a tree, he kept his eyes fixed on Simon's. With all his weight behind the blow, he swung the ski forward low and flat. Teeth flew as the edge of the ski hit Simon in the mouth.

Raging, spitting blood and teeth, his jaw broken, his mouth and beard dripping as Anton swung again, Simon took the second blow just above his staring eyes. Rider felt the skull crack open across the line of Simon's eyebrow.

For a long moment Anton sat on the ice gasping for air. His bullet wound began to ache as the shock passed.

Behind Simon the ice gathered in the current and wedged his upper body in place. Simon's dripping head rested upright on the messy ice, like an undercooked boiled egg set in a cup with the top cracked open and the albumin drooling down the side.

Anton wrenched the ski pole from the dead man's grasp and stepped back to the riverbank. He cleaned his ski and washed his face and hands with snow before drawing on his gloves. Grabbing the skis and rifle, he shuffled slowly across the river.

At the far side, his hunting instincts heightened, he paused and studied the varied sizes of the fresh prints of wolves that had come to the river to drink. Some were young. Perhaps this was the pack that had kept him company through the night. They would know what to do with Simon.

Anton wondered if, like hyena, the wolves would let their young eat first, or whether, like lion, the big males would get the first helping.

Without looking back, Rider lashed on his skis and set off into the hills towards Bihac.

Perhaps it was time for a plum brandy with Marshal Tito.

Chapter Twenty-Five

"Did you enjoy your evening of cards, Doktor?" asked the dwarf as he watched three workmen install the new helm on his quarterdeck.

Although the Cataract Café would never set sail on the high seas, this magnificent adornment was a fitting symbol of command and direction. Created to his specifications at Trimming & Cutler, the finest marine and yachting outfitters in Portsmouth, it was suited to an around-the-world vessel of Napoleonic times. Henceforth its heavy brass fittings and its teak wheel and twelve handles would shine as if Admiral Nelson himself were pacing behind it. Lord Nelson, too, like Olivio himself, was a man who had learned to endure physical infirmities, including one that the two men shared, an eye lost in the conflicts of life.

"I say to you, Doktor, did you enjoy your evening at the Muhammed Ali Club?"

Having completed the ceremony of polishing his gold spectacles, August Hänger replied, "Professor Kotsilibis and I did as you required, Senhor Alavedo."

"How much did you win?"

"One thousand and twenty-two guineas."

Almost rising from his cushion, the dwarf clapped his tiny hands like a child finding his Christmas stocking. "One thousand and twenty-two guineas! Ha! Ha!"

The physician did not speak.

"These winnings are yours, Doktor. Yours and the professor's. You will have your sterling this afternoon." The dwarf slid his thick pointed tongue along his lips. "How did these Englishmen pay you?"

"With a chit, a voucher, signed on a dated gambling note of the Muhammed Ali Club itself." The doctor opened his note case and passed the folded voucher to his patient.

The little man opened the note and held it close to his gleaming merry eye.

"I will have Tariq present this to Major Treitel for immediate collection, at some suitable moment, perhaps at the Officers Club or the Gezira. And if these two men cry for a delay, they will not enjoy what I will require as interest. We will keep this Treitel busy, so he has neither the time nor the means to trouble further the wife of my friend."

"I have no doubt you will, sir," said August Hänger without humor. "No doubt whatever." He looked across the quarterdeck as Tariq hurried up the companionway.

"Master." The big Nubian bowed. "I bring news."

"Speak."

"The old engraver is dead, murdered at his work place in the market. The man who was ordered to watch over him had stepped away to bring a tray of coffee. He, too, was killed."

Olivio frowned at the news. "How did Albrecht die?" he asked sharply.

"Stabbed through the ear, my lord, with one of his own tools. But first his hand was crushed in a clamp. Every bone and knuckle broken from wrist to fingertip."

"This man was under my protection," said the dwarf quietly, alert to the need for an otherwise unimposing man to maintain his fearsome reputation. "This disrespect cannot be permitted. We must bring Albrecht justice. Do we know who did this evil?"

"They say two Englishmen came down the lane towards his booth, effendi. One a very tall man with a peculiar smell." The Nubian added further details.

"The card players," nodded Hänger.

"Leave us, Tariq."

Alavedo turned his eye back to the elderly physician. Long ago the dwarf had learned to provide new enemies for his enemies.

"There is a German prisoner in hospital here who requires your attention, Doktor. He is an old friend of my true friend, Mr. Anton. Captain Ernst von Decken is a man who is not uncomfortable doing the hard things that sometimes must be done."

Olivio paused as the doctor blinked in understanding. "Now this German wishes my assistance to secure his freedom, to escape his imprisonment by the British. For a price, and with your help with the medical authorities, we will give this Hun what he requests. This once, at last, von Decken can provide justice rather than mischief."

***

"Doctor!"

The Sikh sentry at the entrance to the prisoners ward saluted as August Hänger appeared in the corridor. The scarlet and white cockade of the 16th Punjabis brightened the khaki turban of the Indian Army soldier. His buttons shone. His leggings were tight above his polished boots.

The white surgical coat of the Swiss physician was stiff as armor and buttoned to the collar. The toe caps of his black shoes gleamed like polished coal.

Despite his austere demeanor, Dr. Hänger was well received in Cairo's hospital wards, now crowded with military casualties from a score of countries. Some surgeons resented his refusal to consult with other doctors, but the seriously wounded, Rhodesians and New Zealanders, South Africans and Canadians, appreciated his work.

"Where do I find my German patient?" Hänger asked of a passing nurse. "Kapitan von Decken."

"He is the big noisy one, Doctor. In the last bed on the left, number twenty-eight."

"*Italienisch Idioten!*" boomed a German voice as Dr. Hänger approached the end of the ward.

"*Guten Tag, Kapitan,*" interrupted Dr. Hänger.

Ernst von Decken seemed to be the only naked patient. He was sitting up in bed, with heavy shoulders, a large white hairy chest and belly, and thick brown arms. A wicker-wrapped bottle of wine leaned against his pillows. A battered Iron Cross hung around his neck on a dull metal chain. Hänger noticed the German officer had only one leg beneath the bed sheet.

"Guten Tag, Kapitan von Decken," repeated the Swiss more firmly against the noisy background chatter of the Italian patients. They reminded him of the fat yellow canaries twittering in Alavedo's breakfast room when the night shrouds were taken off their cages in the morning.

Von Decken flashed a satisfied smile. "After a lifetime of dealing with the *Mundts* in German East Africa, I know how to manage Mussolini's peasants." Von Decken rubbed both hands over the short grey hair that bristled straight out from his head like the pelt of a hedgehog.

"Kap . . ." Dr. Hänger was not used to interruptions other than his own. Even his bizarre little patient had learned to attend to what he had to say. In Zürich no one wasted words, or anything else.

"The Italian women of Cairo keep bringing them presents. Cheeses, greasy black sausages, disgusting soggy Italian pastries that are making me fat, like their *Duce*." Von Decken slapped his belly, eager to talk. "This revolting Chianti. They bring nothing for me. So I am obliged to forage here for myself like a wolf in the Black Forest."

Dr. Hänger recognized the thick off-Prussian accent of old colonial German as von Decken continued. "In our desert war, of course, all these Italians do is surrender. Here, all they do is drink and eat and boast about women they have never had." Von Decken lifted the Chianti bottle, drank mightily and held it out to the Swiss, who declined it.

"Kapitan," said the doctor quietly in German. "I come to you on behalf of my esteemed patient, Senhor Alavedo."

"That little bastard! Is he still alive? I thought all midgets died young."

"Olivio Fonseca Alavedo is a dwarf, Kapitan, not a midget," said the doctor severely. "It has been my privilege to extend his life, if I may say so."

"Speak up, Doctor. It is a pleasure to be using the language of gentlemen." Ernst scratched himself under the sheet. "No need to whisper, you know. These Italian peasants don't understand anything." He hunkered forward on the bed. "I need your help to get away from here. Far away. Perhaps on a boat up the Nile, with a nurse or two. Get me to the Sudan and then I will manage on my own. I am at home in Afrika."

"Indeed?"

"My father came out to Tanganyika fifty years ago with a young wife and a hunting lodge taken apart in Germany with every beam and board numbered for reconstruction, even the old flower boxes for the windows. He started over. We grew pears and apples and sisal and employed two hundred Africans, a village of them." Von Decken spoke with hard pride, not self-pity.

"Then the English war came to East Africa in fourteen and we fought them for five years from Rhodesia to Kenya and Mozambique, outnumbered ten to one. Of course, they could never beat us. But finally the Kaiser surrendered at home and we lost everything to the damned Britishers."

"I understand." And Dr. Hänger did. Seeing that the conversation was developing in the appropriate direction, he proceeded. "My patient is prepared to help you on your way, the farther the better, with whatever may be required. Passage, documents, currencies, disguises. Perhaps even a young nurse. But there are one or two requirements that will first be asked of you."

"Just like that selfish little devil. Shameful. Always wants something for himself."

"There is no free passage, Kapitan von Decken," said the doctor, annoyed by the grating sound as the German scratched his scalp. "Never."

Aware he was irritating his visitor, Ernst scratched again before continuing. "Your shrunken monster is taking advantage of a wounded man. Damn his eyes."

"Eye."

"What?"

"Eye. My patient has only one eye, Kapitan. And in Cairo they say he sees everything."

"What can he want of a poor crippled German hero?" Ernst finished the bottle and wiped his mouth with the top of the bed sheet.

"There are two Englishmen in Cairo who Senhor Alavedo does not favor."

"Only two?" von Decken exclaimed. "I don't favor any Englishmen, except one, perhaps. I have been killing them for years. In two wars, from Tanganyika to Libya, and there are still too many. Ha! Ha! Why not two more?"

The doctor lowered his voice. "As my patient lives permanently in Cairo, it would not advance him to dispose of two English officers himself. Kap . . ."

"Excuse me, Doktor. First things first." The German lifted a thick cane from the back rail of his bed and banged it twice against the wall.

"*Vino!* Luigi! Giuseppi! Whatever your name is, pass me another bottle. Hop to it." He snapped his fingers repeatedly, hard and sharp as gunshots. *"Pesi! Pesi!"*

Eight beds away along the wall, an Italian patient reached under his bed and lifted a bottle of Chianti from the floor. The bottle passed from bed to bed as the Italians nattered noisily. Finally it reached Ernst von Decken. The German lifted a toothbrush from his bedside table, the only such table in the ward. He ripped off the cap of the wine and punched the cork down into the bottle with the handle of the brush. Wine splashed out onto his bed sheets, red as blood.

"*Wein*, Doktor?" Von Decken politely offered the bottle. "I never share one with these greaser boys. You never know where their mouths have been."

The Swiss physician had never drunk directly from a bottle, but he accepted this one and took a short sip. He passed the bottle back to the German, who wiped it with the back of his hand and drank. Von Decken smiled and belched. Then his face hardened.

"Why does your dwarf wish to kill these two?"

"They murdered a man who was under his protection. An old engraver called Albrecht. And the two are dishonorable in this war you all are fighting. And one of them is a personal adversary, shall we say, of a man who I am told is your only friend."

"Anton Rider! So he is. Let me drink to him, my own little *Engländer*." Ernst lifted the bottle, nearly draining it before he offered it to the doctor, who shook his head. "I have been training Rider at life since he was a boy. Back in twenty I picked him up from the side of the road in Tanganyika. He was eighteen. My foolish old father loved him like a second son. Where is he now?"

"Somewhere in Jugoslavia. Fighting you Germans."

"Of course," said Ernst, as if all had been made clear. "Rider is still an innocent. The boy never knows to take the winning side."

***

"If I am not with you," Nada had told him one evening in the cabin, "and you are not certain whether a village is Croat or Partisan or Bosnian, look for a minaret. Your best chance is a Muslim village with a mosque. The Ustashi do not trust them or wish now to fight them, and the villagers seek only to survive this war in peace."

As Anton thought of Nada's words, he tried to suppress other, more tender memories. Sitting on a rock with his back against a birch, rubbing his still-painful right leg, he adjusted the sight of his telescope. Sometimes he felt he heard her voice, or could feel her touch. At others, their time together seemed distant and impossible. The short winter days had left him feeling alone again. At night, he thought mostly of Gwenn.

He was about to eat the last piece of the back strap of the red deer. Today he must either hunt, steal or beg for food.

An hour earlier, he had found the fresh two-toed tracks of what must be a family of wild boar, almost identical to tracks of the warthogs in East Africa. He imagined them trotting proudly away, heads erect, tails up stiff in the air. The sow would be first with the three little ones in line after her, and the big boar off to one side scouting and foraging on his own. Even their diggings were similar. Here and there the male had scraped away the snow and dug for roots and grubs with his thick curved tusks.

Anton studied the small village below, which had a mosque and no church. Two dozen stone and wood houses were clustered around a square with a well near its center. In the early morning, smoke rose from only one chimney. The absence of motor vehicles in the village meant no

Italians or Germans would be garrisoned there. But the concentration camp at Jasenovac was not far. He must be careful.

Rider got up, striding on his skis just below a ridge line that extended past the village. The boar, he noticed, seemed to be moving his way. He paused again above an orchard of leafless plum and pear trees. Just past the far side of the village he saw what looked like the remains of a burned-out encampment. Anton scanned with his scope, and his heart grew chill. Romanies.

He made out the remains of five small Gypsy wagons. The vardos had been gathered in an arc around a central fire. Three were burned down to their frames and metal-rimmed wheels. One lay on its side. The fifth was charred but almost whole, though broken down at one end with an axle and two wheels dislocated. A large black cook pot lay upside down in the coals of the fire. Only a light sprinkling of snow covered the coals. The destruction of the camp must have happened in the last day or two.

Rider removed his skis and climbed down to the bottom of the orchard. Resting the skis against a pear tree, he chambered a round in the Enfield and made his way down to the Gypsy camp.

The rotten smell of wet burned wood greeted him. The stink reminded him momentarily of the cabin in the mountains, and he brusquely shook the thought away. He kicked around in the snow at the scraps of the camp. The Bosnian villagers must already have scavenged through the wreckage. He found bits of laundry, a torn flowered scarf and the shattered glass ball of a fortune teller. Two emaciated camp dogs lay dead near the fire.

Anton stiffened. He crouched against the side of the least damaged wagon. Something was moving inside. He heard the shuffling sound a small animal might make. Perhaps a dog? The entrance steps were broken off at the end of the vardo where it had settled on the ground near the damaged axle. He bent down and stared up into the darkness of the interior. Nothing. Then he heard a sneeze from inside the wagon.

"Come out," Anton called in Romany, the second language of his youth. "I am a friend. Come out." He stepped back, his rifle ready but not raised.

A boy crawled out of the narrow damaged doorway. He stood up and faced Anton with a small knife in his hand.

The child was perhaps ten or eleven, Rider reckoned, with the long curly hair, dark skin and black eyes of the eastern Gypsies. He was thin and hollow-cheeked, dressed in tall worn black boots, baggy trousers and a thick black wool coat that was too large for him. A dirty red scarf was knotted at his throat, like Anton's own diklo.

"What is your name, boy?" Anton asked, wishing he still had a bit of meat to give the lad.

"Ricardo," the boy replied sullenly

"I am Anton." Rider slung his rifle over one shoulder. "Put away the choori, boy, and tell me what happened here."

The child's voice was numb and hollow as he spoke.

"Two days ago the Germans came and took everyone to the concentration camp, down the river at Jasenovac. Then they burned the wagons." The boy coughed until he spat. "I was in the hills checking the traps when I heard shooting and saw the smoke."

"What did the villagers do, the Bosnians?" Anton put a hand on the boy's shoulder and felt the child shiver. His nose was running. His eyes were old, above dark circles.

"They stayed in their houses," the boy said. "The villagers and the Germans leave each other alone. The Ustashi were only after us, the Gypsies," he explained. "We always traded with the village. Our fresh meat and fish for their coffee and sugar and pears. My uncle used to sharpen their knives."

Rider took that as a good sign. "Will they take care of you, Ricardo?"

"If I can give them something. Here everyone is always hungry. Do you have any food?"

Anton beckoned him with his hand. "Come hunt with me. Then we will bring some food to the village."

Ricardo proved himself a Gypsy. He kept his nose on the boar tracks like a hunting dog. In an hour he pointed up a rocky hillside. Five pigs were climbing towards a cluster of low bushes spotted with dark red berries. Anton shouldered the Enfield and fired once. The big boar snorted and fell, rolling down the slope, leaving a trail of bloody snow. With shrill squeals, his family scattered into the bushes above him.

Anton sat amidst the plum trees and watched the boy gut and clean the pig. Something over one hundred pounds, he reckoned. From time to time he scanned the village with his telescope. When Ricardo was finished, Rider slung the boar across his shoulders. "Come on." He walked down to the village square with the rifle in one hand and the boy beside him carrying his skis.

Reaching the village well, Anton leaned the rifle against its stone wall and lowered a bucket on a rope. It rested at the bottom on a covering of ice. He raised the bucket and dropped it sharply. The ice broke and the bucket filled with water.

"Hold out your hands, boy." First he poured water over Ricardo's bloody hands and rubbed them clean between his own. Then he loosened the boy's filthy diklo and rinsed out the scarf.

Two men emerged from nearby houses, then a woman in thick black robes.

"Good morning," said Anton in the Serbo-Croat that Nada had taught him.

"Who are you?" the older bearded man asked while the other looked at the heavy boar and conferred with the woman. "This is not your boy."

"He is a friend. So am I. Would you like to share our pig with us?" At another time these Muslim villagers might not eat the boar, but they seemed thin and haggard. "Have you bread?"

"Bread is all we have. The German soldiers took our sheep and goats, even our last chickens."

The woman gestured towards the nearest stone house. Anton lifted the pig and followed her. Soon men and women emerged from other dwellings.

The bearded man built up a fire from low coals. The younger man moved a chess board from a table near the fire. The woman set a knife and a thick dark loaf on the table. While the ribs and chops cooked on an iron spit, they shared the crusty dark bread. After a time, the crisp scent of roasting pork began to spread from the fire.

Ricardo wiped his nose on his sleeve and devoured the bread as if he had never eaten before. When he tried to use his bloody knife, Anton took it from him, cleaned it and sharpened it against his own choori, edge to edge, making the blades sing, as the Romanies liked to say. The Bosnians pressed the last of the bread on their guests, though Anton was certain the three were hungry themselves.

A large empty sack lay crumpled in a corner by the fireplace. The woman turned it upside down over the table and shook it out. A few dark beans and some coffee dust settled on the table. Her husband continued to nurse the fire and turn the spit. The woman opened the cylinder of an ancient brass coffee grinder and gathered the coffee into it before closing it and turning the long curved handle. The instrument reminded Anton of his first meeting with Yanko and Nada.

Soon the odors of roasting pig and coffee filled the room. Anton took the opportunity to wash and cover the inflamed flesh wound at his waist.

He wrung out Ricardo's kerchief and spread it by the fire to dry. When the meat was ready, the elderly man opened the door to the house. The entire village seemed to have gathered outside. Two young girls stared at Ricardo as people pressed into the house, some carrying bottles of the village's pear and plum brandies.

Anton Rider was relieved that Bosnia's Muslims drank and ate like Christians. After giving the old man a gold sovereign to look after the boy and a couple of Maria Theresa silver dollars to his daughter and Ricardo, he left the lad with the Muslim family, comfortable that Ricardo would be accepted by them now.

"Keep your diklo clean, Ricardo," he said, kneeling and knotting the red scarf around the boy's neck, squeezing his thin arm. "And your choori sharp."

He saw his own youth in the boy's lonely eyes.

Chapter Twenty-Six

Her grandson was everything she could have hoped for, everything his father would have wished for, thought Gwenn Rider as she opened the door of the hall closet, trying not to be overwhelmed by sentiment. The boy had Anton's sky-blue eyes, the perfect little feet and hands that were so magical in babies, a delicious behind, and the smooth olive skin of the Alavedos. She loved the way he smelled when she tickled him with her nose.

Already exhausted from the hospital, Gwenn began removing suitcases from the crowded closet, hoping she could make a start before Alistair came home.

Saffron and baby Wellie were now staying at Olivio's before they found a place of their own. Cairo was chock-a-block, but she knew the little man would find a way. Gwenn was welcome to stay as well, the dwarf had repeated yesterday. His guest house was hers, but she felt conflicted, not certain she was ready for such a final break with Alistair. On the other hand, this could be the right time to do it, since they were moving anyway. Things were not perfect between them now, but she was tired of always starting over.

The one thing she found impossible was Alistair's occasional bursts of anger. And he seemed so much more distant now, so secretive, though perhaps that was just his job. Of course, everything was more difficult, more intense, during the war. And after all, she thought, the war was not Alistair's fault. Perhaps she should give their relationship a better chance.

This war, of course, was changing all of them, even she herself. Gwenn knew the loss of Wellie had darkened her own spirit to the bone, had made her more irritable and withdrawn, much less affectionate.

Trying to be fair, to understand, she considered again what the war seemed to be doing to Alistair. He was far less the sensitive intellectual man she had first met and respected and enjoyed. More on edge, even his language a bit coarser, short tempered, less confident, perhaps due to the apparent decline in his financial situation, which he never acknowledged but which she detected in the details of each day. From dining and tipping to his annoyance when she bought new flowers instead of cutting and freshening yesterday's. All this seemed to make him drink more, as indeed most men were doing now. And the drink led to his bouts of anger, and once or twice to roughness. That, she could not tolerate.

Moving was always hell, Gwenn thought as she drew an old belted suitcase from the closet. If there were any problems in a relationship, it always made them worse. She walked down the narrow hall to the bedroom and dusted off the case before setting it on the bed.

Even the broad bureau had become a battlefield with Alistair. Her photos of Wellington and Denby as schoolboys and in uniform always seemed crowded to the side by his silver-backed hairbrushes and shoe-horn and by ridiculous pictures of him and Blunt in their robes at Cambridge, and now by his rolled-up excavation drawings of the new dig that the two were considering up the Nile past Abu Simbel. He had been very hush-hush about that, it occurred to her.

Gwenn walked into the sitting room and looked at everything that she had to pack or throw away. At least in the promised new flat there would be space for Alistair's books and she would finally have a small room of her own. That should make things better.

She heard a key click in the lock and felt a gust of musty air as the front door opened. Her stomach tightened.

"Darling?" Treitel called. "Gwenn, are you home?"

"Just sorting out a few things." She offered him a cheek. His handsome face looked lined and tired. "Cup of tea?"

"Whisky, I think. Care for anything?" He lifted a bottle and watched her as she piled up more books and papers on one corner of the desk.

"Please don't touch those things," he instructed sharply, smoothing back his hair with both hands.

"Just trying to get started. You haven't been helping and there's so much to do before we move." Gwenn continued to stack some folders. She was used to running a surgery under battlefield conditions and was damned if she would be bossed about in her own flat even if he was paying for everything.

"Leave those things alone." Alistair pointed a forefinger at her. "I've told you before not to fuss with my papers."

"Don't we have to move next Friday?" she persisted.

"Probably, most likely," Treitel said after a brief hesitation. "But you know I'll look after my own books and papers." He set down his glass and poured more whisky.

He's drinking earlier and earlier, she thought. "You forgot to leave the money for the maid again. It's two weeks now," she said. A shadow crossed his face, putting a doubt in her mind. "Is the new flat ready?"

"Actually, not just yet. They're haggling a bit about the price."

His note of uncertainty disturbed her. "I thought you said it was all settled."

"So it was, mostly. But every day someone offers a better price. It's even worse now that the bloody Yanks are here. They've all got too much money." He took a sip from his glass, then gave the news. "We'll have to spend a month or two in an hotel, I'm afraid, just until things get sorted out."

"An hotel?" She bridled at the notion. "You know I hate hotels, and all the decent ones are full up with the war."

"We'll find something. Perhaps the Bristol or the Hôtel du Nord."

"I don't know, Alistair," she said, discouraged. "Maybe I'll stay at Olivio's for a bit with Saffron and the baby."

"The devil you will, darling!" he cried. "That little toad is the scandal of Cairo. I won't hear of it."

"Olivio Alavedo is my friend. I won't have you speak of him like that," she said hotly, her face red. "And haven't you had enough to drink, Alistair? We are due at dinner in an hour."

"I tell you we are moving to an hotel. I will not have you sponging off that disgusting midget the way your husband does." He strode across the room, glass in hand, ready for a row. "Who would ever marry into such a family? It's shameful enough that the Riders can't even look after their own children."

Gwenn turned and slapped Treitel's face. His glass fell and broke at his feet.

"How dare you!" He pushed Gwenn hard between her breasts with the stiff fingers of one hand. "Who do you think you are? Isn't that darling dark grandson of yours a little bastard?"

She would not stand for such insults. "They weren't married because Wellington was fighting in the desert." She raised her chin and tried to push away his arm. "You yourself are nothing but a coward, ducking all the fighting and playing about and drinking in Cairo."

"The hell you say!" Treitel shoved her against the desk with both hands.

"Anton Rider is twice the man you could ever be. You and that ghastly Blunt."

Alistair Treitel slapped her across the face.

Gwenn staggered back, her lip split and bleeding. "Hitting a woman? What kind of man are you?"

Treitel swung at her again, but she fell back, avoiding the blow and running down the hall towards the door.

***

Later that morning, after leaving Ricardo and the Bosnian village, Anton pressed on. Now that he was separated from the Partisans, he wished to escape Jugoslavia as soon as possible and rejoin his unit in Egypt. But a disturbing sight made him stop.

A dozen figures hung from trees across the river. All were men, most barefoot and half-naked. The body of one, a Gypsy, Anton guessed by its scarf, hung by its feet, not its neck. Several swung from a large oak on the riverbank, as if the Ustashi and the Germans had decorated the tree for Christmas. Crows flapped and hopped in the branches of the trees, occasionally pecking at the eyes of the dead.

A plowed strip of open land began just behind the trees and led to a wire fence at the crest of a hill behind the river. Anton could see the tops of four watchtowers that rose on the far side of the hill. A patrol of black-uniformed Ustashi walked along the cleared strip with two dogs straining at their leathers.

When they had passed, Anton rose and walked through the forest for another two miles or so. Then he settled behind the fork of an oak close to the river. He felt strong again, with bread, plum brandy and pork chops in his pack.

Rider focused his scope on the railroad siding across the river. A water tower and a coal bunker came into his round view. A man in a cap appeared on a bicycle and adjusted the long lever of a switching track before leaning against the water tower and smoking a pipe. The Bosnian family had told Rider that most of the prisoners came by rail.

Anton stood and walked further along the river before sitting and nibbling a bit of bread. The meat would last better in the cold. Soon he found himself drifting off into sleep.

An owl hooted close behind him as he woke. The forest around him smelled of damp rot. Dusk had fallen while he slept. A thin moon rose and gave a rippling brightness to the surface of the river. At first Anton thought he saw a log or large tree stump floating down the Drina between the patchy bits of ice that moved on the water. When he stared through the darkness, though, he discerned a small boat with branches laid across its bow and stern. Three men were crouched in the center of the vessel. They pulled in the oars and drew the boat into the shore directly across from Rider. He tried to follow them with his telescope. When he caught one in the lens, he made out some shadowy detail, but it was difficult to see in the near darkness.

One man held the boat to the shore while the others lifted out a shovel and two packages and carried them to the railroad track. The man by the boat had a weapon slung across his back.

Saboteurs, reckoned Rider, whether Partisan or Royalist, he could not guess, though from his briefings he knew Mihajlovic's Royalists had been active in attacking the rail lines. They were trying to please their British suppliers by inhibiting the movement of Italian and German units from front to front.

Anton could not make out exactly what the men were doing at the rail line, but after an hour they returned to the boat and one of them climbed in. The other knelt behind a tree with what Anton took to be a detonator. The two men in the boat covered themselves with branches.

When morning finally came, a light snow began to fall. A column of open trucks pulled up to the railroad siding then turned around to face back down the road. Ustashi troopers with rifles and light machine guns jumped down from the cabs of the vehicles, sharing cigarettes and swinging their arms against the cold.

An hour later, a battered Mercedes command car pulled up beside the lead truck. Anton heard the whistle of a distant locomotive blast twice. A German driver opened the rear door of the Mercedes. Two men stepped down, a Ustashi officer and a German colonel in a long black leather coat and the death's head cap badge of the Waffen SS.

As Rider checked his rifle and remounted the scope, the whistle blasted again. Twice he estimated the range: one hundred and sixty yards to the staff car. Easy enough shooting, even with a bit of snow and wind, except for keeping the telescopic sight clean. One hundred or a bit less to the boat, but with brush blocking a clear shot. He watched the north wind lifting sheets of snow and settled behind the oak to wait. This might be his chance to do something for the Gypsies. Rider removed the scope and prepared to shoot the way he preferred, over open sights.

Then he heard the engine of the locomotive. A line of dark smoke rose above the trees on the other side of the Drina. An old locomotive with a tall chimney and a wide cow catcher appeared on the track close to the river. It was pushing a short flatbed service car before it, standard procedure for deterring sabotage. These saboteurs, Anton was certain, would seek to destroy only the locomotive, without injuring any prisoners in the six cars that followed.

As the train approached the siding, a small explosion erupted, like a hand grenade, followed quickly by an immense fiery blast. The flatbed car and the bow of the locomotive rose heavily off the tracks. The engine and its coal car fell on their sides, plowing into the ground on the far side of the track. The freight car immediately behind them was pulled off the rails and rolled onto one side. Its sliding doors burst open from the impact. Men and women clambered through the opening. Some helped each other. Others ran into the forest on their own. The five cars that followed, two closed freight cars and three cattle cars with open wooden slats, remained on the track. Anton saw hands and arms reaching out between the boards as prisoners sought to break open the sides of the cars.

The engineer and fireman had been thrown from the locomotive and were scrambling to get clear of the red coals that had been flung from the firebox. The Ustashi guards at the siding ran down the track towards the open cars. The German colonel and the Ustashi officer hurried after them.

Anton removed the glove from his right hand and flexed his fingers.

Doors burst open in another closed car. Prisoners broke through the slats of the cattle cars and began jumping down. Gesturing at them to remain, the Ustashi started firing at the fugitives. In the snow and chaos Anton could not tell how many of the prisoners were Gypsies, though by their scarves and boots he guessed that many were.

The saboteur by the detonator appeared to be wounded. One man, heavily bearded, ran from the boat to help him. A Ustashi trooper knelt by the stream bank and aimed his rifle at the two struggling men. Anton fired once. The Ustashi dropped his weapon and collapsed into the river.

In the meantime, several Ustashi surrounded the last rail car. Both sides of the car had been broken open. Prisoners were running free in all directions. The soldiers fired into the running men and women. Scattered bodies fell. Others dragged themselves away or limped wounded into the forest.

Working methodically, shooting swiftly over iron sights, Anton killed one Ustashi, then another. He continued picking them off with careful shots, as if trying to bring down a herd of Cape buffalo one by one. This was what he knew how to do.

Then he saw the Ustashi officer directing his men to form a cordon around the railroad cars. The SS colonel stood on the far side of the officer, firing his Luger with his shooting arm extended straight before him. Rider steadied the Enfield against the side of the oak and squeezed the trigger. The Ustashi gripped his belly with both hands and fell on his face.

The German colonel looked around, crouching, apparently now aware that someone was shooting from across the river. He returned his Luger to its holster and instead lifted the machine pistol of the fallen Ustashi. In a burst he cut down two prisoners who were running towards the forest hand-in-hand. The wounded man rose and lifted the woman across his arms. The German fired again. The man collapsed before reaching the forest.

Controlling his anger, steadying himself, Rider fired at the SS colonel. The officer dropped his weapon with a lurch and fell forward. He faced Anton as he tried to rise. Rider killed him with a second shot to the chest. He paused to reload, confident that most of the Ustashi were still unaware they were being attacked from across the river. He had not killed the German general Treitel had mentioned in Cairo, but he reckoned a Nazi colonel from the death camp was close enough.

Now the snow was driving hard, whipping down in a fierce wind from the mountains. The two saboteurs, one wounded, had almost made their way back to the boat when several Ustashi ran to cut them off. Their companion waited for the saboteurs on the bank, holding the boat by a rope with an oar in his other hand.

Anton left the oak and knelt by his side of the river for a closer shot in the thickening snow. When one of the Ustashi paused to aim his rifle, Anton shot the man in the throat. The standing boatman stared across the river. Another Ustashi fired at the boatman before Anton could shoot again. The saboteur fell on his face, dropping the oar into the river but with the rope still pinned under his body when his friends reached him. The two struggled into the boat and cast off, guiding the vessel across the Drina with the remaining oar.

Turning his attention back to the siding, Anton picked off one more guard and the driver of the staff car. The remaining Ustashi gathered what prisoners they could into the trucks. Rider killed one driver and wounded another as they climbed into their cabs. One lorry appeared to have been taken over by prisoners who had collected weapons from the fallen guards.

Finally Anton could barely see across the river. He slung his rifle and started to climb back up the hill to shelter under the ledge where he had left his skis. He knew he had been lucky to remain undetected for so long. It was time to try to make his way out of Jugoslavia. He recalled the advice his squadron of the LRDG had received in training: "Never try to win the war on your own."

Just then he looked back at the river and saw that the boat had made it ashore with two men on board. Royalists, he guessed, by the beards. It was almost impossible to see across the water. Slipping in the snow, Anton grabbed the branch of a tree to steady himself as he hurried down to the riverbank.

The bearded saboteur secured the boat to the shore as Rider came towards him.

"I am English. A friend," Anton yelled through the wind and snow, confident the man was aware he had been firing against the Germans and Ustashi.

"*Pomozi mi!*" the boatman hollered back, bending over his wounded companion. "Help me!"

Anton leaned his rifle against a bush and helped lift the twitching figure from the boat. The two lay the groaning man on his back beneath a birch.

"*Huala.* Thank you. I am Zoran," said the short thick-set saboteur. "Did you do all that shooting? I thought there must be several men." Zoran removed his gloves to unbutton his companion's rough jacket. "We are with Mihalovic." The beards of both Jugoslavs were white with frost and snow.

As Anton and Zoran examined the wound, the man opened his eyes and pressed his fist against his mouth to choke back his cries. Could be worse, thought Rider. Wounded in the side with the bottom rib or two smashed at the outer edges. No blood bubbling on his lips, so the wound and the rib fragments probably had missed his lungs. The problem would be fragments of cloth and bone in the wound, and infection.

Anton folded his silk jump scarf and pressed it against the wound as Zoran bound the makeshift packing in place with a length of detonating wire from the boat. Then Zoran stood and squinted up the hill and along the riverbank.

"Nije dobro!" He shook his head. "No good. Marko will bleed if we carry him. We will take him down river in the boat while it snows."

Just as well, thought Anton. He was not looking forward to carrying a wounded man through the forest. He recovered his skis and rifle while Zoran swept the remains of the brush from the boat. Climbing on board, Rider helped Zoran set Marko against the bow with his head resting against the coil of detonating wire.

Zoran pushed off with the oar, and the boat glided into the river. The water was swift but smooth. A froth of snow covered its deep green. Relaxing at last, Anton tasted the flakes on his tongue as the wind-blown snow stung his eyes. It was like sailing through a frozen cloud.

Anton hunched his shoulders and raised his collar, smelling the brisk freshness of the air. He was learning to appreciate the rigors of a different landscape. The cold air and snow brought memories of Nada and the wintry warmth they had found. He knew their isolation had given them a setting that balanced what they could give to each other for a time, as if they required no past or future. He touched the cord of the edelweiss badge that still hung around his neck. Neither Cairo nor Croatia would have suited both of them for long. But what would he give for one more evening with Nada by the fire, to look into her eyes again? To feel the touch of her hand on his face? He felt tears freeze to his cheeks in the horizontal flight of the snow.

Chapter Twenty-Seven

The four armored cars of Denby's troop fanned out as they entered the broad valley. Instead of Eighth Army khaki, the vehicles had now acquired the grey tones of the landscape. The desert of Egypt and Libya had been replaced by the hills and mountains, valleys and passes of Tunisia.

With a hundred and fifty yards separating each vehicle, the Hussars were able to scan a broad sweep of terrain and were less exposed to air attack by the Stukas of the Luftwaffe. Better yet, no crew had to eat the dust of the car ahead. But the six troops of two squadrons manned a reconnaissance line fifteen miles across. The Cherry Pickers of the armored division were spread too thin and Denby was glad to have these American Rangers share the line despite their inexperience.

This land had a way of preserving some traces of man and of blowing others away as if nothing had passed, as if humanity itself could leave no mark. The hills, the wind, the moving sand, the disposition of the underlying crusts and layers of the Maghreb seemed to make choices of their own. Roman stones, deep desert wells, the tracks of chariots and camels and tanks, could either vanish or be preserved forever.

The rocky ground was covered with uneven coats of sand and desert dust. Dry shrubs and thorny bushes with small silvery leaves were clustered low on the ground, as if hunkering down, waiting for the cold and rainfall that came to Tunisia this time of year. Stubby cactus grew here and there. Graham had chopped one open earlier with his bayonet to discover the pods of cool filmy moisture gathered inside.

Denby's lighter rear-engine vehicle was scouting on the right wing, running close to the splintery rocky ridge that extended along the edge of the valley to the north. He stood beside the driver of the Dingo gripping the edge of the forward armored panel and squinting ahead through his desert goggles. His field glasses swung and knocked against his chest. He raised his collar against the sharp morning wind. Like an old hand of the Rommel's Afrika Korps, Lieutenant Rider had learned to wear trousers rather than shorts and long socks.

Occasionally they crossed the tracks of a lorry, or even those of a line of camels or a small herd of sheep. Studying the tracks reminded Denby of early mornings alone with his father in the bush. The old hunter had taught him to distinguish the spoor of oryx and kudu, klip-springer and gerenuk, to follow one animal across dusty red-tinted scrub, or over rocky outcroppings by the tiniest of scratches. "Is that elephant male or female?" his father would ask quietly, kneeling by the trail in a mopane forest, his fingertips gently tracing the footprint the way an archeologist might the inscription on a monument. "How old is he, Denby? How much ivory is he carrying?"

Denby Rider worried about the old boy, wherever he was. His father had always seemed so invulnerable, enduring, but by now Denby knew better. His brother, Wellie, had seemed much the same.

The driver slowed whenever they saw signs of military vehicles, either the deep tracks left by many in column, or the broad well-preserved prints of tanks or half-tracks. But every set of prints was already layered with desert dust. No tracks were fresh.

After two hours Denby felt groggy as he swayed back and forth as the light scout car bounced over the hard bumpy ground. A hawk circled high above the hillside to his right. He followed its flight, hoping to see the bird fold its wings and dive for some snake or rodent. When he looked back down, he spotted something on the open ground that separated his vehicle from the next.

"Stop the car!" hollered Denby Rider. He leaned forward and banged the hot dusty hood with the side of one fist. As the driver braked, Denby jumped down. The fresh tracks of wheeled vehicles stood out boldly, barely covered by sand and dust. But under them, deep and new as well, were jagged tread marks, sharp, deeper and broader than any he had ever seen before. Denby knelt as the driver joined him. He had never expected tank treads so wide. He measured them twice against the twelve-inch length of his own boot. Twenty-eight inches, at least.

"Tigers," said Denby, tracing the tracks with his fingers. It was like finding the sign of a giant tusker in the drying mud of a water hole, crushing out the marks and droppings of every other beast under one unmistakable print. "And no more than one day old."

The driver ran back to the scout car and flicked his lights. The three Humber armored cars and a Ranger jeep turned back towards them.

In minutes all five vehicles were in V-formation. Denby's Daimler led, moving as fast as possible without losing the trail. Whenever they approached a corner in the valley wall, or an eminence that might expose them, they slowed and advanced with care. No one thought of stopping for the customary morning brew-up.

When they came to a tall hill with a wedge-shaped gash near its crown, the Hussar captain in the armored car behind signaled and passed the Dingo. Entering the cut in the hillside, the cars drew up together near some thick bushes. The wireless operator in the captain's Humber tinkered with the whip aerial and put on his headphones as he prepared to test his set.

"Let's go for a climb, Rider, while the chaps top up the petrol tanks and take a wee."

The captain strode swiftly up the hill with his map case in one hand and field glasses in the other, cursing when the acacia thorns tore his bare legs. When he and Denby reached the top, they found the Ranger captain already seated on a rock cleaning his binoculars.

279

The three officers stared down at the broad grey valley that extended to the west and north. The village of Sidi Bou Zid was to their right. The Dorsal mountains and Kasserine were directly before them. A long column of dust rose at the far end of the valley. The British officers knelt and adjusted their field glasses.

"By God, it's them," said the Hussar captain, opening his leather compass case. "Tigers, gentlemen. The finest tanks in the world. Followed by lorries and tankers to cover their tracks. Look at those long barrels. Eighty-eights." He spread a map on a flat rock. "You count 'em, Rider, while I work out their bearing with the map." The captain opened the lid of the compass and set the instrument on top of the map.

"I make it at least five Tigers, sir, and a lot of lighter stuff, mostly new Mark IVs, and several of our captured Valentines, repainted with German markings."

"Right you are, Lieutenant. Let's nip down to the radio. Then we'll try to keep an eye on them until the RAF joins the hunt."

"I'm going to collect my men and try to radio our First Armored Division," said Captain Corrigan easily. "Time they fired a few shots."

The Cherry Pickers were following the Tigers by their dust. The Panzers and their supporting vehicles left a heavy column of airborne sand and haze as the four armored vehicles of the 11th Hussars trailed them at a distance of five or six miles. The captain's Humber led the others.

Denby was not surprised when three dots appeared in the sky above the Panzers, then three more. The tanks would need air cover. During the first two years of the war in North Africa, the campaign had been measured in tank kills. With half of Axis supply ships often sunk while crossing the Med, the Afrika Korps was always short of armor and petrol. The Luftwaffe had to escort the Panzers into battle, especially the precious Tigers diverted to Africa from the Eastern Front. Both sides understood that the new armor represented Hitler's last throw in Africa, Germany's final chance not to lose the Mediterranean and to protect her southern flank.

Fighters, Denby hoped, squinting skyward, perhaps ME 109's, rather than dive bombers. Soon he would be able to make a more precise assessment. The Stukas were easy to recognize by their angled wings and fixed landing wheels.

As a precaution, the four cars spread out more widely. Every man knew the drill. Disperse, then leave the vehicles if more than one aircraft appeared. If it was a single plane, man the guns and try to bring it down.

The Stukas began diving for the British armored cars.

The four cars halted and the crews scrambled out. Most of the men flattened themselves near the thin cover of desert rocks or brush. A few, including Denby, hunkered beneath their vehicles. Only one man stayed aboard and trained a mounted Bren gun at the sky. Graham Walker, trying for his second kill.

Denby lay on his belly and heard the shrill sirens as the Stukas dived. He knew each Junker dive bomber carried up to eight five-hundred-pound bombs and mounted two machine guns under the wings. If one survived the bombs, he should have a fair chance against the guns, unless they caught the petrol tank or the jerry cans carried on the sides of each vehicle.

Denby recognized the welcome chatter of the single Bren as Walker began firing.

He heard bombs burst nearby, then a massive explosion. He saw a black cloud billow out across the desert and smelled the burning oil. A Humber must have been hit. Denby saw a figure running towards him through the smoke, his uniform and hair on fire. He had to help the man.

First Denby rolled to the left edge of the Dingo. He was just standing up when an immense blast exploded near the other side of his scout car.

The right wheels rose from the ground then dropped back and bounced. Shards of metal pinged off the car. The crust of the desert seemed to rise and cover him. Then he heard and saw nothing.

When he opened his eyes, Graham Walker was kneeling beside him.

The trooper squeezed his shoulders as Denby sat up and shook his head. He could not hear a word the Scot was saying. He closed his eyes and covered both ears with his hands. He shook his head again. There seemed to be no wound and only a bit of blood on the right side of his neck below his ear.

"I can't hear you," Denby yelled. "I can't hear anything."

Walker helped him to stand, then pointed to his own Humber, the only vehicle that appeared undamaged. Another Humber lay on its side. The third, the captain's, was still blazing. A smoldering figure lay against some shrubs nearby. Three other Hussars had survived the attack. One was sitting on a rock with his head between his hands and his shirt off while another man bandaged his shoulder.

Denby was the only surviving officer.

"I'll help the others, Walker," he said loudly, collecting himself. "You make sure your car's ready to go. Check the radio. Collect petrol and water from the Dingo and the other Humber." He stared towards the end of the long valley. A column of dust was settling in the distance. "We have to get back on their trail. Looks like the Fritzes are headed for Kasserine Pass to cut through the Dorsals." He paused to consider what this meant. "Then they could either bust through Thala and cut off the Eighth Army in northern Tunisia, or destroy the Allied supply hub at Taberna and sweep on into Algeria. Either way, Kasserine has to be the first stop."

Denby joined the other Hussars as they carefully lifted six bodies and lay them in a tight orderly line on the desert floor, shoulder to shoulder. Two were charred and blistered as if roasted in an oven. Sobbing, the wounded man sat beside one of the dark figures, then leaned over and hugged the blackened body. The soldiers went through each man's pockets and collected the identification chains that hung around their necks.

Denby knelt for a moment of silence. He helped the men gather rocks and pile them neatly over the six figures. He could not hear what the others said, or the sound as he set down each stone. The Ranger jeeps drew up as they worked. Captain Corrigan and the other Americans jumped down and helped with the burial rocks.

Finally the five Hussars stood by the rocky mound, their heads bowed. The Rangers stood facing them on the other side of the graves. Walker looked at Denby and nodded.

"The Lord is my shepherd," said Lieutenant Rider in a loud clear voice. "Therefor can I lack nothing." He glanced up at the other men as he sought to recall the rest of the 23rd Psalm.

"Yea, though I walk through the valley of the shadow of death, I will fear no evil," Denby continued after a moment as he watched the lips of one of the Americans. "But thy loving kindness and mercy shall follow me all the days of my life; and I will dwell in the house of the Lord for ever."

Chapter Twenty-Eight

The killing had not gone as smoothly as one might have wished, thought Alistair Treitel, but fortunately the Cairo police had a full menu. Even in peacetime, the biggest city in Africa was a carnival of crime. Unless the British or the Palace, the Egyptian administration or the military, had some special interest in a matter, conventional crime and ordinary criminals were of little concern, like rats in a dark alley or vermin beneath a damp drain. Working under a British superintendent, Egypt's Special Police were now preoccupied with espionage and security. Of what consequence was the loss of one petty forger in the *souk*?

Even the Department of Antiquities was distracted by the war. There would never be a better time to make off with some of the new uncatalogued treasures. How else to combine one's scholarship with profit? At the Cairo Museum itself, the halls were filled with sandbags and packing cases. Most of the finest vitrines were already empty. Who knew what was really in each crate?

The new dig at Wadi Halfa was a bit out of the way, two days' journey up the Nile into Upper Egypt, past Abu Simbel, near the border with the Anglo-Egyptian Sudan. But the farther away from the Cairo authorities the better. In the end, it might be best to ship a few valuable cases down to Khartoum instead of back to Cairo.

Treitel looked down at his freshly-cleaned jacket with a frown. Blunt's violent zeal had spoiled his new linen suit. Wrinkles and the odd wine stain were one thing. Dried blood was another. The linen itself had proven easier to clean than the fine silk lining that he favored. Like the hands of Lady Macbeth, this jacket would never again be quite clean.

The Don shrugged and picked up the day's stack of ciphers. These damned Jugoslavs were getting greedy. Medicine and explosives, weapons and radios, there was no end to their urgent requests. Now that Tito's Partisans had better radios and even occasional landing fields for light aircraft, the game was getting trickier. Recently the SOE in Alexandria had arranged for several political officers to be flown in to both Mihajlovic and the Partisans, and for a few senior wounded Jugoslavs or British agents to be flown out. He and Blunt were doing all they could to favor the Reds, taking advantage of the bickering and confusion at the higher levels of the intelligence and secret services.

With the time almost at hand to extract Captain Rider from Jugoslavia, they would do what was necessary to extend his service in the Balkans.

Occasionally it was possible to divert some of the Mihajlovic supplies into the contraband pool near Cairo, thus both weakening the Jugoslav Royalists and gaining a few badly-needed quid for Blunt and himself.

Treitel frowned as he thought about Gwenn. He enjoyed her maturing beauty, even her qualities of purpose and intelligence, but her exaggerated sense of independence and high standards, and, above all, her tedious moralizing, made her an overly complicated companion. Even worse, he suspected that at bottom Gwenn still loved her hopeless husband. Of course, she was even more difficult since she had moved out. Cold angry notes demanding the return of her "things," particularly the framed photographs of her boys. No doubt that revolting pygmy was spoiling her.

This morning, the day before he was obliged to abandon the flat, he must drop by and make certain he had collected all of his own kit.

At the apartment Treitel spread the archeological map and sketches of the new dig across the dining room table, holding down the curling edges with four of Gwenn's medical texts. He could see Algernon's

Bartle Bull

finger marks all over the map as well as a few notes and several cigarette burns. Everything else of his had been packed and sent off to the Bristol. Now it was time to find another way to make a few guineas.

He heard Blunt grunting from the bedroom. Drink always made the old boy even noisier. He could smell Fishhead from the hallway. He must be snout-down in Gwenn's favorite small silky pillows, snuffling and drooling on the lace, stinking of whisky.

Algie was always a useful partner, however, from antiquities and intelligence to cards and the rougher bits of everything. Even at the dig, Algernon was comfortable working in the deep narrow airless passages that intimidated Treitel with claustrophobia. But Alistair was growing concerned that Blunt's violent side was getting out of hand, as if the war had raised the standard of what was permissible, as indeed it had in everything from commerce to romance.

A double knock intruded from the front door. Treitel hastily rolled up the drawings and slipped them into a cardboard tube. The knocks came again. Who could this be? They were too loud for Gwenn, and she still had a key. He had been hoping that her need to collect her things would give him one more chance to reason with her.

He opened the door. "Yes?"

"Excuse me, sir," said a slender olive-skinned man in a white gallabiyya and turban. He held a door key in his right hand. Behind him stood a second native carrying two large leather suitcases belted with heavy straps. With a cap, a dark jacket, jodhpurs and gloves, no doubt this was a driver acting as a porter. Two more bags rested on the floor behind the men.

"We are here to collect Mrs. Rider's belongings."

"This is not a good time for it," Treitel said, annoyed Gwenn had not come herself. "She should have let me know." He recognized the first man, some sort of jumped-up servant from the Cataract Café, a mixed-blood Goan, like the wretched dwarf himself. Sustek, was it? Who did these people think they were, calling unannounced?

"I regret, sir, but I must observe my instructions." The second man tried to slip down the side of the corridor as the majordomo continued.

"I believe neither the flat nor these possessions are yours, sir. I understand your arrangement here terminates tomorrow, so these things must be collected now before the new tenant arrives."

"How dare you?" said Treitel as the driver pushed his way past. "Algie! Blunt! Wake up!" he hollered down the hall.

With surprising swiftness Algernon Blunt appeared at the end of the corridor. He seemed to fill the bedroom doorway.

"Algie, stop these men. They've broken in to pinch Gwenn's things."

"Damned cheek!" Blunt exclaimed, barefoot in his khaki shorts, his uniform shirt open and hanging out.

As the driver leaned forward to set down the cases, Blunt struck him under the jaw, nearly lifting the man from his feet.

"No!" cried Sustek, hurrying towards the driver.

Blunt met Olivio's majordomo in the center of the hall. The patch of veins on his neck stood out like a pink monogram on a white towel. Lowering his shoulders like a rugby blocker, grunting with the effort, he punched Sustek in the belly with his entire body behind the blow.

As the Goan collapsed forward, Blunt straightened and kneed him in the face.

Sustek vomited and fell against the wall. His nose was flattened against his cheek. Blood flooded his gallabiyya.

***

Perhaps he'd had a bit too much to drink this evening, thought Major Blunt, taking his ease upstairs above the Club Sheherezade. Even Suda's dancing and more personal attentions were having a difficult time getting him under way. Obligingly, she had set down her favorite *zills*, her brass finger cymbals, to free her hands for more important and intimate work.

Blunt enjoyed the atmosphere of the private room above the night-club. This sort of setting was one of the colonial amenities that made life out here tolerable. The walls and ceiling were hung with thick striped cotton gathered in the center like the tent of a bedouin chief. Worn carpets were layered one atop another. Plump brocade cushions were scattered about the floor near a low copper table and a bubbling hookah.

At least being with Suda gave him an opportunity to talk about his life and his work, the first of which no one cared about, and the second he was not allowed to speak about. Fortunately, the belly dancer seemed to understand only a few English words required by her work, and cared even less about what one of her blokes might have to say. With these people, it was like talking to a camel.

"Must be a trifle fagged out," he said, his eyes half closed as Suda massaged him with expensive patience and his favorite sticky oil. "Cleopatra's Honey," the girls called it, and maybe it was, since they always charged a few bob extra for the treatment.

"Was hard at the blasted shortwave radio all day and half the night," Blunt continued, thinking out loud, really talking to himself, while Suda tried once more to wind him up for the critical moment. Her left hand held him with a grip like a pipe fitter's wrench. The other teased his tip like a cloud of butterflies.

"Had to make certain one of our light planes from the *Ark Royal* didn't help the wrong chaps on the way into Jugoslavia, or pick up the wrong bastard for the flight home. There's one fellow over there who we want to have a nice long winter in those hellish mountains. Chap called Rider."

Suda appeared to be losing her concentration as he spoke. He opened his eyes and saw her pinch her nose as if trying to avoid his smell. Then she paused and lit a pellet of camphor incense in a small copper bowl. Angry, offended by her practice of trying to cover his natural odor with her stinking native perfumes, Blunt gripped the mouthpiece of the hookah.

"Get on with it, girl, or I'll slip this up somewhere it doesn't belong," he said, slightly dizzy from the mixture of strong tobacco, drink and some deadly weed. "What's the matter with you this evening?" He swung with his other hand, a bit harder than he intended, and smacked her glossy behind with a blow that knocked her over. "Think I'm about to pay you for nothing?"

Suda screamed as she fell against the bowl of the hookah. Knocking it over, she collapsed with her belly on the edge of the glowing fiery coals.

"Dog!" she yelled, rising instantly. A few tiny bright embers were stuck to the perspiration and oil that greased her shiny stomach. "Bastard dog!"

Suda struggled to brush off the burning embers with the hem of her veil, then with the edge of her hand. She grabbed her brocade slippers, opened the door and plunged down the narrow steep stairs to the public nightclub below. Each one of her client's words was branded in her memory.

***

A white crown of soapy foam covered Ernst von Decken's head like a chef's toque, or the fluffy top of a sack strapped to the back of a cotton picker in the Delta. A filthy blue towel draped his chest and belly.

The Italian prisoners in the nearby hospital beds chattered and stared as the gaunt dark *muzaiyin* sharpened his cutthroat razor on a wide leather strap hanging from his waist. The itinerant Egyptian barber extended the strop straight out from his belly with his left hand, drawing the long blade along it with swift strokes, edge by edge. He turned over the leather strop and drew the straight razor more gently across its smoother side.

The muzaiyin leaned over the German with the handle of the instrument bent between his fingers. He drew the razor in one long stroke from hairline to crown with a sound like a wire brush scraping rust from an ancient boiler. The barber wiped the blade on the towel and gripped his client's nose, turning the large ridged head towards him as he prepared for a second stroke.

At that moment a British medical orderly entered the prisoners' ward with a clipboard in one hand.

The barber shaved in a straight stroke from above one ear to the back of von Decken's head.

"Beds number eleven, seventeen, twenty-one, twenty-eight, twenty-nine and thirty-six," called out the orderly at the end of the prisoners' ward, reading from his clipboard in a cockney accent. "Hospital days are over for you lot. It's back to the prisoner-of-war camps. No more tea and cookies."

"*Impossibile! Madre di Dio!*" cried out several Italian voices, each one demanding more days of care. "*No! No, e no!*"

"We need the beds," answered the orderly before calling out the numbers once again. "More of you wounded Huns and Eyeties dropping in every day. Get your filthy kit together and jump up. We have to boil your bedding. Hop to it! Up and out."

From the far end of the ward there was a crack-crack like gunshots as Kapitan von Decken banged his cane against the metal foot rail of bed number 28.

"Attention!" cried the German prisoner, pushing aside the barber. "*Achtung*! This is an outrage. I require an operation. I have already lost one leg. Where is the Red Cross inspector? What of the Geneva Convention?"

The orderly walked down between the beds to number 28.

"We need your bed, Captain. This is a ward for prisoners with serious military wounds, not for babying old injuries. You can have that missing leg of yours fussed over in Baden-Baden when this show is done." He looked down at the two straw-wrapped empties on von Decken's bedside table. "And we're not running a pub for drunken Jerries."

Dr. Hänger appeared at the head of the ward. A stethoscope hung around his neck. An elderly nurse walked behind him. He examined the patient in the first bed and dictated notes to the nurse.

"Doktor! Doktor Hänger! *Bitte sehr!*" roared von Decken, wiping his half-shaved head with the soiled towel. "*Was is das?* I am a German officer, not a peasant from Calabria! These idiots are trying to send me to a prisoners' cage to die in the desert. It is against the Geneva rules. It is your duty to see I receive the care that I require."

The physician ignored the hollering and continued slowly down the ward. He passed by the patients who had been ordered to leave and dictated instructions to the nurse regarding each of the others.

"Ah, Kapitan von Decken," he said finally. "Is there something you require before you leave for the camp?"

Then Dr. Hänger dismissed the nurse and conversed quietly with von Decken. The grizzled head of the German officer bore two bare stripes like harvested lanes in a wheat field.

***

It was a very different sort of camp. Instead of Tito and Stalin, the heroes were Mihalovic and King Peter II of pre-war Jugoslavia. Rather than political lectures from the commissars, a grey-bearded priest from the cathedral in Sarajevo conducted twice-daily services. Only the cold mountains and the plum brandy were the same.

Anton Rider made a point of establishing friendship with the radio crew. Each morning and evening at the scheduled time, which rotated twice daily in half-hour cycles, he would join other men sitting in silence near the radio. A long wire antenna ran up into the trees. The radio operator, a fine-featured middle-aged woman with thick grey hair in a bun, sat on a log with a headset over her ears and a code book resting on her knees. A music teacher, she spoke five languages and had the sensitive ears of a violinist. The radio had been dropped to them by British intelligence three months before and was intended to keep the Royalists in touch with Allied operations and support.

But each day the messages seemed less frequent and more disappointing to the men in the camp.

Six signal fires waited to be lit on the floor of the valley below them. The narrow sloping field they surrounded was just long enough for a light single-engine aircraft. The angle of the field would slow down a plane landing and assist acceleration on take off, provided the wind was favorable.

The commander, General Ludovico of the old Royal Army of Jugoslavia, had been wounded two weeks before and appeared to be paralyzed from the waist down. He rested fitfully in the mouth of a shallow cave, conferring with his officers and drafting messages for several hours each day. A crucifix and a photograph of King Peter in uniform hung from spikes driven into cracks in the rock behind his head. The camp's only medical officer did not dare operate on the general's spine, but he did his best with the gunshot wound at Anton's waist. "Sorry we've no antiseptic or disinfectant," he said as he rinsed and trimmed an old bandage before dressing the flesh wound.

The second morning General Ludovico received Anton. Two men helped him to sit more erect as Rider approached. A grey blanket covered his legs. The general reached down for his red-braided field cap and set it on his head when the British officer saluted. His trim beard reminded Anton of the late King Edward. He wore a black band around one sleeve.

"Welcome to you, Captain," said the general in stiff schoolboy English. "And God bless you for assisting my men at the river. The third man from the boat, the one who was killed near the train, was my nephew."

"I'm very sorry, sir . . ."

"It's the war, Captain." The general rubbed his forehead. "They tell me you killed your share of Ustashi and Huns, even in the snow and firing from across the Drina. Very fine shooting, they say. Remarkable."

Anton deflected the praise. "That is what I came to do, sir."

"Are you a hunter, by any chance, perhaps a sporting man? May I ask where you learned to shoot like that, Captain?"

"Mostly in BEA, sir. British East Africa."

"Elephant? Buffalo and leopard?"

"Yes, General."

"Anything else?"

"A few Italians in Abyssinia." Rider smiled. "And some Germans in the Western Desert."

The General's eyes brightened before he replied.

"If the weather stays clear, we are expecting a flight one of the next three evenings. Hopefully with a new radio, medical supplies, detonators and, if I'm fortunate, an English surgeon to fix me up. Your intelligence headquarters in Alexandria offered to fly me out, but I like to think the men need me here. I'm hoping you would fly out instead of me. I want a letter delivered personally to General Wavell in Cairo. And I would appreciate your telling them what you've seen us doing to the Nazi rail system."

Anton was grateful for the opportunity. "That would suit me very well, sir. It's time I got back and rejoined my squadron in the desert." He smiled. "The weather in Egypt agrees with me rather more."

General Ludovic raised his hand in a pouring motion, then two fingers. An aide brought tin cups and a bottle of brandy.

The two men drank, and drank again. The general took only sips.

"Frankly, Captain, I am more concerned about my country's politics than the war. We are fighting the Germans and Italians as best we can with what we've got, but we do not seem to be getting our share of the weapons and ammunition that are being sent here. The Reds are holding back, waiting for tomorrow, getting stronger, leaving my men to fight the Germans. When this war is over, Tito wants to be the Josef Stalin of my country." A spasm struck him and the General clenched his hands. He closed his eyes, leaning back his head until it touched the rock. In a strained voice he said, "Ah! Now you must excuse me, Captain."

Rider rose, saluted and returned to the radio. Twice the old Marconi crackled and stuttered as men gathered around. The operator held up a hand for quiet, but no message arrived.

After a time, Zoran came and sat beside Anton. "Our friend from the boat is stronger, but we need antiseptic and bandages, and morphine. That's why the General and the other wounded are getting all the brandy." Hearing that, Anton felt guilty for all he had just drunk. "This evening I am ordered to escort you to the strip after the General gives you his dispatches. You and I will wait for the aircraft in the forest with the beacon fire parties."

For three nights they waited for the buzz of a single-engine plane. Rider carried the messages in a leather pouch under his shirt. Torches were lit, waiting for the bonfires, but no plane arrived. He wondered what was happening with flight arrangements in Cairo. Each day more casualties came into camp, both from scouting parties and sabotage teams sent against the bridges and railroads. The fourth day, Anton helped the camp break up and prepare to move higher into the mountains. He knew the General would not do well on a litter. Every man and officer in camp, perhaps three hundred altogether, believed that the Communist Partisans were advising the German and Ustashi hunting parties.

The final evening, the Royalist commander took back his handwritten dispatches and replaced them with a coded message.

"Since you cannot fly out, Captain, you are obliged to sail. So perhaps it is time you enjoyed a holiday on our Dalmatian coast." General Ludovico tapped Dubrovnik on the map that was spread across his legs. "Zoran will be your escort. He has family there. I suggest you start growing what we call a fisherman's mustache. If our radio works, we will try to arrange a sailor's rendez-vous for you as soon as we can."

Chapter Twenty-Nine

"Where else could such a party be?" said Gwenn Rider with delight as the maroon Benz approached Mena House. She sat in the back seat between Olivio and the intended wife of her dead boy. It was Saffron's first night out since the birth of baby Wellie. Gwenn's mind turned with annoyance to Anton having been the first to call Saffron "Mrs. Rider." She shared the sentiment, but resented her occasional husband declaring it on his own. Anton, however, had never raised a hand to her. For a man so used to violence and killing, he had always been gentle at home. This evening she had tried to cover the bruise on her cheek with face powder. Gwenn was ashamed. How could she ever have tolerated such treatment from Alistair?

With every Luftwaffe base captured all the way to Tunisia, Cairo's blackout finally had been lifted. Two years had passed since the heavy bombing of Alexandria, two years since the Suez Canal had been closed by mines dropped by the Luftwaffe and two hundred ships had waited in the Red Sea to be unloaded. Tonight the grand hotel by the pyramids was illuminated as it had not been since the celebration in 1935 of Prince Faruq's sixteenth birthday.

"*Le tout Caire* will be dining with us tonight, my dears," said Alavedo, patting Saffron's hand. "*La haute Copterie, la haute Juiverie, et la haute Mussulmanie du Caire.*" Although he had no regard for the French, like many distinguished Cairenes, the little man occasionally displayed his familiarity with the language of diplomacy.

Olivio checked the pocket of his double-breasted white dinner jacket to be certain it held something special for two guests in whom he had a particular interest.

Alavedo was insulted by Blunt's beating of his majordomo and embarrassed by the murder of the engraver who had been under his protection. But a lifetime of self-control had taught him to turn outrage to deliberation, Olivio reflected as his motorcar drew up the sweeping drive of the hotel.

Death had come to Albrecht a mere two days after his cards had transformed the bridge evening at the Muhammed Ali Club. Coincidence? Only children and old ladies believed in coincidence. Jamila had advised him of what Suda had told her regarding Treitel's scheme to abandon Mr. Anton in Jugoslavia. Soon he himself must act on his friend's behalf. He must investigate the archeological enterprise of Blunt and Treitel at Wadi Halfa.

Only the Combined Hospital Dinner could bring together the military, the Palace and all Cairo. The city's old civilian hospitals were now essential both to Egypt and to the Eighth Army. Each day planeloads and convoys of fresh casualties were arriving from the front.

"They will be honoring the principal benefactors of each hospital tonight, Papa," Saffron said, anticipating the proud moment, aware her father had already rewarded the Anglo-American for saving both her baby and herself.

Tariq stepped down from the front seat as a doorman, elegant in emerald fez and sash, opened the rear door. His master was gripping with both hands the braided cord that hung across the back of the front seat. With the intensity of a man dragging himself into a lifeboat in a raging sea, the dwarf hauled himself forward to the front edge of his seat.

Tariq reached in and lifted out Alavedo. Olivio settled into the Nubian's arms, as erect as he could manage, straightening his sleeves. Gwenn and Saffron followed them up the broad entrance steps. The excitement and power of the evening greeted them as if they were passing through a waterfall into a different world.

The high-ceilinged Moorish lobby was resplendent with the evening dresses of pre-war Paris, black and white dinner jackets, and the dress uniforms of the Anzacs and South Africans, the Indian Army and Horse Guards Parade, the King's African Rifles and the Royal Rhodesians and Canadians. Rumors were that the PM and the American president, Mr. Roosevelt, might be planning a conference at the same hotel.

Olivio's party joined the long receiving line waiting to be introduced to Ambassador Lampson, General Auchinleck and Prime Minister Hassan Sabry Pasha. Portraits of King George and King Faruq rested on easels behind the hosts with the flags of Egypt and the Empire on either side. Two white-gloved announcers, French and borrowed from the Abdin Palace, inclined their heads towards the approaching guests as each one whispered his or her name to the announcer.

When but one couple remained in line ahead, Tariq bent down and set his master on his feet. Alavedo took a moment to steady himself before he advanced with measured steps and intractable hauteur. As he approached the dignitaries, the dwarf thought of how he had begun his life, as an unknown orphan in Goa, crawling about for lost coins beneath the pews of Sé Cathedral.

"Monsieur Olivio Fonseca Alavedo," announced the French attendant, emphasizing the incorrect syllable of each word. The little man strained to bow as best he could. Reaching up, he shook the fingertips of each offered hand, confident that only the commanding general was not aware of who he was. No doubt the entire room was staring down at him. Tariq collected him again, and Alavedo and his ladies moved onto the terrace for drinks.

An orange crescent moon shone like a crown above the lion head of the Sphinx as four hundred guests gossiped and sipped champagne. A line of tall torches flared at the base of the Great Pyramid of Giza. Just before dinner was announced, the kilted pipers of two Highland regiments slow-marched toward the pyramid. "Scotland the Brave" echoed against the great stones. Each piper stamped his feet as he turned and formed in single file before the line of torches.

Even Olivio's tortured spine tingled like an English schoolboy's as the powerful haunting sound of bagpipes filled the desert night with "Rule Britannia."

Alavedo's table was positioned proudly on the edge of the dance floor, though not quite as centrally placed as he might have wished. But with ambassadors and generals common as lusty rabbits in a hutch, what was a modest gentleman to expect? At least an adjoining table of important Kopts was positioned behind his own. Most of the table seatings suffered from the usual wartime shortage of presentable women. Dried dowagers were courted like ripe debutantes. Elegant Levantine ladies acted as table hostesses. Distant tables on the periphery of the room were crowded close together, each filled with less distinguished families and the more common ranks of officers and diplomats. Majors Treitel and Blunt among them, Olivio noticed with anticipation. He guessed that it was Miss Gwenn's lover who was responsible for the bruise on her face. She was the mother of his grandchild. A blow to her was a blow to the house of Alavedo.

The main dish, thanks to the generosity of the palace, was lamb from the royal flocks at Zifta. With the king owning one tenth of the most fertile land of Egypt, some said his breeds ate better than their shepherds. But even the most spoiled diners did their best to clean their plates, perhaps conscious that elsewhere the world was hungry, even starving.

Following the royal toasts, the Minister of Health stepped to the center of the dance floor. A small dark Egyptian in a wing collar that pressed against his chin, the man had a surprisingly strong voice as he welcomed the guests in drawing-room French and English. Alavedo guessed the man's black shoes were artificially heightened, a moral concession the dwarf himself had always abjured.

The minister spoke briefly of each hospital: the Victoria, Qasr el-Aini, Kitchener Memorial and the Anglo-American. How each had increased the number of its staff and beds, and what each was doing for the kingdom and for the Empire.

"A special thanks," he declared, "to the sixty ladies of Number Eleven Convoy of the Motorized Transport Corps who at this moment are waiting at Main Station for the midnight ambulance train from the Western Desert. Each of their new Dodge delivery vans has been converted into a two-stretcher ambulance and bears a plaque with the name of the club or business in the United States of America which raised the money to purchase it."

He thanked those donors who had chosen to be anonymous. To Gwenn's surprise, her host was one of those modest givers. After reciting the most important recent contributions to each institution, the minister called for the announcement of any new gifts made in honor of the evening. Waiters passed between the tables collecting envelopes and notes on silver plates.

Olivio Alavedo reached into his white jacket and drew out an envelope that he placed on a salver.

"Five thousand guineas to the Qasr el-Aini from his majesty King Faruq," announced the speaker to standing applause as a man at his elbow opened envelopes and passed their contents to him. Olivio remained seated, aware that "gifts" from the palace were always announced but rarely received.

Some messages the speaker set aside. Others he chose to read aloud.

"One thousand guineas to the Victoria from the Wissa family in honor of their distinguished grandfather, Ambassador Wissa." Applause followed each announcement. "Fifteen hundred pounds from the Suez

Canal Company." The minister pinched his nose. "Eight hundred pounds from the directors of the Cotton Exchange."

He then accepted the contents of yet another envelope and hesitated before speaking.

"And a special gift on a card of the Muhammed Ali Club. A personal note for one thousand and twenty-two guineas on the credit of Major Alistair Treitel, signed over to the Anglo-American by the generosity of Mister Olivio Fonseca Alavedo." Applause rose. Curious heads turned to identify the donor.

Gwenn Rider raised her eyebrows at Olivio, who was seated on a cushion on the seat beside her, his face just above the edge of the table. No wonder Alistair could not pay the rent. August Hänger stared down across the table at his host. The normally-impassive face of the Swiss surgeon brightened in understanding. Never had Alavedo seen the physician smile as he did now. Presented as generosity, probably at no cost to himself, his little patient had converted a private debt into a public humiliation.

The bankers on the boards of the hospitals, famously rapacious in charity as in commerce, would now pursue every farthing of the bridge debt like grave robbers ripping gold from a dead man's teeth. The British administration, and particularly the military, would find it intolerable that a debt to a hospital not be honored promptly by a gentleman in uniform. The intelligence staff, especially the SOE, would be alarmed by any evidence of gambling or financial irregularity in a senior officer.

The dwarf had learned a lesson as a boy, and he applied it throughout his life with the force of a commandment: give your enemies new enemies. How else had a small poor man been able to prevail in life? As a tiny youth, smaller than every other boy at the orphanage but with a magnificent round head its present size, and a brain to match, Olivio had recruited the biggest bullies to punish his own tormentors.

At first Alavedo had thought to send Tariq to collect the bridge debt from Blunt and Treitel. But then, he considered, why not let other men do it for him, while adding public humiliation and career risk to the debt?

Gwenn began to smile. Turning to her small friend, she said, "That was handsomely done, Olivio."

***

"Even the Germans need food." The old Croatian trawler captain coughed deep in his throat. "They can make *ersatz* coffee. They squeeze sugar from beets. They can invent artificial rubber and replace petrol with alcohol, charcoal and firewood. They mix sawdust with tobacco." He spat into the sand at the idea. "But even the Krauts cannot make artificial fish."

Anton listened patiently, then asked, "When do we sail, captain?"

The tide was flooding into a narrow beach in front of the rocky Dalmatian cliff near Slano. He stank like a fish himself, he thought, like a bucket of old sardines. An empty pipe in the corner of his mouth, wearing rubber boots and a frayed pea jacket, the thick collar raised against his chin, Rider felt ready for the sea, though he had never liked it. He glanced at the cliff top where Zoran, a cousin of the captain, leaned against a dead tree, staring down at the cluster of fishing boats waiting to be lifted off by the evening tide. Each vessel had a lantern at its stern and the required flag of the fascist Independent State of Croatia hanging at its bow.

With Zoran as his escort, the journey from the mountains to the coast had not been so difficult. Staying off main roads, avoiding large towns, they had travelled like Boy Scouts, sleeping in forests and fields, fishing and hunting as they travelled. Zoran had been astonished by Rider's field

302

craft and instinct, his ability to think like an animal, to track and set snares. For his part, by the time they saw the Adriatic, Anton felt lean and fit again. Even his leg was stronger, as long as he did not have to run or climb.

He knew Zoran would make good use of the Enfield. Now Rider's only weapon, apart from his choori, was the long curved fish knife in a wooden sheath at his waist. Sharp but soiled, it too smelled of fish guts and the sea.

"We sail now, Englishman," said the captain when the first wave lapped against their boots. Rider clambered in as the two other fishermen stood in the cold water and gripped each side of the boat to keep her head into the waves. Anton looked up at the cliff and raised his black cap. Zoran waved the sniper rifle above his head. Three or four boats were stirring with the tide to port and starboard. All raised their sails.

As they lifted off, the captain whistled and pointed to the west. A swastika and the eagle of the *Kriegsmarine* flapped in the setting sun as a German patrol boat sped towards them along the coast. A heavy machine gun was mounted near the vessel's bow, probably a Mauser 42, Anton reckoned, with the usual 50-round belt and a prodigious rate of fire. A sailor removed the gun's canvas shroud as the launch approached.

"The Huns come by every day as we're setting out and coming home," said the captain. "Usually check one boat and take half of its catch on the way in. The Bosch and Ustashi like whiting and porgy," he noted, resigned to the thievery. Anton sat on the gunnel at the stern and began fussing with the oil lamp. His shipmates sharpened their knives and filled buckets of salt water.

The German launch approached the last vessel in the small fishing fleet. Its air horn blasted twice. A naval officer stood on deck with a megaphone in one hand. The fishing craft lowered its sail, and the Nazi patrol boat pulled alongside. A sailor wearing the red-and-white-checked arm badge of the Croat Naval Legion jumped down to the deck of the fishing boat, then crouched to enter the low forward cabin holding a Schmeisser machine pistol. Two men stood by the bow gun. After a few moments the uniformed sailor climbed back onto the launch with one of the fishermen under escort. The two craft parted and the fishing boat turned back for shore.

The other boats continued out to sea as the evening darkened. Soon six lanterns were casting bright moving circles on the water as their nets were dropped over the side. The night was uneven, with a crescent moon and thin drifting clouds blocking most of the stars. The captain joined Rider at the stern and stared back at the diminishing cabin lights of the German vessel. Finally they vanished.

"We have three hours if we are going to meet your navy," said the captain. Anton helped the crew pull in the cork-rimmed nets. Soon his hands were numb and he was wet from the chest down. Sea water dripped into his tall boots until his feet were soaked. This must be a harder life than he had thought. Somehow one never appreciated the hardships of another man's trade.

The swells became deeper and longer as they sailed farther out to sea. Once again, Rider was not at home. To Anton, the small vessel seemed to catch every pitch and roll. The black line where the inky sea met the dark blue of the sky rose and fell like a child's yo-yo. After trying to hold himself until no one was nearby, Anton retched and emptied his stomach over the side. He washed his face with icy sea water, spat out the acrid taste and breathed deeply. Taking a seat on a fishing net, he watched the sea rise and fall around him for the next two hours.

He considered how life might be if he got back to Cairo and made it through this war. With one son, and a grandson, and hopefully even a wife. Somehow it always came back to Gwenn. He still wanted her back, but in a way that might work, sharing a life together in Kenya, where he knew how to make his way. Her trade, of course, she could practice anywhere. He knew the first step was to stop messing about with other women, to be able to give Gwenn what every woman wanted, a dedicated heart. If he could not offer Gwenn the comforts of money, or what women called security, at least he must give her all of Anton Rider. Nada, and their time together, already seemed a distant gift, almost an illusion.

Like a breeching whale, a dark looming shape forced a circle of waves a quarter mile to starboard. The captain hurried to the stern lantern and removed his pea jacket. Rider recognized the profile of the submarine. The fin, sprouting two radio masts and a periscope, remained above the swells as water filmed down its sides from wide horizontal weep holes. Each time it rose with the sea, the high bulbous nose drained water from the mouths of its torpedo tubes. The three-inch deck gun appeared to be mounted on the water. Rider was dreading the suffocating confinement of a submarine, even one of the large Thames-class boats he had seen in Alexandria.

"Take off your boots, Englishman," said the Jugoslav captain. "You may have to swim."

Anton pulled off his boots, then his coat. Three times the captain draped his own jacket over the lantern and lifted it swiftly away like a bullfighter's cape. A running light blinked three times from the front of the sub's sail, as submariners called their conning tower.

A rubber raft was soon bumping alongside. Never much of a swimmer, Rider sat precariously on the gunnel of the fishing boat, gripping the edge, his legs over the sea, waiting to choose the moment. One submariner tried to grab the rope bumper of the fishing craft. Another reached up to help as Anton leaned forward.

"Now, sir!" hollered the British sailor with his arms outstretched. "Jump!"

Rider pushed off with his feet just as the vessels parted. He plunged into the gap of icy sea water. Black ocean swallowed him. He kicked upwards desperately and his head hit the bottom of the rubber raft. In a panic, he clawed for the edge of the raft. One hand found the raft's outboard rescue rope as he opened his mouth gasping for air. He swallowed a huge gulp of salt water. Instantly a submariner jumped into the sea beside him, one hand gripping the rope and the other seizing the back of Rider's belt.

"Welcome aboard *HMS Utmost*, Captain," smiled a short lean officer a few moments later as Anton released his grip on the ladder that led down to the control room beneath the sail. "Commander Dawson. Would you like to strip or have a drink?"

"Both," said Anton, shivering in a puddle of sea water.

Two other officers and a seaman were crowded into the small cabin. Busy with their dials and controls, they ignored the new arrival.

"Prepare to dive," called the mate, lowering the periscope. The Aegean was still heavily patrolled by Italian torpedo boats and light destroyers. It would be a long run past Brindisi and around the boot of Italy and Sicily to Malta, and they would surface only at night to recharge batteries and breathe fresh air.

Anton bent over as he coughed and spat repeatedly into a bucket clipped to a bulkhead. The cabin smelled of oil and salt and sweat. A klaxon sounded twice. Disturbed by the shrieking sound, Rider straightened too quickly and cracked his head against a dripping pipe as the submarine flooded her tanks and began to dive.

"Sorry, Captain. You're not a good fit," said Dawson. "Too much of you for undersea work." He eyed the tall soldier head to foot. "Don't know how we're going to squeeze you into one of our triple-decker bunks. We're a **V** class. Only seven hundred ton, four tubes and not an inch to spare. We're built for training, patrolling and torpedoes. No room for a chess set."

Both men knew better than to speak of Rider's mission. The boat shuddered as she turned, then settled into a steady trembling as she sailed south.

Shivering, Anton stripped off his filthy wet clothes. Introducing himself, the medical officer handed Rider a towel and filled a mug with Pusser's Navy Rum. "Looks like you've been bumped about a bit over the years, Captain." He peered at Anton's wounds as he handed him the rum. "Anything we should take care of before we deliver you to Valletta? That wound at your waist looks a little hot. Infected, I'd wager, and that scar at the back of your hip looks rather raw. Could do with some neater darning. Perhaps the galley cook and I should set to work on you and start over . . ."

Cleaning up after Simon's .45 was one thing, but Anton was having no more butchery on his hip. "Rum is the best thing for it, thank you, Doctor."

Chapter Thirty

As always, Major Algernon Blunt preferred it when Suda came upstairs directly after her performance. He could wait in his shorts in the tent-like private room having a double gin or two and lounging on the brocade cushions in the lamp light, smoking some fine native hemp. After dancing, she would arrive glistening and slightly sweaty, still excited by the noisy adulation of her drunken audience downstairs at the Sheherezade, and slightly aroused by her own sensual exertions and display.

Suda, he knew, was not considered the best belly dancer in Cairo. Usually, while she worked on him upstairs, they could hear the music and the roaring crowd below as Jamila or one of the other top girls performed the final dances.

Alistair was right this time. On his last visit, Blunt never should have told the dancer that Treitel and he had been disobeying orders and cutting off supplies to the Royalists in Jugoslavia, not to mention redirecting any escape flight intended to bring back Captain Anton Rider. A single mistaken drop was one thing, but a pattern like this must be close to treason. Fortunately, this sweaty tart was too stupid to understand anything deeper than her navel. All the same, it was a mistake to tell her anything that could be harmful if repeated. No matter what they promised or intended, women always talked to someone. The thought itself made him angry. There had been no consequences as yet, but the possibility that Suda might talk was too dangerous.

For the first time Blunt had the sense that things were out of control, and that some enemy was behind all this. The loss at cards was disaster enough. Paying the debt would require either cheating at a higher level against men who took such things seriously, or managing some other scheme that would create new hazards and possible exposure. Expanding the contraband operation was too dangerous. He did not see how he and Treitel could patch things over. Worst of all, the public display of their obligations at the Mena House banquet had stripped away the possibility of working out some discreet delayed arrangement. Treitel had told him that somehow that scheming midget, Olivio Alavedo, had been behind that embarrassment.

Blunt recalled the surprise he felt when he saw the card-playing physician, Dr. Hänger, seated together with the dwarf and Treitel's mistress at the Mena House celebration. Suda herself was friendly with Jamila, the personal tart of that hideous little cretin. Somehow that damned midget was at the center of it all. His single eye and bald dome reminded Blunt of the bulbous yellow hairless head of an octopus. Even his tentacles were similar.

Anger and frustration rose in Blunt like boiling water in a kettle as he tried to think through the problems that were bedeviling him. He drew on the water pipe and closed his eyes, breathing deeply, deferring panic, absorbing the familiar mixed sensation of lethargy and excitement.

The music and the cheering stopped. Applause echoed up the stairs from the Sherezade, even louder than normal. The door opened behind him as the band started up again. Blunt turned his head and watched Suda's heavy slick breasts as she bent over and placed her tambourine and finger cymbals on the table beside the hookah without acknowledging him. She seemed sullen after their last time together. But she owed him her attention. He reached up and twisted one of her long dark nipples until the woman gasped.

Suda's transparent dancing scarf was wrapped twice around her neck. It swung against her belly as she lit some incense before pulling off his socks.

"Who is dancing?" he said, insulted by her habit of masking his odor.

She knelt between his legs and began working on his first foot. He might as well wait until she had finished. Why not first get some benefit from the evening?

"Who is dancing?" he repeated, growing woozy and unbalanced.

"Jamila," said Suda with some annoyance in her voice. "Their favorite."

He knew the crowd always loved it when Jamila bent a thin gold coin in her navel.

Suda paused to open a bottle of oil. She warmed a splash between her palms, then oiled her long supple fingers, so important to all aspects of both her public and her private trade. She could make her hands and fingers ripple like ocean swells or work their magic with her cymbals. In private, they provided different, even more satisfying services.

He turned over and lay on his back, his head raised on two cushions so he could still use the pipe. He scratched the network of veins on his neck. Sometimes they seemed to be pulsing.

"Who did you tell?" he said with no preamble.

She straddled his belly on her knees. "What?"

"I said: who did you tell? What I told you about my work in Jugoslavia."

Hearing the menace in his voice, she stiffened. "No one, Major." She shook her head. "I say nothing." She accelerated her work, no doubt surprised he had not settled into his usual spirit of indulgence: smoking, drinking and chattering about nonsense while she spoiled him. "I do not understand."

Blunt could tell she was lying. He sat up abruptly and gripped her right wrist. "Who did you tell?" With his other hand he bent back her fingers, knowing how her work depended on them.

Suda grew afraid and began to fight him. Strong as he was, her dancer's body was remarkably fit and limber.

"Tell me!"

"I said nothing, sir. I . . ."

Suda screamed as two of her fingers snapped. Pain and fear and anger joined within her. With whip-like speed she kneed him violently between the legs. She struggled to rise.

Though the crowd below would not hear over the music, he hated her shrill cries.

"Bitch! I will teach you not to talk."

Blunt gripped Suda's thick glossy hair close against the back of her head and forced the woman to her knees with her head cast back. With his other hand he lifted the small bowl that held the smoldering incense. As she opened her mouth to scream, he dumped the glowing incense down her throat.

Choking and thrashing, violent with pain, Suda fought him. Welcoming the challenge, he grabbed her scarf in both hands. He twisted it into a cord and pulled her to him. A wisp of smoke clouded from her mouth. Her eyes swelled and protruded like enormous wet marbles. He wound the scarf around her neck again and again and rose to his knees, then his feet.

Unable to scream, Suda writhed and flailed with her hands while he dragged her into the corner of the room behind the door. She struggled to force her good hand into the tight coils of the scarf and pull it from her throat. But she could not match his strength. Finally, on her knees before him, staring up at him with popping eyes, Suda clawed at Blunt, then grabbed his testicles, clenching and squeezing them in a death grip as she expired.

The applause and cheering from the crowd downstairs reached a crescendo.

"Ah! You stupid bitch!" hissed Blunt, releasing the scarf at last and prying away her fingers. He was stepping back from the body when the door opened. He had neglected to bolt it.

Jamila entered the room, glistening with sweat. Her eyes and face were smiling and excited until she looked around.

"What . . ." she started to exclaim.

Blunt slammed the door and slipped the bolt. Then he lunged for her.

With a dancer's speed Jamila eluded him. In jumping aside, though, she stumbled against the table. As she fell back against the hanging cotton of the wall, Blunt lifted the water pipe from the floor by the long cloudy throat of its glass bowl. With a quick swing he bashed it against the side of her head. The pipe splintered into a rainbow of fragments and cut her cheek and neck.

Jamila released an agonized scream. She clutched a handful of the cotton as she staggered to one side. Anxious to keep her quiet, he swung again with the jagged broken stem of the hookah but missed her. Even with the music and noisy crowd downstairs, a scream like hers might bring men running.

The dancer dashed about the room like a wounded animal, quick on her feet, madly ripping the cotton from the walls, hurling pillows, screaming curses in Arabic. But Blunt, crouching, always remained between her and the door to the stairway. At last he heard the drum and tambourines grow silent and the crowd grow noisier as the club began to empty out below.

Suddenly Jamila lifted the copper table by one leg. She swung upwards with the table as Blunt rushed at her once more. The narrow edge of the table struck him across the forehead. Stunned, the big Englishman staggered back against the door. Blood flooded over his eyes from a long cut.

"Pig!" screamed Jamila as she swung again. "Pig!"

Blunt blocked her second blow with his left arm and struck at her with the broken circle of glass.

The thick shards caught Jamila in the throat. Blood gushed from rough gashes in her neck. She collapsed on her belly with the remains of the broken hookah beneath her.

His chest heaving, Blunt wiped his hands and bloody face on a scrap of hanging cotton. He hurriedly put on his clothes. The bright coals of the hookah started to ignite the loose cotton. By now the nightclub would be empty, he guessed. Blunt glanced down at the two women, then knelt by Jamila and tore off her necklace of small gold coins. He ripped the long gold hoops from her ears. He opened the door and slammed it after him as flames and smoke rose behind him. It was time to get out of Cairo.

Chapter Thirty-One

The battered Humber continued east and north, her engine stuttering, driving along the base of the line of hills that rose steadily towards the Tunisian towns of Sbeitla and Kasserine. Denby Rider was determined to locate the enemy's heavy armor and then radio in the location. After that, his armored car could run for it. Their radio was worse and worse, though, barely audible in fragments of scratchy transmissions. The operator reckoned it was good for one or two more tries, probably after dark. Denby, still deafened, could not even hear the static.

The signs left by the Panzers had grown more dense and confusing. In the early morning they passed two camps where enemy armor must recently have laagered. The Germans had left little behind except used bandages and empty tins of Italian sausage meat, both remains alive with busy sand flies. One camp was marked by rows of depressions in the pocked gritty sand where tank treads had been laid out, repaired and refitted by teams of German mechanics travelling with the armor. Mark III's and IV's, Denby reckoned, by the size of them. But not a crowbar or a spanner, not a bolt or a jerry can or an ammunition case had been left behind. At another messier encampment, they found an abandoned Fiat lorry with a fasces painted on the driver's door, and signs of lighter Italian armor, probably Ansaldo's, perhaps the Centauro Division, Mussolini's best. There they found a heavy wrench and chucked it into the Humber.

Emerging around the end of a steep chain of hills, they were surprised by a long column of dust rising to the west. Denby raised a hand in warning and Walker stopped the scout car in a cluster of acacias. Denby glassed the broad valley as best he could. He made out the profile of a tank he had not seen before except on recent armor recognition sheets: a new Sherman. Thirty-six tons, a 75mm gun, 25 mph. These American-made tanks had made the difference at El Alamein because their thick armor protected them against the older German tanks. But these Shermans had not yet met a Tiger. The American machines, a white star painted on each turret, bounced and jarred as they pounded down a rocky slope into the wide valley before the defile of Kasserine Pass. Had they been German or British, even Italian, faster scout cars would have checked the route first, Denby noticed with alarm.

But at last the Yanks had joined the war, not just sold weapons. The Hussars watched as squadrons of the American 1st Armored Division dispersed into the valley near Sidi Bou Zid, in a rough V formation, but in some disorder, mixed in with self-propelled guns, trucks, half-tracks, tankers and even several jeeps sprawling out onto the flat lower ground. Many vehicles had a large American flag painted on the front to distinguish them from British armor, in the hope that the French would then be less likely to fire on them. Huge clouds of dust rose due to the speed of the machines, making vehicle coordination more difficult.

Denby's fears came alive as German anti-tank guns, hidden in olive groves on the plain, suddenly opened up enfilading fire as the Americans roared past. From north northwest, a flight of Messerschmidt 109's appeared. Then nine Junker bombers streamed towards the valley from a higher altitude. Sticks of bombs plunged down. Lines of explosions crossed the paths of the vehicles. Where was the R.A.F.? And the American Army Air Force? wondered Denby. Could these tanks not have aerial protection?

Bursting bombs brightened the dusty valley. Hit dead-on, an American oil tanker flared like a giant torch then rolled and tumbled down a slope, crashing into a half-track and soaking its crew in flaming petrol. Black oily smoke seethed through the low clouds of dust. Denby, unable to hear the sounds, had the sense of watching the scene on silent film.

As the Luftwaffe flew on, the American armor began to regroup near Sidi Bou Zid. Again the American tanks, half-tracks and tank-destroyers began to charge across the valley.

"Let's join them," yelled Denby, though he could not hear his mates' reply. "Perhaps we can help with the wounded and borrow a wireless to call the regiment."

Denby and the three Cherry Pickers climbed into the Humber and started forward, leaving the shelter of the thinly wooded hillside. Then a terrible sight stopped his breathing.

"Stop!" Denby hollered. He banged the side of the scout car. "Stop!"

Through a cleft or pass in the hills at the far side of the valley near Kasserine, a second line of armor was advancing in precise formation through yet another cloud of dust and sand. Massive tanks ground forward in arrow-shaped groups of three, with half-tracks on either flank and sidecar motorcycles scouting ahead like ancient skirmishers. Well dispersed, troop transports followed close behind. He knew at once this must be the enemy's main force, Germany's last iron fist in Africa. He bowed his head and frowned. The Hussar scouts had located the enemy but had failed to make a difference.

Gun muzzles flashed as the Tigers fired into the confused flank of the American armor spread before them. Quick-firing rounds of eighty-eights streaked flat across the scrubby rock-strewn desert. A few American tanks, mostly old tall-silhouetted Grants, turned to face the enemy and return fire.

In minutes many of the Grants and Shermans were brewed up, hit and on fire. One by one, two by two. The enemy fire was faster and more accurate. Like experienced hunters, the German gunners tracked their targets with their barrels. PAK 75mm anti-tank guns fired at the American armor from camouflaged emplacements.

The Tigers rumbled into the valley. Rommel had arrived, thought Denby, still not beaten. Behind the big tanks, lighter Mark III's and IV's roared through the pass in the hills. These old veterans knew the game. They were agile on the sloping entrance to the valley, firing steadily with their smaller cannon, short-barrelled 75's for the Mark IV's and 50mm cannon for the older Mark III's. Behind the tanks came the troop carriers, both lorries and tracked vehicles. English, Italian and German, all dusty over their sand-yellow paint, and packed with Panzer Grenadiers. Though he could not make them out, Denby knew that these survivors of the Afrika Korps, hardened by three years of seesaw victories and defeats across North Africa, would be lean and tan and hard in their worn sand-yellow tunics. They had not been softened by the luxuries of Cairo. Radio trucks, self-propelled guns and tank recovery units would follow directly behind them.

At Denby's command, the Humber pulled back to the shelter of its earlier position. Now they could do nothing. The four Hussars stepped down and raised their field glasses. They watched the German column punch into the chaos of American vehicles. They knew enough to recognize defeat and slaughter in the desert. Columns of dust mingled with clouds of oily black smoke and drifted eerily across the valley.

Erwin Rommel himself could not be far, Denby thought. The Desert Fox was always famously at the front, either piloting his own Fieseler Storch low over the battlefield or standing beside the driver of a lead armored car or half-track, lean and alert, squinting through his British sun goggles, a checkered scarf knotted at his throat above his Iron Cross, one hand gripping his field glasses, the other holding the top frame of the windscreen. The Tommies knew his image better than they recognized their own commanders. Even England's Prime Minister had spoken glowingly of Rommel in the House of Commons.

Here and there the turret hatches of the Grants and Shermans were raised in surrender. Yanks climbed down with their arms high and leather helmets in one hand. Truckloads of American infantry pulled up. Men dismounted hurriedly without their weapons.

In minutes, German tank crews were busy siphoning fuel from the American vehicles. Rows of jerry cans were being collected into captured trucks. Everywhere squads of Panzer Granadiers were gathering American prisoners. Denby stared helplessly through his binoculars. Men of the Afrika Korps were searching their prisoners, probably for cigarettes.

He saw troopers dismount from the sidecars of two motorcycles and scan the surrounding hills through field glasses. Light reflected from a pair of binoculars as one German scout appeared to look directly into Denby's eyes.

"Saddle up!" he shouted as two heavy eight-wheeled German armored cars detached from the battle and turned towards them. Nimble across rough country, the envy of the Eighth Army, said to be the best all-terrain fighting vehicle in both the Western Desert and the Eastern Front, the all-wheel-drive Achtrads mounted 20mm cannon and heavy Mauser machine guns.

The Hussars climbed up in a hurry. Walker pressed the ignition. The engine turned and scratched but did not catch. Seeing his frustration, Denby unlimbered the Boys anti-tank gun, checked the five-shot box magazine and trained the weapon on the approaching Germans. Still the vehicle would not start. Steady, he reminded himself as if hunting lion or buff with his father. Wait. Again the engine turned and died. Batteries? Sand? Fuel line? There was no time for repairs.

The first light shell exploded in the nearby bushes. Shrapnel hit the side of the Humber. Denby's mates jumped down and knelt behind some rocks with a Bren.

The two Achtrads advanced rapidly towards them, faster now on the flat ground. Denby could make out the crews of the big vehicles in their sun goggles and tropical helmets. He waited until the lead machine was within range, then fired. The Boys tore up the ground between the armored cars. Feeling the heavy punch of the recoil, he fired again. But both Achtrads came on, their cannon and machine guns sparkling through the dust.

Then another column emerged from the right. Heavy machine gun fire blazed through the dust from a weapon mounted on a jeep. The long grey tube of an American bazooka extended across the dash of another jeep beside it. The bazooka flared, the jeep shuddered and Denby watched its 3.4-pound rocket strike the engine panel of the lead Achtrad. The jeep stopped to steady its aim for a second shot. The front of the heavy armored car rose in the air like the head of a heart-shot buffalo.

As it crashed down, the 20mm cannon of the second Achtrad turned its aim from Denby's Humber to the Ranger jeep. But the bazooka fired first, striking the Achtrad amidships just above its wheels. The smoldering armored car collapsed on one side. Armed men jumped down from both German vehicles.

The jeep had emptied first, though. With a pistol in his left hand, Captain Corrigan lobbed a grenade into one of the open armored cars. Armed with submachine guns, the other Rangers ran for the Germans, crouching and firing, crouching and firing.

Denby's crew gave support from the Humber, firing the Boys over the heads of the Rangers. The Germans were soon annihilated. There would be no prisoners.

"We won this little one," screamed Corrigan when Denby pulled up to him, "but the Krauts have taken Kasserine Pass and given our First Armored a damn bloody nose. We lost about two battalions each of armor and infantry."

Shaken by the fight, still unable to hear, Denby waved and replied in a loud voice, "We'll get another crack at them."

***

In some ways the submarine had been like an undersea safari, thought Rider as he rested his elbows on the sticky surface of the bar in Malta. Closely confined, with a few people travelling together across a vast space, and obliged to observe a number of strict rules to ensure safety. But he had missed sunrise and the stars.

They had surfaced just before dawn eight miles from the port, then cruised north along the eastern coast of the island in the Med. He had been relieved when the captain invited him up on the sail as the boat approached the port of Valletta. Never had Anton appreciated fresh air as when he climbed the ladder to the narrow open bridge of the sub, relishing the salty smell of the sea with every step.

As first light brightened the water, a coastal defense aircraft flew out to escort them to the island. The twin-engine Wellington wagged its wings as it made a pass over the submarine. A seagull alighted on the barrel of the deck gun, rested and flew off.

Few of the thirty-seven men on board had slept much the night before. Lying on his back in his borrowed hammock, filling it rather like a sow in a sling, Rider smelled the man swinging a few inches above him and heard every grunt and gurgle of the sailor suspended beneath him. All had been waiting for the sound of the draining pumps being started by the diesels, the first confirmation that the *Utmost* was surfacing. Every now and then cold drops dripped on his head from the hammock ring, condensation leaking from the rivet heads shaken loose by the perpetual trembling of the engines.

Now he understood why submariners on leave were said to be the most tightly wound of any servicemen, ready to explode when they stepped ashore. Each man on board seemed compressed by the same pressure of the sea that had caged their vessel. For two days the crew had spoken of little else than the Gut, Valletta's rough district along Strait Street.

Pity the bars and the girls, Anton thought, remembering some of his own foolishness when he came back from the bush to Nanyuki or Nairobi. No wonder Gwenn had often been upset with him. But in Malta he was determined to behave himself. Soon enough he would be back in Cairo. And he was getting older, perhaps twice the age of the ratings on board.

Rider expected to find an intensity of life waiting in Valletta. As the base for British attacks on the convoys that were the lifeline of the Afrika Korps, Malta had been the Stalingrad of the Med, besieged for two years, enduring a blitz longer and more intense than London's, often bombed eight times each day from the Luftwaffe bases in Sicily. Malta and Tobruk were the keys to the early battle for North Africa.

As the *Utmost* ran past the outer rocks and approached Valletta harbor, her nose, deck gun and sail just above the oily water, she passed the grounded angled wrecks of two destroyers and a cruiser. Anton looked up at the town's ancient towers and bastions and ramparts, wondering whom they had withstood before this war. Finally the *Utmost* tied up beside her sister, *HMS Uproar*, docked alongside the submarine depot ship *Maidstone*. The mate of the *Uproar* saluted and raised his cap. Rat rings protected the *Maidstone's* hawsers. As Anton stepped onto the deck, tugs and lighters and small boats were busy all around them. The iridescent dark water was thick with garbage and marine waste.

Rider was among the first ashore, stumbling when he stepped from the gangway of the *Maidstone* onto the pier. He stopped on the dock beside a line of canvas-covered lorries. He stared up at the steep hillside of the city, then across Grand Harbor where the carrier *Formidable* was unloading Spitfires.

He had time for a stroll and a drink, he decided, before reporting to the aerodrome at Luqa for a flight south to Derna or Alexandria. He was in no hurry. What was he going to report about the American officer he had killed in Jugoslavia? Perhaps he had never seen Captain Simon again after they had parted on the hospital march.

Soon Anton found himself picking his way across the ruins of Queen's Square, where every building had been bombed out, but where the statue of Queen Victoria on her throne was untouched amidst the rubble. Finally he made his way to Strada Stretta, deep in the Gut, at a pub with a black wooden entrance. Small window panes and a cheery flower box hung over the door.

"That'll be two bob or a roll of the cup," said the barman, setting a glass and the leather dice cup before Anton. The Barca Pub seemed to have a tradition of wagering for drinks, a custom not uncongenial to a man raised by Gypsies. With a smile at the bartender, Rider spilled the dice along the counter. They rolled to a stop between two of the short thick candles that lit the bar. Five and six.

"Lost again," said Anton cheerfully, reaching in his pocket, not surprised by the unfriendly dice. Every currency was said to work in Malta, and so it seemed. Rider still had two gold sovereigns and a handful of Maria Theresa silver dollars, and he passed over one of the latter. The barman held the silver coin against a candle, squinted with approval and gave him a ten-shilling note and some coins.

Several Maltese girls, the celebrated "Butterflies of Valletta," eased about the low-beamed smoky room, attentive to the fortunes of the winners. A couple of silver dollars would make a girl very friendly, he thought, though determined to behave himself. Most were dark, but no

322

two shared a single look, perhaps reflecting the island's varied conquerors, Phoenician and Carthaginian, Roman and Arab and British. They were the usual painted blousy heavy-armed women who would leave one with a sense of shame and an urgent need to wash. But one or two drew Anton's eye, especially a slender girl with short dark curls, a high backside tight and round as two large cricket balls, and cheekbones that could split your chin.

Backgammon and darts were settling the wagers of some drinkers. Six sailors were gathered at a card table. Three were submariners from the *Utmost*, including the sailor who had hauled him from the sea. With a Gypsy's gift for card play, Rider thought of joining the game but did not want to empty the pockets of his shipmates. He sent over a bottle of dark rum and returned a cheerful wave.

He watched the slender girl step to a corner table where a heavily-built Maltese was seated on a bench against the wall, taking on all comers at arm wrestling. A young sailor from New Zealand faced him on a stool.

Rider thought back to an evening over twenty years ago at the old White Rhino Hotel in Nanyuki. Young and strong, in a contest that had nearly killed him, he had arm-wrestled the brother of the Irishman who had raped Gwenn on board the old *Garth Castle* on the way out to East Africa. In the end he had held Paddy Reilly's hand over a burning candle before slamming it down onto the flame. Then the Reilly brothers had attacked Anton, and the dwarf barman had intervened, firing a shotgun into the ceiling. That was his first encounter with Olivio Alevedo, and he was still grateful.

Rider lifted his drink and stepped closer to the corner. Defeated, the New Zealander left the table. The Maltese rose briefly and flexed his powerful shoulders. Anton noted that the man's own seat was higher than the stool.

A young RAF pilot, tall and solid enough, took the low stool opposite the strongman. He grinned, looked up at several friends in air force blue, then at the girl before slapping a half crown down onto the table.

The Maltese lifted both hands and joined his thick fingers, cracking his knuckles like gunshots. The man was built for this work. Like Reilly's at the old White Rhino Hotel, his right forearm was huge, pink and round as a ham. It appeared substantially bigger than the left. His arched back had the thick humped shoulders of a buffalo. He set his right elbow on the table. The pilot did the same, bending his wrist to meet the grip of the shorter-limbed man. The wrestler grabbed the pilot's fingers and slammed his hand down on the table, hard enough to split the knuckles of a weaker man.

"Again?" said the Maltese as he collected the coins.

The airman looked up at his friends. Anton caught the eye of the girl. He sensed they shared regret for the outcome of the match. She seemed to simmer as they held each other's look.

"Come on, Charlie, we'll stake you," said one of the pilot's mates, throwing down several coins. They all seemed so young. Like Denby, Anton thought. Like Wellington. Anton blinked and lifted his glass to both his sons. These pilots must be the boys who were defending the island, fighting the Luftwaffe for control of the Mediterranean, always aloft in their Beauforts and Spitfires, sinking Rommel's supplies on the way to North Africa, winning the war, one flight at a time.

Twice more the Maltese won. With the final victory, he stood and rolled his shoulders, stepping aside to speak to a barman. The young pilot rose from the stool, nursing his hand and wrist.

The girl eyed Anton again and pointed at the stool. He stepped to the table and sat down quickly in the winner's seat on the raised bench instead of the stool. He felt the old excitement rising in his blood.

"That's my seat there, boy," said the Maltese, first in English, then in his own language. "That be my seat." Two burly doorkeepers stood behind him, nodding. Each had a leather-wrapped cosh hanging from his belt. One of them stared at Rider and pointed at the stool.

Anton threw his ten-shilling note onto the table and stretched his fingers. "Any takers?" he said, glancing up as the Maltese kicked the stool. "Ten bob?"

Piqued by the wrestler's cheek, the submariners gathered next to Rider, as if facing off against the doorkeepers. One sailor clapped Anton on the shoulder, joking cheerfully. The girl came and stood on his other side, leaning against the wall with one hand, almost touching him as a crowd collected.

The champion lowered himself onto the stool. He squinted through the smoke at Anton with angry red eyes. For him this was no lark. This was what he did and who he was. The doorkeepers stood behind him. "Give it to the bloke, Theo," said one. "Give 'im a taste of the Gut. Snap 'is wrist."

The Maltese set his right elbow on the table.

Rider finished his drink and thrust it at one of the doorkeepers. Startled, the man accepted the empty glass. Anton felt at home with this sort of game, feeling the electricity of the moment, but he was getting older. He rolled up his sleeve. The old hawk tattoo showed on his forearm. He glanced casually around the room with his elbow on the table before looking down at the strongman.

Suddenly Rider seized the man's fingers and slammed his hand down on the table with a crash. He held the hand there for an instant as the wrestler tried to raise it. At last Anton released him. The thick arm jerked upward as if beyond control.

The man rose from the stool as the young submariners cheered and hooted.

"Another go, you bleedin' bastard," said the Maltese, enraged. "I weren't ready. You didn't let me get my grip. Another go it is."

"You haven't yet paid for the first go," said Rider in a steady, almost friendly voice, taking back his banknote.

The girl touched Anton's shoulder as if in warning.

The wrestler threw down a handful of coins. "Another go," he said. "And you get the stool."

"No quittin'," said a doorkeeper.

"Another go?" said Anton. "Only if we go left-handed." He rose and stepped to the bar. The girl reached for his hand as he passed.

Theo tried to get past the arm-wrestling table to his old raised seat against the wall, but the three submariners blocked his way. Anton picked up two bar candles and set one on each side of the table. Hot wax pooled onto the wood.

"We go left-handed," Rider repeated, not yet seated, "and we'll use candles to confirm the loser. That's the game if you want it, Theodore. Left hands this time. Double or nothing."

"Right hands." The champion shook his head from side to side like a bull before the charge.

Anton bent and scraped the coins into one hand. He turned his back to the table and took a step towards the bar. He felt his stomach harden.

"The game's not done," said a doorkeeper, grabbing Rider's arm and lifting the cosh from his belt.

Flaring at the touch, Anton lowered his body. He knew the handful of coins would harden his fist. Rider swung as he turned. Rising, he hit the man low in the belly with all his force. Someone else punched Anton hard in the side. Instantly they were all in it. Wrestler and pilots, doorkeepers and barmen and sailors. Rider lifted the stool.

The girl slipped along the bar. She called to him and pointed towards the door. Anton wanted to go with her, but he could not leave the others to finish his fight. He waved to her with the bar stool in his hand.

It felt good to be back in civilization.

Chapter Thirty-Two

"You don't understand, Blunt. You never do. We're in Cairo." Alistair Treitel leaned forward to see around the coral tree in the copper planter beside their table. He snapped his fingers for a suffragi. Service was famously slack at the Continental-Savoy, but the old caravanserai in Opera Square was never as crowded as the Semiramis or Shepheard's, which were always chock full of officers from GHQ and the better regiments.

"You're making things too messy again, Algie. You're panicking. The way you killed that card forger, and both those dancers, the night-club fire . . ."

Fishhead snorted in contempt. "Good men are dying every day in this war. Who gives a damn in hell what happens to a few tarts and hoodlums?"

Treitel pinned Algernon in his gaze. "I will tell you who cares. That blasted midget cares."

"Who cares about him? He could be next." Blunt's face reddened as he banged down his empty highball glass. "Don't you see, Treitel? We can't afford to be caught. These debts, the contraband, the mission to Jugoslavia, the people you've made me kill . . ."

"Lower your voice." Treitel's mood was not enhanced by the knotting cramps in his belly and the looseness of his bowels, so typical of life in this filthy country.

Blunt snarled at the criticism. "You always want me to do your rough work, Treitel. Then you whine when it gets done. Just like at school. You told me we had to . . ."

"Algernon. I said, lower your voice."

Trying to defuse the antagonism, Treitel pointed at his glass as a bar boy approached, elegant in a crisp white gallabiyah and lime sash and fez. The Englishman slowly lit a cigarette before continuing.

"That second girl you did was too well known. She was called Jamila. I hear she's danced for the king at the Palace. And she was some sort of whoring mistress of that filthy toad Alavedo. They even say she loved him. Loved that creature! Can you imagine!" The Don crushed out his cigarette. "And you bashed up his servant at my flat. I tell you, Olivio Alavedo is behind all this."

"Yes, I know," nodded Fishhead impatiently. Parts of his face flushed as he grew heated. "He started it all by cheating us at cards with that bloody forger."

"And helped Gwenn to leave me. Having his cotton broker rent my landlord's flat at double the price. Getting me chucked out while he gives her his guest house."

"At least we've seen the last of her husband, rotting somewhere in Bosnia."

Treitel handed a letter to his friend. "And now Alavedo is setting the hospital's solicitors after us, hounding my bank manager for that bridge debt." The bar boy appeared with fresh drinks and a dish of black olives while Blunt read the dunning letter from Taheri & Lawrence.

"Where are we going to find nearly eleven hundred quid?" exclaimed Blunt, picking up a handful of olives before tossing the greasy letter on the table. "And the contraband game is getting too dangerous. And the intelligence chaps and the SOE aren't going to sit about whilst we get dragged through the Mixed Courts for our debts. They'll chuck us back into the army. We'll end up crawling ashore on some rock in Sicily while the Eyeties pour down machine gun fire. I won't be able to look after you there, Professor."

Blunt leaned closer to his friend and said harshly, "You won't make it up the bloody beach."

Treitel ignored the threat. "Don't you know where the money is, old boy?" He slipped the letter back into a pocket before stirring his scotch and soda with his middle finger. "We are in the land of the Pharoahs. The money is buried in the sand." He looked away, hating to watch Fishhead spit olive pits into his left hand. "Three interesting digs have been interrupted by the war. Two of them are too close to Cairo. The Department of Antiquities may be all messed up, but they've still got some ragged guardians pacing about near those ruins, or asleep in the shade, at any rate."

"So it's back to Upper Egypt," said Blunt, calmer now as he drank. "The Second Cataract. Wadi Halfa." The two men nodded in agreement. "We still have our authorization papers for the dig. I've been studying those early drawings of the site. They've done a bit of digging all around the place, just to sketch out the parameters. Most of it seems to be Middle Kingdom . . ."

Treitel nodded. He was always surprised by his friend's scholarly interests, the incongruity with his other tastes. Despite Blunt's filthy manners and annoying habits, where else would he find a partner who combined his own cerebral tastes with the requisite appetite for occasional violence, even if he overdid that part of it now and again? It was like finding an ape who could compose sonnets with a pencil between his hairy toes. Why complain about the verse?

"We have a fortnight of overdue leave," said Treitel more patiently. "If we get lucky, Algie, we can bring anything small and precious back to Cairo to raise the money. Anything else we can crate and ship south to Khartoum."

He looked away as Blunt tossed several pits into the planter and wiped his fingers on the shiny heart-shaped leaves of the coral tree.

***

The director of the orphanage of St. Francis Xavier bowed as Olivio Alavedo and Gwenn Rider entered the hall. "Each one of our boys considers you to be his father, sire." And perhaps a few did so with reason, reflected the dwarf with pride.

Naive watercolors and crayoned drawings brightened the cool corridor of the orphanage with vivid village scenes of water wheels, baby camels and tall-wheeled donkey carts. Each picture was pinned low on the wall, at a height suitable for viewing by a small child, or a very short man.

For the visit, Alavedo was dressed *toute à l'Anglaise*, in a three-piece ivory linen suit and perfect small brown toe-cap shoes burnished like tortoise shell. Dr. Rider and Tariq followed a few slow paces behind Olivio. Prepared to visit the private clinic at the rear of the orphanage, Gwenn carried her black medical bag. Tariq carried a wicker picnic basket filled with presents for the sick children and prizes for the winning artists.

Surely, thought Alavedo, King George must feel something like this when he visits hospitals and orphanages in wartime London.

The dwarf hesitated at the end of the corridor. Tariq reached one hand to steady his master as Alavedo appeared to rock on his feet. Then Olivio collected himself, pulling down the points of his vest before he turned back and paused before each picture a second time. He was pleased to observe the results of his instructions to the arts teacher: require that each child select one single subject, then draw and paint that one over and over again, rather than flit from one subject to another and not learn to make the very best of whatever one chose to do.

This academy provided the dwarf with the opportunity to instill into the dross of Egypt the spirit that drove him, and that four centuries ago had protected golden Goa herself when a few fighting Jesuits, Portuguese soldiers and their African slaves defended that Indian island against an eleven-month siege by hundreds of thousands of Muslims. In 1559, the Inquisition in Goa had appointed a Judge of Orphans to direct their education. How could Olivio Fonseca Alavedo not do his part here on the Nile? How could he not name his orphanage after St. Francis, who himself was buried in the Basilica of Bom Jesus in ancient Goa?

At Olivio's signal, Tariq gathered up his master in his free arm, then followed the director into the narrow crowded dining hall. Centered on the facing wall was a photograph of Egypt's handsome prince before he became king. Young Faruq, perhaps fourteen, dressed in white naval uniform, stood erect on the bridge of the royal yacht, *Maroussa*, a pair of binoculars in one hand, as if staring out to sea to survey his fleets. On one side of the door was a large framed photograph of the patron of the orphanage, Olivio Fonseca Alavedo himself, and five of his six daughters. Four of the girls stood in a row behind the seated dwarf. The youngest, Cinnamon, sat cross-legged at his feet.

A gilt-framed painting of St. Francis Xavier hung on the other side of the doorway. An auto-da-fé sparkled in the distance behind the saint as burning heretics, Muslim and Hindu, perished at their stakes in the halo of the sacred public fires. One day the dwarf, too, would be buried in Goa near the bones of that same great saint, the Conqueror of Souls.

"Welcome home, sir!" chorused forty boys as the director lifted one hand. "Welcome home!" The children set down wooden spoons and rose from five tables in their white gallabiyahs, like a flight of young swans taking wing. The dwarf's eye moistened. Then the boys began to sing. Hearing the clear young voices, their patron beamed like a sunrise.

The director called out two names. The young artists stepped forward to receive their prizes: for the second winner, a wooden paint box and brush set from Gibbon's of London; and for the first, a framed portrait of

Albrecht Dürer, an image that formerly had hung in an engraver's workshop in the Khan el-Khalili. Olivio Alavedo did not believe in waste.

"Now, sire, and madame doctor, if I may show you our clinic." The director guided them with one hand.

Six beds were set in what once had been a conservatory. The head of one bed was hidden behind a screen. Sunlight filtered in through dark wooden shutters. Flowering plants flourished in four large tubs. Three beds were empty. Two boys, perhaps ten and twelve, occupied the beds near the door. Olivio reached down from Tariq's arms and presented a grapefruit to each boy while Gwenn examined the youths in turn. Only a small round lemon with a greenish cast remained in the bottom of the basket.

"A fresh gift for you lads from my family's farms in the Delta," said the dwarf with rare gentleness as he distributed the grapefruit. He had learned that the full extension of his influence required a reputation that combined fear and generosity, and occasional unpredictability.

From constant pruning, selection and grafting, one of his farms was close to developing a nearly seedless lemon. Small and almost round, with a thin fine skin and little of that useless white liner, the new lemon yielded a particularly tart and pungent juice. The dwarf had been contemplating what might be a suitable name for such a perfect acid fruit. After the war he would have them packed in straw in flat wooden crates and sold in specialty stores that would soon be serving the newly rich. Perhaps at Harrod's, and Fauchon?

"Mein Gött!" exclaimed a loud voice from behind the screen. *"Die Zwerg!* The wicked dwarf himself."

"Our new patient, a crippled German prisoner," explained the director as if apologizing for some ill-behaved creature in his household. "Part of the overflow every clinic is obliged to accept from the military hospitals in these busy times. They just sent us this one." At my instruction, Olivio thought as the man continued. "The government provides us a trifling consideration, of course, towards our extra costs."

"How much?" said the little man, his eye narrowing. "For each bed, each day? How much?"

The director's eyelids blinked nervously. "Ah, I will send your office an accounting, sire. We do not perform surgeries. They send us only the disabled for whom little can be done." He pointed at a wooden leg hanging from a leather strap at the foot of the bed. "Last week they sent us two Italians and one Canadian. Now we have this . . ." He gestured with a thumb at the prisoner.

"*Guten Morgen* to you, *Herr Alavedo,*" called the German patient, leaning forward from his pillows. "I must thank you, I believe, for from a British prison camp sparing me. They understand not how to treat a German gentleman and heroic officer." He tapped the Iron Cross that hung from a chain outside his nightshirt. "All they provide are flies and dry English biscuits."

"It is too soon to thank me, Captain," said the dwarf, asking himself how this villain could be the friend of his friend. "Far too soon." He glanced at Gwenn Rider and the director. "Leave us, if you please." As the two turned for the door, he took the lemon from the basket and handed it to the director. "This is for you. A young Fonseca Citron."

Alavedo pointed. "And Tariq, prepare a seat for me there at the foot of this creature's bed. Then take that filthy stinking leg with you and wait by the door." He had too many painful infirmities of his own to be sensitive to this man's hardships. What would he himself not give for one sound full-length leg?

Tariq pulled away two pillows from behind von Decken's head despite the German's protestations. He plumped up the pillows, reversed them and set them against the foot of the metal frame of the bed. Then he seated his master against them as the other two left the room. Von Decken grumbled as he rested his head against the bars of the bed. How could he, a German officer, share a bed with this troll? But this was not the moment to complain.

"Very well," said the dwarf, settling himself comfortably, his little feet resting not far from the German's only foot. He was not displeased to soil this man's white bed sheet with the soles of his own small shoes.

"At my request, Dr. Rider has had you transferred temporarily to this clinic of my orphanage. But a military prison still awaits you. They provide no feathered pillows. They do not serve fresh figs or tender lamb. It will be back to prison with you, Captain, without your wooden leg, unless you accomplish certain duties that should assist that gentleman who is the best friend to us both."

The German shook his head. "You and I have no friends."

"I am blessed with several," Olivio said firmly. Who did this hulking Hun think he was addressing? Perhaps he should return to him a different wooden leg, splintered, and several inches shorter than his old one. "You, however, have one friend, one more than you deserve. I speak, of course, of Mr. Anton."

"That damned Rider again." Von Decken scratched his grizzled head with a sound like a metal file grating glass. "Why is this *Engländer* always such a burden to my life?"

"You are fortunate to have the opportunity to share his burden. Otherwise you would perish in the desert on the way to prison camp. Even your own army, the Afrika Korps, would have no use for you."

Ernst grumbled but he knew that what Alavedo said was true. The British always wanted their wounded back first. The Germans wanted the fit ones back. "What do you want from me, an honest old sisal farmer from Tanganyika?"

"What you are best at, Captain." The dwarf paused and waggled his head from side to side. His eye twinkled. "Killing people."

Alavedo's bluntness startled even von Decken. "I think I need a drink."

"There are two English officers, probably now in Upper Egypt at a dig," Olivio went on, ignoring him. "They have done much wickedness and are enemies to our friend. You must see that they never return to Cairo. Never."

The dwarf missed Jamila, perhaps more than he himself acknowledged. He was reluctant to admit, even to himself, how much the dancer had meant to him, to his lonely heart. She had the gift of making him feel younger, and alive. He liked to believe that Jamila had truly cared for him. But there were other important reasons to avenge her. His own influence depended on his reputation, and his reputation was based on fear and fortune. The murders of Jamila and Albrecht were, above all, offenses directly against Olivio Fonseca Alavedo himself.

"Who . . ." began von Decken.

"Listen to me," said the dwarf sharply, annoyed by the disrespect of interruption. "Listen." He lifted his feet from the bed and clacked together the heels of his little shoes like cymbals.

"First, you will join me on my yacht, sailing from Aswan to Wadi Halfa. You will stay below deck. Near Wadi Halfa you will find these two English devils, probably engaged in looting a neglected dig near the Nile, stealing the national treasures that should belong to better men. After you complete this work, I will see that you continue on to the Sudan with suitable papers and sufficient currency to accommodate for a time even a person of your low appetites."

Captain von Decken nodded, shrugging off the insult. "You are an evil little man." He drew back his foot further from the dwarf. "But I understand you."

"Are we agreed?"

"Jawohl," nodded the soldier, pinching his medal. "Now give me back my leg."

"You will have it when you need it. In the meantime, we will have it cleaned. Boiled, most probably." Without his wooden leg, this coarse German would never manage some other method of escape.

Alavedo clapped his hands. Tariq stepped over from the doorway. He lifted his master and set him on the floor.

The Nubian took the little man's hand, and the two walked slowly down the hall to the entrance to the orphanage. Children stood back, smiled awkwardly and touched their foreheads as their patron passed. Eight boys and a tutor stood by the steps in the courtyard. There Tariq lifted his master in his arms and they descended to the forecourt as the children sang.

Chapter Thirty-Three

Captain Corrigan removed his headset and stepped down from his communications jeep. "We lost over a hundred and fifty tanks and half-tracks at Kasserine and Sidi Bou Zid," the American yelled at Denby, who had Graham at his side taking notes. "They want our recce team to move back towards Thala and provide screening and reconnaissance for the British armor defending the town. If Rommel breaks through there, he'll capture central Tunisia and our whole campaign falls apart. But if the Krauts can't break through at Thala, they'll lose Tunisia and Africa as well."

With Kasserine Pass behind them, the five light vehicles of the Rangers and Hussars climbed between the rocky djebels towards the town. The rough narrow road was a chaos of damaged and abandoned transport. English, American and French troops and equipment struggled past in both directions. There was an atmosphere of near-panic, or at least confusion, thought Denby, as if the old Desert Fox was once again invincible.

Every man was conscious of their vulnerability to enemy aircraft and was disappointed at the few friendly flights, mostly American P-38 fighters from a new runway built nearby. Denby noticed that the Arab boys were hawking eggs and dates to the British, were begging chocolate and chewing gum from the Americans, and were asking nothing of the French, who they knew well.

Denby and Corrigan found the British 26th Armored Brigade laagered down in defensive positions on both sides of the road near Thala. The reconnaissance team of Rangers and Hussars filled their cans and tanks from a petrol wagon before turning to scout for the expected Panzers. They pulled up onto the shoulder of a higher djebel on the south side of the road and settled down for tobacco and a brew-up, coffee for all the Yanks, tea for most of the Brits. While they drank and smoked, they watched American engineers laying mines further down the approach road. Hasty shallow work, thought Denby, not the way the Jerries did it.

At about 15:00 hours the first shells whistled in.

"Seventy-fives," said several Rangers and Hussars at the same time.

"Gunned-up Mark IVs, by the sound of them," said Graham. "Should do a nice job on the old Valentines and Crusaders holding Thala,"

"If we wait 'til they're close, our bazooka should help," said Corrigan. "Perhaps your Boys rifle could pitch in, too. We might settle into that olive grove just before dark and see if we can have a little fun." Graham wrote this into a briefer message and showed it to Denby.

"Aye, aye!" nodded Denby eagerly, trying not to scream. "Let's feed the lads and do it."

A late cold rain began to fall as the day darkened. The Leicestershire regiment was camping nearby. The road grew slippery. The shallow wadis soon filled.

Corrigan and Denby positioned their transport deep in an olive orchard below the town, with the bazooka jeep and the Humber closer to the edge of the grove. They hung camouflage netting and cut branches to cover the exposed sides of the autos. Except for two gunners in each of the armed vehicles, the other fifteen men were scattered on foot through the orchard.

At 17:00 hours the ominous slow grind of German armor advanced along the line of the road. Sappers moved ahead of the tanks, clearing mines from the muddy ground under the protection of machine-gun fire from half-tracks and armored cars. Whenever there was light resistance, infantry advanced to clean up ahead of the tanks. Out-gunning and out-ranging the defending Valentines and Crusaders, the Panzers Mark IVs prevailed, but slowly, as if carefully conserving each tank and half-track. This was not Rommel's usual rush of concentrated armor. He could not replace his losses.

Finally the German sappers and skirmishers reached the edge of the olive grove. Sheltered by the falling light, the rain and the trees, Denby and Corrigan waited impatiently, hoping that valuable targets would come in range before they themselves were spotted by the men on foot.

Just as a squad of German infantry entered the edge of the olive grove and turned to search through the gnarly trees, two half-tracks ground up along the edge of the road. The first was loaded with three rows of Panzer Grenadiers. The second, carrying artillerymen, pulled an 88mm cannon with many white rings around the long barrel to record its kills of tanks and aircraft. Behind the two half-tracks came a Kübelwagen dragging a six-tubed Nebelwarfer rocket launcher. Following that, Denby was surprised to see a British Valentine tank leading the advancing German armor. Where were the Tigers?

Corrigan tapped his chest and pointed at the 88mm cannon. That left the first half-track and the Panzer Grenadiers for the Hussars.

Denby fired the Boys at forty yards. The shell exploded in the driver's compartment of the half-track, killing every man in the front row and destroying all control of the vehicle. The wheels and tracks continued turning, the wheels inclining to the right on the slippery shoulder of the road, steering the big machine into the edge of the olive orchard. Two rows of Panzer Grenadiers jumped down.

Corrigan fired his bazooka, severing the connecting bracket that secured the .88 to its tractor. The heavy artillery piece rolled backward, barrel first, and crashed into a wadi that was running fast with new rainwater. The half-track stopped. The gun crew leaped down to see if they could save their cannon.

Denby and Corrigan each fired once more, but the moment of surprise had passed. Denby missed as his Humber came under small arms fire from the dismounted Germans. Corrigan's second bazooka shot hit the half-track amidships, smashing its left tread from the driving wheels. By now the Rangers and Hussars were engaging the Germans who were sweeping through the olive grove.

Back on the road, the men in the Kübelwagen had stopped to arm the Nebelwarfer and turn its tubes to face the orchard. Between the trees the Rangers and Hussars were fighting off the German heavy infantry. Then a horn blasted twice and the Germans ran back to the road in the rain.

A sheet of orange flame flashed as the rockets went off with a rolling explosion that Denby could not hear. The six rockets tore into the trees. All three jeeps were struck. Running back from his vehicle, Denby stumbled into Graham. The Scot had been hit twice, once by a bullet and now by shrapnel from a rocket. His throat was torn open. Blood soaked down his neck and chest as he collapsed in Denby's arms behind a tree. Graham died before Denby could speak or assist him. Denby closed the soldier's eyes and set him down.

"Come on!" Corrigan, a .45 in one hand, grabbed Denby by his arm and dragged him to the far side of the olive grove. Only three other men seem to have survived, and two of those, both Rangers, were wounded.

The battle was continuing behind them along the road as the Germans broke through the outer defenses of Thala. Near the town the defenders were firing smoke shells to enhance the confusion and deny the enemy the advantages of their superior weapons.

Corrigan and Denby gathered the other men into the Humber. Denby cautiously drove out the back of the orchard, then climbed the slope of the djebel and turned towards Thala on a rough track that ran parallel to the road below. By the light of gunfire and explosions and burning vehicles, they watched the German armor push into Thala. The Valentine they had spotted earlier seemed to be leading the assault.

"That Valentine is now a Panzer," said Corrigan, squinting down at the muzzle flashes. He squeezed Denby's shoulder and pointed insistently towards Thala's inner line of defenses.

Denby drove the Humber down the slope towards the town. In minutes they found themselves in a melee in the darkness. Allied and enemy troops and armor were intermingled, fighting at close range. Always better at combined arms, the Germans seemed to have the advantage, both in men and weapons.

Denby stopped the Humber near a burning Crusader as a German stick grenade landed on the hood of their vehicle. Denby and Corrigan flung themselves from the armored car as the hand grenade exploded. Stunned, Denby lay on the ground. Flames and gunfire filled the air around him.

The Crusader was belching orange flames from every hatch. Its hull was torn by violent internal explosions as its tightly-stored ammunition exploded. Fireballs erupted from its turret and gun barrel. Still stunned by the grenade blast, Denby crawled away from the heat around the rear of the Humber, searching for Corrigan. He found the Ranger officer sitting with his back against a wheel of the armored car. Wounded in the chest, with his .45 raised in both hands, he was searching for a target as blood bubbled from his lips. Lung-shot, Denby knew at once.

Corrigan emptied his pistol towards the German column on the road just below them, then fell on his side, dead. Denby sat down beside the American. For a moment he closed his eyes against the thick oily black smoke and flashes of iridescence rising from the burning lubricating oils and the rubber of the tank's tracks and bogey wheels.

When he opened his eyes, he saw a strange reflection sliding along the ground towards Corrigan's body. The orange and reds of the exploding shells were reflected in the silver pool of molten aluminum that was pouring from the Crusader's engine onto the ground and spreading towards them. Raindrops steamed as they fell into the hot bright liquid. Denby staggered up and dragged the body of his friend further from the molten pool. Finally he collapsed on the ground. He felt one eye twitch and his body begin to tremble. Only then did he realize that he, too, had been wounded.

***

Cairo's Main Station was a bedlam of soldiers, porters, beggars and pedlars. English women, some Cairo's lady volunteers, others cheery "Naafi girls" in pleated uniform skirts and side caps, offered tea and biscuits to swarms of New Zealanders and South Africans, Canadians and Rhodesians. They seemed young as boys, cheerful and untroubled, more like scouts than soldiers. Or was he just older?

Anton Rider had no kit and not much of a uniform. Only the long tan socks, khaki shorts and bush shirt he had found in Malta. Taking off in an old Lancaster from Valletta by moonlight, they had evaded the German night fighters based in Crete and finally been escorted to Alexandria by a flight of Hurricanes on patrol over the sea lanes to Port Saïd and Suez. A train from Alex had brought him home to Cairo.

He tipped a porter who hustled Anton into a waiting gharry. The driver jabbed his thin horse with a long stick and they were off to the Cataract Café. It was time for a cocktail.

He saw instantly that Olivio was away. The dwarf's personal pennant, a clove on a green field, was not flying on the main mast. Increasingly, Olivio was now observing the salty customs of an admiral of the Royal Navy. A young suffragi had been trained to pipe him ashore and aboard. Trusting nothing less for authenticity, Alavedo had provided an

English cruiser's bo'sun with a fountain of gin at the café and with what one might call a romantic introduction, in order to have the English sea dog train his suffragi with the proper naval drill.

"*Kattar kheira*k." Anton paid the driver and patted the bony shoulder of the horse. He was tired. Taking a cigar from a pocket, he sat on the parapet of the embankment and looked down the ramp to the Cataract Café, recalling old adventures before the war.

Two women were seated on the quarterdeck with their backs to him. A small child was playing beside them on what appeared to be a bed-spread. The blond boy was wearing a blue and white sailor smock. The child glanced up at the embankment and smiled. His grandson, Wellie.

Anton waved back. He felt himself soften. His eyes filled. He clenched his jaw and wiped his face as he observed on the deck so much of what he had always wanted but had never been smart enough to make complete or lasting.

He rose and walked down the gangway, smelling the sweet coolness of the Nile.

Sustek, beaming, was waiting at the bottom of the gangway. "Welcome home, effendi!"

"How nice to see you, Sustek." Anton clapped Olivio's majordomo on the shoulder, making no mention of his bandaged nose. "Could I have a gin, please? A double, if you don't mind."

The women looked around. Saffron rose and rushed first to greet him. They hugged, rocking a bit from side to side, almost as if Anton were his son, and she belonged with him. Both knew this was what each felt and meant. She was wearing the ring he had given her on behalf of Wellington.

When the two pulled apart, Gwenn rose and smiled, but there was some distance in her eyes. She placed one hand lightly on each of Anton's shoulders, touching him hesitantly, recalling their past intimacy.

She looked up at him to see clearly how he was, as if he were a patient for whom she especially cared. He leaned and kissed both of her cheeks, wanting to do more but feeling restrained by her self-control.

"It must have been hard." Gwenn touched his arm. "I heard that several of those missions were lost, either over the Med, or in Jugoslavia." She did not identify who had told her. Anton noticed a bruise on her cheek.

"I'm all right," said Anton Rider nervously. Typical Treitel, he thought, saying more than he should when that served him.

Anton knelt before the boy, quietly, then sat on the bedspread and spoke gently to his grandson, letting the child come to him. Tickling him, he saw his lost son in the boy's eyes and in the sunlight of his smile. "Wellie," said Anton, hugging him and lifting the grinning boy against the sky. "Wellington, it's you!"

"We have news of Denby," said Gwenn from her chair. "He's with the Hussars somewhere in Tunisia . . ."

"He was wounded," interrupted Saffron with animation. "But not too badly, we think."

"He should be all right, then," said Anton, relieved, and gratified by Saffron's concern for Denby.

He glanced at Gwenn as he spoke. She looked tired, lined around her eyes, but still herself, with a slender body, a sculpted face and the best legs in Cairo. He wanted to ask her to dinner. "It's not over yet," said Gwenn. "They say Hitler is sending fresh troops to Tunisia. Tanks and paratroopers under General von Arnim."

She is still so beautiful, he thought, looking into his wife's green eyes. How could she be sleeping with a man like Alistair Treitel? What he would give for three days of camping with her by a water hole, to share an African evening as the animals came in, to listen to the night sounds as they whispered under canvas and loved one another as once they had.

"Where is Olivio?" asked Anton, poking his grandson in the tummy.

"My father said he was taking a little cruise up the Nile to Upper Egypt. Aswan and Wadi Halfa," said Saffron, handing Anton an envelope. "For his health, he said, or something like that. He left a letter for you. If you got back, he was hoping you might join him as quickly as possible. I think he wanted a bit of help with something. Said there might be a need for some 'stout work,' whatever that means."

Anton had an idea. "I'd best drop in on the Army first."

"And he said to tell you that an old friend of yours, a one-legged German rogue, is joining him on this mission."

"I believe I know the man he refers to." Anton hugged Wellington and rose. Gwenn smiled at him and touched his arm as he kissed the cheek she offered. He found neither invitation nor rejection in her touch.

"Are you free for dinner, Gwennie?"

"Sorry. I'm due at the Anglo-American this evening. Should be a long night, with another hospital train coming in."

Anton nodded and turned to leave. Before she could react, he stepped back to her, took her face between his hands and kissed her gently on the lips. "I would like to see you when you're free."

Chapter Thirty-Four

"Damned idle wogs!" Treitel wiped the back of his neck with a damp handkerchief and squinted down at the dig from the shelter of the canvas. Even the dust and stones seemed to carry their own heat and glare. "Who'd ever believe these wretched fellahin built the pyramids?"

"We've six days left to sort out whatever we can find here." Blunt flexed the thick knuckles of his right hand and stared down at the entrance of the tomb. "Pack up several big crates for Khartoum and take the best smaller bits back to Cairo with our baggage. So far we might have just enough to pay our way out of debt." Fishhead removed his shirt, bunched it in one hand and wiped his sweating face.

Treitel turned away, recoiling. The garment smelled like an old dressing torn from an infected wound.

"But there must be something more in there," said the Don, trying to disregard the stink as he stared at his own sketch of the dig. "Something truly precious."

Below them, a line of diggers was carrying away baskets of sand and debris balanced on their heads. Some had rags pressed between the baskets and their heads. Others labored with long-handled shovels, removing sand from the approach to the entrance. The back cloths of their turbans hung down over their necks. Every man's robe and face was layered with dust. Occasionally one of two heavyset foremen stroked the shoulders of a worker with the lash of his qurbash, not brutally, just chivvying the man back to the excavation after he had dumped his load down the adjacent hillside.

Treitel recognized wedge slots in the next rocky hill from where he sat. There ancient quarrymen had hammered wooden wedges into slots cut in the stone, then soaked the wedges with water until they swelled and split the rock along the chosen lines. An early substitute for explosives.

Both Englishmen knew they had no time to do their work as it should be done. Like generations of thieves before them, they were going at it rough and fast, like tomb robbers, not archeologists. "If we don't rip this thing open," Blunt had said at the end of the second day, "some other bastards will."

Every grain of sand should have been strained through sieves, every wall painting protected from dust and smoke and moisture, every fragment inventoried and catalogued. Numbered notes, drawings and photographs should complete the record, all to be filed later with the Department of Antiquities.

But they had little time, and war had thinned the Department and weakened its procedures, both in Cairo and especially in the field. Dozing guardians had replaced teams of scholars from a dozen countries. Energetic work had been suspended at fourteen major sites on both sides of the Nile from the Mediterranean to the Sudan. By selecting a secondary site, Treitel and Blunt had made the robbery easier. Marked down on the Department's draft map as a lesser tomb, perhaps that of a minor wife or a deceased child, this ruin near Wadi Halfa was far enough down the list to deny it proper protection during wartime.

Presented with credentials, a letter from the Department and an envelope of cash, the senior guardian at the dig had been relieved to surrender his authority to these visiting archeologists and to return to his village and complaining wife with some money folded in one shoe. Blunt and Treitel had established themselves under canvas on the rocky hillside overlooking the site. Now the trick was to reward a few of the hard boys and have them flog the rest of the diggers until they dropped. Most were unauthorized workers from the Sudan. The two foremen were well-paid dependable brutes who would do whatever was required. Both carried heavy knives in their belts.

Treitel and Blunt had wasted two days excavating out a false passage that led to nothing. The ancient priests and architects had anticipated the character of the men and civilizations that would follow them. Even the lesser tombs employed some of the tricks and deceptions of the larger and later tombs and monuments. After fifteen yards or so, the overly steep angle of descent and the unfinished nature of the stones of the walls had identified this one as another ruse, a trick path. The true passage was parallel to the false one but at a gentler grade and with smoothly finished walls cut from the living rock. The first challenge had been removing the huge vertical wedge-shaped stone that had plugged the entrance.

Using oil lamps, saving their two battery-powered military torches, Blunt and Treitel took turns directing the front men toiling at the head of the passage. The laborers worked in teams of four, two digging with picks and hoes, two scraping the debris into baskets to be collected and taken back to the entrance by other men.

Finally, on the fourth day, they arrived at an impenetrable block, an immense limestone slab the size of a double door, nearly six feet across, though only four feet tall.

Blunt held the smoking lamp as Treitel examined all four edges of the stone. He felt along each one with gloved fingers. Instead of the perfect flush corners characteristic of Egyptian masonry where a blocking slab met the stone of a side wall, the left and right edges of the slab were smoothly rounded. Treitel removed his gloves and stroked along the edges with his fingertips. He could feel the marks of the copper chisels that had beveled the curves.

From their studies in the Valley of the Kings, both men recognized the reason for these rounded edges. They would permit this giant stone to pivot on some fixed point near its central axis, like the panels of a modern revolving door.

Blunt directed the careful sweeping of the margins of the stone. Even a handful of gravel would impede or prevent the perfectly balanced masonry from pivoting cleanly as it should. Typically, the top and bottom of the massive limestone slab would have been cut away to a smooth finish, except for two stone pivot knobs left at the center of the bottom and top of the great stone. These knobs would be set into fitted depressions in the framing stonework.

While Blunt supervised this preparation, Treitel returned to the canvas shelter and refilled the largest of the oil lamps and trimmed its linen wick. The oily smoke would damage any hieroglyphics formerly protected in the clean dry air, but this could not be avoided unless they had a portable generator, electric cables, proper bulbs and considerable time.

Treitel selected the two burliest fellahin, brothers with the solid dark look of men from Upper Egypt or the Anglo-Egyptian Sudan. He directed one of the brothers to cut a thick four-foot plank, and the other to bring two large wooden mallets and a maul. To strike the stone directly would crack the edge of the stone without moving the mass. Better to use a plank to spread the impact of the blow where it was needed.

Accompanied by the two men, he returned to the head of the passage, where his friend was now directing a thorough sweeping of the stepped sloping corridor. A foreman, Massoud, joined them.

"Lean into it, you bastards," said Blunt as the two large fellahin pressed their shoulders against the right edge of the blocking stone. Massoud gave one fellah a sharp flick with his qurbash. Still there was no movement. Then they tried the left edge of the stone. It would not budge.

Treitel set the plank against the right edge of the stone and directed the laborers to hammer it with the mallets, one at the top, the other at the bottom. "Again!" he shouted. "Again!" Every grunt and blow echoed in the narrow stone passageway. Nothing moved as the men pounded and sweated, encouraged by the blows of Massoud.

"Stop!" yelled Blunt. "Enough. I will do it myself." He picked up the heavy maul, its handle longer than a woodcutter's axe, its steel head shaped like a giant tack hammer. "You," he pointed to one fellah. "You! Lie down and hold the plank flat against that edge of the stone."

Treitel stepped back several paces. In this confined space he could not avoid the odor of his friend.

The worker lay on his side against the slab and pressed the plank flat against it with both hands near the bottom, his thick dark fingers close together. Blunt swung and struck near the center of the board, his eyes closed at impact to protect them from the flying fragments of rock.

Treitel thought he heard a slight scraping groan of stone against stone as if the slab were complaining at the impact. A small cloud of dust emerged along the right edge of the slab.

"Damn you!" said Blunt to the prone Egyptian as he gasped and leaned against the handle of the maul. "The board was not flat against the stone." He kicked the man's back and pointed. "Press against it higher up."

The dark fellah gazed up at him with weary red eyes. Lying on his right shoulder, facing the stone with his back to Blunt, he reached higher with his left arm and pressed his hand flat against the plank with his fingers spread.

Fishhead stepped back and leaned the handle of the maul against his belly. He spat into his left palm and rubbed his hands together as he measured the distance in the tight space. Then he turned sideways to the stone and slowly swung the maul back and forth before his legs like a cricket bat. Using the momentum, he raised the implement back behind his right shoulder then twisted his entire body like a discuss hurler uncoiling. With his thick arms fully extended, his eyes shut at impact, Blunt slammed the head of the maul towards the center of the board.

The fellah screamed as the maul crushed his hand against the plank. The stone, however, did yield from the blow.

"You've done it, Algie!" cried Alistair Treitel as the slab shuddered to a stop, perhaps six inches forward at its edge. He glanced down at the injured screaming worker. "Take your brother outside and send along two more men," he ordered the other fellah, who now was kneeling beside his wounded brother. The man's hand had the shapeless red pulpy look of a bowl of rotted tomatoes. Massoud herded out the two brothers.

Blunt set down the maul and leaned his shoulder against the stone, pressing hard, grunting like a beast, gaining another inch or two as the stone scraped and grated. "Now we'll use the mallets," he said huskily, repositioning the bloody plank as Ali, the other foreman, led two fresh men into the tunnel to assist the work. One stepped carelessly in the slick trail of blood on the floor of the passage. Everyone knew that an injured digger meant employment for another man.

Thirty strokes later the slab pivoted to nearly ninety degrees in the center of the passageway. Treitel noted that the knob at the bottom center of the stone appeared to have been damaged during the work, cracked near its base. He doubted that it could endure further service as a pivot for the great weight above it. Then again, he did not care what happened after they left.

Intensely curious about what treasure they would find, Treitel raised the wick of the oil lamp. Something precious must be concealed behind that great stone.

The flame flickered and bloomed higher. He felt his body thrill. He was, after all, a professor, not a soldier. Everything he had always dreamed of, both scholarship and fortune, could be waiting in the chamber on the other side of this single stone. This lamp might show him what the future of his life would be.

The two Englishmen crouched to pass beneath the four-foot lintel, breathing in the cool dry stale air that no man had used in nearly four thousand years. "Take these men outside, Ali," said Treitel, "and see that no one enters the passage."

**

After eight years on board the Cataract Café, Olivio Fonseca Alavedo felt at home at sea, or at least on the River Nile.

Vasco da Gama, Columbus, Leif Ericsson, even the great Nelson himself, had all been men of courageous spirit, far-sightedness and with a need for understanding obliging women. Fortunately, he had provided for that delicate requirement on this voyage up the river.

Although Jamila herself was lost to him, two of her most dedicated students, one a dusky Sudanese, were at this moment preparing themselves in the captain's cabin. No doubt these disciples knew that their efforts must be a fitting tribute to Jamila's tutoring and a suitable dedication to the spirit of their teacher's memory. And Jamila herself would never wish him to be unsatisfied.

After her cruel death, it had seemed appropriate to call together, in the hold of the Café, the more accomplished young women of Jamila's belly dancing academy. Excited by grief, anxious about their own prospects, they had arranged themselves mournfully in what one might call a *tableau vivante* as he gave each one a sympathetic caress, his personal diploma of appreciation for the promise of each flat belly and high tight derriere. Each of the trembling beauties understood, of course, that her future depended on the tastes and appreciation of Senhor

353

Alavedo himself. While none could replace Jamila, he thought mournfully, each could do her best.

The difficulty on board this steam yacht would come from keeping that filthy Hun, Captain von Decken, apart from the two dancers he had selected. Olivio must focus the creature's strengths on providing physical justice for the murderous villains that awaited them in Upper Egypt. Disposing of Treitel would also be a handsome act of friendship on Olivio's part: Mr. Anton's wife would not be able to blame her husband for the death of her lover. Shortly before sailing from Aswan, the dwarf had learned of Treitel's violence towards Miss Gwenn. Murder and betrayal were crimes enough, but this would add an even more personal element to the reckoning.

Kapitan von Decken was secured in the aft cabin, without his wooden limb, and with an ugly cousin of Tariq's seated on a stool against his door. Alavedo had procured a new leg for the crippled Kraut. Carved from a lighter and stronger Lebanese wood, it had been fabricated by the same master cabinet makers, father and son, who were employed by Cairo's cricket teams to make bats for important matches. The leg would be given to the German when the man's mobility would be a requirement, not a risk. There was always the danger that von Decken would flee before he had executed his assignment, though Olivio did not think the old soldier would find the work itself uncongenial. Naturally, the brute's need for money and documents would bind him more than his word.

The dwarf sat on a thick cushion in the captain's chair in white shoes and trousers, a braided navy-blue cap over his eye as he rested on the bridge of the *Quarenfil*, or *Clove*, the name of his daughter who had perished in a hideous conflagration some years before. The ancient symbols of Upper and Lower Egypt, lotus and papyrus, were painted on either side of the black funnel of his yacht.

Olivio smelled the sweet cool air of the river, cleaner than in Cairo, because of the freshness of its unspoiled headwaters deep in Africa. He watched the Nile glide by as they steamed south against the current. The layered sandstone of the west bank glowed pinkly in the bright sunlight as shadows bathed the yellow sand of the opposing shore. He watched women harvesting golden corn in the cultivated fields beyond. Birds and men fished in the moving water. A red-bellied male baboon sat on a ledge above the milky green river, scratching himself and eating an orange with both hands.

Occasionally the dwarf reached from his seat and gripped a spoke of the teak and brass wheel with which the captain steered the yacht. There was no need to do more. Admiral Nelson himself, after all, did not captain the *Victory*, his own flagship. He, too, had greater concerns.

With von Decken and Tariq to assist him, Olivio was confident he would be able to overcome the two English rogues at Wadi Halfa, savage butchers though they were. Yet he would be more comfortable if Mr. Anton were with them as well. But he realized military matters might detain Rider, and no doubt it would be best for relations with his wife if Mr. Anton were not directly involved in the disappearance of her lover. Nonetheless, he had left a suitable letter and map for his friend.

Early in the evening, after sunset, the *Quarenfil* would tie up near Wadi Halfa, shortly before the Second Cataract. Fortunately, as a benefactor of the Cairo Museum and of certain projects favored by the Palace, notably the bronze equestrian statue of Muhammed Ali at the Rond Point in Alexandria, he carried a letter of introduction from the Minister of Antiquities and a certificate of authority as an Honorary Inspector of National Monuments. In Egypt, the subtleties of generosity were well rewarded.

In the meantime, he thought, glancing downward, he had an obligation to Jamila. He would go below as she would have wished and give her students the opportunity to demonstrate all that Egypt's greatest dancer had taught them. As a generality, he preferred the attentions of a single woman, though occasionally an active gentleman had to tolerate exceptions. Perhaps the competitive enthusiasms of the two attendants waiting below might fuel them with a spirit of enterprise and even a spark of sexual ferocity. Both were approaching twenty, and must have some concern about their future.

What these two dancers would not expect was that he would devote himself to providing them with sexual pleasure rather than requiring that of them. Everything these women had learned, whether dance or disrobing, massage or the arts of teasing, was premised on the effort to provide men with stimulation, pleasure and arousal. As a bald, one-eyed dwarf, Alavedo had learned long ago that he must provide women with what other men, especially Englishmen, did not: the patient development of their own fulfilment. With this he would reward these dancers today. At least one of them should understand, and so herself become a candidate to replace his lost Jamila. If all went well, perhaps the other could continue south with the Hun.

As Wadi Halfa came into view along the Nile, village dogs barked from the shore. A line of open stalls and one-story shuttered shops with corrugated tin roofs extended behind the dock. Barefoot vendors sat on mats between stacks of baskets. Sandals and European-style undershirts, the favored work garments of many fellahin, dangled from nails above their heads. Gallabiyahs and a crocodile skin hung from a cord stretched between two stalls.

The dwarf looked forward to his adventure ashore. He felt young again, stimulated by the threat of violence and the possibility of retribution. After getting as far as one could by motorcar, he would approach the dig under a parasol in a donkey cart, but with Tariq and Ernst von Decken for escort. He expected an arduous final ride over a dusty rocky trail after they had left behind the mud walls and dwellings of Wadi Halfa and the cultivation near the river.

First, however, he must attend to his romantic obligations on board.

"Tariq," called Olivio. "Carry me to my cabin."

Chapter Thirty-Five

As an archeologist and working scholar, Professor Alistair Treitel had never had a finer day in the field. For once, ahead of any other man, he had been the first to uncover an important monument or tomb. In two days, Blunt and he had secured objects enough to make any man proud and rich. After entering the first secret chamber on their own, they had examined its contents as best they could before calling on one of the foremen and several fellahin to assist them.

Even Fishhead had done his best with every aspect of the work in the first chamber: bullying the laborers as they dug and moved the fill, assisting with his own hands as they levered off the lid of what, at first, had seemed to be the outer stone coffin of some child of distinguished family. Best of all, *pour encourager les autres*, he had caught and thrashed a digger who had attempted to pinch a small canopic jar.

Already they had packed many small objects into the two large wood-framed brass-cornered trunks that had carried their personal effects and important provisions to the site. The work within the dig had been made doubly difficult due to the tight dimensions of the approach corridor and the scale of the two chambers, which evidently had been designed and built to accommodate a child and his requisites in the afterlife.

The only disappointment was that it had not been the tomb of an important royal child. Instead, they had found the first mausoleum dedicated to Bes, the Egyptian god of dwarfism. The casket inside the small sarcophagus of Aswan granite contained the mummified skeleton of a dwarf. Large-headed, short-necked and club-footed. One could feel the creature's life of pain.

They had not fully unwrapped the mummy, but the Don was aware of the ancient skills that had been employed under the inspiration of Anubis, the jackal-headed god of embalming. Bathed, drained of fluids, organs removed, cavities washed out with palm wine and cedar oil, then stuffed with resins and coated with pitch or natron, the body would have been wrapped in linen bandages treated with myrrh, olive oil, honey, wax and astringents. Each toe and finger would have been separately encased and treated, the penis itself wrapped in a state of proud erection.

Small gold and inlaid objects, cast and carved to scale, celebrated each of the dwarf god's five attributes. One was celebratory, the sponsorship of wine and music and dancing. Four were protective: the protection of warfare and the dead, and of sleep and women, particularly during childbirth. These five trophies were now wrapped in cotton and packed in straw in the smaller of their two trunks. They'd had no time to study them yet. The mummy had been left standing erect in a corner of the funerary chamber. The larger trunk, half-filled, rested on top of the smaller one inside their round tent, a shelter that the outfitter at Wadi Halfa claimed had once accommodated Lord Carnarvon himself.

As they worked, either Treitel or Blunt always occupied a folding canvas stool at the entrance to the tunnel, a holstered Webley at the waist. A pot of tea and two cups rested near the seat on a round copper tray set on a flat stone. From there, while the others worked inside the tomb, one of them could both watch the tent and be certain that no one of the fellahin left the entrance with anything of value.

From now on, thought Treitel as he flicked away the persistent sand flies with a horsehair lash, he would have to keep a sharper eye on Algernon Blunt. Old friends though they might be, Algie was not above trying to snitch more than his share of the fortune they had uncovered. After all, it was Treitel himself who had conceived this effort in the first place. It was he himself who deserved more than half the reward. No doubt, he thought with distaste, Fishhead had left his smell in the tight airless confines of the tomb.

Just then Blunt appeared at the mouth of the tunnel, wiping his sweating neck with a rag, his face flushed from bending over inside the dig.

"I've found something else!" Algernon cried as he straightened his back and flexed his hunched shoulders. "As usual, I've done all the hard bloody work, Professor. While you've been out here sipping tea in the shade, I found it."

"And what is that?" said Treitel calmly, putting down his cup, still seated, though his nerves were tingling.

"It's a small litter, a sedan chair, or sort of throne set between four ivory handles. Stones, lapis lazuli, enamel. Perhaps two foot long, a little less, maybe a foot and a half." His face perspired heavily as he continued. "And a small squat statue of a dwarf, like a little toad, that sits on the chair under a parasol. I think it's solid gold."

Treitel stood up instantly. "Where is it?" That single object could be the answer to their financial difficulties.

"In the small back chamber. I couldn't stand up and the light was bad. I didn't want to break it trying to get it out. It's fixed somehow, secured to a stone platform, right beside a sort of doll house made from some dark wood. Ebony, most likely." Fishhead arched his back, stretching it out. "Everything made to tiny scale for that damned dwarf god, Bes."

"Will the sedan chair fit into the bigger trunk?" Treitel asked eagerly.

"If we empty out some other rubbish. But first we have to free it up without harming it."

Alistair Treitel knew that he himself was far better suited for that delicate task. "Catch your breath, Algie. Sit down and have some tea while I have a look."

Treitel disliked entering the narrow dark passage with its low square-cut walls and the imprisoning atmosphere of the two rock-cut chambers. They lacked proper lights and a fan to circulate the ghastly dead air. Each time he passed the entrance stone he was concerned about the damaged pivot on which it rested, even though they had braced the slab in place with two thick wooden wedges. Now there were fewer men to help if anything was needed. Most of the diggers had been paid off and sent home to the Sudan, diminishing the number who might inform against them. Only three were left, plus the burly foremen.

Blunt poured himself a cup of tea before sitting down. Massoud and Ali were seated at their small fire between the tent and the tunnel entrance, eating flatbread and sipping a tea of their own.

Treitel entered the tunnel. The brother of the injured fellah was waiting to lead him in with an oil lamp. Hard to trust this chap, though they had paid off the injured brother well enough. At least Treitel had his small army-issue electric torch clipped to his belt for emergencies, though he had not checked its flat rectangular battery. Long shadows moved along the walls and floor as the two men bent and entered the passage.

Treitel pressed one hand against the door slab as he passed. The limestone felt cold and smooth, secure and immovable. He bent as he entered the first, larger chamber. A wooden ladder leaned against the sarcophagus. An oil lamp flickered from a nail driven into a crack in the wall. Its dark smoke was already damaging their find. The casket had been emptied, but the Englishman was privately embarrassed by the hasty rough nature of their work as archeologists. The dig-and-grab style was more suited to grave robbers than scholars. But of course, if they did

361

not do it, someone else would. Even in England, only a few years ago, Roman ruins had been pillaged and sold off in fragments. Parts of Cambridge itself were built on top of uncared-for Roman ruins. What could one expect at Wadi Halfa?

The two chambers were separated by a narrow double switchback tunnel, shaped like the letter **W** and walled with green and blue tiles. "Go back to Mr. Blunt," said Treitel to the fellah, pointing the way. As the man turned away, the Englishman took the lamp from the wall and continued on alone. The lamp was only half full with oil, he saw, annoyed. Blunt should have had it filled.

The stagnant air grew worse as he advanced, not foul or thick, but strangely lifeless, empty, as if the natural elements that composed it and made it breathable had lost their potency. A deep breath did not freshen one's lungs. Short of oxygen, the flame burned lower as he turned the final corner and approached the second chamber, his back bent and the lamp held before him.

There he found the stone platform at the end of the smaller room, two feet above the dusty floor. The reliquary atop it seemed to sparkle in the lamplight, as if it provided an illumination of its own.

Treitel's breath caught as he stared at the masterpiece. He began to sweat despite the chill. The object, a ceremonial sedan chair, a sort of moveable throne, was finer than Blunt had described it. The ivory carrying poles were tipped in gold and banded with small gold rings.

Probably Middle Kingdom, the period of the finest jewelry, from the 12th Dynasty. The chair was made of gold, set and decorated with lapis and semi-precious stones. The delicate pleated parasol was also gold with a pointed ruby at its tip.

Drawn to the prize, Treitel set down the lamp in one corner. He knelt before the platform and removed his gloves. Gently but unsuccessfully he tried to raise the throne chair by its carrying poles. He could see where that idiot Blunt had damaged one handle while trying to lift it.

Treitel moved the lamp directly beneath the platform. He had never felt so concentrated. His body and mind were consumed by a single impulse. He brushed the top edge of the platform where the sedan chair rested. Two bumps on the stone blocked his fingers. Elated by the discovery, he adjusted the wick of the lamp and lowered his eyes to the level of the bumps. Each one was the head of a tiny stone dowel that had been driven through holes in the platform and into the supports at the bottom of the sedan chair. To free the chair, he must either remove or destroy the dowels. He needed a pair of pliers or a small wrench. He cursed softly for he did not believe that they had either tool at this hasty informal dig. Had there been electric cables, there would have been a set of pliers.

Alistair took out his pen knife and opened the shorter blade. Using its thicker dull edge, he tried to lever out the head of one dowel, first prying up one side, then the other. Slowly the first dowel came free. It was slightly smaller than a cigarette.

The second one resisted him. He dug the tip in deeper, but the blade snapped when he tried too hard. Treitel opened the second, larger blade and worked more slowly, first levering out one edge of the head of the dowel, then the other.

Finally the second dowel started to come free, then froze in place with an inch left to go. He tried again, but the rod was truly stuck. When he applied more pressure, the second blade snapped. Treitel cursed loudly this time. In desperation he pinched the free part of the dowel in his fingertips and struggled to pull it out. The beveled head of the dowel snapped off in his hand. Enraged, he hurled the fragment across the chamber. Then he regained control of himself. He must be patient. He sought to pull on the sharp broken stump. Impossible. He tried again to lift the sedan chair but it was still secured to the platform. Wrenching it free would destroy the object.

What else could he use to draw out the stump of the dowel? He glanced at the lamp. The oil was getting low. His knees ached. To remove the dowel he must either shatter it, lubricate it or pull it out by force. Perhaps he should go back outside and get a nail with which to smash it. No, he decided, this was the greatest find of his life. He would do it now, himself. He knew which muscles were, for their size, the strongest in the human body: the muscles of the jaw.

Treitel used the longer of the broken blades to cut off the end of his shirt tail. He folded the cotton fragment into a small pad and fitted that into his mouth to cover the edges of his front teeth.

Alistair Treitel lay almost on his side, raising his head on his right arm. He wiped the edge of the platform with his sleeve. He set his mouth against the platform, his nose just above the top edge, almost touching the golden chair. He scraped his upper front teeth along the edge until they met the jagged dowel. He adjusted the cotton pad and bit hard. He felt the solidity of the stone dowel squeezed within the cotton. He clenched his teeth as tightly as he dared. He was heartened when he was able to jiggle the dowel a bit from side to side. The lamp flickered. Finally he closed his eyes and bit down tight. In one surge he pulled back his head. He split an upper front tooth as the dowel came free. Treitel sat up, trembling with the painful effort. He spat out the pad and felt his chipped tooth. Then he focused his eyes on the treasure.

Kneeling down again, trying to ignore the sharp pain in the exposed nerve of his tooth, he slowly lifted the chair with both hands. A pair of tiny ivory carrying poles rested across each palm, as they must have done when the artist set this moveable throne in place thousands of years before. He was astonished by the dense weight of the object. Bending low, he set the treasure back down, determined to keep it to himself. But how was he to carry both the lamp and the sedan chair?

Treitel rose in a crouch and carried the lamp to the entrance to the chamber. There he jammed his pen knife between two tiles in the wall, using the stump of the larger blade to anchor it. He hung the lamp from the knife. Only a low pool of oil remained in the lamp. He removed his shirt and set it folded on the floor of the tunnel as far into the zigzag passage as the flickering light permitted him to see. He returned for the object and rested it carefully on his shirt. Then he took down the lamp and the knife and repeated the process at each sharp turn in the passage.

Finally he reached the large chamber. By now his back was aching frightfully. His sweat seemed frozen to his skin. He took long deep breaths without being able to fill his lungs. Feeling dizzy, his tooth throbbing, Treitel set the sedan chair on his shirt and leaned against the edge of the slab. It was cold against his skin. Stone dust scratched his body. He dropped the remains of his knife into a pocket of his shorts as the flame of the lamp lowered and almost died.

Short of breath, terrified in the silent near-darkness, Treitel collapsed with his back against the stone casket and his legs extended before him. He stared in shock when he found himself at eye level with the mummy of the dwarf. Bes himself seemed to be staring at him from the corner, as if monitoring the theft of the possession that had accompanied him in the afterlife.

Treitel calmed himself and pulled his small battery-powered torch from his belt case. The modest yellow light barely made shadows on the walls. Treitel remained seated for a moment and tried to breath slowly and steady himself. The light dimmed. He stood and leaned against the sarcophagus.

Feeling along the wall with one hand, with the dying torch in the other, Treitel entered the passageway planning to pick up the sedan chair and hurry out. Then he felt an angle in the wall. He was going the wrong way. He turned around abruptly, returned to the chamber and started along the correct passage. The torch died just as he discerned natural light waiting at the head of the tunnel.

The Don leaned against the wall, gasping in the better air as he considered what he would tell Blunt. As he stood there, the golden artifact at his feet, he heard the sounds of argument and then of violence echoing down the passage towards him. A strange voice cursed in German.

Fearful, Treitel drew back. At last, he had found the treasure that would change his life. But what was happening? Who could this intruder be?

Chapter Thirty-Six

"I can take you no more, effendi," said the donkey man respectfully. He wore a shabby brown gallabiyah over a filthy torn undershirt. His sandals were cut from rubber tires. His cracked toenails were thick and hard as the shell of a turtle. His donkey, its head low as a feeding chicken picking at scraps, had stopped and relieved itself when it came to a pile of sliding rock and blown sand blocking the narrow trail along the edge of the hill.

Olivio Alavedo sat in Tariq's lap on the bench beside the driver. A grey silk bandana covered his nose and mouth beneath the wide-brimmed straw hat that rested nearly on his ears. The dwarf knew the combination gave him the rakish look of an elegant bandit. He wore brothel creepers, tan twill trousers and a perfectly fitted khaki safari shirt with buttoned epaulettes.

Ernst von Decken sat grumbling in the bed of the cart behind them, adjusting the straps of his new wooden leg. The thick Moroccan leather was remarkably supple, and the dwarf vowed that this leg was far superior to the previous one.

"You will wait here," the dwarf ordered the donkey man. "You will not leave. You will be paid when I return." Alavedo wiggled away from Tariq to the edge of the bench. His servant stepped down, then reached back to pick up his master, lifting him piggy-back onto his shoulders.

"Here, Captain, is a present for you from the Third Reich," said Olivio to the German as Tariq handed him a Luger. "To help you with your work. It must be clear that a Hun has killed these officers. Then it is war, not murder." He pointed to the hillside ahead. "Now you will follow us."

"Are you mad?" Von Decken stared down the steep rocky hillside. "How can you expect a wounded Prussian officer with one leg to climb around these mountains in this heat? You must bring these Englishmen to me. Then I will deal with them like enemies of the Kaïser, or the Führer, as you prefer."

"A little exercise will improve you, Captain," Olivio said severely. "Those young sable tarts in Khartoum will like you better without your hospital belly."

Ernst examined the black 9mm German pistol. He racked the slide and checked the magazine. "This Luger is half empty. It has only four bullets."

"Nazi ammunition is not fashionable in Cairo just now. It is difficult and costly to acquire, and you have only two men to kill."

"You never know," shrugged the German. "Sometimes you must kill more to kill two."

Dismissing all objections, the dwarf tapped Tariq's shoulder. The Nubian set off around the obstacles that blocked the trail.

Tariq slowly picked his way down the steep slope, following a zig-zag path made earlier by other animals and men. Fearful that Tariq would slip and fall, Olivio leaned back and gripped him tightly around the forehead, his fingers locked together across the man's prickly eyebrows. Von Decken followed distantly, grumbling like an old woman cleaning the kitchen of her daughter-in-law.

"Perhaps I should leave the little monster here," von Decken mumbled to himself as he stumbled down on his new leg.

***

Anxious to catch up with his two friends and share their adventure, Anton Rider stepped from the fast steam launch onto the dock at Wadi Halfa.

It had been a comfortable journey from Abu Simbel on what in peacetime was a canopied boat used to transport privileged travellers to ancient sites along both banks of the Upper Nile. He had studied the map Olivio had left for him. He had also read the note warning that their enemies were dangerous and had killed both women and men in brutal ways. Then Anton considered what he had learned at GHQ about Denby and the Hussars.

It seemed that the battle of Kasserine Pass might be Rommel's last victory in Africa. His Panzers had crushed the Americans and taken the pass, but failed to get beyond the town of Thala in the Dorsal Mountains. Thala had been the Field Marshall's high watermark. Inadequately supported by the new German forces commanded by General von Arnim, short of petrol and ammunition, and no longer in total independent command, the Desert Fox for once had been tentative rather than bold. Instead of following up on Kasserine by thrusting deeper into Tunisia, Rommel had paused at Thala while British reinforcements, artillery and armor, arrived to confront him. Now he was in retreat, first to the Mareth Line, then beyond, towards the final German base of Tunis.

Denby, wounded again in one shoulder and probably permanently deafened, was reportedly on his way back to Cairo with other wounded Hussars.

Anton strode along the modest waterfront of Wadi Halfa, looking for some sort of transport. As he searched, he was advised that three strangers, including one very small one, had left Wadi Halfa that morning by donkey cart. He checked the width of the track left by the cart, as he might the footprint of an elephant he had to follow. There were no motor vehicles suitable for a rough trip into the hills, save one old lorry with its engine block suspended by chains under a tripod made from what appeared to be sections of old railroad track.

Rider found a pony, apparently part horse, part mule, that was tied to a post that held up the canvas roof of a shop on the waterfront. He knelt and shook his head as he examined the feet of the unshod animal, while its elderly proprietor offered the dozing creature for either sale, rental or dinner.

Finally Anton found two young Arab boys slick with grease as they worked on a Triumph motorcycle. Rider negotiated for the bike then studied his map and devoured a bowl of couscous and some hot flatbread while the boys finished tightening the drive chain and pumping up the tires. For a few more piastres, they found a third tire which they tied to the pillion with a container of spare petrol. Anton opened the container and sniffed to confirm the contents.

It was a dusty uneven ride. The bike was noisier than a Bren gun carrier and exhaled plumes of dense black smoke. Anton tried to avoid the sharpest stones and deepest pits as he climbed into the hills and paused frequently to check the map and tighten the fuel line. After two hours he came to some donkey droppings between two lines of cart tracks. As in the old days, he brushed away the flies and probed the patties with his fingers. The centers were still damp. The cart tracks were the same width apart as those he had measured in Wadi Halfa. He was on the trail.

Another half hour passed and he came upon a donkey cart. The animal, head down, was dozing in the sun. The driver, asleep beneath the cart, was not wakened even by the racket of the approaching motorbike.

"Yes, effendi," nodded the driver finally, leaning up on his elbows and accepting a handful of dates. "I am waiting for the three men who left me here without my money hours ago to walk down in that direction." He pointed to a steep jagged path down the hillside.

"Stand up," said Anton, starting to think like a Gypsy rather than a British officer. "Stand up."

The man climbed out and stood facing Anton with awkward deference. He was nearly Rider's height though not as solidly built.

"Take off your clothes and sandals," said Anton firmly, bending to unlace his own boots, then stripping off his khaki shirt.

The driver started to protest, then looked at Rider's wounds and muscles and did as he was told. Anton pulled on the shirt and gallabiyah, which hung down thickly over his army shorts and pistol belt. He slipped his feet into the well-fitting sandals and pulled the cowl of the gallabiyah over his head. He checked inside the cart and found the driver's heavy staff with a knotted leather whip tied to its handle.

Rider gave the man some coins, then left the motorbike and the cart and set off along the zigzag trail, sometimes leaning on the staff.

***

Resting for a moment, the dwarf and his two escorts found themselves looking down on a large round tent pointed at the center. Nearby, a canvas canopy was stretched between six poles. Piles of new waste from an archeological dig were gathered around the messy camp.

"You must carry me down there, Tariq," Alavedo said in hushed tones, "as quietly as we can go."

They had almost reached the bottom when the big man slipped. Tariq threw up one hand to save his master as he tumbled forward on his belly. Alavedo gripped Tariq's ears just before they went down. As they fell, Olivio saw a large red-faced man rising from his sleep in a chair under the canvas awning. The man was drawing a pistol as the dwarf's head struck a rock and he lost consciousness for an instant.

Alavedo awoke lying on his bad shoulder at the edge of the canvas. He saw the Englishman, Major Blunt, he believed, fire his pistol into Tariq's side as the two men grappled. Then Tariq seized Blunt's gun

371

hand in one fist and his elbow in the other. In a single downward motion the Nubian snapped Blunt's right arm across his knee like a man breaking a branch for kindling. The Major screamed and cursed. But blood was flooding down Tariq's belly. He fell back as Blunt bent and lifted the Webley with his left hand.

Two gunshots, crisper and lighter than the Webley's, sounded just behind Olivio. The first missed, kicking up a spurt of sand. The second struck Blunt just above his left ear and creased the side of his head. Blunt stiffened and dropped the Webley and collapsed forward on his face.

The dwarf struggled painfully to rise. Blunt did not move. Dead? Olivio hoped. He saw that his own trousers were torn through at both knees. He watched von Decken limp towards him with surprising speed, holding the Luger.

"Check the tent! Then down there!" cried Alavedo, pointing at the entrance to the dig. "There is nowhere else the other devil could be." Though weak and not yet standing, Olivio felt in command, youthful and on fire again, with all of his capacities ready to be engaged. Alavedo rose slowly, gripping a pole, blinking as he entered the shade of the canvas. He collapsed into the camp chair and watched von Decken limp from the tent, Luger still in hand.

"A few little treasures in there!" called Ernst as he descended to the entrance of the dig. Olivio frowned, wondering how many the German had already stolen. He tasted blood at one corner of his mouth. He licked his lips with his thick pointed tongue before feeling the open cut on his cheekbone just below his false eye. The lash-less eyelid was painful from the grit and dust collected on his ivory eye. He must find a moment to bathe it.

Then the little man was assailed by a different sense that nearly overcame him. A sudden feeling that, after all, he was indeed old and weak and slack. What, he asked himself, would Mr. Anton do in such a situation? He would not sit in a chair while others fought on his behalf.

Olivio gripped the arms of the seat and rose, fortifying himself with determination. He looked about for his hat, but it was too far from him to be recovered now.

He stumbled over to the body of Algernon Blunt and knelt beside it trying to reach under it to secure the man's pistol, but the weapon was hopelessly pinned beneath the smelly brute's massive frame. The body was still warm. Alavedo succeeded only in exhausting himself and soiling both his hands in Blunt's blood. Irritated, the dwarf wiped his hands on the villain's shirt sleeve before crawling to Tariq. His servant was unconscious, bleeding but alive. Olivio unknotted his own silk kerchief and pressed it against Tariq's wound as a compress. Then he saw the nearby cup of tea and used it to moisten the lips of the Sudanese.

Finally the dwarf left the shelter of the canvas and walked unsteadily down to the mouth of the dig. Von Decken had already passed inside. An oil lamp hung from a nail several yards into the entrance. Alavedo leaned against the wall to steady himself as his eye adjusted to the gloom. He walked slowly forward, occasionally bracing himself against one wall.

After a moment the dwarf heard two angry voices echoing towards him along the narrow passage. He could not tell how far away they were. He came to a corner where two dim cones of lamplight seemed to meet. He looked down at something glittering near his feet on a piece of cloth. He knelt in the dust and touched the object with two shaking hands. A tiny bejeweled sedan chair with a golden misshapened dwarf seated as if enthroned.

Bes! His god!

Olivio rose as a gunshot and a scream echoed towards him. If that was the Luger, the German would have only one shot left. Alavedo crept along the darker wall and turned another corner until he came to a slab of stone ajar at the entrance to a chamber. Two wooden wedges appeared to secure the massive stone in its position.

In the chamber, von Decken and Treitel faced each other across the corner of a sarcophagus. He could only see the shadowed sides of their heads above the stone coffin. Terrified, weakened by his injuries, for once the little man was uncertain what to do.

Resting in the corner directly facing him, Olivio Alavedo saw what he had never seen before: the mummy of a dwarf, the distortions of its head and body clearly evident through the ancient linen wrappings. The outsize round head could be his own. The creature was exactly his height. This could only be Bes himself, the god of his ancestors.

Short of breath, with his injuries, the echoes, the setting and the thin air all serving to incapacitate him, Olivio fell backward against the slab that split the entrance to the chamber. He crawled back to the tiny sedan chair and collapsed beside it. He struggled to breathe and collect himself. Which man would emerge from the chamber? His killer or his savior?

Mr. Anton had always told him that Ernst von Decken was a man who could manage in a violent crisis, especially when his own well-being was at issue. This German had already survived three wars in Africa.

For several minutes, Olivio sat on the floor of the passage with his back against the wall. His heart had not pounded so rapidly since his last challenging encounter with Jamila. His spine and neck throbbed as if he had survived a massive electric shock. He closed his eyes as he listened to the sounds of two men fighting several yards away in the chamber he had left. From where he sat, near the first corner of the passage, he could just see the edge of the entrance slab. The magnificent sedan chair lay cradled in his lap and arms. He stroked the golden dwarf with one short thumb. A reviving current seemed to charge through his own body as he touched it.

He saw the back of Alistair Treitel and the long shadow of his figure cast down the corridor by an oil lamp inside the burial chamber. Horrified, the dwarf watched Treitel kick away one of the two wooden wedges that were holding the entrance stone in place.

"Damn you!" cried a voice in German as the second wedge was kicked into the passage. Shadows moved like puppet dancers across the wall as the two men struggled and knocked against the slab.

Olivio heard the glass of a lamp shatter, followed by a harsh grinding sound as the slab began to pivot towards its closed position. Then the damaged stone of the pivot point gave way. With a final slamming crunch the massive limestone door settled into its blocking position, slightly lower, perhaps an inch or two from flush at one end and slightly higher at the other edge where the top corner jabbed into the ceiling and precipitated a long crack in the roof of the corridor. A thin stream of lamp oil leaked into the passage beneath the raised corner of the slab.

One crouching figure had escaped from the chamber into the passage. In the darkness and the cloud of dust falling from the damaged ceiling, the dwarf was not able to see which man it was.

Foe or friend? Alavedo prepared himself to offer the victor either a bargain or a reward.

He heard the tapping of a peg leg on the stone. Kapitan von Decken?

"Help me!" called a weak echoing voice. Alistair Treitel must still be inside the now-sealed chamber.

"*Ja vohl.*" The German holstered his weapon and struck a match. He squinted down at the little man seated in the dust with the gleaming artifact resting across his legs.

"Can that be you, Mein Herr? We need light," said von Decken as his match guttered down. He tossed the match aside, but it fell near the small opening at the lower corner of the slab.

The trail of oil caught and flared. There was a whooshing sound as the flame, sucked in by the draft, carried and ignited inside the sealed chamber, no doubt allowing Professor Treitel a final moment of illumination. Truly, thought the little man with a quiet chuckle, his fate was sealed.

In a few minutes Ernst von Decken blinked as he stepped out into the bright daylight with Olivio Alavedo a few small paces behind him.

"Don't touch that Luger," ordered Blunt in a strong voice from his left. One side of Blunt's face was swollen and dark with dried blood. A stained strip of cotton was wrapped around his brow and knotted just above one ear. The patch of veins on his neck appeared to be smashed and leaking blood like a swamp being drained of its murky waters. He sat in a camp chair at one side of the tunnel entrance gripping his Webley revolver in both hands.

Ernst considered stepping back into the darkness of the tunnel, but the dwarf was directly behind him. The German hesitated, his hand already near his belt.

Suddenly a blow crashed down, smashing his right shoulder. Von Decken screamed as he heard his own bone break.

"Well done, Ali," said Blunt to the foreman who stood against the other side of the entrance and was preparing to swing a long-handled steel-tipped pick for a second blow. "That should be enough for him for now. Give me his pistol and tie his arms behind his back."

On his belly, von Decken cursed through the pain as Ali roughly bound his arms together from wrist to elbow.

The dwarf stood framed in the tunnel entrance, the magnificent antiquity in his hands. His body was still, unthreatening, but his mind was working like a conjurer. His eye appeared to be weeping.

"Good afternoon, Major Blunt," Olivio said quietly, nodding to the big man as he recalled the deaths of Jamila and the forger. He must handle this devil with care, not with anger or weakness. Instead, he must appeal to the man's true nature: greed. First, he must calm the scene, diminishing the atmosphere of adversarial violence that would bring out the worst in this English killer.

"May I sit down and speak with you, Major? And might I have a glass of tea, if you please?"

"Give the midget a stool," Algernon Blunt ordered the first foreman. "And fetch us some water, Massoud."

"We have each lost a partner," said Alavedo slowly, gesturing with a thumb at von Decken as if the injured German were already dead. "Perhaps now you and I, Major Blunt, can share in this opportunity, doing business together in these difficult times, as contending gentlemen sometimes must. I have many relationships who could be useful to you and me in the world of marketing antiquities with uncertain provenance." The dwarf almost smiled as he continued. "Of course, without our partners, sir, there will be more for you and for me."

"Lost a partner?" exclaimed Blunt, leaning forward. "What do you mean? What's happened to Treitel? He should be out in a minute."

"I think not." The little man settled on the stool and shook his head. "I believe Professor Treitel is still alive, and well enough for now, although resting in darkness and probably somewhat scorched." Olivio sighed thoughtfully before continuing. "But he will never be what you might call 'out.' It would require at least a locomotive or a pair of elephants to move the great stone that now secures his final privacy."

The dwarf paused and sipped the water offered to him by Massoud. "Kattar kheirak," he nodded gratefully to the Egyptian before continuing.

"Your friend is alone in the burial chamber at the end of the passage. Should he seek repose, there is a splendid carved sarcophagus in which the distinguished professor may rest whenever he chooses, either for a nap or forever. Of course, he will have to bend his knees, as the stone coffin was prepared for a far shorter man."

"Why, you little bastard!" exclaimed Blunt, rising, now fully understanding who his adversary was and had been. He holstered his Webley and seized the sedan chair from the dwarf. He drew his rhino-hide swagger stick from his belt. Bending, he struck the dwarf twice across the face, right and left. Once across the eyes, once across the mouth. The first blow knocked the dwarf's ivory eye from its socket. The second blow knocked the dwarf from the stool and onto his back in the dust.

Olivio Alavedo was accustomed to pain, his own and other men's. He lay curled tight on the ground like a snail in its shell. Blood ran down from where his eyebrows once had been and flooded over his torn eyelids. He volunteered no sound. Though he could speak, now he could not see.

"Tie that little freak to the tent pole, Ali, and bring me the big oil lamp that is in there between the cots. Make sure it's full."

Blunt wound a strip of cotton tightly around his damaged right arm, using a slat from a camp chair as a splint. He split the end of the cotton with his teeth and, with Ali's help, tied a firm knot before flexing his fingers and gritting his teeth against the pain.

Ali," said Blunt, "rip off the German's wooden leg, then drag him into the tent and make sure he is properly tied down to both ends of the big trunk. Have Massoud keep him and the midget in there out of sight.

Gag them both. One of you stay there. You must guard the entrance to the tunnel while I go inside."

Blunt checked his pistols before picking up the lamp. He jammed von Decken's Luger into the back of his belt, noting that the fine weapon contained only one shot. "If anyone else appears, you and Massoud take care of them. Do whatever you must. I will be back out in half an hour."

Algernon Blunt was soon deep inside the passage, the lamp raised before him, his Webley holstered. Finally he arrived at the great stone that blocked the entrance to the burial chamber. He bent and examined the corners where it met the floor and walls, each one just a bit off center and with one edge slightly raised. A snake, perhaps a lizard, or even a human hand might be able to slip through the narrow cavity.

Blunt raised the lamp to examine the two corners at the top. The higher one was jammed into the damaged ceiling. The lower corner exposed a flat narrow opening only slightly larger than the gap at the diagonal corner of the floor. He held the light to it.

"Who is that?" cried the weak voice of Alistair Treitel from the other side of the stone. "Help me!"

"It's me, Professor. The man you call Fishhead behind his back."

"Help me, Algie! Help me. I'll do anything. We've always been friends, more than that. They burned me with the lamp oil before they left me here." Treitel began to sob. "You can't imagine the pain, Algie. You must collect all the boys now and force open the stone."

"There is nothing I can do for you," Blunt said brusquely. "Our fellahin have all gone home. The pivot stone is destroyed. This big stone is jammed in. It's immoveable, part of the mountain again. You know how they built these things." He hesitated, as if confused by recollection. "Alistair. Truly, I cannot do anything."

A long pause hung between the two men in the silence of the dead air.

"At least slide your revolver through this opening so I can kill myself. Please, Algernon. Please. I'm already thirsty. I couldn't bear to starve to death."

Blunt considered it. Why not? The old bastard couldn't take advantage of him anymore, or split the money, and he would not want Treitel to talk about everything if someone came along and found him before he died. And he still had the Luger in the back of his belt.

Blunt set down the lamp and used his good arm to slide his Webley into the crack. But the revolver was a bit too thick. The six-shot chamber jammed against the stone. He dusted the Webley clean and put it back in its holster before setting the Luger on the flat stone. He pushed against the long barrel and shoved the German pistol forward as far as he could.

"Got it?" he asked.

"Nearly," gasped Treitel. "Just let me stretch my arm a bit. There we are! Got it. Thank you." There was a pause before Treitel spoke again more quietly, almost whispering.

"One more thing. Can you hear me, Algie? Please try and listen closely."

Blunt craned his head forward against the crack.

There was a deafening explosion.

A bullet ricocheted towards his head along the narrow opening. Stone splinters cut Blunt's face and neck as the bullet whistled past his ear.

Fishhead leaned against the wall and closed his eyes for a moment. The tricky bastard had not changed since they were schoolboys. With a bloody hand Blunt felt the cuts on his neck. Then he lifted the lamp and made his way back down the passage.

A man in a gallabiyah seemed to be waiting for him in the shadows just inside the entrance to the tunnel.

"Ali! I told you to keep watch outside!" yelled Blunt.

There was no reply. The man stepped forward to meet him with the cowl of his robe over his head and a cart driver's whip in one hand.

"Ali?" Blunt paused as the man came closer. He could not raise the lamp which dangled low from his fingers at the end of his damaged right arm. But he lifted the Webley in his left.

The leather of the whip flicked out around his left wrist. The weapon and the oil lamp fell to the floor of the passage as the man pulled Blunt to him with a painful jerk of the lash.

"Rider!" yelled Blunt as Anton pistol-whipped him across the face with his own service revolver. Rider holstered his weapon and went after Blunt with his hands.

"Mr. Alavedo has told me everything," said Anton, slamming Blunt against the jagged wall with blows to his face and belly. "Your crimes in Cairo and Jugoslavia, your cruel murders and your treachery."

Blunt dragged his good hand down Rider's face, raking his eyes before seizing his throat.

Rider punched him twice more in the belly, but Blunt held his grip. Gasping, dizzy, Anton began to lose his sight. He lifted one knee as hard as he could into the big man's groin. Blunt cried out and loosened his hold as his head fell forward. Anton chopped his fist into the bridge of Blunt's nose. The bone gave way.

Blood flooded down his face as Blunt collapsed on his back onto the oil lamp, knocking his head against the wall. For a moment there was darkness and near silence while Anton gasped for breath.

Light flickered across Blunt's shoulders and down the sides of his tunic as he sat up. He screamed and rolled over across the broken glass and flaming oil that had been under his back.

Blunt stood, covered in fire from neck to knees. He tried to brush himself with bleeding hands cut by the glass. He rolled once more on the floor to suffocate the flames, but instead collected more oil before getting to his feet and running screaming back down the tunnel, his hair now a fiery crown.

"Alistair!" was the last word that Anton heard echoing back to him down the passage. "Alistair."

Chapter Thirty-Seven

Denby Rider could not hear his small nephew, but he was certain the boy was laughing. Wellie sat on his knee, grinning and wiggling as his uncle tickled him. The infant gripped a stuffed camel in one hand and used the other to try and pull off the heavy dressing that covered Lieutenant Rider's left ear.

"Careful, Wellie," said Gwenn, thrilled to be with her son and grandson but still saddened that Denby might be permanently deaf. She knew he could not hear the wartime news and music that were coming over Olivio's new Zenith radio in its polished walnut cabinet. She glanced again at the exquisite object centered on the nearby table: a miniature golden sedan chair on which a tiny figure sat beneath a gold parasol topped by a single ruby.

Somehow an injury like Denby's seemed less severe during wartime, when so many suffered so much. But Gwenn knew how it would impede his life and worried what her son would find to do. All the same, he was more handsome than ever. Lean and tan, desert fit and neat in his Hussar uniform, though with his left shoulder still bandaged. Wounds enough, she knew, to keep him out of the game.

Denby's looks were so much like Anton's once had been. His voice reminded her of his brother each time he spoke. If Gwenn were not looking at Denby when he talked, she would think that Wellington was still alive.

Perhaps that was why Saffron had been so quiet. She had cried and hugged Denby when he first appeared on the ramp to the Cataract Café. Now Wellington's young widow sat across the table next to Olivio's usual high seat on the quarterdeck. There the little man could watch who came on deck. He could also be certain that the setting sun was blinding someone else's eyes.

On the radio, the war news was over for the day. The familiar voice of Vera Lynn followed softly. But Denby could not hear her words.

Gwenn reached for the pad, wrote and passed it first to Denby. Saffron tucked her hair behind one ear and glanced quickly at Denby as she waited to read the words: "Shall we all dine together here tonight? Olivio likes it when we keep his staff on the jump."

"Of course," said Denby a bit too loudly, passing the message to Saffron. His left eye twitched as he lit a cigarette.

"I'd love to," nodded Saffron. "It's sundowner time. I'll go down to the galley and order something. Let's eat early with Tiago and my sisters." Acting as the Alavedo hostess, she tapped Denby's glass. "Another cocktail?"

"Gin and tonic, please." Denby nodded and smiled.

He is already drinking and smoking too much, thought Gwenn, nettled, but with a sense of understanding and affection. Just like his father and all those boys in this damned war. What else could one expect when they had everything to lose? Without thinking, she rubbed the wedding band on her finger, slowly turning it around.

The two youngest Alavedo girls appeared, Thyme and Ginger. Each took one of Wellie's hands and they swung their young nephew between them as they carried him to the hammock on the main deck. There their brother Tiago was practicing shuffleboard like a boy at war, knocking enemy pieces off the board with sharp hard slides of his pucks.

A few minutes later, two suffragis stretched a checked cloth over a long table. One set out whisky and gin, ice and a siphon of soda. The other brought out a tray of silver and linen napkins.

Just as Denby rose and walked to the table, a maroon Daimler pulled up to the embankment. The driver descended and opened a rear door. For a moment no one emerged.

Then, declining assistance, Olivio Fonseca Alavedo slowly stepped down, back first, his left hand gripping the edge of the seat as his feet reached down for the curb. His right arm was in a sling. A bandage covered his left cheek. He had resolved to accept no physical assistance until Tariq was well enough to provide it. The little man had no doubt that knowledge of his own determination would accelerate the healing of his faithful servant. He himself took pride that his own injuries and dressings made him so much more like other men, as if he himself were a casualty of war.

Erect at last, the dwarf turned carefully and faced the Nile as Anton Rider let himself out the other side of the automobile. Olivio and Anton had travelled together from Aswan, exchanging narratives after they left Tariq and von Decken at the local clinic. Anton and Ernst had shared a drink or more before the German was surrendered for medical attention to his shoulder, but the two old Africa hands had not had the opportunity for extended conversation.

In a lucid moment of negotiation, Olivio had arranged for the second young dancer on his boat to remain in Aswan and to assist with Ernst's recuperation on his forthcoming voyage south to her home in Khartoum. With Alavedo brokering the understanding, the enterprising woman accepted the proposal with even more enthusiasm than the German officer. She had already oiled his new wooden leg and massaged the other. Soon, no doubt, she might dance for him.

"And what of Major Treitel?" Rider had asked Olivio, unable to feign disinterest. Both men knew it was his way of enquiring about Gwenn.

"Difficult to say with certainty, Mr. Anton." The dwarf shook his head from side to side. "But never again will this Treitel trouble your wife, or you. His life is complete. If he is still with us for a bit, the professor will be singed and very hungry. But living or dead, he will always be in the most distinguished company." What more could a man ask than to share a tomb with a mummy of the dwarf god, Bes?

Olivio waited on the esplanade of the embankment for Anton Rider to join him. He could just hear the voice of the English singer rising from the radio below.

> *We'll meet again,*
> *Don't know where,*
> *Don't know when,*
> *But I know*
> *We'll meet again*
> *Some sunny day.*

Their grandson grinned up at them as the two friends walked to the parapet side by side and gazed down at their family. Denby and Saffron were standing close to each other, casting a single shadow across the deck. The Nile sparkled behind them in the setting sun.

Gwenn rose and smiled, looking over at Anton as if she had been waiting for him all of her life. She looked as lovely to Anton Rider as she always had. To his surprise, her eyes only on his, Gwenn raised one hand and blew him a kiss.

Author's Note

Like my other novels set mostly in Africa and Shanghai, writing *We'll Meet Again* has enabled me to combine several things I relish: research, adventure and special relationships.

World War II in North Africa always reminds me of my father, Captain Bartle B. Bull, who died of his war wounds when I was twelve and who had served in the Coldstream Guards in Egypt, Ethiopia and Libya while still a Member of Parliament. After being grievously wounded, he helped lead the Coldstream breakout before the British surrender of Tobruk in 1942.

As the Coldstream war history put it, "The gallant Bartle Bull, having fought his way back to the battalion after receiving a wound which would have killed most men, was soon stirring up trouble on the road above Sollum." And later, "A welcome reinforcement at this juncture was the quite irregular return of Bartle Bull, who had been sent away once already as unfit after being wounded, but who now thought the tempo of the battle warranted his desertion from a staff appointment in Cairo seven hundred miles away." The regimental war record stated that after being "wounded Bartle Bull was saved by Ralph Lucas, who had the rare experience of killing three of the enemy with three successive revolver shots."

Several years after my father's death in 1950, the senior regimental sergeant-major of the British army, RSM C.I. Smy of the Coldstream Guards, said that my father was "the bravest man that he had ever seen."

Many years later, General Harold Moore, who commanded the 7th Cavalry in Vietnam and wrote *We Were Soldiers Once and Young*, wrote to me that, "I wish I could have served with your father; my kind of leader."

During his service in World War II in North Africa, whether in the desert or in the hospital, my father, like all of his friends in the British military, found great company and comfort in the lovely wartime songs of Vera Lynn, the "armed forces sweetheart," both *There'll Be Bluebirds Over The White Cliffs of Dover*, and, of course, in her magnificent heartbreaking song, *We'll Meet Again*.

My son, Bartle Breese Bull, also provides me with adventurous and literary inspiration. After leading the first horseback expedition ever to circumnavigate the world's largest lake (Lake Baikal in Siberia), he became the youngest member in the history of the Explorers Club. As an independent journalist covering the second Iraq war, he wrote for the six most distinguished newspapers in our language. In a ceremony on an American aircraft carrier, General David Petraeus gave Bartle the Centcom Medal, saying he was "very courageous, brilliant and a vision-ary." Earlier, General Hal Moore had written to me about his work in Iraq: "Bartle- I hope your son makes it out of there OK. That guy's got balls." Now we are awaiting, in 2023, the publication of my son's second book, *Babylon*, a history of Iraq.

In researching the second part of the North African campaign, I spent time in the Tunisian desert, trying to learn what the war there must have been like. Short of water, I acquired kidney stones while studying the battlefield of Kasserine and its approaches. Along the coast, I visited the well-kept military cemeteries that hold the American and British soldiers killed by the French armed forces who fought the allies as they landed in North Africa in 1942.

My description of winter in the hard mountains of Bosnia comes from the winter war in Jugoslavia of 1992-1993, when I worked with the International Rescue Committee as a volunteer helping refugees in the towns of Travnik and Vitez near Sarajevo. The setting of the hospital scenes in my novel come from my visits to a hospital in Travnik just before Christmas, where I heard the cries of children being operated on without anesthetic. Before leaving Travnik, I gave black market food and cash for medical supplies for their son to a brave Bosnian family that had welcomed me with hazardous hospitality. In return, they insisted on giving me a family treasure, an old cylindrical copper coffee grinder that I still enjoy, and that is a detail in this story.

Early each morning in Bosnia I would visit the mountain base of the Cheshire Regiment, taking strong dawn tea with the young British soldiers as their armored map truck printed out the day's assessment of where it was safe to drive supplies to the refugees. There I had the privilege of spending Christmas Eve in a frozen mountain bunker, sharing plum brandy and scraps of cheese and sausage with my courageous interpreter and four young volunteers of the Bosnian army, one of whom was the lead violinist of the Sarajevo Symphony Orchestra. He had brought his guitar to the bunker, and we all cried at midnight as he played the Battle Hymn of the Republic in honor of their American guest. I have never had a finer Christmas Eve.

The next morning, I watched the nine-man band of the Cheshires parade through a mountain village playing their instruments, their automatic rifles slung down their backs as they ignored the Serbian snipers and played for the hungry children on a freezing Christmas morning.

The bear incident in my story was inspired by a bear I shot at the request of local villagers while on a *shikar*, an Indian safari, in Kashmir in 1962.

The description of Gypsy wagons is drawn from the old crumbling *vardo* that my friend Michael Blakenham kept for years on his lovely place, Cottage Farm, in Suffolk, England. And of course Cairo's Khan el-Khalili market, the largest market in Africa, is a setting that I have enjoyed for many years, most recently with Kathleen Augustine, before visiting it again in this book.

The details of sniping are partly drawn from the expertise of my friend Major John L. Plaster, for many years the senior sniping instructor of the United States Marine Corps and the author of *The Ultimate Sniper*. Major Plaster is a man in whose sights one would not wish to be. The legendary Enfield/Holland & Holland Number 4T sniper rifle used in my story was manufactured in my father's parliamentary constituency, Enfield, in Middlesex County, England.

The American Ranger officer, Jack Corrigan, is a composite of two old soldiers with whom I have hunted wild boar: Pat Corrigan, the rugged gentleman rancher of Vero Beach and once the heavyweight boxing champion of three army divisions based at Fort Riley, Kansas; and Jackson Campbell May, a West Point "ring knocker" and Army Ranger. In his youth, Jack commanded the Reconnaissance Company of the 82nd Airborne Division, a top assignment for a young officer. Later in life, Jack took up Ferrari racing, and set the record driving across the United States in his Dino when he won the Cannonball Race in 35 hours and 53 minutes.

The name of Olivio Alavedo's majordomo was the name of my American grandmother's hard-drinking Polish butler, Sustek. As a young boy, when I visited my grandmother in Chicago, Sustek would escort me to Comiskey Park, where he would drink beer and grumble as my Yankees beat the White Sox.

Other details in the book also arise from various fragments of my personal history, including the references to pigeon-shooting at the Fayum oasis, climbing the steep casbah in Algiers, wine storage in Oporto, and the sleeveless khaki sweater that Gwenn knitted for Anton, as my mother had done for my father during the war, a garment he treasured until his death. Knitting a sweater was a unique domestic gesture for both ladies.

Many of the specifics of fieldcraft contained in *We'll Meet Again* come from my experiences in Africa with the legendary professional hunters Robin Hurt, Alan Elliott and John Stevens. A few of their exploits are recorded in my book *Safari - A Chronicle of Adventure*.

In 2014 I once again had the privilege in Zimbabwe of sharing trails and camp fires with Alan and John. But this time both experiences were enhanced by the spirited and courageous company of Kathleen Vuillet Augustine, who helped make this a better book, and who brightened every camp fire, as she still brightens every day. In 2019, Kathleen and I travelled extensively in Egypt, working on this book, and spending five special days sailing up the Nile on a felucca from Luxor to Aswan.

All these adventures aside, of course, *We'll Meet Again* is about what finally matters between one man and one woman. With that in mind and in my heart, it is an honor for me to dedicate this book to Kathleen.

Bartle Bull

About the Author

Bartle Bull was born in London and educated at Harvard University and Magdalen College, Oxford. A student of Africa for over thirty years, he is a Fellow of the Royal Geographical Society and a member of the Explorers Club. A former publisher of *The Village Voice*, Bull wrote an environmental column for the *Voice* and later for the Natural Resources Defense Council. He is the author of the widely praised novels, *The White Rhino Hotel*, *A Café on the Nile*, *The Devil's Oasis*, *Shanghai Station* and *China Star*.

BARTLE BULL'S
ANTON RIDER SERIES

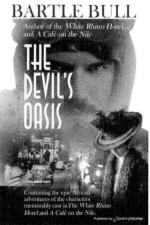

For more information
visit: www.SpeakingVolumes.us

BARTLE BULL

"Bartle Bull brilliantly brings to life post-WWI Shanghai. Great tale from a great writer." —*Forbes*

BARTLE BULL

**The master of the exotic adventure novel
returns with a tale of romance, vengeance and intrigue…**

**For more information
visit:** www.SpeakingVolumes.us

Printed in Great Britain
by Amazon

17911776R00233